Untamed

Books by Crystal Jordan

CARNAL DESIRES

ON THE PROWL

UNTAMED

SEXY BEAST V
(with Kate Douglas and Vonna Harper)

UNDER THE COVERS
(with Melissa MacNeal and P. J. Mellor)

Published by Kensington Publishing Corporation

UNTAMED

CRYSTAL JORDAN

APHRODISIA

KENSINGTON BOOKS

http://www.kensingtonbooks.com

APHRODISIA BOOKS are published by

Kensington Publishing Corp.
119 West 40th Street
New York, NY 10018

All Kensington Titles, Imprints, and Distributed Lines are available at special quantity discounts for bulk purchases for sales promotions, premiums, fund-raising, and educational or institutional use.

Special book excerpts or customized printings can also be created to fit specific needs. For details, write or phone the office of the Kensington special sales manager: Kensington Publishing Corp., 119 West 40th Street, New York, NY 10018, attn: Special Sales Department, Phone: 1-800-221-2647.

Aphrodisia and the A logo Reg. U.S. Pat & TM Off

ISBN-13: 978-0-7582-3829-0
ISBN-10: 0-7582-3829-0

First Kensington Trade Paperback Printing: November 2009

10 9 8 7 6 5 4 3 2 1

Printed in the United States of America

Acknowledgments

For Michal. Of course.

I must give a special nod of filthy appreciation to Eden Bradley and Sam Saturday for inspiring the Space Race game in this book. I won't say more, but they deserve all the credit.

To those who read this for me and beat it into submission by deadline despite winter storms, burst pipes, apartment floods, family meltdowns, and other natural disasters: Robin L. Rotham, Rhiannon Leith, Bethany Morgan, Kate Pearce, and Dayna Hart. Y'all rock. Many, many thanks for responding to the call for help of, "Holy crap, this is due tomorrow. Can you drop everything and critique hundreds of pages right this very second?"

And, as always, to John Scognamiglio and Lucienne Diver. Editor Extraordinaire and Agent Awesome Sauce. None of this would be possible without you both.

Contents

Stolen
Temptation

I

Delilah Chase perched on the corner of the building, her hand braced on the ledge in front of her as she swept her gaze over the city below. From ninety stories up, it looked clean, beautiful, an ocean of multicolored lights against pure ebony.

But Delilah knew the truth. Up close, it was gritty, dirty, and dangerous. A place where someone like her flourished.

She grinned and let the adrenaline humming through her body take over. Her claws slid forward, scraping against the slick metal ledge. She ran her tongue down a long fang, her smile widening. It was always this way when she was on a job. Half cool, calm professionalism, half unadulterated thrill seeking.

Schooling herself to patience, she tilted her wrist and checked her chrono. A few more minutes and the virus she'd seduced a young computer techie into feeding into the building's security system would kick in. She'd have a quarter of an hour to get in, steal the priceless ruby her client wanted, and get out again.

Kitten's play, this job.

Still, every case had its risks, and the moment a thief got too cocky was the moment they slipped up. If all went well, by the end of the night, multitrillonaire Hunter Avery would be missing a gem and Delilah would have a sizeable commission in her encrypted cred account. So, things had better go well. She gauged the distance between the skyrise she stood on and the one she needed to break into. Tricky, very tricky. Timing was everything. The lynx within her purred at the challenge.

This was going to be fun.

Balconies circled the entire penthouse. Not surprising a family of red-tailed hawks would build the glass and mercurite sanctuary for themselves in the middle of the city. High enough they couldn't see the grime of the real people below.

The newsvids had reported on every aspect of the Avery family's lives for as long as she'd been alive. Their fortune was one of the few to survive the Third Great War, which made them newsvid darlings, beautiful people in an ugly world.

Delilah had heard all about it when Hunter's parents were killed in a tragic industrial accident. A few years after that, Hunter's uncle died, and Hunter had all but disappeared from public view. The buzz on the street whispered that Hunter had done the killing himself, his mind twisted from seeing his parents' death. A bitter little smile curled Delilah's lips. Figures that he'd get away with murder. The rich always did.

Now, Hunter was practically a recluse in his tower penthouse, only allowing a trusted few in for business purposes and only leaving for a few business meetings or high-society parties a year. This meant conning her way in wouldn't work, so breaking in was her best option. Her client said Avery was in Los Angeles at a board meeting and wouldn't be home until the next day. Her intel had confirmed it, so tonight was the night to get what her client wanted.

If a tiny part of her was curious to see the inside of the Averys' ivory tower and got a malicious thrill from stealing from the richest man alive, she'd never admit it to anyone else.

Her chrono vibrated against her wrist, letting her know the

window of opportunity had opened. Reaching behind her, she pulled her grappler gun out of her knapsack, aimed it at the balcony railing, and fired. A gossamer-thin strand of mercurite shot from each end to form molecular bonds with the railings on both buildings. She flipped a setting so the grappler would move along the wire. Taking a breath, she said a quick prayer that the virus worked and she wasn't about to get fried by the security field that electrocuted any unauthorized life-forms attempting to enter.

Then she tightened her grip on the grappler, jumped, and let gravity carry her down the wire with a soundless rush of speed and wind. Her heightened vision took in every detail as she went. She knew the exact moment something started to go wrong. The mercurite was designed to dissolve after one use. It left no evidence behind. The wind was especially intense this evening, and she might just reach the end of that one use before she reached the other building.

Shit, shit, *shit.*

Heart pounding so loud in her ears it drowned out everything else, she tilted her feet forward and hoped for greater speed. Tensing every muscle as she hit the perfect spot in her downward flight, she kicked her legs hard. She swung up and around the wire, launching herself into the sky. The cable slackened, and she knew it was no more than silver powder beneath her. She twisted midair, flipping until she landed lighter than a cat's paw on the edge of the railing. Triumph rushed through her, making her grin. Perfect.

She loved it when a plan came together. Almost as much as she loved it when the plans went awry and she had to think on her feet. It was why she was the very best at what she did.

Stepping down onto the balcony, she turned to make sure she'd left no evidence of her passing. The shoes she wore were specifically designed not to leave a distinct footprint. Cost a load of creds, but totally worth it. A quick brush of her fingers across the railing and what was left of the mercurite cable dispersed into metallic dust that swirled away in the gale-force breeze of New Chicago. She'd thicken the wire's setting and shoot another one across when she needed to leave, but there was no need to advertise while she was here. She wasn't the only predator who could see in the dark.

And everyone was a predator.

She knew it, and so did everyone else. It made life more dangerous and a whole lot more exciting than it had been before the war. Biological warfare early in the twenty-first century ripped the planet apart. What scientists never expected was the effect long-term exposure to their weapons would have on humans. It twisted their genes, morphed them into shape-shifters.

Jungle cats, bears, wolves, birds of prey, every imaginable predator on the planet. No one knew why, but the chemicals brought out the most feral instincts in mankind. Nearly a century later, everyone accepted that inside each human lurked an animal, a beast who might take control at any moment. It meant Delilah had to be even more careful not to get caught. A small sigh slid past her lips. Her ancestors had it so much easier when they tried to steal something.

Then again, if it was easy, it wouldn't be so much fun.

The balcony door was laughably easy to get through. The problem with most people was they assumed if their security system was expensive enough that they didn't have to take care of the simple protections for their property.

Stupid, but their mistake was her gain.

She slipped inside the penthouse and froze for long, precious moments. Every feline sense went on alert for any movement, any noise.

Nothing.

Even if there was someone here, it wouldn't stop her. She had a nasty little surprise she used on those who interrupted her work. She slid her hand into her vest, running the pad of her thumb over the trigger of a tiny, pressurized canister of poison. It wouldn't kill them, but it left them with nothing but a headache to remember her by.

Creeping forward, she eased into the master bedroom where this particular hawk kept his treasures. A bit of digging had turned up the fact that his safe had been installed along the west wall. There was a painting large enough to cover a safe hanging on the wall. Picasso. Original, too, unless she missed her guess—and she rarely did. A pity she didn't have any way to take it with her. It would fetch an excellent price with several of her regular clients. In fact, most of the decorations in this penthouse would bring in more than a few creds.

Her eyebrows arched and she gave a low, appreciative hum. "Prime."

Business must be even better for Avery than the buzz said, because the whole penthouse was a study in the rare and valuable. Polished wooden floors when most people had concrete, marble sculptures and ancient artifacts sat in precise arrangements on mercurite and polyglass furniture. The man's bed was wide enough for ten and draped in deep blue microsilk.

What she wouldn't give for a few hours to take her pick from Hunter's collection, but a glance at her chrono made it clear she didn't have time to admire the man's pretty toys. Slipping her bag of tools off her shoulder, she set to work disarming the safe.

The Windy City was the best place to fly. The breeze that kept Lake Michigan at a constant ripple swirled around Hunter as he skimmed above the water in his hawk form. He stretched his wings further, pulling out of his glide to spiral higher and higher in the night sky. The wind cut sharper up there, whipped at his body. It was one of the few times he was *free*, the stink of the city and the weight of his responsibilities falling away as he soared into the moonlit clouds.

He glanced down at glittering metal and glass cityscape of New Chicago as it whizzed past. The Lakeshore District and the downtown areas of the city had been built over the grave-yard of the old. Most of Chicago was reduced to rubble in the urban riots of the Third Great War, which had ended long be-fore his birth. Many who lived before the war said New Chicago lacked the grace that history lends a city, but there was little left of the world that could be called graceful. Most people struggled to survive. He was one of the lucky ones, and even he had more than his share of problems. A heavy sigh slid from his throat.

The meeting with Pierce Vaughn hadn't gone well. A wolf-shifter, the government agent was as ferocious and relentless when he pursued his prey as Hunter was. He liked that about the man, respected his judgment. Even so, Pierce had been try-ing to nail Tarek for over a year. A viper in every sense of the word, Tarek had done things that would make most humans' stomachs revolt.

As Tarek's biggest business rival, Hunter was a prime target for industrial espionage and sabotage. This last trip to Los An-geles had proven that someone was sabotaging his business ef-forts there. Both Pierce and he knew who was doing it; they just couldn't prove it. Yet. But they would.

Privately, Hunter suspected the wolf kept him informed as a way to ensure he didn't take the law into his own hands when he finally had undeniable proof of Tarek's perfidy. Once he did, there was little Pierce could do to stop Hunter. He would relish ripping the viper apart, but he would wait until his suspicions were grounded in fact. If that meant Pierce and he had a rela-tionship of mutual information sharing, then he was willing to listen. Each of them were in this for their own ends, and he re-spected that they were up front about it. No games, no toying with each other.

The arrangement worked for him.

Slow, deep beats of his wings carried him toward home. He wasn't going to be able to outdistance the problems plaguing his mind, so he wouldn't waste his energy trying. Frustration boiled through him. He was a patient man, but a year was too long for any rival to get the better of him.

Tarek. The viper-shifter redefined cutthroat, and his inability to beat Hunter and drain profits from Avery Industries had made their rivalry personal for the viper. Hunter snapped his beak. It was business; ruthless, cool-minded efficiency was the best approach to business decisions. Lack of objectivity was going to trip Tarek up sooner or later; Hunter just had to hold tight to his patience and wait for the best time to strike.

He had to admit it pleased him how galling it must be for Tarek that he hadn't succeeded this time any better than he had in his other attempts at sabotage. Hunter had been attending an annual board meeting in Los Angeles when word of problems at a local manufacturing plant had reached him. He'd gone to investigate and found that someone had been caging half-starved illegal immigrants as slave labor. In his facility. It brought back nightmares of the last time an Avery plant had been used for criminal activity. His parents' faces flashed through his mind, twisted in terror as they had been the last time he'd seen them. His stomach churned and he shoved the memories aside, as he always did.

He'd cleaned up the mess, fired the traitors who were obviously on Tarek's payroll, let Pierce sort out the illegals, and returned home a day ahead of schedule. He was more than ready to enjoy the peace and solitude of his private tower. Circling slowly, he tucked in his wings to land on his balcony. He shifted quickly, heat vibrating through his muscles as they stretched and twisted into the shape of a man. Shrugging his shoulders to settle into the new form, he scrubbed a hand over the back of his neck.

The restless feeling that had eaten at him for weeks intensified. It wasn't just the business problems—it was something deeper, something he couldn't pin down. An instinct he had no name for. Not for the first time, he wished his father were still alive to ask. But he wasn't. The only two people he'd ever trusted were dead and he was alone. Always alone. Anyone who met him now wanted something from him. He was nothing but a name, a fat cred account, and an opportunity. He didn't bother reining in his disgust at the other man that he should have been able to trust. His uncle. Thankfully, that blight on the family tree had been cut away.

The only lesson his uncle had ever taught him was that there were worse things than being alone.

He was used to the loneliness, but this new instinct was something else. He tried to step back, to look at the unwanted and unwarranted feeling logically. The restlessness was new. But it was more than that. The unfamiliar instinct that crawled over his skin, like an itch he couldn't reach. A foreboding of some kind? Some people claimed they could sense their own death, but . . . that didn't sound right. Deus knew he'd had enough troubles lately. Deliveries going late or missing, a rash of fires, accidents that had become too common to be coincidence. He could lay it all at Tarek's feet.

The only thing he knew about the instinct is it had nothing to do with business.

There his thoughts hit a wall. Nothing. He had no idea why or where the instinct came from or how to get rid of it. So, he did what he always did when he didn't care for something . . . he pushed it away, distancing himself from what he couldn't control.

He stepped into his flat, reaching for the pants he'd left lying over the chair by the door in his main space. Then a sound caught his attention. He froze and tilted his head, letting his extra senses take control.

There was someone in his home.

Rage ripped through him that someone would enter his domain uninvited. His hands balled into fists, hawk talons digging into his palms. The mood he was in, he welcomed the chance to shred an intruder with his bare hands. Then he'd let the hawk have its turn.

Anticipation hummed in his veins and a tight smile curved his lips as he left the pants where they were and followed the whisper-soft sound of movement coming from his bedroom.

A tall, thin young boy with baggy black cargo pants on and a padded vest covering his chest stuffed the Avery ruby into a bag slung over his shoulder. The jewel had been in his family since before the war—his mother had loved it and kept it on display. After she died, Hunter couldn't look at it and had a safe built for it. Hunter's nostrils flared as he throttled another wave of anger.

He glanced at the vid monitor that should be following anything that moved, but it stood frozen. The little bugger had disabled his security system *and* broken into his safe. His eyebrows arched; he was enraged and almost impressed despite himself. Almost. It wouldn't stop him from teaching the boy a lesson and then having him thrown in prison.

No one took what belonged to an Avery.

Lunging through the door, he caught the thief around the waist and tumbled with him across the rug. Lightning-fast reflexes were all that kept Hunter from slamming the boy's face into the floor. A snarling, distinctly feline hiss issued from the body beneath him. Shit. A cat.

The boy lashed back with his foot, almost catching Hunter in the balls. He moved his leg to block just in time, sucking in a sharp breath. The kid scrambled away, swinging out a blind hand. A soft *snick* sounded and Hunter caught the skinny wrist just before a white powder spewed into the air. He held the breath he'd taken and twisted the boy's limb until he arched against the painful hold and cried out.

"Drop it," Hunter growled. The kid tried to kick him again, and he retaliated by jabbing his fingertips into the boy's ribs. His breath whooshed out, but Hunter felt the vest harden to prevent further attack. Body armor. Expensive stuff. He should know; Avery Industries invented it.

The kid gagged on a breath and the canister with the noxious powder hit the wood floor with a sharp *ping*. Grabbing the boy by the scruff of the neck, Hunter hauled him to his feet and backed him against the four-poster bed.

He noted two things at that moment. The first was that the boy was a woman; even with the vest, her slim curves molded to his front. The second was that the woman in question was his mate.

Double shit.

Shock made his grip loosen, and she took advantage, thrusting the heel of her palm into his solar plexus. He choked, sucking in air. He stumbled back, taking her with him as he hit the wood floor on his side. Sharp pain reverberated up his shoulder and into his brain. Reacting automatically, he rolled her beneath him and pinned her arms above her head. She hissed at him, bucking against his hold. He pressed his weight down to keep her still, but he couldn't stop his body from reacting to his mate's nearness. The moment his instincts had kicked in, every ounce of his awareness noticed her softness, her scent, her beauty. His cock went harder than a mercurite rod, and her squirming only made the situation worse.

His talons punched through his fingertips again, the hawk struggling for freedom. The deadly points pressed to her wrists, but he didn't trust her enough to relax his grip. Her eyes widened and she froze. He noted the emerald shade of her irises, the ring of black that rimmed the green. Thick loops scored each ear; the rings appeared to be filled with phosphorescent liquid, and he'd wager that they glowed when she turned them on.

She was lovely. Those wide eyes dominated her face, tilting up exotically at the corners. Her pale blond hair was no more than a few centimeters long, but it looked soft to the touch. He wanted to find out.

He wanted to stroke all of her. He could feel every micrometer of her underneath him. She was tall for a woman. Tall enough that he'd mistaken her for a young man. Her body was slim, her legs long. They'd look good wrapped around his waist, or, draped over his shoulders, or, hell, anywhere as long as it meant he could get inside her.

His cock throbbed, urging to fuck her, take her, claim her as his own. His instincts clamored an insistent agreement.

Mate.

He'd never imagined finding one. Only a few shifter species could sense their mates—those that mated for life. Red-tailed hawks, gray wolves, black vultures, condors, a few species of eagles. There weren't many who did. It was only his poor luck to be among those species, the hawk's instincts always seeking something the man preferred not to find.

But now he had.

His silent study of her had taken long enough that she fidgeted beneath him, her gaze wary. He smiled down at her, and the wariness turned to suspicion.

Well, she wasn't stupid, he'd give her that. She should be suspicious. Now he had to figure out who she was and how to keep her here without revealing the truth about what she was to him. He wouldn't give her the upper hand. Ever.

The vid monitor whirred softly, pointing at where they lay on the floor. His smile widened. "The game is up, kitten. Whatever you've done to disarm the system seems to have worn off. Your window of opportunity closed, didn't it? Now I have your face scanned into my system. I bet if I send that to the police, they'll know who you are without even running a check through the ident files. Won't they?"

Her gaze flickered for the briefest of moments, and he knew he had her. He should probably feel guilty, but she *had* been robbing him. Those exotic green eyes narrowed to dangerous slits and she hissed at him again.

He ignored her ire and settled himself more comfortably against her, digging his talons a bit deeper into her wrists as he stretched her arms higher to press her body tighter to his. The feel of her was almost enough to cloud his mind with lust. If he relaxed his attention for even a moment, she was the kind of woman to take advantage. He respected that. He would do the same.

Then again, she was supposed to fit him perfectly.

And that was a thought he didn't want. He wasn't interested in becoming dependent on anyone. He knew how it could gut a person to lose those that mattered most. Despite his parents' loving relationship, mates were for breeding, nothing more. That's all she would be used for, and she would be comfortably kept for her efforts.

"Tell me your name." His gaze bored into hers. "One way or another, I'll find it out."

Tugging at her hands, she shot him a fulminating glare when she couldn't break his grip. "Delilah."

His lips twitched against his will, amusement winding through him as he gave her short blond locks a pointed look. "I thought Delilah cut off Samson's hair, not her own."

"Hilarious." A derisive snort underscored her disgust.

"You've heard that before?"

Her eyes widened theatrically. "No, not once. You're so original and clever. Really prime."

"Thank you." He pretended not to notice her sarcasm. "And your surname?"

He could hear her teeth grind together before she spat, "Chase."

"Delilah Chase. Lovely to meet you. I'm Hunter Avery."

He knew her name, and that was one objective down. Now to force her to stay.

"I know who you are, Hunter." The sound of his name on her lips sent a peculiar warmth winding through his chest. No one called him Hunter anymore. He was "Mr. Avery" or simply "Avery" to anyone who addressed him. Once he'd taken his father's place in the company, he'd ended up with his title as well, for all that he was only sixteen at the time. He pushed away the thought, struggling to stay focused for the first time in his life.

Delilah squirmed again, twisting at her captured wrists. He could all but hear the gears spinning in her head as she calculated how to get out of her current predicament. Her body softened beneath him, her legs lifting to clasp his hips. So that was the way she wanted to play it? He fought a grin. She couldn't make this easier for him if she tried.

"I'm certain, if we really want to, we can come to a . . . mutually beneficial arrangement to resolve this issue." When she tilted her hips up to rub her sex against his, he had no idea how it was possible, but his cock grew even harder as he settled into the crux of her slender thighs. Fire fisted in his belly, spreading until he thought his body would explode out of his skin. He wanted her. Every part of him craved her. A knowing little smile curved the corners of her full lips, and something close to triumph flashed in her green eyes when he couldn't stop himself from thrusting against her softness.

"An arrangement?" He slid his tongue over his teeth. "You might be right about that."

"What did you have in mind?" she purred. Her grin widened. He allowed her that small moment of victory before he smiled back. With teeth.

"You, in my bed." He stroked the pad of his thumb over the inside of her wrist. The skin there was soft, warm. He wanted to explore the rest of her and see if all of her felt as good. "In exchange, I won't alert the authorities to your little breach of my security system. Then the ruby stays with me, and you're free to go."

"I think I can handle some time in your bed." She glanced over his shoulder to the wide mattress. Her shoulder lifted in a delicate shrug, her grin never wavering. "It looks comfortable enough."

He waited a beat. "The deal is for a full week of your time."

"A week?" Wariness slid over her expression again, the smile winking out as though it had never been.

"It's a very valuable ruby." He lifted his eyebrows. "Maybe it's worth a bit long—"

"A week is fine." Her lips lifted in a snarl; she was obviously not pleased by this new turn of events. Her fangs slid out of her gums. "How do you know I won't kill you in your sleep?"

Easing his grip on her arms, he moved away from her to sit back on his heels. "They'd catch that on vid, too, wouldn't they?"

"You'd still be dead." Raising herself up to her elbows, she didn't try to escape.

He rolled his shoulder in a shrug, rising to his feet. "Some things are worth the risk, kitten."

Sliding his gaze down her body, he let it heat with appreciation. Her mouth formed a moue as she sat up and rubbed her wrists. His talons had left red marks on her creamy skin, and he felt an unprecedented pinch of remorse. It must be the mating thing. He rarely regretted anything he did—he planned too well for that to be a problem.

She leveled him a frank look. "I don't know what your kink is, but if you think for a nanosecond that you get to hurt and humiliate me, you're going to find yourself gutted like a fish." She slid out her razor-sharp claws to emphasize her point. "*That* isn't part of our deal."

"I don't hurt women." His gaze was drawn to the redness around her wrists and he fought a wince. "Usually."

"Just coerce them into having sex with you?" She shot him an incredulous look as she pushed to her feet.

He let a little grin kick up the side of his mouth. "When the situation warrants it."

"How do I know you won't go back on your word and turn me in after you have what you want?" Her blond brows rose, and she propped a hand on her hip.

He chuckled. "Believe it or not, I keep my word. You'll just have to decide if it's worth the risk."

"Fine." Her hands relaxed at her sides, and she made no move to leave.

"Good. You can start now." He stepped back to settle into a comfortable chair. He steepled his fingers together and pressed them to his lips, watching to see what she would do. It was easier if she stayed by choice, but he wasn't above keeping her by force. He did have her on vid, as he'd said. He was sure he could have her found if he needed to. It would be an inconvenience he didn't want or need. Having a mate at all was an inconvenience he didn't want or need. A humorless smile formed on his lips. "Strip."

Shrugging, she slid her nail in the seal of her armored vest, and it parted down the middle. Dipping a narrow shoulder, she let it fall to the floor. Then she pulled a tight, long-sleeved shirt over her head. Her breasts were high and firm. The nipples were a soft pink, and he wanted to suck them into his mouth until they darkened to raspberry. The thought alone was enough to make his cock jump. Her gaze locked on that portion of his anatomy as she unsealed her pants and pushed them down her legs. Her hips were a small flare from her waist, her body long, lean, and willowy.

When she bent to unfasten her shoes and remove the last of her clothing, he saw that a green dragon nanotat, which matched her eyes, wound around her ribs and up her back. The tattoo moved beneath her skin, the beast looking real. Another nano-tat, this one a small monarch butterfly, fluttered on one hip. A tiny gem sparkled from her navel. Interesting. He wanted to tug on it with his teeth and see if she gasped. He wanted to lick the tats, slide his tongue over every delicious micrometer of her smooth body.

Anticipation made his heart pound and his cock ache, but he schooled himself to patience. He was very good at waiting for the right moment to act.

She stepped toward him, her body a study in feline grace, the light kissing her skin as she moved. When she was within a meter of him, he held up his hand. "Stop."

A pale brow lifted at the command, but she obeyed. She slipped a fingertip down her cleavage, around her belly button, and over the butterfly nanotat. "Does the pretty birdie just want to watch? I can put on a very good show."

Her smile and her movements were too practiced. He didn't want to be seduced as he was sure she'd done with other men. They might have been satisfied with that, but he was her mate. He wanted her genuine reaction.

And he would have it. Now.

Crooking his finger, he had her bend toward him. When she was within reach, he bracketed her jaw in his fingers, holding her in place. She went rigid, her muscles tensing. His lips brushed over hers gently, and he could feel her tiny jolt of surprise.

Her eyes fluttered closed as he licked his way into her mouth, and he shut his eyes to focus on the flavor of her. His mate. His tongue twined with hers, and the taste of her sank into his senses. He'd never rid his mouth or memory of the essence of her, some instinct locking it in forever.

He let his free hand skim over her shoulder, his fingertips brushing her collarbone before slipping down to the upper slope of her breast. He cupped the curve, rubbing the pad of his thumb over her velvety crest. A grunt of pleasure came from his chest as he was rewarded by the tightening of her nipple. The little point stabbed into his palm, and he flicked his nail over it. She made a tiny noise in the back of her throat, set her hands on his naked thighs, and raked her teeth over his lower lip.

The scent of her wetness reached his nostrils, and he bit back a smile. Didn't think he could turn her on, did she? This wasn't going to be a duty she suffered through.

Then her fingers slipped up his leg to wrap around his dick. He groaned at the contact, her touch enough to make his thoughts evaporate into nothingness. It was a reaction he'd never had with a woman before. He didn't like her effect on him so soon, yet he wanted more.

He broke the kiss, his chest heaving with each breath. Clinging to his control by the thinnest thread, he pulled her hand away from him. He wanted it wild and possessive, but he wanted her with him every moment of the ride. Everything within him screamed with the need to claim. The woman was his, whether she knew it or not, whether she accepted it or not. She'd just have to get used to it.

So would he.

Shaking away the disturbing thought, he forced his mind to focus on the task at hand. Fucking his mate for the first time. He sank to his knees before her, lifting one of her legs over his shoulder.

She wavered on her foot, but the cat kept her balance. "Wh-what are you doing?"

He just flashed her a wicked grin, set his mouth against her sex, and licked.

She screamed, high and thin, standing on tiptoe to get away from his mouth, but her fingers fisted in his hair, holding him to her. He chuckled against her clit, and she moaned.

The sweetness of her flooded his tongue, and he drank the wetness that coated her sex. He worked her with his lips, teeth, and tongue . . . suckling, tasting, biting gently. He cupped her ass in his palms, pulling her closer to him. She gasped, the muscles in her legs shaking against him. Her pussy contracted around his tongue, her cream slipping over his taste buds.

"I-I . . . Hunter, Hunter, *Hunter!*"

Hearing her scream his name made lust burn through him, made his cock harden to the point of pain. If he didn't get inside her soon, he was going to explode. He hummed against her clit, nipping at the little nub. He moved one hand up her thigh until he could stroke her damp lips and ease his finger into her tight pussy. He added a second digit, loving the snug clasp of her inner walls. Her hands tugged on his hair as he began pumping his fingers inside her. Hard.

The frantic sounds she made told him exactly how close she was to orgasm, and he worked her faster and faster with his hand and mouth. He wanted to feel her come against his lips, wanted to taste her satisfaction. Pulling his fingers from her pussy, he trailed the moisture to her anus and teased the rim of the small pucker.

"Hunter . . ." She shuddered in his arm, her hips pressing back into his hand.

He bit her clit and sank his thumb into her ass. She screamed as she came hard. He continued to move his tongue and fingers over her, in her, until she moaned and pulled at his hair. Her hands closed over his shoulders, pushing weakly. He chuckled, licking and suckling. The taste of her would drive him mad.

With sudden force, she shoved him back and toppled him onto the area rug. He frowned as his back hit the floor. "This isn't what—"

"I don't care." Passion flushed her face and made her eyes sparkle. "I want to fuck you right now, and I'm not going to wait until you're ready. Deal with it."

He grinned, folded his arms behind his head, and licked her wetness from his lips with relish. "Then by all means, have your way with me."

She laughed, a low husky sound that made his cock throb. "I will."

Straddling his hips, she positioned her herself above him and closed her fingers around his dick to stroke the shaft. She rubbed the head over her slick lips. He gritted his teeth until they ached, the muscles in his neck cording as he fought the need to slam home into her tight heat.

She sank down on him slowly, squirming and twisting her hips until he was encased in her pussy.

Perfect. Deus, it was fucking perfect.

His hands lifted to cup her pert breasts, his thumbs chafing her dusky pink nipples until they were tight and flushed. Her hips rolled against his, lifting and lowering herself on his cock. The slickness between her legs coated his shaft, and the glide was so smooth he had to laugh.

Bracing her hands on his chest, she leaned forward to change the angle of his penetration. He groaned, arching between her slim thighs to rock his pelvis into hers. She shuddered, her claws extending to dig into his pecs. He grinned. "Watch the claws, kitten."

She blinked and withdrew them. "Ah. Didn't mean to hurt you."

"A little scratching from a pretty she-cat isn't even enough to qualify as real pain." He rolled his hips, grinding his teeth to keep from coming before she did.

He'd never had to fight so hard for control in his life. It was unsettling, but he didn't have the time or attention to spare to examine it.

She clenched her inner muscles around his cock and laughed when he groaned. The sound hit his chest like a blow, and watching her face light up and her eyes dance with mirth made it difficult to breathe. Deus, he wasn't going to last much longer. Reaching between them, he extended his talons and flicked the tip of one over her hardened clit.

She jolted, orgasm strumming through her body. Her wetness sealed their bodies together at one central point as she arched. Her thighs locked tight, and he knew he'd never in his life forget the look of ecstasy that swept over her face just then. A low cry spilled from her lips, and her pussy milked the length of his cock as she came. Retracting his talon, he worked her clit with a fingertip, dragging *more* from her.

"Hunter!"

His name on her lips broke his control. He bracketed her hips with his hands, flipping her underneath him so they were half on the carpet and half on the wooden floor. She gasped at the quick movements, but he was beyond caring about anything except the drive toward orgasm.

Catching her wrists in one hand, he held them over her head and pinned them to the floor. His hips bucked hard, driving deep inside her sweet heat. It felt so damn good, he was going to go off like a biobomb.

His jaw locked as she arched under him, her beaded nipples rubbing against his chest. Their mingling scents combined with the musk of sex and sweat in the room, dragged out the primal hungers, and the hawk fought for dominance within him. He slammed his cock into her over and over again, no finesse, no concern for her comfort, just the white-hot need to come inside his mate's soft body. But her long legs clamped around his flanks, lifting her into his thrusts. Her voice chanted in his ear, calling his name, urging him on.

That was all it took to send him flying, to push him higher than he'd ever been in his life. Her pussy clenched around his cock again, and she hissed as she shattered in his arms. His fingers bit into her wrists, his back bowing as he came in powerful jets inside her.

"Delilah," he breathed. Shudders racked his body as he released her hands and sank down on top of her. He buried his nose in her throat, inhaling the fragrance of her with each ragged breath.

She flung her arm around the back of his neck, panting. Her legs relaxed, her thighs falling open against the floor. His cock slid from her pussy, and he grunted. He knew he'd want her again. Soon.

First, he should probably get them both up and off the floor. A self-deprecating smile curved his lips. Certainly not how he could have ever contemplated taking his mate the first time. Then again, he'd never imagined having one—hadn't even wanted one. But she was here now and he had to deal with her.

He gathered her against his chest and stood. She stirred when he laid her on the bed, yawning catlike. "I should . . ."

"No, you shouldn't." Crawling onto the microsilk sheets next to her, he pulled her back into his arms. "You're here for a week. Stay there." He settled against her, throwing his thigh over hers. "Sleep."

She sighed, a little purr rumbling in her chest. Her body relaxed into boneless sleep. It was amazing how felines could do that. He let out a slow breath, stroking his fingertips down her side. The restlessness that had ridden him for weeks had dissipated, and his muscles loosened by degrees, his eyes sliding closed. If he was taking the wrong risk and she gutted him in his sleep, at least he'd die having had the best sex of his life.

Not a bad exit strategy.

2

When Delilah woke up, the man was wrapped around her like a boa constrictor. She smirked. Afraid she'd get away, was he? Smart man.

She'd stay the week, though, if for no other reason than to find a way to get around his security system and snatch his ruby. She knew it was back in the safe. When he thought she was asleep in the middle of the night, she'd watched him take it out of her bag and return it to the safe. A frown pulled at her forehead as confusion swamped her. He had to know she could get into the safe again if she'd done it before. Faster this time, probably. So why put it back? His actions made no sense.

Then again, when did the rich make sense to anyone but themselves? Maybe he was just stupider than she assumed. It didn't matter, so long as she could get enough time alone in this room to steal the ruby.

Once she made that happen, she'd offload it before anyone could prove she'd had her paws on it. If anyone asked why she'd been in Hunter's flat, she could always claim to be a hired jade. It wasn't like the police wouldn't believe she was a prostitute. Her mother had been, and so had her sister Lorelei—until she'd clawed her way to the top of the food chain as a madam. Now Lorelei owned the most notorious technobrothel in New Chicago. Hell, the world, maybe. As unsavory as the life of a jade was, it wasn't illegal. She couldn't be arrested for getting paid to fuck a wealthy man. And, really, part of the fun of Delilah's own job was taking from wealthy men. They'd taken so much from her and her family, it was only fair to return the favor. She'd have to lay low for a while after this, though. The money was definitely good enough to make it worth her while. Her client obviously wanted the ruby bad.

So, now it was a challenge. Figure out how to take the gem right out from under Hunter's nose and not get caught. She ran her tongue down a long fang and grinned. She'd been paid to do a job and she was going to do it. She never failed, which was why she got the prime commissions. And playing with the hawk wasn't going to be a hardship. He was good-looking, had an acre of microsilk sheets to roll around on, and had the most talented mouth she'd ever come across.

The things she did for her job.

It surprised her how he'd seen to her pleasure before he'd taken his own. Not what she expected from a spoiled rich boy like him who'd grown up with anything and everything he wanted. Then again, did she really care why? He was a mark, nothing more. She'd use him and he'd use her, but when it was over, she'd be the one on top. She always was.

Hunter sighed, his warm breath whispering over her neck as he snuggled in deeper. His arms tightened around her torso, pulling her even closer to him. The hard arc of his cock pressed against her ass. A low purr soughed from her throat. Now, there was a toy any cat would like to play with.

Reaching behind her, she let her fingertips feather over the length of him. He groaned against her skin, giving a tiny jolt as he woke. Peeking over her shoulder at him, she winked. "Good morning."

"Mmm. Yes, it is." His palms cupped her breasts while his hips thrust into her hand. "Don't stop."

She chuckled. "Hadn't planned on it."

"Good," he grunted.

Extending her claws, she lightly ran the tips up the long shaft of his cock. He groaned, his hips thrusting into her touch. She rubbed the pad of her thumb over the tiny opening at the head and smeared the bead of moisture there, massaging it into the bulbous crest. His ragged breath brushed her ear, and he rubbed his palms over her nipples. Heat wound through her. The man knew how to touch a woman.

She loved the power that raced through her when she held a man's cock in her hand, when she sucked it into her mouth. At that moment, rich or poor, smart or stupid, the man was hers. He would do *anything* for her. Her pussy clenched at the thought, moisture slicking the lips. Her fingers tightened around Hunter's dick, but the angle at which she had to twist her arm made it difficult to stroke him the way she wanted to. She moved to roll over, but he stopped her, pulling her hand away from his cock.

"I wasn't done yet." Wriggling in his arms did little for her—he was bigger than she was, and unless she wanted to damage him, she wasn't going to get away.

"I nearly was," he growled. She couldn't stop the grin that formed on her lips. She liked how he reacted to her. Not as a mark, but as a man to a woman. It was surprising, but chemistry like this wasn't something she ran across often. Especially not while she was on a job. Best not to question it.

Reaching past her, he lifted a small, carved stone statue from his bedside table. He held it in front of her eyes and let her get a good look at it. Standing on a flat base was an ancient warrior in ceremonial garb—loincloth, headdress, and an eagle symbol carved over his chest. It was compacted, so that the figurine formed a long cylinder.

"What are you doing?" She shot a confused glance over her shoulder. There were a lot more pressing matters to take care of than a miniature Mayan statue.

"As if you couldn't guess." He tilted the top of the statue so that it parted her curls and rubbed against her clit. "Spread."

He couldn't possibly . . . but he did.

Rolling her hips, she kept the constant contact against her clitoris. Her arm reached back to fist in his silky hair. A moan exploded from her throat and her thighs eased apart. He pressed the small statue to the entrance of her sex, pushing in one slow micrometer at a time. It stretched her, and a helpless whimper echoed in the wide room. If she weren't so wet already, it would have been painful. As it was, the pleasure was going to kill her.

"That is a *twelve-hundred-year-old* figurine," she gasped, horror and excitement rippling through her. Stealing things like that were how she made her living. The man was clearly insane, but Deus this felt too good to stop now.

"At least. From the ruins of Palenque, I believe." He pulled it out, only to push it back in again. Faster this time, harder. "You know your ancient artifacts."

A shudder racked her form, and she twisted in his arms, clinging to sanity by the barest margin. "It's my business to know."

He chuckled, the sound vibrating against her back. "It's never been put to better use."

The ridges in the stone pressed into the walls of her sex, slightly rough, utterly exciting. Her fingers dug into his forearm, but she was careful not to let her claws scrape him again. A shudder rippled through her. "Hunter . . ."

He hummed in the back of his throat. "I like it when you say my name."

Her head rolled against his shoulder, arching her torso. "Move. Faster. *Hunter*."

A rough sound burst from him as she gasped his name, and he gave her exactly what she'd demanded. She lifted her leg, curling it back over his thigh. It left her wide open, gave him all the access he could possibly want. She didn't give a single thought to how many creds she could get for that figurine, or how this was the kinkiest thing any man had ever done to her.

Her hips snapped forward to meet each of his thrusts, working herself as quickly as he would allow. Contractions rippled in her sex, tension building deep within her until she thought she might scream. The way her heart pounded made the sound of blood rush in her ears. She panted for breath, each lungful of air dragging his hot, masculine scent to her nose. It aroused her even more. Her head pressed back against his shoulder, her body bowing as she moved closer to orgasm.

He buried the figurine deep inside her, angled and twisted it as he pulled it out again, then did the same in reverse. The maddening scrape of the smooth edges against her most delicate tissue was more than enough to break her control. Her pussy convulsed around the statue, her walls closing on it while he kept pumping the thing inside of her.

The world faded around her until there was nothing left but the harsh sound of her own breathing, the heat of his erection pressing against her backside, the wide expanse of the figurine inside her. Her sex pulsed around it one last time, and she moaned.

"Did you enjoy that?" Hunter's warm voice vibrated in her ear, and she could hear his smile.

She shuddered when he rubbed his thumb over her swollen clit, a purr slipping from her throat. "That was . . . creative."

"Thank you, kitten."

She shot an incredulous look over her shoulder, extending her claws to dig in to his arm while she flashed a smile at him. With fangs. "I'm no one's kitten, rich boy."

"You purr like one." He kissed the nape of her neck, and she had to fight another purr. Something must have given her away, because he laughed. She hunched her shoulder and glared back at him.

He just smiled and twisted the figurine still buried inside her, making her gasp and shiver. Pressing it deeper, he slowly worked her with it again. He slid his hips back enough to slip the hand not holding the statue down her back and between her thighs. Rubbing her vaginal lips on either side of the thrusting figurine just emphasized the hard stone length of it moving within her. Her hands balled into fists, her claws digging into her palms.

Trailing her own moisture to the recessed pucker of her anus, he eased a finger inside her ass. Her breath caught, dark ecstasy charging through her system. He slid a second finger in, widening her. "I'm going to fuck you here, Delilah."

"Yes," she moaned, nodding for emphasis. The mere thought of being penetrated by both him and the statue made wetness surge between her thighs.

The statue stopped moving for just a moment, long enough to make her anticipation shriek. His cock nudged against her ass, entering in one long, slow push. She hissed, felt her fangs slide down, and struggled to keep a grip on the wildness inside. Her back arched and shudders ran through her muscles. "Don't. Stop."

"I haven't even started, kitten." His mouth opened on the back of her neck, sucking on the sensitive flesh. But he didn't move within her. She was stretched past bearing, his long cock throbbing in her ass, the figurine lodged in her pussy.

She held herself still, agony and ecstasy balancing her on a razor's edge. The need twisted tighter and tighter until she was ready to scream. "What are you waiting for?"

"For you to relax." His palm slid up and down her side, the touch soothing, but did nothing to alleviate the tension building within her body.

Concentrating harder than she ever had in her life, she un-balled her fists and forced each muscle in her body to loosen. When he moved within her, sweet pain followed in his wake. She was so *full*. The movement of his cock pressed the thin wall separating her anus and her pussy against every single ridge and curve of the figurine.

She could feel every detail.

She moaned. The hot, vital feel of his flesh inside her along with the hard stone was exquisite. Gooseflesh broke down her limbs and she shivered, liquid flames coursing through her veins. He rocked his hips against her, his thrusts increasing in speed and force until the hard muscles of his lower belly spanked against her ass. His hand worked the figurine within her at a tandem rhythm until there wasn't a moment where she wasn't penetrated by one or the other. Or both.

Beads of sweat rolled down her body, sealing her back to his front. The scent of him intensified, deep and masculine. It filled her nostrils, sinking her into every sensation. Smell, touch, feel.

He chuckled, his hand moving the figurine as he stroked into her. "Say it."

His name. He wanted her to say his name. She grinned and, shaking her head, refused to give him what he wanted. Instead, she clamped her anus tight around his thrusting cock, giving as good as she got. They both groaned at the increased friction.

Then he drove himself and the statue deep inside her, pressed his hand to her lower belly to still her movements, and froze. "Say it."

She wriggled, trying to get free, trying to *move*. She couldn't. He was bigger than her, stronger. Raking her claws up his arm, she hissed. "Move."

"No."

"*Move*." She bucked and twisted, but her struggles only stoked the fire inside her higher and higher. Even without movement, the fit was so tight that her pussy spasmed around the figurine. Her muscles fisted around his cock. A choked breath rasped past her throat at the sweetness of it, but it wasn't enough. Not nearly enough. "Deus."

His voice dropped to a silken whisper in her ear. "Give me what I want and I'll give you what you want."

A whimper was the only response she could manage as he used his free hand to pluck at her nipples. Then he pinched them hard, and she broke. "Hunter!"

"Yes." He pistoned inside her, his cock stretching her almost as wide as the statue did.

She almost cried out in relief as pleasure ripped through her system. Shoving her hips forward and back to meet each thrust, she could do nothing more than moan. His hand stroked her nipples, and the combination was enough to make her shudder at the ripening tension.

His mouth opened over her shoulder, sucking on the sweat-dampened flesh. He bit down, and she screamed, shock and ecstasy flashing through her. Her body bowed hard as she came, and her sex clenched rhythmically as she exploded in his arms. His cock hammered inside her, his arms locking tight around her to hold her close, and a harsh groan ripped from his chest as his fluids filled her.

When orgasm finally eased its grip on her, she relaxed, her face pressing to the pillow. Her lungs burned as she tried to gulp in needed air. Shivers still racked her body many moments later, and she whimpered. "Deus."

"Did I hurt you?" It almost sounded as though he were concerned, and she fought a snort. Any man concerned about a woman who'd tried to rob him was clearly out of his skull. Then again, any man who'd fuck a woman with a priceless figurine was also out of his skull, so Hunter wasn't faring well on the sanity scale. He pulled both the statue and his cock out of her, his hands sliding over her as if looking for damage.

Peeking over her shoulder, she saw the same closed expression she'd noted the moment she'd met his gaze. He laughed and smiled, but there was a remoteness about him that warned people away. She doubted it was there solely for her benefit. It intrigued her—she'd never been one to heed warnings or obey rules. She wouldn't be in her line of work otherwise.

A few moments passed while she looked him over, rolling so she could see all of him. He wasn't hard to look at. At well over two meters tall, he made her feel petite. It was unusual. Unsettling. She wasn't sure if she liked it or not. Something to consider later.

His shoulders were ridiculously wide, tapering to a narrow waist. There wasn't an ounce of fat anywhere on his body. She'd put her hands all over his pretty muscles the night before, so she knew firsthand how well built he was. She'd never met a man with a nicer body except one of her sister's jades, Nolan Angelo. But . . . something about Hunter made him stand out in her mind. Nolan was as close to human perfection as a man came, and he'd never affected her this way.

It was Hunter's face, she decided.

A slim scar ran from the corner of his eye and curved down to disappear under his jawline. Interesting. She wanted to know how he got it, wanted to run her fingertips over it to memorize the shape and feel. His eyes were a rich brown, flecked with amber, gold, and ebony, the look in them intense and focused. And they usually focused in on her. It made her feel stalked, hunted. Like prey. Also unusual, since she was usually the one doing the hunting.

His hair was also brown, a little long, but nothing special. Average coloring. He should have been easy to overlook and dismiss. He wasn't.

He was imposing, but he didn't scare her. He fascinated her. It was within his power to hurt her, and he hadn't so far. Instead he'd made her come more times in one night than she'd ever imagined possible. And wasn't that just a nice little bonus to their arrangement?

Nothing about him should fascinate her, and the fact that he'd more than captured her interest sent a niggle of worry though her. She pushed it aside—it would pass, and once the week was over and the job was done, she'd never see him again. That would be the end of it, no matter how intriguing she found him. It was just another reason she was good at her work. To put it mildly. She was the *best*. She took great pride in being the best. She'd worked her ass off to get the kind of reputation that said she never failed, that she could steal anything from anyone at any time. Nothing was going to change that. She wouldn't let some rich little hawk smear her reputation. No one was that good-looking or that good in bed.

Putting any lingering uncertainty aside, she gave a contented cat-stretch and yawned until she thought her jaw might crack. "So, what shall we do for the rest of the day?"

"I'm sure we'll think of something." A smile curved his lips and he reached for her.

Just watching Delilah walk was an erotic experience. The feline grace in every stride and every smooth swish of her hips captivated Hunter, and he was unable to tear his gaze away. Her small breasts bounced, the pert nipples a lovely shade of pink. He recalled clearly the satin texture of them in his mouth, the way they'd darkened and puckered.

His cock began to fill, the flesh firming with every step she took toward him. She settled herself on a stool topped with plush kleather padding. The kelp leather was prime grade, imported from Asia. The contrast of the black fabric against the pale flesh of her ass drew his gaze.

Everything about her drew his gaze.

And he liked having her here in his home. His instincts

flickered to life at the reminder of what this woman was to him. Mate. The hawk within reveled at the claiming of her. He'd reached for her so often in the night that his body ached, but he'd woken again and again, the hunger so sharp he'd had to have her.

He blinked and swallowed, forcing his mind away from the heated memories before he bent her over the countertop to fuck her once more. "Are you hungry?"

She nodded, crossing her legs demurely. Considering her complete nudity, the gesture made him smile. He caught himself, the grin fading. He'd smiled more in the last day than he had in . . . years. Yet, it felt natural to smile at her, to laugh with her. She seemed to take such joy in living, throwing herself wholly into what she did and said. Whereas he was much more cautious.

Life after his parents' death—life with his uncle—had taught him the value of caution. Nothing had changed his mind since. But he rarely changed it once a decision had been reached.

"Hunter?" She tilted her head to meet his gaze, the corners of her eyes crinkling. "Are you going to offer me food just to tease me?"

He shook himself out of his reverie. "No. Of course not." Turning to retrieve the required sustenance, he paused and looked back. "What do you like to eat?"

It was one of many things he didn't know about this woman who was his mate. He knew she was a criminal, knew she was passionate and beautiful, but that was the extent of his knowledge. He would have to change that.

The deep craving inside him to know everything, to know all of her, had to spring from the mating instinct. He'd never been the least bit curious about his lovers. They were a means to a mutually satisfying end, nothing more. He'd never allowed any of them to be more.

The very notion of *needing* anything from anyone, of caring, was enough to make him break out in a cold sweat. He knew how the loss of someone he needed would feel, how it could make him pray for death himself. No one got close to him, not really. He preferred it that way. Swallowing hard, he stuffed the cravings into the darkest corner of himself, never to see the light of day again. He would deal with this as he did everything else in his life—rationally.

Regardless of where the desire to know the particulars of her life sprang from, it was a practical need as well. If he was going to be near the woman for the rest of his life, it was necessary to understand what kind of threat she might be to his company, what kind of weakness she might present to his enemies. She would eventually find out she was his mate, though he'd hold off telling her as long as possible, but it was best he had all the salient details at his disposal beforehand.

It would make her easier to control.

"I'm a cat. I like fish best." A gamine grin lit her face, and her fingers spread over the shiny metal surface of his kitchen counter. "But, I'm hungry enough to eat anything you put in front of me."

The soft rumbling of her stomach reached his ears, underscoring her words. He nodded and reached for a cutlery drawer, plucking two sets out to drop them on the counter. She picked up a utensil to examine it and he narrowed his gaze at her. "Don't steal that."

She didn't even bother to feign indignation, just gave him a thoroughly feline grin and set it back down. "I won't." She waited a beat. "I don't bother with the petty thievery. You have much more enticing pieces here."

"Don't steal those, either." He flicked his gaze over her torso, staring at her breasts. "Though I do recall how much you *appreciated* my collection this morning."

Stroking her fingertip across her collarbone, she flashed a sinful look. "You have very unique uses for your collection. I couldn't help but admire it."

"That's good to know." Moving away from her again, he keyed his food storage unit for two plates of Alaskan rockfish and fresh greens. It took a few moments for the information to uplink into the system, and then the unit's door unlocked with a soft click. He opened it, pulled out the gently steaming dishes, and set one in front of her.

Her eyes widened and she gave the air a delicate sniff. "Mmm. That looks prime."

Hauling a kleather stool around to his side of the counter, he was about to sit when he paused. "I have ice wine, if you'd like."

"I'd like. Thank you." She set down the bite of food she'd scooped up and waited for him to return to resume her meal.

Sitting, he watched her. He rarely had anyone in his house for anything other than business or sex. Or both. They didn't stay long enough to share a meal with him. It didn't feel wrong, just . . . odd. He took a drink of his wine and contemplated her for a moment. She dined as gracefully as she walked. It didn't fit with the mental image he would form of an experienced criminal—and she had to be very experienced to have gotten into his home.

Another question he couldn't answer about her.

Now was as good a time as any to start unearthing the mystery of his mate. He picked up his utensils and began eating, casting her a casual glance. "Where are you from?"

She froze, her wineglass halfway to her mouth. For the first time since she'd sat down, she seemed discomfited, and gave him a guarded look. "Why do you want to know?"

"Just curious." He frowned, disliking her reaction. He took another bite of food, trying to bank his reflexive annoyance at her reticence. The spices on the rockfish burst over his taste buds, perfectly complementing the dish. He might as well have been chewing on polyglass for all it did to still the unwelcome emotions roiling through him. He'd done nothing to cause the amount of distrust in her gaze. "Appease me."

"I can think of better ways to appease a man." The expression of practiced seductress molded her features again, and it irritated him even more this time. He took a breath, reining in the unwarranted feeling. It wasn't like him to overreact about anything. He didn't care for it.

"We'll get to that." His brow arched, and he issued a quiet order, "Answer the question."

"I grew up in the Vermilion District." Her shoulder lifted in a shrug.

He blinked, uncertain how the woman before him could have come from the cesspool that was the Vermilion. "You don't . . . the way you speak isn't . . ."

She met his gaze, her green eyes open and frank. "My mother made sure my sister and I knew how to speak well, use the correct utensil, and waltz like a lady. To entertain rich men. Not that I use those skills very often, but I do have them."

"Ah." He understood what she meant by "entertain" without having to ask for an explanation. It did slide a few more pieces into place. The amount of contempt in her tone when she said *rich men* was surprising, though. Every answer raised more questions. "How often do you end up *entertaining*?"

"For money? Never. My sister didn't want me to enter that line of work, so I found something that interested me more." She took a deep swig of her wine and focused on her food, clearly dismissing the subject.

Her sister was a jade. Likely her mother as well. It was so far removed from his own existence and the environment he was raised in. Despite his instinctual response to her, he forced the ruthless reminder into his mind. He couldn't trust this woman. She was a thief, the sister of a whore, and she had even more to gain than the normal socialites who scrabbled for his attention and cred account. No matter how true it was, it made his belly cramp. How desperate must her childhood have been growing up in the Vermilion? He swallowed hard and cleared his throat. "Prostitution is at least legal. You chose a life of crime."

She snorted, pausing to finish chewing before she spoke. "Strange how that turned out, isn't it?"

"Why?" Leaning back on his stool, he pushed his plate away and picked up what was left of his wine.

Her blond eyebrows lifted. "Why what?"

"Why would you choose to become a thief?" He sipped the sweet liquor, savoring the flavor.

A breathy laugh escaped her. "You know, no one has ever asked me that."

"Not even your sister?"

She licked her lips, mimicking his pose as she sat back. "We have a mutual agreement not to ask about the dirty details of each other's work."

"I can understand that." He coughed into his fist, fighting another smile. A jade and a thief—he could definitely appreciate the problems of full disclosure inherent in either of those professions.

She just smiled.

"You haven't answered my question." He arched a brow at her. "Why a thief?"

"I'm good at it." Her narrow shoulder lifted in a shrug, which made her breasts sway, drawing his gaze like a targeting missile. "My nature makes it easy, my personality makes it fun. Isn't that what I should look for in a good job?"

"It's still illegal."

Her gaze narrowed to green slits and her voice dropped to a purr. "Laws only matter to people who have the luxury of following them."

"True." He'd struck a sore point with her there, but it was

hardly a false accusation. What she did was illegal. That would have to stop. He had no desire to deal with the legal entanglements of having a thief for his mate—and she would hardly be able to keep her face from the newsvids. He certainly couldn't. Then again, he didn't have to marry her to breed with her. With her family background, she might even prefer being his mistress. He'd have to think about it. He rubbed his free hand over his forehead. This mating business was far more complicated than he liked.

The silken edge to her tone sharpened. "So, you've never broken a single law?"

Tilting his head, he decided to see where she was going with this. "I try not to."

"Only try?"

He shrugged and grinned. "I have a corporation to run. I do what I have to, and sometimes rules need to be bent."

She huffed a breath and crossed her arms over her breasts. "You're as bad as I am, Mr. *It's Illegal*."

Lifting his hands to ward her off, he chuckled. "That wasn't a condemnation, just an observation."

"Hmmph." She recrossed her legs in the other direction, and the soft brush of her thighs against each other reached his ears. He'd rather those thighs were brushing against his. "Well, then . . . I think that's enough serious conversation for the day, don't you?" Her glass clinked against the countertop when she set it down and stood. A sensual little smile formed on her face as she moved toward him. The erection that hadn't fully eased during their meal came roaring back, lust fisting in his belly. He set his feet flat on the floor, using them to swivel his stool so he faced her when she came around the counter.

He cupped her hips in his palms when she neared, pulling her between his knees. Her nipples rubbed against his chest, making his breath hiss between his teeth. The feel of her was amazing. He'd never known anything like it with any other woman. There hadn't been a single moment since he met her that he hadn't wanted her, the need always on the edges of his consciousness. Even in his sleep, even in the quiet moments after he'd just had her. The little smile that formed on her lips made his cock ache with the need to be inside her any way that he could. "Kiss me, kitte—"

Her mouth slanted over his, and he chuckled against her soft, soft lips. Her tongue thrust into his mouth boldly, demanding a response his body was more than eager to give. He jerked her closer until the hot, damp curls of her sex rubbed against his cock. He filled his palms with her ass, lifting her into his body. Their breath mingled as they panted, their heads tilting to change the angle of the kiss. Deus, he loved kissing her.

The scent of her intoxicated him, headier than the finest wine. Soon his home would smell of her . . . and him. Them. Together. The hawk rippled to the surface, its pleasure matching the man's at the very idea. His fingers burrowed inward until he could touch her slick heat from behind. He loved how wet she was for him, how responsive. She rubbed her torso against him, catlike, and a shudder ran through him.

Pushing at his shoulders, she leaned back enough so that she could drop to her knees before him. The height of the stool was just right to leave her mouth level with his throbbing dick. Anticipation coursed through him at the wicked look of delight on her gamine features.

She flicked out her tongue to catch the pearly beads of fluid sliding down his dripping cock. His fingers slid through her short hair, cupping the back of her head to hold her close. "Take me in your mouth, kitten. Suck me."

Slipping the head between her lips, she purred an agreement. Her eyes danced as the vibrations ran along the length of his cock. He choked off a groan. She took as much of him into her mouth as she could fit, sucking hard enough to make every muscle in his body jerk in response. "*Delilah.*"

Her fingers wrapped around the base and she moved to slide her tongue down the underside of his shaft. "I love the look on a man's face when I suck his cock."

He growled at the thought of her doing this to any other man but him. She wouldn't ever again. She was *his*. Pure male possessiveness ran through him, something else that was so unlike anything he'd ever experienced before it made his hands shake. Any other woman was cut off before she started to cling, but any other woman wasn't Delilah. His mate.

Pushing her back, he slid off the stool and dropped to his knees with her. "Lay back."

She rolled to her back, propped herself on her elbows, and spread her legs for him. He lunged forward, bracing his arms on either side of her shoulders. The tip of his dick nudged at her slick labia, probing for entrance. She thrust her hips up, taking him in one hard push. A hiss escaped her, but she wrapped her legs tight around his waist. "Hurry."

"Yes." Thanking Deus she was so wet and ready for him, he rode her like a man possessed.

Mine. His mind growled the word, but he managed to keep it from passing his lips. She couldn't know she was his mate yet. It was too soon. Too soon to tell her, too soon to feel this way, too soon to crave her like a bliss addict craved his drug. His body and his relentless instincts didn't care what his mind knew. The word, the claiming, pounded through him as he pounded into her. Mine, mine, *mine*.

"Delilah," he breathed.

An annoying chirp sounded over his head and the small vidscreen in his kitchen lit up. The smooth, electronic female voice announced, "Incoming vid. Downlink?"

He groaned, holding himself still inside Delilah's tight sheath as he tried to catch his breath enough to speak, to think, to react calmly when the predator inside him wanted to shred anything that interrupted his time with his mate. "Deny vid."

The chirp sounded in recognition of his command. "Store any messages in vid cache and power down for—"

"Ignore the fucking vidscreen." Fisting her fingers in his hair, Delilah pulled his head down to kiss her. She bit him and he tasted the coppery flavor of his own blood. Her tongue plunged into his mouth, desperate little moans vibrating under his lips. He loved the sounds she made, the way they made his heart pound and his blood roar in his ears.

His hips bucked, driving his dick into her wet heat. He slid his hands under her, curving his fingers over her shoulders to hold her close. Her palms cupped his ass and pulled at him to urge him on. Hunching his shoulders, he slammed his pelvis forward. The need to come fisted deep within him, and he knew he couldn't hold on much longer. He shifted his weight to one arm, slipping the other between them to stroke her hard little clitoris.

"Hunter!" She cried out as orgasm took her, her pussy pulsing around his cock.

He exploded, the sharp ecstasy in her voice as she screamed his name shoving him past his endurance. His come filled her, and he kept thrusting until his cock went soft, wanting nothing more than to lose himself inside her welcoming heat.

It wasn't until hours later, curled around Delilah in his wide bed, that he realized this was the first time in his life that he'd ignored his business. He wasn't certain what it meant that his mate could wipe all thoughts of everything except her from his mind. He wasn't certain he even wanted the answer.

He doubted he would like it.

3

Hunter jolted from a nightmare, his heart pounding and sweat rolling down his chest. His muscles shook with adrenaline that had no outlet. He clenched his teeth until the horror faded, wiping a weary hand down his face. He'd had the nightmare so many times, he knew to the nanosecond how long it would take for his body to cool, for his pulse to stop racing. If only his memories were as easy to predict and contain. If only the nightmares were nothing more than a figment of his imagination, but they were not. The images of his parents' last moments on earth were lasered into his mind, their power never fading. The feel of his uncle's blood streaming through his fingers when he meted out his own form of justice for the abuse . . . and for the corruption that had cost his parents' lives. The two incidents were separated by years, but always tangled in his dreams.

He was only glad Delilah had slept through it. She was an intelligent woman, and she was bound to ask questions he didn't intend to answer. Maybe it was better that he moved her to her own place after the week was over. A mistress didn't need to live with him . . . or sleep through the night with him.

The idea of having her whenever he wanted her and never having to admit to anything other than lust was so appealing it made his teeth clench. He could have everything he wanted, needed, craved. He could keep her forever.

Glancing to his left, he saw the tangle of covers where her slim body should have been.

But he was alone in his bed.

Terror fisted in his gut. She was gone. Lost. Like his parents. He leaped to his feet, kicking aside the covers that threatened to trip him up. He had to find her, had to protect her. His mate.

Whether she wanted him to or not. He couldn't lose someone else. He simply . . . couldn't.

The wide vidscreen embedded in the wall across from his bed chirped to alert him of an incoming message. Delilah? Had she crept away and left him a message for when he woke? He knew little of her, but it didn't seem like the feline's style to leave anything behind.

"Display message." His voice was little more than a hoarse croak, and he worked his tongue around in his mouth in an effort to generate some moisture.

Pierce's serious face greeted him on the vidscreen. "Avery, it's Vaughn. The Los Angeles incident looks like a deliberate attempt to recreate the circumstances surrounding your parents' death. Tarek's looking to rattle you. Don't do anything rash." Those gray eyes seemed to look right through him, much the way the man did in person. "More information when I talk to Forensics. Contact me when you get this."

"Huh." He shook his head. One more reminder of the worst time of his life. But as much as the past haunted him, it was his future he was worried about.

Where was Delilah?

Whirling for the balcony doors, he was a nanosecond away from shifting to his hawk form to hunt her down when he caught sight of her in the moonlight. It turned her into a pale goddess, gleaming on her hair and skin. No one should have skin as flawless as hers with the acid rain and pollution in the city, but moonbeams kissed every perfect millimeter.

She crouched on the balcony railing, her hand braced in front of her on the figure of a carved gargoyle. A breath rushed out of him as relief almost took him to his knees. Swallowing, he struggled for the calm that usually came so naturally to him. All he knew was that he could never let her leave him. Now that he'd had her, now that the hawk had had a taste of its mate, he had to protect her. The way he hadn't been able to protect his parents all those years ago.

"Leaving so soon?" He leaned against the open balcony door, arms crossed over his chest.

Tilting her chin down, she shot him a dirty look over her shoulder. "I keep my bargains, Avery."

"Call me Hunter." He frowned, annoyed now that his panic was receding. He'd been more terrified than he'd ever be willing to admit and she was perching on his balcony. "I don't want you calling me Avery."

She snorted and stepped down onto the balcony floor. "Then don't insult me."

A small sigh eased past his lips when her feet touched a solid setting. She wasn't a bird; she couldn't shift and fly to safety if she fell. He arched an eyebrow, forcing his body to relax. "It's insulting to think a thief might be less than honest?"

"If I make a bargain, I keep it." She gave a disdainful sniff. "I make bargains with my clients, not the people I steal from."

That made him smile—something he'd never have guessed he could do so soon after the nightmare. "You did with me."

"I also don't get caught." Her nose wrinkled and she folded her arms, the picture of annoyed feline.

He pushed himself away from the door, letting himself savor the most beautiful sight he'd ever beheld. His nude mate framed by the night sky and the lights of New Chicago. Lovely.

And cold. The chill wind swirled around him once he'd moved outside the buffer of the door. Not cold enough to make him walk away from her, though. His grin stretched wider. "I caught you."

"You're an exceptional man." But her tone was dry enough that no one could consider her words a compliment.

He stepped close enough that he could feel the heat of her curves. "Who was your client for my ruby?"

"I don't always have clients." She twitched her shoulders in what might have been a shrug, staring down at his rising cock. The heat he'd felt from the moment he touched her was always there, waiting for her to rouse it. "If an item is valuable enough on its own, I know I can move it if I steal it."

She didn't need to tell him that the Avery ruby was more than valuable enough to fit that category. She licked her lips and he forgot about clients and rubies and anything other than the craving he had for her and the need to burn off the fear of finding her gone.

Fear he'd never wanted to feel again. It was one thing to be plagued by a nightmare of events long past, another to be haunted by the reality of it every day because of his mate. He hated it, but the hawk inside him wouldn't allow him to send her away—for once, the beast won the battle of wills with the man.

He craved her too deeply.

Cupping her biceps, he turned her to face the city lights. The smooth globes of her ass brushed against his cock and he had to fight to keep from dragging her to the floor and burying himself inside her. Instead, he bent her at the waist to place her fingers on the balcony's railing, holding her there with his palms covering her hands. "I love this view."

"What do you think I was out here admiring before you woke up?" She shivered, arching her back to rub against him. His cock slipped into the cleft of her ass and further forward until her damp heat drenched the head of his dick.

"Let's enjoy it together then, shall we?" He spoke the words softly in her ear and saw goose bumps rise on her flesh. She tilted her head, baring her throat to him. The trust in that gesture from any natural predator shook him. Whether she knew it or not, some part of her had faith that he wouldn't hurt her. He swallowed hard, his fingers twining with hers where they lay on the railing. The ever-present breeze swirled around them, ruffling his hair. "Are you sure you're not too cold?"

"I don't mind." She wriggled against him, and he could hear the edge of wicked laughter in her tone. "But you can warm me up."

He pressed his mouth to her throat, flicking his tongue out to taste her flesh. Her pulse raced, he could feel the beat of it under his lips. The way her body writhed, her hips already moving to a carnal rhythm, told him how much she liked what they did together. "How do you want it, Delilah? Fast or slow?"

"As long as I come, I'm game for anything you've got, birdie." She shoved her ass back, opening herself to his penetration. He couldn't resist and slid his cock into her until she'd taken all of him into her tight, wet channel. Her muscles clasped him snugly and he shuddered, biting down on her neck. She cried out, her body jerking against him, her dampness increasing in a hot rush. "Deus, Hunter! Fast. I want it fast. Now."

"Good." At this point, he wasn't sure he could go slowly even if he had a gun pressed to his temple. He plunged deep into her pussy, her slickness coating his cock with each thrust. Molten heat flooded his body, and he barely clung to his sanity . . . and his control. Touching her was better than any pleasure he'd ever known—he couldn't get enough, and he didn't want to. The thought alone should have worried him, but he was beyond caring about anything other than the ecstasy he found in possessing her.

Their bodies shuddered with the impact of his thrusts, his

hips driving hers against the railing. She met each of his move-ments with her own. A low, husky laugh slipped from her throat. "I really. Love. This view."

"It's the best." His fingers tightened around hers, and his breathing hitched every time he slammed into her. Her slick sheath clenched around him each time he withdrew, as though trying to keep him inside her, and the fire racing through his blood reached a boiling point. He was going to come soon, but he intended to take her with him. Rolling his pelvis against her, he changed the angle to one that never failed to make her scream.

"Yes! Deus, yes!" Her slim body bowed and her pussy fisted around his dick in rhythmic pulses that dragged him into orgasm with her. He came deep inside her, grinding his pelvis into her with each hard jet of come.

The lights of the city blurred before his eyes, and he knew he'd never look at it again without thinking of his mate. Her cries were lost in the relentless wind off Lake Michigan, and only his ears would hear their sweet sound. He pressed his sweat-dampened forehead to the back of her shoulder and breathed in her scent. His muscles shook with the effort it took to remain upright, but he didn't want to withdraw from her. Not yet . . . not yet. She was here, she was safe, and she was his. That was all he needed at the moment. Everything else could wait.

It wasn't until she stirred against him that he pulled away from her, gritting his teeth at the drag of his flesh in hers. He drew her pliant body against his, nudging her in the direction of his bedroom. Every room in the house except the kitchen had indestructible polyglass doors that led out on to the bal-cony. The main space had several. There was another set be-yond his room before the building curved around a corner. He never went in there.

"Where does that lead?" As if she'd read his thoughts, she jutted her chin toward those doors.

He considered not answering her, but thought she'd investigate on her own if he didn't. And the last thing he wanted was the cat's curiosity prying into his past. "That was my parents' room before they died."

"Oh. Well, what's in there now?" Glancing down, he saw her head had cocked in question.

He blinked and frowned, nonplussed by the odd question. "It's their room. What else would be in there except their things?"

"I see." Something close to sympathy glimmered in her wide green gaze. "They died in an accident, right?"

He smoothed his hand over her silky hair, bending forward to kiss her forehead. "No, it wasn't an accident."

"How did they die, then?"

Sighing, he let her go and stepped around her to enter his main space. The whole evening had his insides churning. The nightmare. His fear for Delilah. Pierce's message. Tarek trying to bring back the worst moment of his life while destroying the business the Avery family had been building for generations. His hands shook, rage and terror and a million other emotions he always avoided coursing through his veins.

Delilah's palm stroked down his back. "Hunter?"

He pulled away from her, pacing in a tight circle. "My uncle was using one of our factories as a front for the slave-labor trade." A fact Hunter hadn't known until much later, that a man his father had trusted *because* he was family, because he was his beloved mate's brother, had betrayed them all. "There was an escape that turned into a riot when my parents and I were visiting. We got caught in it. They didn't survive."

Her eyes widened, latching on to the scar on his face. The question was there in her gaze, but she didn't give it voice.

Scrubbing a hand down the old scar, he sighed. "I got this as a memento of the occasion. A lovely reminder every time I look in a mirror."

He hoped to Deus she dropped the topic, but that didn't keep the memories at bay. There was a riot, true, but it was much, much worse than that. His father had discovered the truth about the factory when he arrived and nothing the manager told him made sense. They'd been on vacation, and his father decided to spot-check the site on their way home. Only an hour out of their day, he'd sworn.

They'd lost far more than an hour.

The air of desolation about the place had made both his parents suspicious. While his father had gone to question the manager, Hunter and his mother had looked around. She found a double reinforced mercurite door that latched from the outside and popped the seal on it.

His father and the manager had come around the corner then, their argument heated. Every scrap of color had left the shorter man's face when his gaze locked on that door. He'd shouted for them to close it, but it was too late.

Shifters of all species came boiling through that opening. An enormous man, half-shifted into a grizzly bear, swung his hands around wildly as he fought for balance in the melee. His roar echoed over the crowd, a claw ripping through Hunter's flesh as he rushed past. Hunter's young body had flown back, slamming into the side of the building. He watched his father dive after his mother and into the mass of emaciated shifters, their sunken eyes bereft of anything except an animal's survival instinct. No humanity remained there.

It had taken only moments for Hunter to lose sight of his parents, and for the people to scent the manager who'd caged them. They'd turned on him so fast he'd had no real chance of escape. When Hunter finally regained his footing in the rioting mob, it was to see the one memory he would give his entire fortune to erase.

His parents' deaths.

They hadn't just been killed, they'd been ripped limb from

limb. When the authorities arrived to clean up the mess, they'd found the corpses mangled and half-eaten.

Bile rose in Hunter's throat, and he desperately shoved the waking nightmare away. It shouldn't haunt him anymore, shouldn't have the power to make him sweat and shake. He balled his trembling hands into tight fists, dragging in slow, clean breaths that didn't carry the acrid stench of blood and fear and death.

"How old were you?" Delilah's voice sounded from a distance, but when he turned to face her, she was right behind him.

He cleared his throat. "Fourteen. The trip had been to celebrate my birthday with just the family. It was so rare that we had time to ourselves."

"I thought . . . If your uncle . . . Did you stay with other family after that?"

"No, my mother's brother received guardianship of me. And the company." The man had done everything in his power to make sure Hunter would never take over his inheritance. Two years of beatings and abuse, of fear so sharp he could taste it, of being paraded in front of board members and the newsvids when his uncle wanted to assure others of how well the young heir was doing had ended in more violence, more bloodshed. The day he'd overheard his uncle bragging about the unexpected bonus the slave trade had granted him by taking care of Hunter's parents had unleashed a rage he hadn't known he was capable of. Rage that had cauterized his fear and made him turn on his uncle as surely as the slaves had turned on their manager. It was the last time he'd ever truly lost control, and he learned exactly how dangerous emotion could be—the good and the bad.

Delilah's green eyes hadn't left his face. "You killed him, didn't you? It's not just pure buzz."

"No, it's not." Something so sweet it was painful sliced through him. He'd never confessed this to anyone in his life.

The police had called it self-defense, the board of directors hadn't wanted a scandal for Avery Industries, and they made all of it disappear. Only Delilah knew the truth from his own lips. "He beat me, stole from me, and was responsible for my parents' deaths."

She nodded, and there wasn't a hint of recrimination in her eyes. Perhaps a woman from the Vermilion, a criminal herself, was one of the few who could truly understand. "You feel guilty for living when your parents didn't. It's why you work so hard."

It wasn't a question, but he answered it anyway.

"Yes." He swallowed, rubbed a hand over the back of his neck, and tried to suppress the guilt of surviving, of not doing enough while his family died. "I emancipated myself and took over the business. I was sixteen."

"It doesn't sound like it was your fault. A riot, a bent uncle. Nothing you could do about any of that."

"Does it matter? I'm still alive, and they're not." He took a deep breath and let it out slowly. "My uncle, I don't regret. He had it coming." A bitter smile twisted his lips. "Even in the wealthiest of families, there are a few bad apples."

"You don't have to tell me that. I know firsthand." The bitterness he'd come to expect when she spoke of the wealthy was barely discernable. She sighed. "That's rough. I'm just saying maybe you should let up on yourself a little, get out of this ivory tower a little more often." She slipped her hand into his and squeezed. He stared down at it, wondering when the last time was that someone touched him as a show of support, affection. He couldn't remember. Perhaps his mother was the last one to do so.

He brushed his thumb over her knuckles and let her lead him to his bed. They lay curled on their sides facing each other before he spoke again. "I can't imagine your childhood was any easier."

"Yes and no." She swallowed and looked away. "I didn't have any of the money or the privilege, but I always had my sister to look out for me, and I always looked out for her."

Curling his finger under her chin, he urged her to look at him again. "She needed you to look out for her?"

"She's a mink-shifter. A lot of predators out there could take her in a fair fight." The ghost of a smile danced across her mouth. "Not that she ever plays fair."

He chuckled. "Smart girl."

"She is, at that." The smile bloomed more fully, and he could see the love Delilah had for her sister reflected in her gaze. Something wrenched deep inside him. He remembered that kind of affection for family, but more than that, he wanted her to look at him that way, to feel that way for him. Not as a sibling, but as a woman loves a man.

He swallowed, cold sweat breaking on his forehead. This was foolish. He shouldn't crave her love and devotion. He'd already told her too much, let her in too deep. No matter how good and right it felt to do so, it would have to stop. Immediately.

The next day, Hunter seemed distant, more distant than he normally did. Delilah had woken to another round of explosive sex, but he'd left her gasping in bed, made an offhand excuse of work, and closeted himself in his office. She hadn't seen him again until dinner. She hated to admit that it bothered her.

After dinner, she wandered into the main space of Hunter's penthouse and watched him settle onto his big kleather couch with more work scrolling down the screen of his palmtop computer. During the *hours* that he'd left her by herself, she'd retrieved her own palmtop from her bag and left Lorelei a vid message that her latest job was taking longer than expected and not to worry.

She sighed, tilted her head, and squinted at the whorls of mercurite mounted to the wall next to Hunter's office door.

They seemed to form a spiral leading to a centerpiece that . . . wasn't there. "Something is missing from that sculpture."

Glancing up, he froze, grunted, and looked away.

She narrowed her gaze at him, then stared at the sculpture for another moment. The size and dimensions for the missing piece was just right for— "The ruby."

"Considering why you came here, you can understand why I removed it and put it in a safe." He gave her a sour smile and the way it curved his mouth made the scar on his face stand out. Her heart twisted as she remembered where'd he'd got it, but that didn't dissipate her annoyance at him for ignoring her today. He was the one who'd insisted on her staying a whole week. He was the rich man who always got his way, and if he thought she would cater to his moods because of who and what he was, he could kiss her ass.

She propped her hands on her hips. "No, I don't think so. For you, everything seems to have its place, and you like things to stay in their place. There has to be another reason you took the ruby down."

His mouth worked for a moment before he gritted out, "My mother loved it. It was her favorite piece."

"Why not take the whole sculpture down, then?"

He shrugged and went back to reading his palmtop screen.

Her gaze swept the whole room. Everything here reflected an older taste, and considering he still reserved his parents' room for them when they would never sleep there again, she had a sad suspicion about whose taste the room reflected. "You never moved anything after your parents died, did you?"

"I liked it the way it was."

She doubted that. Every piece of furniture was arranged to face the incomplete sculpture. She could understand why his mother might have laid the room out that way—the ruby encased in gleaming coils of mercurite would have been breathtaking. Now, it was just heartbreaking.

She swallowed and shook her head. It didn't matter. He didn't matter. She shouldn't get involved in his problems. After this week was over, she would never see him again. And she was going to steal something his mother had loved.

He would hate her for it. Forever.

The whole flat was a museum, a way to showcase his many collections. It went beyond that, though. The way the furniture was arranged, the way everything was exactly as his parents had left it. His entire home was another piece in a collection of things he'd frozen in time when he'd lost his family. A reminder of the past with no hope of a better future.

Hell, that was depressing. Even in the worst moments of her life, in the shittiest gutter of the city, she'd always had a glimmer of hope that things could change and get better. Hunter didn't even have that.

How had he lived this way without suffocating?

The one thing she'd learned first and learned well in the Vermilion is that everything changes. All the time. It was the one constant. She turned when his palmtop clattered to the surface of the low table in front of his couch. His dark eyes narrowed at her. "You can stare at it forever, and the ruby isn't going to appear for you to take."

She took a step toward him. "I wasn't—"

His broad shoulders jerked in a shrug and he strode past her toward the doors that led out on the balcony. It was difficult to imagine that only the night before he'd pleasured her so thoroughly on that balcony. "I'm going for a flight. Stay out of trouble."

Her hand lifted in supplication. "But—"

She didn't get to finish as he flung open the door and shifted to bird form. The hawk screeched, a deep beat of dark red-brown wings allowing him to hover in the breeze for a long moment. The creamy feathers on his chest flashed in the sunlight as he tilted his body into the wind and was gone. Irritation and sympathy warred for dominance within her. Obstinate male. Poor, lost man.

She watched him through the floor-to-ceiling windows until he was no more than a speck on the horizon and even her cat eyes couldn't make out his shape. He loved this view, he'd said. Loved the city, the skyline, the lake, the lights at night. Her gaze swept the room once more, and an idea formed—one that was guaranteed to ruffle the hawk's feathers.

Maybe it was time someone ruffled them.

A wicked grin formed on her lips as she got to work, pushing, nudging, and scooting the furnishings and rugs until the room no longer faced the reminder of his long-dead past, but the living, changing, vibrant city he loved so much. She was panting with exertion when she was done, sweat sheening her skin. She wiped her brow with her forearm as she surveyed her work.

Oh, yes. He was going to be more than a little annoyed. She didn't bother to hold back a chuckle, the lynx inside her purring at the challenge.

The more rational human woman argued that she should have left well enough alone, that she should put everything back before Hunter returned. It was stupid. She shouldn't get involved. She shouldn't even care enough to want to get involved. This was a disaster waiting to happen. What could she hope to gain from doing this? Nothing. It wasn't as if she wanted a future with Hunter. He was everything she despised in a man. Rich, powerful, controlling. He wouldn't survive a day in her world, and she had no interest in his. Kicking him into a better headspace wasn't going to save her from his disgust, his hatred, when she stole something precious from him. She wasn't going to get more creds for trying to help him, and he wasn't going to thank her for her efforts.

Cursing herself for the moron she knew she was, she didn't move the furniture back. Instead, she stripped out of her clothes, lay on her side on the table, and propped her chin in her palm to wait for Hunter to come home. Dusk fell, the lights of the city flickering to life as the sun faded behind the horizon. A few overhead lights turned on automatically, but she left the flat dim otherwise.

The barest flutter of movement and a large shadow detaching itself from the dark told her he'd returned. His scent reached her nose the moment he opened the outer door. Lust hit her with the masculine smell of him, the sight of his large, naked form. Her sex dampened, some muscles tightening, others loosening as her body prepared itself for sex . . . and the coming confrontation.

She didn't have to wait long for the second one.

He blinked, his gaze taking in her and the rest of the room. "What did you do?"

A sound between a chuckle and a purr escaped her as she moved her shoulder in a nonchalant shrug. "I rearranged the furniture."

"I can see that." He folded his arms and frowned. "Put it back where it belongs."

She grinned and twisted into a stretch, noting the way his gaze locked on her nude body as she moved. It made her heart speed, made heat wind through her. Her hand cupped her hip, slid down and inward until her fingers brushed through her damp curls. "Why does it belong there? You like the view of the city better anyway."

"Because that's where it's supposed to go." His tone was distracted, his arms relaxing at his sides as he swayed toward her.

"Everything in its place." And then she dipped her fingers between her thighs. Her muscles jerked at the delicious contact, and she caught her lower lip between her teeth.

"Yes, damn it," he groaned, and she wasn't certain if he was talking about the furniture or encouraging her to continue touching herself.

"I know of one very good place for you right now, Hunter." She rolled to her back, letting her legs fall open so he could see all of her. Her sex would be gleaming with juices, and she parted her lips with her fingers, slipping her finger into her slick channel.

He shuddered when she said his name, his gaze following every movement of her hand as she toyed with herself.

Arching herself in offering, she added a second finger to the one fucking her pussy. "Come enjoy the view with me."

"Delilah," his voice held a low warning she ignored.

"I promise you'll love it. Give it a try, Hunter." She watched his pupils expand until only the thinnest rim of brown remained. The scent of his excitement was the most intoxicating aphrodisiac she'd ever encountered. A ragged moan tore free as she panted for breath. "I'm so hot for you, Hunter. So wet and ready."

"Deus save me." He reached her in three strides, scooped her off the table, and sat in the middle of the couch. His hands jerked her thighs apart, positioning her so she straddled his lap, but they both faced the view of the city. The heavy muscles of his chest burned into her back, and she arched as he surged inside her with one hard push.

Deus, he was big, but she was so wet, it didn't matter. He slid deep with each plunging stroke, stretching her wide. She loved it, loved the feel of him, the scent of him mingling with her and sex. The sheer carnality of it made her even wetter.

Leaning forward, she braced her hands on his knees, shoving her ass back until her skin slapped against the hard muscles of his abdomen. He groaned, his fingers biting into her hips as he urged her on. "Delilah."

She flicked a glance over her shoulder, noting the dark flush of lust that ran under his tanned skin. "Isn't this the best view ever, Hunter? I love it."

A laugh tangled with a ragged groan. "You're evil, kitten. A menace."

"I've heard that before." She tossed a grin at him, rotating her hips to torment him.

His palm smacked against her ass, and she squealed and laughed. Her back arched reflexively, pressing her backside into his hand. He swatted the other cheek. The sting added another layer of sensation to the ecstasy skimming through her already. She flexed her pussy around his cock, increasing both their pleasure. He groaned each time he thrust into her, and she could feel the moisture between her legs rolling down the insides of her thighs. Her heart slammed in her chest and her lungs burned as she struggled to pull in enough oxygen. She needed to come so badly, every sense she had focused on the central point that joined their body. The pressure within her built until she had to clench her teeth.

He jerked her back against his chest, one hand fondling her nipple while the other flicked over her clit until her sex clenched tight and the tension within her snapped. She moaned and shattered in his arms, her body shaking as she came. Pleasure so hot it burned exploded inside her, and her orgasm went on and on until she screamed.

"Hunter, Hunter!"

He groaned, ground his hips into hers, and spilled his fluids deep in her pussy. His arms tightened around her, his lips nuzzled into the crook of her neck, and shudders racked his big body.

They stayed that way for a long, long time. Finally, he shifted beneath her, moving them until they were spooning on the couch. Since they were both so tall, she was grateful it was long enough for both of them to lie on. Their legs tangled and his cock was still nestled inside her, his arms around her. She rested her cheek on his bicep, watching the ocean of city lights twinkling beyond the edge of his building. She sighed, quiet contentment winding through her. "This is more comfortable than the balcony."

"Mmm." His chest vibrated against her back as he hummed. His free hand cupped her breast, his fingers idly plucking at her nipple. "Warmer, too."

She grinned, brought his hands to her lips, and kissed the center of his palm. Then she put it back where it was, stroking her nipple. He chuckled, but the semi-hard erection inside her began to thicken, stretching her pussy. She sighed, subtly arching her back to press her breast into his hand and her sex into his cock.

He thrust into her, his rhythm unhurried. The tension within her built as his hands and cock moved over her, in her. Tingles broke down her limbs as the pleasure began to reach unbearable levels. She shoved her hips back harder, twisting under the harsh lashes of ecstasy. Deus, she needed him to hurry up.

Shivers rippled through her with each slow movement of his cock inside her, his fingers on her nipple. She was going to die, it was so good. Swallowing, she licked her lips and tried to find her voice. "Hunter?"

"Yes, Delilah?" His hot breath brushed against the back of her neck and made goose bumps rise on her flesh.

She whimpered and bit her lip hard enough to draw blood when he rotated his hips while twisting her nipple hard. "Could you . . . move a little faster? Harder, too?"

"Since you asked so politely." His body flexed, slamming against her.

She choked, working her hips as fast as she could to encourage him to increase his speed and force even more. "You like it when I'm demanding."

"I like touching you whether we're wild or civil." His breath hissed out when her hand reached back to clamp on his thigh. "I like it when you touch me, too."

"Yes." She slid her grip up until she could sink her claws into his ass. The feel of his flexing muscles under her palm was exhilarating. She loved the leashed power, and loved driving him out of control. Whimpering with every hard push he made, she closed her eyes to focus on the play of his flesh against hers, the hair-roughened thighs, the smooth buttocks, the hard pecs sliding against her back. It was the most perfect thing she'd ever experienced. The rush was better than pulling off the biggest heist of her life.

"I'm going to come." She heard the way he gritted his teeth and hissed the words, felt the way his fingers shook where they gripped her hip.

He reached around her, pinching her clit hard, working it fast and rough until she couldn't hold back any longer. Her thighs tensed and her body jerked as every single sensation rolled over her and dragged her under into orgasm. Starbursts exploded in pinpricks of light behind her eyelids, and shivers raced over her arms and legs until every micrometer of her body was consumed in ecstasy.

The sound of his harsh breathing and deep groan sounded distant over the buzzing in her ears, though she knew he still held her tight, still moved inside her. Every stroke he made into her pussy set off another tidal wave of orgasm, sending ripples through her inner muscles. He sank into her over and over again before he froze, his cock buried deep, and she felt his come fill her.

His forehead rested against the back of her head, and sweat sealed their bodies together. He brushed his lips over the nape of her neck. "Delilah."

Lifting herself, she rolled in place until she could press her front to his. She threw her leg over his thigh and settled against him. A low purr soughed from her throat, and the deep, undeniable feline urge to sleep swept over her. He tugged her closer, his arms around her protectively, and she set her palm over his heart as her eyes slid shut.

"Hunter," she breathed.

"Sleep now, kitten."

And she did, feeling safer and more content than she ever had in her life.

4

She liked him too much.

Time had blurred in an endless orgy of pleasure and heat and sensation. Three days in Hunter's bed and she woke up reaching for him automatically. She lay in his bed now and could smell the fading musk of his scent while she watched the newsvids scroll across the vidscreen. But her focus had turned inward and she no longer saw the screen.

He drowned her in sensuality, and she had to admit, having every ounce of his intensity turned to her pleasure was enough to make her wet just thinking about it. She loved it, loved the way he touched her, the way he kissed her, the way he fucked her until she screamed his name. He liked that best, she'd found. Whispering his name in his ear could make him shudder, his long cock expanding even as he fucked her hard. It was amazing the effect that one word had on the man. A purr slid from her throat. She liked that, liked that she could make him react so strongly to her.

She liked *him*. She shouldn't, but she did. She'd tried to

deny it, but it was there anyway. It was going to be a problem, and as much as she'd kicked herself for it, she couldn't turn it off. Closing her eyes tight, she sighed. Self-disgust twisted within her, cinching around her soul.

The only good thing in this whole mess was that she knew it would be over soon. Her heart clenched at the thought.

Why did it matter? Why did *he* matter? How had he done this to her so quickly? She was the best at her job. She never became emotionally involved. Her job was to take, not to give. He was a rich man like all the others, and he'd see her as nothing more than a toy. That's how they all were with women. She knew it.

And yet. And yet, she couldn't stop herself from reaching for him as often as he reached for her, couldn't stem the cravings she had for him, couldn't make herself want to stop talking to him, couldn't deny the need to make him laugh and rid his eyes of the shadows for a few moments.

It was obvious he wasn't accustomed to speaking to anyone about anything besides business, and his gruff awkwardness was more endearing than it should be. He'd sketched out the minor details of some sabotage he was dealing with in his business, and she'd discussed some security measures he might try. She was, after all, an expert in security systems and how to get around them. Trivial things. Things you discussed with friends or family. They felt far too natural with this man, but she couldn't help it. She wanted to know why Hunter was Hunter. There were times he seemed so alone, so . . . lonely.

The cat was fascinated by him, and the woman more so.

It was as if she'd set a biobomb off in her life, and everything was morphing into something grotesque and unrecognizable. A bitter chuckle spilled out. The worst part was she'd done this to herself. She'd taken the job, she'd propositioned him to keep him from turning her in, she'd agreed to stay. None of this was his fault. If there was any innocent party in this whole mess, it was him—though she hesitated more than a little to apply the word to the lascivious hawk.

A shiver rippled through her, and her nipples tightened as a parade of erotic memories marched through her mind. She grinned and wondered what Hunter was doing now. He'd said he had to get some work done today, but that was several hours ago and she found that was longer than she was willing to wait to fuck him again.

She sat up in bed, flicking a fingertip over the controller to turn off the vidscreen. Plucking one of Hunter's robes out of the clothing refresher built into his bedroom wall, she slid it on and belted it as she strode across his flat to his open office door.

"Hunter?" He glanced up from the vidscreen he was reading. It looked like it scrolled nothing more than random numbers. "What's that?"

He sat back in his chair, the kleather creaking under his weight. "Quarterly reports."

"Ah, my business doesn't come with anything quite that official." No, in fact the less documentation she had, the better. She had enough encrypted that if any of her clients burned her, she could take them down with her, but other than that it was in her best interest to cover her tracks and leave no evidence of her work.

"Money is money. Numbers are numbers." He shrugged. "Business is business. It all works the same way, in the end."

"True." She'd never thought about it that way. Having anything in common with the wealthiest man alive was . . . unnerving. She liked him too much as it was, without any common ground to stand on. Twitching the folds of the oversized robe, she walked into his office. His eyes locked on where the robe parted to reveal her legs with each stride.

She smiled, her body beginning to burn. Damn, they had chemistry that could put a nuclear reaction to shame. The best she'd ever had. Her step faltered. No. She needed to stop think-ing these things. There was *no* future with this man, no matter how much she liked him, how much they had in common, how much she enjoyed the sex. It didn't matter. This was business, she reminded herself ruthlessly. A job. That's all he was, a job. An opportunity.

The way his brown eyes heated made her heart twist. The smile that tilted up one corner of his mouth warmed her, and she felt guilty for even thinking of him as an *opportunity*. She couldn't remember the last time she'd felt remorse about any-thing, let alone her work. Or a man. She used them the way they used her, for sex, for entertainment. It didn't mean anything, *they* didn't mean anything. Hunter was no different. He was a diversion while she finished this job. She was a toy for him to play with for the week. A dirty little alley cat from the wrong district of the city. Cheap thrills for a rich man.

Knowing it was true didn't make it hurt less.

She swallowed and shoved all those ugly thoughts away. She'd known the score her whole life—growing up a whore's daughter didn't allow for a lot of innocence—so she knew she couldn't change reality. It would be foolish to think otherwise, and she always needed to be one step ahead of everyone else. No time for silly, stupid feminine wishes.

Hunter's knuckles rubbed her cheekbone, and she started. "Are you all right, kitten?"

"Yes. Fine." She hadn't even noticed when he stood, let alone approached her. Her instincts hadn't warned her of the danger. Because they didn't consider him one? Another unfor-tunate revelation she wanted to forget.

Luckily, Hunter was nearby to divert her attention. She forced a smile to her face, laying her palms to his broad chest. "I want you."

"Anytime, anywhere." The gold flecks in his eyes shim-mered the way they did when he was aroused.

Her grin became more genuine, turning wicked. "Here and now work for me."

"Delilah, are you sure nothing is wrong? I can help." He covered her hands with his, and she felt comforted and protected rather than trapped. When had anyone else ever made her feel protected, *safe*? Never. Even with Lorelei looking out for her, she'd always known they were one wrong move away from disaster.

Stop it, Delilah! It was an illusion, no more real than a hologram. Think about something else. Something better, less disturbing to her sense of calm.

She moved her fingers against the microsilk that covered Hunter's chest until she found a nipple. His breath froze in his chest, and his face got that intent look she liked so well. His dark eyes glittered and his skin flushed. She grinned, meeting his eyes so she could watch him react when she flicked her nail over the small, flat disc.

His big body jerked, and his hands tightened around hers. "You're trying to distract me so you don't have to tell me what's bothering you."

She was trying to distract them both. It was for the best, which he'd agree with if he knew the way her thoughts were running today. She stepped closer, looping one leg around his thigh. Tilting her face up, she kissed the skin beside his mouth. "Let me distract you."

"Delilah—"

She rubbed her foot up and down the back of his leg, her mouth a whisper away from his. "I want you inside me. I want you to make me scream and claw your back."

He swallowed, and she watched his pupils dilate as she spoke. He made a rough, desperate sound in the back of his throat, and his lips captured hers. She twined her tongue with his, sucking it lightly. His hands dropped to her hips and pulled her flush against his long, hard body.

She moaned into his mouth, jerked the hem of his shirt out of his pants, and ran her hands up his bare chest. Her senses delighted in the tactile pleasure he offered; his skin was smooth velvet over the hardened mercurite of his muscles. His taste flooded her mouth and his scent filled her lungs, drowning her in *him*.

Still she wanted more.

Breaking the kiss, she gasped. "I want this shirt *off* you, or I'm going to shred it."

She scraped her claws lightly over his abs to emphasize her point.

He laughed, took a step back, and yanked his shirt over his head to drop it on the floor. He ripped open the seal on his pants, shoving them down his legs. "Now you. I want my robe back."

She couldn't tear her gaze away from his naked body. Every micrometer of him was gorgeous, the light sprinkle of hair on his muscular legs, the tight pecs. She wanted to swirl her tongue around the flat brown nipples, wanted to suck his long cock until he let out that rough, helpless groan that gave her the most intense rush of power.

He reached for her, unknotting the belt. His fingertips grazed her collarbone as he pushed the microsilk off her shoulders to let it slither down her body to pool on the floor. The movement of the fabric raised gooseflesh on her skin, peaking her nipples tight.

"You are so damn beautiful, kitten." The heat and masculine appreciation in his gaze warmed her from the inside out, made her crave him even more.

Shrugging, she ran a hand down her hip. Lorelei had always been the womanly one; Delilah was too tall and athletic to ever be beautiful. Not that she didn't like her looks, but it was nice to hear that Hunter liked them, too. It shouldn't matter, but it did—though she'd never confess it to anyone else, least of all him. "You can look all you want, but I like it better when you touch."

"Me, too. Though the view is amazing. Even better than the one from my balcony." They both chuckled at that while his fingers closed around her biceps, swinging her around until she faced his desk. He pressed her palms flat against the slick poly-glass surface, his heat searing her from behind.

Her sex clenched tight, excitement twisting through her when his palms cupped her hips. His lips brushed over her shoulder. "This is a lovely nanotat you have, Delilah. I like looking at it while I take you from behind."

She flicked him a mischievous glance, lifting an eyebrow. "I'm thinking about having it reconfigured."

"Into what?" His tongue traced the line of the dragon's tail, leaving a trail of dampness behind. He blew on the wet skin, and shivers racked her body. She had to lock her knees to keep her legs from buckling beneath her. He nipped at the skin at her waist. "Delilah?"

Swallowing, she tried to hold on to the conversation. Her shoulder jerked in a shrug. "I-I don't know. A phoenix, maybe. I'll probably decide when I get to the tattoo shop."

"You don't care what's on your skin permanently?" His hands slipped between her thighs, nudging them open.

Her breath hissed out when his cock replaced his hand to slide against the hot lips of her sex. "It's not as if I can't change it later. Besides, in my business, it's never a good idea to keep the same distinguishing marks for long."

"I can see your point." He paused as if considering, and she thought she was going to scratch his eyes out if he didn't slide that thick cock inside her soon.

"Speaking of getting to the point . . ." She arched her back, rubbing herself against his cock.

He teased the lips of her sex with the tip of his dick, sinking just the head into her. His fingers stroked her wet lips, emphasizing how wide he stretched her just with the bulbous crest of his cock. She sucked in a deep breath, waiting for him to fuck her. Anticipation made her pussy clench, and she dropped her head between her bent arms.

Working only the first few centimeters of his dick inside her, he moved his fingers up to circle her anus. He slipped his finger into her ass, using her own moisture to ease his entrance. He added a second finger, widening her.

Her breath caught and pleasure wound through her, insidious and weakening. She pressed her forehead to his desk, her breath fogging the clear surface. "I don't care where you put it, but your cock better be all the way inside me in the next minute or I'll—"

"I don't normally find threats arousing, but I'll make an exception for you." He pressed his cock to her asshole and sank in one infinitesimal micrometer at a time until his entire length was deep within her. Her breath hissed between her teeth, and the pain was so good it sent hot and cold tingles over her skin. When he moved, her fangs slid forward, her claws scraped over the polyglass desk, and her back arched like that of a cat in heat.

"Harder, faster. *Now.*"

He gave a short laugh, his cock pistoning in and out of her ass. The sensation bordered on agony, but it twisted and tripped over the ecstasy until they were one and the same. She loved it, loved the wildness of it. Loved that she could drive him to the very edge of all that control of his.

"Kitten, you feel so fucking good." His breath bellowed out, matching the harsh rhythm of her own. His hands moved around her waist, one gliding up to fondle her breast while the other slid down to flick across her clitoris.

He stroked her hard. In her ass, over her clit. His fingers twisted her nipple until her body exploded into a trillion little pieces. She closed her eyes to savor it. Her muscles fisted every time he thrust his cock into her ass, sending another wave of contractions through her pussy. The polyglass squeaked under her claws as she dug them in with each pulse of orgasm that strummed through her.

His pelvis slapped against her ass, shoving her against the edge of the desk. She whimpered, not sure how much more she could take before she begged him to stop . . . or to never stop. She wasn't even sure what she wanted anymore, she just knew it was good with Hunter. He pinched her clit, making her jolt and flex her inner muscles around him. He groaned, pushing deep one last time before he came with a harsh shudder.

She stayed where she was, bent over the table and panting for air. A bead of sweat slid down her temple to her chin and dripped on to the polyglass. She swallowed, waiting for the pleasure to ease its grip on her, but shivers still rippled through her body. Hunter managed a tortured groan before he slid his cock out of her ass. "You're going to kill me."

She glanced back over her shoulder at him, not bothering to hide her smirk. "Can you think of a better way to die?"

"Not one." His voice was slow and rough, the very essence of a well-satisfied man. "Delilah, I—"

"You?" Pushing herself upright, she turned to press herself against his chest.

He sighed and cuddled her close. "I've been thinking . . . we might want to continue our arrangement after the week was up."

She pulled back a bit to look at him, but his expression was a controlled mask. "I'm not sure what you mean."

But she had a few ideas, and she doubted she wanted to hear what he had to say. A tiny, treacherous part of her dared to hope he wouldn't reinforce all her ugly memories of privileged men.

"Things between us are so good. I've never had anything like it." He pulled her closer, and she felt the jut of his still semi-erect cock against her stomach.

Shaking her head a little, she lifted her eyebrows. "So, you want to what . . . date me? Keep me on call for when we both have an itch to scratch?"

"I was thinking something a bit more solid than that." His gaze met hers, the look serious. "I know you're not a jade—"

"But you thought you might like to add me to your collection? Your personal whore?" And the crashing sound in the back of her mind was those thin shards of hope shattering into nothingness. It made her angry. At herself, at him. This was the first indication she'd really had of him being like all the others, and it hurt so badly she wanted to wrap her arms around herself and cry. But she never cried, and she wouldn't give him the satisfaction of watching.

"It's not like that, Delilah." His hands pressed to the small of her back.

"Oh, yes, it is." She shoved her way out of his arms. "You collect things, Hunter. You keep them and preserve them and put them in their place and expect them to stay there and to always be the same. The only way that works with people is if they're dead. I can't do that. I can't be that for you."

Pain, anger, and denial flashed in his eyes. It was so obvious he didn't understand why what he'd offered was beyond insulting. The same way he didn't understand what a mausoleum his penthouse was. "Delilah—"

"Besides, I told you I'm not a jade." She turned away, humiliated by the disappointed tears that welled in her eyes. Blinking them back, she refused to let them fall. The sad, pathetic fact was this was probably the most intimate he'd ever let himself get with anyone since his family died. It wasn't his fault that it wasn't enough. Her anger died, and her voice emerged a flat monotone. "I won't turn tricks for you or anyone else. I certainly won't be your bought-and-paid-for mistress."

"Fine. Then our original arrangement for the week stands."

"Yes. Just for the week." Then she'd escape back into sanity.

As she moved toward the door, she caught an unfamiliar scent just before a male voice she didn't recognize sounded in the penthouse. "Avery? Where are you?"

"Ah, shit. Carnac. I have a meeting. Now." Glancing back, she watched a very nude Hunter scramble for his clothes.

She bent to snatch the discarded robe off the floor, jerked it on, and spun for the open door. "I'll distract him, but hurry."

Something about Carnac's scent bothered her, and it hit her the moment she closed the office door behind her. The man's small black eyes locked on her, and he looked her over, the expression on his face making her skin crawl. After Hunter's offer, she was more than a little on edge. Her muscles tensed, preparing her for anything. Business associate of Hunter's or not, that didn't mean she could trust this Carnac. No one was who they seemed in her world, and her defensive instincts vibrated along her nerves. She bared her fangs at him when she smiled. Poising herself on the balls of her feet, she braced for an attack.

"How did you get in here?" Hunter might be upset at her rudeness to his guest, but she didn't care. Her unease intensified by the moment. Hunter really needed to hurry and get dressed.

Carnac's thick, dark eyebrow rose as his eyes narrowed. "The doorman let me in the lift. I'm here to speak to Mr. Avery. He's expecting me."

"Mr. Avery will be out in a moment." She tilted her head toward the office door, but gave no details about what Hunter might be doing in there.

"That's too bad." Carnac sniffed the air delicately. "From the smell of things, Avery might take quite a while to recover." He stepped forward, a cruel smile lighting his face along with a masculine interest that made her belly cramp. She'd seen that look on one too many of her sister's clients' faces. The one that said they thought Delilah was for sale, and that even if she wasn't, they could have her anyway. "I suppose we'll have to find ways to entertain ourselves."

Fangs still bared, she brought her clawed hands into view. She hissed a sharp, feline warning. "Come any closer and the only one you'll be entertaining is a medic."

He blanched and dropped the hand that had been reaching for her. Angry red mottled his fleshy face as he straightened the front of his pale green microsilk shirt. He wore the mandarin collar so popular among the fashionable, and his jowls bulged over the edge. "You're rather inhospitable for a jade."

"She's not a jade." Dark fury was stamped on Hunter's face when he entered the room, the heavy door to his office slamming into the wall. His fists clenched at his sides, his nostrils flaring with each breath.

A chill rippled down Delilah's spine. She'd never seen him look so angry in the time she'd known him, not even when she'd been trying to rob him.

But this proved how right she was. Hunter's desire to keep her as a mistress, Carnac's assumption that she was a whore . . . it was a reminder she needed. No matter how much she liked him, all he saw when he looked at her was a sexual commodity. And no matter what little fantasy world they'd been living in the last few days, ensconced away from the rest of reality, this was a reminder of what his life was truly like. He wasn't just a hawk who fit her like a glove, he was the richest man alive and the distance between them yawned wider than Lake Michigan. She was a thief from the Vermilion District. He was a multitrillionaire who owned half of the Lakeshore District.

They were nothing alike and they never would be.

The message finally sank in.

"I'll let you get to your meeting." She pulled in a deep breath, smiled the kind of smile her sister reserved for placating customers, turned on her heel, and walked through the bedroom and into his wash closet. She shed his robe, dropped it on the floor, and keyed the control panel to give her a scalding hot water flow.

The last ten minutes flooded her mind, made her skin crawl, and she felt dirty. It reminded her too much of things she'd rather forget, and a shudder ran through her. She rubbed her hands up her arms, wishing the water could wash away her ugly memories. This was why she hated the rich, why it was so much fun to take what was theirs.

Spending time with Hunter had confused her, twisted things around in her head. And even he thought she was his to keep. She needed to get away from here, get back to reality. The problem was she had no doubt that if she didn't keep her bargain, Hunter would definitely have her hunted down. He was just stubborn enough to do it, even if she didn't take anything with her. But she *was* taking something and he would have her tracked. In this job, timing was going to be everything.

She ignored the nasty twist of guilt as her long-dormant conscience reminded her how much the ruby—and anything that belonged to his parents—meant to Hunter. She was a criminal; it wasn't as though she lied to herself about how what she did might hurt people. She stole from people who could afford to lose what she took, but that was the only leeway she could grant herself. The price her victims paid wasn't in money. It was in a feeling of vulnerability, personal safety, security.

Things people in the Vermilion dealt with from birth. Things she had had to survive the nightmares about . . . nightmares caused by the same rich people she stole from now. They didn't know how vulnerable she could make them. They thought their money made them invincible, and she made it clear how untrue that assumption was.

She'd never questioned what she did before. It was Hunter. He was spinning her around, muddying things up in her head.

She had to get away from here. Tonight. Now.

* * *

Hunter was still shaking with fury when he was through demolishing Carnac and sending the bastard on his way. The man would never work for Avery Industries or any of its subsidiaries ever again. If Hunter was just as angry at himself and had taken some of that out on Carnac, he wasn't about to admit it. The man deserved what he'd gotten for insulting an Avery mate.

The look on Delilah's face when she'd realized Hunter wanted her as his mistress flashed through his mind, and he felt sick to his stomach. He should have known better. It was the coward's way out of keeping a mate, and Delilah deserved better. He was a fool. He should know by now that she wasn't the kind of woman to accept less than she gave. And she'd want it all. He wanted her to have it . . . he just didn't know if he was capable of giving it to her. There'd been no one who mattered in his life for so long, and he'd deliberately shut out anyone who tried to get close after his uncle's death, that he wasn't sure if he could be a real mate to her.

He just knew he didn't want to lose her, wanted years to develop this *thing* between them that was so sweet it made him ache, but he knew he was running out of time.

Swallowing, he pushed into his bedroom and found it empty. For a moment, his heart seized with the same fear he'd felt the night he'd awoken alone. It twisted together with the self-loathing he couldn't escape. So many emotions since Delilah had stolen her way into his life, none of which he wanted to feel. He missed the numbness, the cool rationality that he'd operated under for the last decade. Only the nightmares had ever broken his calm.

And now Delilah.

He couldn't bring himself to wish he'd never met her, to send her away so he could get back to the life he'd been comfortable with. He closed his eyes. Deus, what the hell was he doing?

He sucked in a deep breath, finally hearing the patter of water droplets from the wash closet over the pounding of his heart. She was still here. In his shower.

A picture formed in his mind of her naked body dripping with water, and his cock swelled painfully in the confines of his pants. The lust sliced through the dark fear and fury, leaving nothing behind but the need for his mate. The only peace he'd have now was burying himself in her soft body.

Yes, he wanted that so much.

His fingers quaked when he hurried to unseal his pants, shoving them down his hips until he stood as naked as she no doubt was.

A smile touched his lips when he followed the sound of running water and saw her, her long body caressed by curls of steam, her hands braced on the slick polyglass walls, her face turned into the shower stream. She was so beautiful, fierce and uncompromising in her desires. He loved that about her.

Droplets of water splattered against his skin as he stepped into the shower behind her. She spun with a hiss and a baring of fangs and claws. "Hasn't anyone ever told you it's stupid to try to sneak up on a cat, birdie?"

He narrowed his gaze at her, set his hands against her shoulders, and shoved her back to the wall. She didn't resist, but neither did she retract her claws. He sensed the churning of deep emotions inside her. He felt the turmoil as well. His offer and Carnac's visit had upset her, which angered him all over again.

Clenching his fingers in her short hair, he jerked her head back until her throat was exposed to his mouth. And then he bit her there. Hard.

She cried out, her hands gripping his shoulders as she tried to climb him. Her claws dug into his flesh, but he didn't give a damn about the pain. He wanted her now, fiercely, desperately.

Then her ass was in his hands as he lifted her, and her pelvis tilted toward him so he could thrust inside her tight sheath. She was already wet and ready for him, and he thanked Deus for that. The last person he would ever want to hurt was her. Delilah. His mate. A shudder ripped through him and he began to work his cock in her pussy with short, hard jabs.

There were no words between them, not this time. Only the water that ran over their bodies, caressing their flesh as they caressed each other. It sealed them together, adding sensations to their already intense coupling. She wound her fingers into his wet hair, pulling his mouth down for a kiss. He plunged his tongue between her lips to the same rhythm his hips set for their bodies. The slap of wet skin on wet skin echoed in the wash closet, the scalding water pounding over his flesh making him burn hotter, move faster. She whimpered into his mouth, suckled on his tongue, bit his lower lip. It only fueled the fire roaring inside him.

Tension coiled low in his belly, made him thrust deeper and harder into her sleek pussy. Moving his hands down to cup the underside of her thighs, he hitched her higher on the slippery wall and changed the angle of his penetration.

Her legs clenched around his hips, her torso twisting to rub her beaded nipples against his chest. He ground himself against her, stimulating her hard little clit. She shuddered, her body jolting in his arms as she reached orgasm. The feel of her tight walls milking his cock was all the encouragement his body needed to explode within her. He seated himself inside her and never wanted to leave, ecstasy making streaks of fire run over his skin. It went on forever and ended too soon.

He ripped his mouth away from hers, dragging oxygen into his starved lungs. "Deus."

A sound that was almost a sob made him glance sharply at Delilah. She'd turned her face away from him, and by the time she looked at him, her face was a composed mask. "I need to finish my shower."

Easing his grip on her thighs, he set her on her feet gently.

He wasn't sure why it disturbed him so much when she faced the shower spray and ignored him. Had he been too rough with her? She'd seemed to enjoy herself. Was she angry with him? Or was it Carnac that still upset her? He didn't know. He didn't even know how to ask. It had been so many years since he'd needed to connect with anyone that he hadn't the words left for kindness.

She shrugged away from his hand when he stroked her shoulder, but she turned to face him, her arms crossing defensively over her breasts. "I need to go out for a few hours tonight."

His hands clenched at his sides, and he fought the urge to demand she stay here where he knew she was safe. The closed expression on her face warned him that it would be unwise to make demands. "Where and why?"

"I have to check in."

He shook out his fists and tried to relax. "You can—"

"I already checked in on vid." An impatient sigh punctuated the sentence. "You have to understand in my line of work why they might want me to check in in person to be sure I'm safe."

"So, not your client?"

"I never said I had a client for this job." Her jaw jutted pugnaciously. "The ruby would get a lot of creds on the open market."

He just looked at her, waiting for more information. She swallowed and glanced away.

Crossing his arms, he watched her step out of the shower and engage the dryer. He waited until she was done to speak. "Then you won't mind if I come with you."

Her expression showed wariness, distrust, and fear. Her hands lifted as though to ward him off. "I'm going to the Vermilion, Hunter. It's no place for someone like you."

The disgust she'd aimed at rich men in general was now for him, specifically, and he swallowed the bile that rose in his throat. He deserved it. He'd tried to make her his personal whore. His *mate*. He wanted to kick his own ass for letting the words come out of his mouth, but it was too late. He'd already hurt her.

He didn't try to touch her, though he wanted to. He always wanted to. Instead, he kept his face blank and made his body language as unthreatening as possible. "I want to know you're safe, too, kitten."

"I tried to rob you, you do realize that, don't you?" She shook her head and huffed a small laugh. "My mother was a whore. So was my sister until she slept her way to the top of the garbage heap and now owns a technobrothel."

He frowned. She was his mate. Seeing how Carnac treated her, and how much he wanted to rip the man's heart out for insulting her, only reinforced how little her background or his mattered. His instincts said she was his, and the rest was circumstantial. Then again, was he really any better than Carnac? Delilah's stinging words about him needing to collect things and keep them in their place struck home. Hadn't he assumed that she'd be content with whatever place he designated for her *because* she came from a family of prostitutes? Hadn't he assumed she'd stay in her place because everyone did what he told them to? Arrogant fool. "I know all of this already."

"I'm a professional thief. You're a rich man. I *steal* from people like you *for money*. As my job. All the time. And not only do I *like* my work, but I'm very, very good at what I do." She swung away from him, exiting the wash closet to rifle through his 'fresher closet until she came up with the clothes she'd arrived in.

His shoulder lifted in a nonchalant shrug when she finally looked at him. "You'd have to be good at your work to have gotten past my security system. It's prime. Top of the line."

"I know what your security system is like. I specialize in getting around them." She shoved a hand through her hair, gripping it tight as she ground her teeth in frustration. "I'm nothing more than a momentary diversion for you, Hunter. You don't really give a damn if I live or die, if I'm safe or in a boatload of danger. Let's just be honest about what we're doing here."

"I'm still coming." Only he knew that he'd been anything but honest with her since the moment they met. He picked up her pack, which was lying in the chair where he'd sat when he first tasted her. He willed his body not to react to the memory. Convincing her to let him go with her was paramount. He could follow her, hunt her, but he wanted her to be willing. He understood, finally, how essential it was that she *want* to stay with him rather than that he *keep* her as his mate. But he would do what he had to do to make absolutely certain that she was protected. He gave her a hard look. "You spend the week with me; that was the deal. You go out, I come with you."

She hissed at him, gripped her clothes tight, and stomped back into the wash closet. "Stubborn, bird-brained blisshead."

"I heard that."

She slammed the door behind her.

He dressed in all black, the same way she did. Heavy black boots, black pants and shirt that molded to his body, and a bulky black jacket topped it. Nothing flashy, nothing to indicate who and what he was. The jacket had a nanosheet built into it that hardened to an impenetrable layer if it was pierced with a bullet or blade. Since he knew Delilah's vest did the same, he didn't have to insist she wear his.

An hour later and he was a world away from his penthouse skyrise. Men in tattered clothing stood around burning trash heaps and corroded old canisters from the war era. They watched him with the defiant eyes and skittish demeanor of animals caged. People in ostentatious garments paraded through the night streets, separating them from those lower on the food chain, but even they had the hardened edge that spoke volumes about what they had done and would do to keep their place in the pecking order.

The Vermilion District.

It was as dank and filthy as he remembered from his few visits here as a wild youngster. That was before his parents died, before his uncle, before he had to assume responsibility for Avery Industries.

A lifetime ago.

"This is The Rogue's Gallery." Delilah motioned to the front of a brightly lit building deep in the heart of the Vermilion. His gaze followed the smooth sway of her hips, admiring the way her pants cupped her ass for a moment before he glanced up to see what she was talking about.

Curved windows belled outward into the sidewalk at regular intervals. His eyebrows arched at what he saw. He was no innocent, but he'd never been one to visit a jadehouse. He'd never had to pay for trim in his life. Whatever he'd imagined wasn't this. People hung by clamps on their nipples, their vaginas, their dicks. Some were mummified in black kleather and hung upside down like wriggling corpses.

A few steps took him to the first display case. He slid his hands in his pockets, keeping his face carefully blank because he sensed Delilah was waiting for him to react with shock . . . or revulsion. A well-endowed woman hung suspended by strips of shiny polymer. She wore a mask so that the only feature he could discern was her light brown eyes. Her nipples and pussy lips were clamped with electrical probes. Others were implanted deep in her pussy and anus. Lighted cords ran from the probes into the wall and ceiling. Blue neon light indicated when each of the clamps activated, the woman shuddered at the unpredictable rhythm.

"Like what you see? She's for sale." Delilah's tone was meant to be casual, but he caught the edge of acidity in her words.

Jealousy. He liked it. He wanted her to want him exclusively, and to want him to be exclusive to her. It was excellent progress. The hawk within him preened.

He arched an eyebrow at her, pulling his gaze from the window display. "Thanks, I'm otherwise engaged for the week, but I'll keep her in mind as a future option."

Flashing him a nasty look, she strode toward the door. The scenery of wriggling, bound bodies blurred as he stepped up behind her. The word TAIL was etched into the metal surface. Delilah swished her ident card and the huge iris door spun open. The middle point split into nine curved slices and retracted into the walls.

Loud synthrock pumped into the room they entered. He let his gaze sweep the wide space, wary of any new surprises. People in various states of undress littered the room. Wrapped around one side of the room was a translucent polyglass bar, lit with the same neon blue light as the probed jades in the windows outside. Behind the bar were more iris windows that opened from the middle to reveal a decadent variety of carnal acts. Men and women, women and women, multiple men and women.

Interesting. Not necessarily to his preference, but interesting to watch just the same.

Delilah nodded to the opening and closing windows. "That's the Peep Show."

"Indeed." He couldn't think of a better name for what he was seeing.

A woman behind the bar snapped around the moment they drew near. From across the slight distance, he could see the relief that washed over her face when she caught sight of Delilah. They had the same eyes, same shade of green, same exotic tilt at the corners. The sister. She had to be. Delilah swung around the long bar and folded the woman in her arms. "I'm really okay, Lorelei."

The woman—Lorelei—clung tight for a moment, then stepped back and cleared her throat. What she wore could be called clothing only by the most generous definition of the word. Metallic lace covered her from breasts to mid-thigh and barely disguised her nipples and pussy. Her hair hung in a sleek auburn curtain all the way to her waist, and she wore cosmetics that highlighted her wide green eyes. She was indescribably lovely, but he had to work to keep his gaze on her and off her sister. It was Delilah he wanted, and if he'd had any doubts about ever desiring a woman besides his mate, this certainly answered the question. Lorelei wore the smooth mask that her sister had also learned to perfect, and she turned it on him when he leaned against the bar.

She arched an eyebrow at him and gave him an artful grin. "What's your pleasure tonight?"

His gaze moved around the room, and he offered up a truly salacious grin when he settled on Delilah. "I came in with her and I'm leaving the same way. Nice place you have here, though. I've heard about it but never been inside."

He wasn't lying either. *Everyone* had heard of Tail—it had a reputation for being a safe haven for every imaginable sexual deviance. He couldn't believe Delilah's sister owned *this* techno-brothel. Pieces began to click into place in his mind. Things Delilah had said, what her last name meant. Who hadn't heard of Lorelei Chase? Men were supposed to have begged the woman to use her skills at pleasure on them. They'd paid fortunes for the privilege of touching her. And now, they paid fortunes to fuck the jades who worked in her technobrothel.

"Welcome to Tail, then." Lorelei tapped a manicured fingernail on the sleek bar. "Can I get you a drink at least?"

"A bottle of synthbrew, please. I'll open it myself." Whether this was his mate's sister or not, he was in the Vermilion and he'd rather not end up sick, poisoned, or drugged.

Lorelei's grin relaxed into a more natural one, and it crinkled the corners of her eyes as they danced with amusement. She reached under the polyglass surface and pulled out an unopened bottle to set it in front of him. "Enjoy."

"Thanks." He slid his ident card across a scanner to transfer enough creds for the drink.

Lorelei's eyebrows almost reached her hairline when she glanced at the name attached to his account. "You're welcome, Mr. Avery."

"Hunter." He grinned, popping the top off the bottle. "May I call you Lorelei?"

"Of course."

A cheer went up on the far side of the room, and he turned to see what caused the commotion. It was difficult to imagine in this wild amusement park of pleasure that any one thing might generate that much extra excitement.

But he was wrong.

His eyebrows arched and he had to work to keep his jaw from dropping to the floor at the spectacle he saw. An enormous vid screen was split in two, with each side trying to blow up the other's animated spaceships. The two contestants stood on motion-sensing pads with controllers attached to each hand as they played.

What made the game intriguing wasn't the players locked in mortal combat, but the two jades mounted on polyglass stands beside each player. A large phallus was built into the stand, and every time the jade's contestant destroyed a ship on the screen, the stand vibrated and thrust the phallus into the jade's body.

Each jade seemed wildly enthusiastic about the fated demise of the animated spacecrafts. They screamed encouragement to their contestants and screamed for other reasons when their contestants scored points.

Clearing his throat to keep his voice mild, he glanced back at Lorelei. "What is that?"

Her gaze followed the direction he jerked his chin, and a wicked little grin lit her features. "That's the Space Race 5000. My jades love it when clients want to play."

"Where can I get one?" He sipped his brew, slanting her a sly wink. "It would look great in my flat. I have the perfect spot for it."

She wrapped her arms around her waist as she laughed, a deep belly laugh that made her eyes light up and dance with merriment. It was the first unpracticed expression he'd seen on her face, and it made her even more beautiful—which seemed impossible. Then he realized it made her look more like Delilah and grinned at his own transparent fascination. Every man in earshot turned, entranced, to stare at the madam. Lorelei hiccupped, dabbing tears from her eyes. "You know, I think I like you, Mr. Avery."

"Thank you. Likewise." He saluted her with his bottle of brew, took a swig, and turned back to enjoy the show.

When the game had reached its inevitable conclusion, he found himself searching out Delilah. She stood behind the bar speaking to a woman who was obviously a jade. Lorelei worked her way down the bar until she stood before him again. "May I get you another synthbrew?"

"No, thank you." He dragged his gaze away from his mate to focus on the madam. Her glance slid between him and her sister, and Delilah poured herself a glass of liquor while studiously avoiding her sister's gaze. Lorelei focused on him, her eyes narrowing, and he could see the sharp intelligence behind the flawless features. "You're a red-tailed hawk, is that right?"

"Yes, it is."

He watched realization dawn on her face, the shock, the wariness. All the emotions flashed in rapid succession before her expression went carefully blank. "I see."

"Good." He nodded. It was fairly obvious that she had

guessed why he wanted Delilah. Why else would a steadfast recluse follow a professional thief into the Vermilion? Did he care that Lorelei had figured out what Delilah was determined to ignore? No. He didn't care if everyone knew, but he knew by now that Delilah was cautious enough about him and his wealth that if he told her outright, she would run. That, he wouldn't tolerate. He wanted her by his side.

"What are the two of you talking about?" Delilah sidled up beside her sister, leaning her shoulder against the shorter woman. The two of them were so very different, and yet it was obvious they were sisters. Delilah was long, lean, pale, and carried herself like the dangerous woman she was; Lorelei was petite, curvaceous, charming, and used her looks to make people respond any way she wanted. Both were beautiful in their own way, and both drew sidelong glances for very different reasons. Delilah would make people fear she'd gut them for fun, but the risk only made them want to touch her more. Lorelei gave the impression of softness, warmth, comfort. Until a man looked in her eyes. There were secrets there, knowledge of sins he could only dream of committing with a woman. And a man could tell she'd let him touch . . . for a price.

"We weren't talking about anything special, baby. Don't worry about it." Lorelei popped a kiss on her cheek, looping her arm around her sister's waist. A dimpled grin parted her lips.

He chuckled and rolled his eyes at them. "You know, if I tried that, she'd skin me alive."

"I'd help her." The gorgeous smile sharpened to a dangerous beauty.

"Ouch." He saluted them with his bottle of brew. He had no doubt that Lorelei would do whatever she had to for her sister. He was glad Delilah had family who loved her, regardless of what either of them did for a living. Family and the connections they offered were a blade that could cut both ways.

He knew that better than most.

5

The stubborn male had insisted on following Delilah to her room. Hunter didn't want her out of his sight tonight, and while he hadn't hovered protectively, he'd watched her like the hawk he was. She was torn between being annoyed that he thought she needed protecting and touched that he cared. Neither of them had mentioned his offer to make her his mistress, and she was just as happy to pretend it never happened. This would all be over soon anyway, so she might as well enjoy the great chemistry and follow her original plan for the rest of it.

She swiped her ident card across the scanner mounted beside the door to get into her room, and he stayed in the open doorway while she went to gather a change of clothing. "So this is where you live."

"Yep, home sweet home among the jades." Old steel lockers were mounted against one wall, and she rifled through a few of the compartments, tossing articles of clothing over her shoulder in the general direction of the bed. Boots, two belts to crisscross over her hips, a kleather bracelet that hid a very deadly little blade.

"Those lockers are real steel. Prewar." His tone was somewhere between musing and slightly confused. "There are collectors that would fill your cred account for those."

"Not everything is for sale, rich boy. No matter how much you're willing to pay." She'd said those words—or ones just like them—a million times to men over the years. Her muscles tensed as familiar weary anger washed over her. Great, Delilah. That was the perfect way to avoid having to talk about his mistress faux pas.

"I'm sorry about what I said this afternoon, Delilah. It was wrong and insulting and I had no right to say anything like that to you. I know you're with me right now because you choose to be." He pulled in a deep breath and it escaped in a snort. "Not that I gave you any better options to choose from when we met, but it *was* your choice."

"I know. I . . . forgive you for insulting me." She closed her eyes for a moment and swallowed. Her reaction had been more reflex than anything else, and she believed his apology was sincere, which just made what she had to do harder. Everything about him wasn't what it should be. He confused her, and that scared her. She wanted to push him away—she wanted to pull him closer. Shaking her head, she sighed. This was a prime example of why she should never have any real contact or involvement with her marks. Get in, get out, get the goods on their way. That's what she did best.

This job was well beyond disaster and into the destructive territory of a biobomb. A cluster of biobombs.

When she glanced back at Hunter, she saw that his gaze moved around the room, taking in the tumbled covers on the bed, the metal arms that held the bed frame in place as they ran attached to the bottom corners and ran diagonally to where the ceiling met the wall.

"Nothing touches the floor." His dark brows drew together in a frown.

She gave a quick shrug before turning away again. She didn't want to see his reaction to the reality of her world. "Helps keep the bugs and rats out of our things."

"I'm assuming you don't mean rat-shifters."

Her weak chuckle echoed in the long metal compartment she was rummaging through. "No, I don't."

"I see."

"Scared yet?" She kept her face clear of expression when she turned around.

He arched an eyebrow, folded his arms, and propped his shoulder against the doorjamb. "You don't really expect me to say yes, do you?"

"Mmm." She avoided the question and ran an impatient hand over her short hair. Her senses shivered when Hunter began moving around her room. He didn't touch anything, just looked at everything. It made her uncomfortable. Part of her wanted him to know her too much. The other part warned that letting him too close, letting him know anything at all about her, would only end in greater disaster. She fought an angry hiss. Conflicting emotions weren't something she was used to dealing with. She didn't like it. Her life was simple, straightforward. She knew her world, knew her place in it and how to survive, she knew what mattered, she knew how to get what she wanted.

She didn't know what to do about Hunter. He mixed things up, made her want things she couldn't have, made her *feel* something so powerful she didn't even know what name to put to the emotion. She'd met blissheads with more direction than she had right now.

He approached her from behind, and she flipped the door closed on her locker. The security system keyed automatically. There were things in there no one should see, and even then they weren't her most confidential pieces of information. It would be dangerous to keep that kind of information anywhere near her sister. What her sister didn't know meant she couldn't give that information to anyone else. It kept her safe.

The irony didn't escape her that Lorelei had spent so many years trying to spare her from the danger and degradation of her work, and Delilah had chosen a career far more hazardous.

She kicked her shoes off. They were designed to leave no tracks behind, and were expensive. She didn't use them unless she was on a job. Anything that made her distinctive wasn't something she could afford. She quickly shucked the matte black clothing she'd worn to his house. Then she turned to grab the slick, shiny kleather bodysuit and the matching boots with silver buckles up the sides she'd thrown across the bed. She'd look like a high-priced jade instead of a cat burglar. Just how she needed to look in order to get away with his ruby. At least she'd finally fit the part he'd cast for her in his mind. A pang went through her and she ignored it. She always completed a job when she'd been contracted for it. There were no exceptions, not even for a pretty hawk with a painful past. Not even when everything about him called to her.

She didn't want to think about that. She'd come back to Tail to check in with her sister and get a dose of reality, but her world colliding with Hunter just showed her how very much he was out of her league and she was in over her head.

Hunter glanced at her and then over her shoulder at the closed locker. His gaze slid down her nude form, and her body tightened and throbbed with want. Well, then. Time to make good on the promise to herself to enjoy the sexual attraction. She tilted her head and met his eyes boldly. "You're overdressed, Hunter."

"So I am." His long fingers slid down the seal of his jacket, opening it until she could see the skintight shirt he wore underneath. He shrugged and the jacket hit the floor with a soft thud, then he peeled the shirt off and it followed the jacket to the ground. The light danced across his hard pecs and sloping abs.

She wanted to touch the ridges of muscle, taste the small masculine nipples. He bent and unfastened his boots, tugging them off his feet before he straightened and flicked open the fly of his pants. A light sprinkling of hair trailed from below his navel down to his groin. The thatch of crisp hair widened to surround his long, hard cock. A bead of moisture seeped from the tip to slip down the length of his shaft.

"Deus." She took in every micrometer of him as his clothing was cast aside. The ache in her body rose to a fever pitch, and she squeezed her thighs together to prolong the sweet agony of it.

She set her hands on his chest, backing him up until his legs hit the edge of her bed. Then she pushed, tumbling him backward. He propped himself up on his elbows and grinned at her. "Now that you have me here, what are you going to do with me?"

"Guess." Her hand folded around the rigid arc of his cock, rubbing the dripping come into his hot flesh.

"I have a better idea." His fingers rose to grip her hips, and before she even had a chance to protest, he'd pinned her underneath him on the mattress, his heavy thighs straddling her waist. One hand wrapped around her wrists and held them over her head, while the other reached for the two belts she'd tossed onto the bed.

"What are those for?" But they both knew what he was doing. She just wasn't sure it was a good idea. She'd never enjoyed being tied down before.

His white teeth flashed as he smiled. "Guess."

He wrapped the thick kleather around her wrists, binding her to the support bars that held her bed off the ground. She blinked and tugged. The kleather held. "What are you doing?"

This time, he just laughed at her. "Whatever I want, since you're a little tied up at the moment."

"Funny. Untie me. Now." She twisted her hands, trying to finesse her way out of the kleather.

"Are you sure?" He slid down her body until he could kiss the butterfly nanotat on her hip, lower until his mouth hovered over her pussy. His fingers parted her heated lips, holding her wide. Blowing a stream of air over the damp flesh, he had her arching off the bed.

She swallowed, jerking at the binding. "I—I want . . ."

"You want?" He kissed the very top of her pussy. His tongue flicked out until the tip pressed against her clit.

"That." It was unbearable. Deus, she needed to come. Her heart slammed in her chest, blood rushing hot and fast in her veins. "Kiss me, make me come with your mouth."

He chuckled. "Whatever you want, kitten."

He settled in to feast, suckling her hardened clit until she screamed. She closed her thighs around his head, fire streaking through her body. The man had the most incredible mouth she'd ever had on her. Every thought slid from her mind as he licked, sucked, and bit at her hot, wet flesh.

"Let me touch you. Untie me." She ripped at the bindings around her wrists, but she couldn't escape the pleasure, the need. When he pulled away, she thought she would die. "Hunter!"

Lust hardened the planes of his face, flushing his skin. His eyes glittered as they swept over her body. He jerked her thighs open, pressing them flat against the mattress. Then he plunged into her tight sheath with one hard, fast thrust, and it sent spasms rocketing through her. Her body bowed hard enough to lift him with her, but the kleather bindings snapped tight and caged her movements.

She expected it rough and wild. Perhaps a little pain to accentuate her pleasure. She couldn't stop him, couldn't get away unless she shifted while he was inside her. But she wanted him to fuck her, wanted to touch and be touched. She didn't want to get away.

Arching her hips, she tried to take him as deep inside her as possible. He grunted, his cock seating to the hilt. His talons raked the skin on her thighs. Wildness flashed in his eyes, and she saw the hawk there, saw the struggle for dominance between man and predator. He shuddered when she smiled at him, and she let her fangs show for a moment before she retracted them.

A soft sound of surprise escaped her when he kissed her, his mouth soft, his touch gentle. A shiver raced through her and her hands flexed inside the kleather bonds, her claws punching through her fingertips. His tongue slid against her bottom lip before he sought entrance in her mouth. Curling her legs around his hips, she felt the bunch and release of his muscles as he moved over her, in her. The slow pump of his cock inside her pussy would drive her to madness, but there was little she could do to speed him up. Instead, every moment intensified. The drag of his hard flesh inside her, her inner walls clamping around him. The crisp hair on his legs stimulated her thighs as she strained toward him. The scent of his arousal, her wetness, the hot musk of sex. Her beaded nipples rubbed against the rougher skin on his chest, their sweat-slicked skin clinging and sliding as they moved together. His tongue stroked into her mouth, twined with hers, one more sensation to try to hold on to and savor.

She moaned into his mouth, her need peaking. Her legs cinched tighter around his lean waist, and she arched under him, silently begging him for more. He ground his pelvis against her, the rough hair at his groin only adding to her excitement. Breaking the kiss, she gasped for breath. "Please, Hunter. I need to come."

"Mmm." He nipped and suckled her bottom lip, dragging his teeth down the sensitive tissue. It hurt. It made her wetter. Her sex flexed around his cock as she quivered on the edge of orgasm. She twisted, jerking at her bonds. Desperation screamed through her.

"I love the feel of you inside me, Hunter. I want you deeper,

I want to feel you come inside me. Hunter, Hunter, *Hunter.*"
She chanted his name, sobbing for breath as she clamped her
inner muscles around his thrusting cock. "Hunter, I need you.
Hunter!"

The sound he made was like a volcano erupting, pressure
locked deep within exploding forth. He sat back, his hand gripping her hips so tight she knew she'd be bruised in the morning. But she knew she'd won. Her eyes slid closed as she all but
sobbed her relief. Yes. Thanks to Deus. Oh, *yes.*

His large body bowed between her thigh, his hips ramming
against hers. On the third thrust, she came hard, lights bursting
behind her eyelids. Her sex milked the length of his cock as her
walls closed around him in rhythmic waves.

When she opened her eyes, she saw the muscles in his chest
gleaming with sweat and his hips pumping faster and deeper.
Her desire built again, and she whimpered. Her over-stimulated
senses reeled, and she didn't know how much more she could
take.

He had to stop. She was going to die. It was too much.

The sound of blood rushing in her veins drowned out the
sound of her own voice, but her throat was soon hoarse from
screaming his name, demanding he never stop, demanding he
fuck her harder. Somehow, in the back of her mind, she knew
that she'd gone well beyond enjoying sexual chemistry with a
man, but her body reacted without any direction from her mind.
Her hips lifted off the bed and she froze, her pussy spasming
around the hot length of his dick. He groaned, thrusting into
her twice more before he followed her over the edge into orgasm. Sinking down onto her, his weight pressed her deep into
the mattress, his forehead dropping to rest between her breasts.

Reality returned in slow increments, and her arms twitched
in the uncomfortable bonds, her lungs starving for oxygen as
his heavy form made it difficult to breathe.

He reached up blindly to unfasten the belts, leaning away

from her to kiss the raw skin on the insides of her wrists. "I didn't mean to hurt you, kitten."

Heavy remorse filled those brown eyes, and her heart squeezed. She cupped his cheek in her palm. "It wouldn't be so bad if I hadn't pulled on them so hard trying to come as many times as you'd let me."

A lopsided smile quirked his lips. "Are you sure you're all right?"

"Better than all right." She closed her eyes, linked her fingers together, and stretched against the mattress, bowing her body in a way that she knew would make him stare at her breasts. When she opened her eyes, she saw his gaze focused exactly where she wanted it. "I need to get dressed."

He made a small noise of protest in the back of his throat, leaning down to kiss one of her nipples. Pleasure wound through her in a slow wave of heat. He plucked at the other nipple for a moment before he straightened. "Then again, this means I can watch you undress when we get back to the Lakeshore side of town. I like that."

"You are such a male." She rolled her eyes and sat up, reaching for the kleather bodysuit that now hung halfway off the end of the bed. She wriggled in to the tight, shiny outfit and sealed the front before she reached for her boots. Even in the heels, Hunter would still be taller than her. There weren't many men who made her feel petite, but he managed. When she stood, he was already dressed and her two belts dangled from his fingertips.

"Give me those." She snatched them from his hands and stuck her tongue out at him.

A low chuckle rumbled up from his chest. "That outfit should be illegal."

Fighting the desire to preen a little at the appreciation in his gaze, she arched an eyebrow. "This is a technobrothel in the Vermilion District. Nothing is illegal here."

"You have a point there." He grinned. "Take me back to civilization, then."

She snorted. "Civilization. As if rich people aren't as filthy and perverted as all the freaks in the Vermilion. At least we're honest about it."

"Another point for the lady." His eyes narrowed, but he didn't say anything about her snide tone.

"Right. Let's go." She spun for the door, engaged the security locks on her bedroom as they left, and led him out of the employee living hall and back into the main room of Tail.

A familiar, welcome scent reached her nose just as they turned the corner.

"Nolan!" A wide smile parted Delilah's lips and she threw herself into a tall man's arms.

The man was stripped to the waist, wearing nothing except a pair of kleather pants and heavy boots. Nanotats formed dark red, gold, and yellow flames that danced up his forearms. Both of his nipples were pierced with the same glowing rings that Delilah wore in her ears. His dark hair was tied back in a short, tight ponytail. He had the most unearthly handsome face Hunter had ever seen. He wasn't attracted to men, but even he could tell this one was exceptionally good-looking.

And he had his hand on Delilah's ass.

Hunter gritted his teeth, throttling the need to rip her from the other man's arms.

Nolan spun her in a tight circle, and they both laughed. She grabbed his face and popped a kiss on his cheek. "How've you been, sexy?"

"Working hard for the money, honey. You know how it goes." His tone was light and flirtatious, white teeth flashing and dimples tucking into his cheeks. But when he looked at Hunter, there was something in those eyes that said this man was much more deadly than he first appeared.

It was the same look he'd seen in Pierce's gaze. It set off every defensive instinct inside him, the hawk rising to the surface of his consciousness. This was a predator that was very, very dangerous. Something dark lay beneath this man's pretty exterior.

All the more reason to keep him away from Delilah.

"Hello. I'm Hunter." He didn't supply his last name as he held out his hand to the man, who hesitated for an almost imperceptible moment before he offered his hand and that same flirtatious smile.

"Nolan Angelo. I work for Lorelei." He looked Hunter up and down, interest lighting his gaze. Hunter arched a brow, gave a firm shake of his head, and released the man's hand. Nolan's gaze flicked between Hunter and Delilah, absorbing the possessive, protective stance Hunter had taken behind his mate. Understanding filled Nolan's midnight eyes as he nodded easily and turned his attention to a customer walking into Tail. "Have a good night. See you around, Dee."

The man might be a jade, but Hunter would wager this quarter's profits on the fact that Nolan was into something entirely different than selling his body for sex. He wondered if Lorelei knew. He wondered if it would put his mate or her sister in danger.

The prospect wasn't a pleasant one, but reality often wasn't.

Still, he'd do what he had to in order to protect his mate. It was abundantly clear how important her sister was to her, so he included the other woman in his protection as well.

He frowned. He wasn't certain at what point in the last few days Delilah's emotional needs became so vital to him, but there it was. His mate should have the comfort and protection his money provided. What she wanted, she would have.

As they moved through the room, more than one man reached out to touch Delilah or made lewd noises at her. She shut each of them down before Hunter could say anything, and

the way she moved told him just how frequent that kind of reaction was.

A growl reverberated in his throat. He didn't like other men
staring at her. He didn't like any of this. She was his. And he
didn't like the jealousy ripping through his system. It was ac-
ceptable for her to feel that way, but the lack of control went
against his grain.

But he was the only one who had to contend with the mating instinct, wasn't he? Lynx didn't have them. No cat that he
knew of did.

Damn it.

He bit back a snarl. She glanced over her shoulder at him,
the way she'd slicked back her hair making her eyes stand out
even more. Deus, she was beautiful.

They stepped out of the iris door, and he caught her arm to
spin her toward him.

"Wha—"

He slammed his mouth over hers, cupped the back of her
head to tilt her face up, and shoved his tongue into her mouth.
It was possessive, wild, needy. It made him angry that he felt
the need to brand her this way, but he craved her, needed her
forever, and he knew she planned to walk away from him at the
end of the week. There was little he could do to stop her. There
was nothing to keep her with him, no instinct that drove her
into his arms.

He expected her to struggle and fight the way she had when
he'd tied her down, but she melted against him, a soft purr
soughing from her throat. His grip gentled, his fingers massaging the back of her neck while his other hand dropped to cup
her ass and arch her into his erection.

Her head fell back on her neck. "Again?"

"Yes." The word was a barely audible growl.

Her booted foot curled around his leg. "Let's go back to my
room."

"No, to my house." He bit the delicate curve of her neck, just hard enough to make her jolt. "I have plans for you."

"Plans?" Her voice was high and thin with need. Just how he wanted her—needing him.

"Dee." A sub-bass voice sounded to his left from deep in the night's shadows.

Both Hunter and Delilah snapped to attention, and his lust died a swift death. What had he been thinking to touch her when they were exposed and in the Vermilion District? But he hadn't been thinking. He'd been jealous. Shit.

Delilah sniffed the air, her nose wrinkling. "Tank."

"Gotta problem." The huge, grimy man stepped out of the dark, and the garish blue light cast from Tail's windows gleamed off his very bald head.

She tilted her chin toward the alley beside the techno-brothel. "Step into my office."

The ghost of a smile crossed the man's lips.

When Hunter fell into step behind her, Tank's face hard-ened. Delilah glanced back at him, making a decision. She didn't trust Tank as far as she could throw him, and the bastard was three times her size. The look on Hunter's face clearly said he expected her to argue with him and that he was going to fight her on it. Between him and Tank, it was no contest. She gave Tank a cold look. "He's with me. Is there a problem with that?"

Tank grunted, jerking his chin to indicate they precede him into the alley. Not the way she normally would have demanded it, but he'd already conceded on the Hunter issue, so she didn't push her luck.

Extending her claws to their most deadly, she glanced at Hunter to see that he'd done the same, his nails curving into the sharp black talons of a hawk. He flexed his hands at his sides. "Friend of yours?"

"Business associate." She shrugged and focused on Tank.

The man was a blisshead and he was obviously looking for money to score more drugs. His information had been very useful in the past, but his addiction made her wary.

"I see." Tension vibrated through Hunter's body, so she forced herself to relax into a nonchalant pose. She hummed low in her throat, whether he understood or not was irrelevant. They could argue about it later.

"Got a tip on a piece you were looking for last spring." Tank wiped sweat from his shiny pate, his gaze darting between her and Hunter, clearly not certain which was more dangerous.

"What piece?" She lifted her hand, curling the fingers to examine her claws.

He shifted his weight from one foot to the other and looked ready to bolt any moment. "Gutenberg Bible. Original. Nice."

"Whose?" That drew her attention, and she gave Tank a sharp glance. She'd had a buyer on the line for that piece for over a year, and he'd had promised her a hefty commission if she ever ran across one.

Tank's gaze narrowed, calculation flashing in his beady eyes. "What do I get for the snitch?"

She tilted her chin, assuming her relaxed pose again. "Depends on how accurate the tip is."

"It's prime." Tank's tone turned to one of outrage, but they both knew his intel wasn't always as prime as he claimed.

"We'll see." She sniffed and almost gagged on the stench of his clammy sweat. "Five percent cut of what I get for it if you're right."

"Twenty."

She snorted. "For twenty, I could dig up the information myself."

"Fifteen."

"Ten, and that's final."

He smiled, revealing cracked yellow teeth. "Prime."

"Where is it?" Delilah's tone was bored enough to make it

clear how much she wanted to know without giving anything away.

Tank twitched, his fingers tapping a staccato beat on his thigh. Classic sign of a blisshead coming down off a high. "Coming in a shipment to an auction down in the Lakeshore District. Charity. Private bidders only. Two weeks from now. You want to know more, you gotta ask Tam. She knows."

A smile curled her lips. The timing couldn't be more perfect, though she usually liked to space her jobs out more than this. It helped to avoid any unwanted attention. But anything involving Tam usually panned out to a very lucrative score. The woman was her sometimes rival, sometimes ally, and the feline inside her was curious to see which it would be this time.

The usual shiver that went through her at the prospect of a new job, a new adrenaline rush didn't come. It scared her to think she was losing her edge because Hunter was the best rush she'd ever found. Maybe another job right after this one wouldn't be such a bad idea. It would get her back on solid footing. "I'll check it out."

"Tankie, my favorite little tweaker." The side entrance to Tail burst open into the alley and spilled out a puffy man in an expensive suit. He reeked of alcohol, his veins tracing purple lines on his nose. "I thought I smelled you from inside, but I couldn't be sure it wasn't just the garbage."

A glance at Tank showed that he'd gone whiter than a ghost. His shaking grew more pronounced and he began sidling toward the front of the alley. "Shit."

"You owe me money, old friend."

"Come back in, honey. We were just starting to have fun." One of Lorelei's jades—Dara—stood silhouetted by the light.

The man didn't even pause, whipping a hand out to slap the woman hard across the face. She fell back with a scream, her hand pressed to her face. The man cackled and shoved a finger at her chest. "You shut your hole, whore."

Hunter's big body went rigid, and Delilah could smell the anger he didn't bother to hide. His talons clicked together when he shook out his fists. "Another friend?"

"Never seen him before." She knew the look, though. Men like that usually had one or two knuckle-draggers with them to handle any kind of real confrontation. And there they were, two big thugs, pushing past Dara into the alley. Normally, she'd have let Tank deal with his own issues, but the man had hit one of Lorelei's girls, and he deserved an ass-kicking just for that. Adrenaline pumped in her veins as anticipation for the games ahead roared through her. This was exactly why she'd said the Vermilion was no place for someone like Hunter. The only good news was that Hunter had beat her in a fight the first night they met, and she'd never been so grateful to have her ass handed to her in her life. It meant he knew how to handle himself, and she had a feeling he was going to need to. Very soon. "I'll take the one on the left."

He grunted in protest. "He's bigger."

"You get the other two." She glanced up at him, a grin parting her lips. Snapping her hand out, she shoved her fingers in his hair and yanked him down for a hot, hard kiss. A shudder ran through his body, and her heart was pounding for more than just a fight. "For luck."

He barked out a laugh. "You are insane."

There was no time for her to respond before the men were on them. She didn't know if they were trying to get to Tank or if they just considered Hunter and her collateral damage, but she didn't really care.

Moving on cat's feet, she positioned herself directly in front of the bigger thug. He grinned, rolling his shoulders. "You used to be so pretty until you messed with me."

She didn't even bother to roll her eyes, just sank down and swept one leg out to knock him off his feet. He went down hard, grunting, but he was on his feet in a matter of moments, his face flushed with anger. He didn't shift, which told her he was probably bigger and stronger in human form than in animal. One of her poison canisters would be nice right about now, and she could definitely use that bracelet with the knife in it, but she'd forgotten it in her room. Shit.

Hissing low in her throat, she circled him and waited for the moment to strike her prey. There. He dropped his shoulder and his arm moved back just enough to expose his ribs. Her clawed hand lashed out, slicing through his shirt and flesh.

He snarled, but didn't back down. The man moved like he had some training, but not like a professional. Good for her, but not great. She swung out again and he blocked with one hand, using the other to backhand her across the mouth. She tasted her own blood. Slamming the pointed heel of her boot down on his instep, she winced when his howl pierced her sensitive ears. But the pain didn't stop her from striking with the butt of her free palm, crushing his nose and knocking him out. She shoved him away, and he slumped slowly to the ground, his eyes closing. "I wish I could say the same for your ugly ass, but you weren't any prettier before you messed with me."

When she turned around to look for Hunter, she saw him hauling himself to his feet. The other thug lay drooling and unconscious on the ground, half-changed into what looked like a gorilla. She grinned and wiped the blood off her lip. "Looks like you got the big one, after all."

He smirked. "You could at least break a sweat and pretend that wasn't almost as fun for you as sex."

"Aw, honey. Fighting doesn't even come close to fucking *you.*" Which was probably one of the truest statements she'd ever uttered. Batting her eyelashes, she stuck her tongue out at him. "But if you wanted a girlie girl, you should have caught some other female breaking into your place."

He arched an eyebrow and opened his mouth to retort, but Lorelei stepped out the side door just then. "Are the two of you all right?"

"Of course," Delilah replied, and Hunter nodded his agreement, stepping over the gorilla-shifter to stand beside her. She leaned into him, and he wrapped his arm around her waist. The contact was reassuring. Everything was fine.

"Don't get too spun, baby girl." Her sister drew her attention away from Hunter, and she felt a flush heat her cheeks. Deus, Lorelei was right. Delilah was beyond spun over Hunter if she'd bring him to Tail and trust him to watch her back in a fight. She knew she was in serious trouble if a rich man could ask her to be his mistress and it did little to cool her ardor. Returning home hadn't help clear her head at all. In fact, it may have made the situation worse. She gave her sister the nod she was expecting, but wasn't as confident as Lorelei obviously wanted her to be about pulling out of the spin.

"Spun?" Hunter slanted her a questioning glance.

She snorted a laugh and shook her head. "It's not about you. Don't worry about it."

No, it was all about her and how stupid she was being.

Dara hovered in the open door, her left eye already swollen shut. "Thank you. Both of you."

"You should go." Lorelei's gaze swept the scene. "The brigade will be here soon, and neither of you want that kind of attention."

"They respond to calls in the Vermilion?" Hunter brushed at the dirt and slime on his clothes.

A perfectly sculpted brow arched. "Of course. Their commandant is an old friend. He likes to make sure Tail stays safe."

"Say hello to your friend, then." Delilah grabbed Hunter's arm and dragged him down the alley. She had no desire to be around when any kind of authority was asking questions. "We'll be off now. Hunter promised he had *plans* for me, and I'm dying to know what they are. See you later!"

6

There was a lynx lounging on Hunter's bed. A combination of dark brown spots and stripes broke the sand-colored base of its sleek coat. The ears had long, pointed black tufts.

Its amber gaze locked on him, an unblinking stare that only felines could manage. It sent a chill up his spine, and the bird inside him tensed in the presence of a cat. He controlled the reflex and lifted an eyebrow. "You're getting cat hair on my sheets."

The lynx yawned, running its tongue down a long fang. It stretched its spotted forelegs, its body bowing into motion. A few twists and pops of bone and muscle and a nude woman lay in the place of the cat. "You're no fun today, birdie."

After the insanity in the Vermilion last night, he was still nursing a few split knuckles. He sat on the edge of the bed and rubbed his hand over his hair. He didn't feel like much fun today. He'd spent the morning in conference vids with Pierce and other investigators trying to sort out the Los Angeles mess. It felt like a million years ago, but it had been less than a week. Because Delilah was still here. He could feel the time sliding away from him, and he was no closer to coming up with a way to make her *want* to remain with him permanently.

"Hunter . . ." She propped herself up in bed, hugging a pillow to her chest. It covered her nudity, which was a shame. "Are you going to the Conservator's Gala tonight?"

He blinked at the non sequitur. "I can't think of anything I'd enjoy less. I have more pleasurable things to occupy my attention lately."

She turned a beatific smile on him, walking her fingers up his arm. "Is it too late to change your mind?"

Catching her fingers, he brought them to his mouth for a kiss. "They want my money, kitten. It's never too late for me to change my mind."

"Ah, the rich." That same mocking cynicism she always used when referring to wealthy people flavored her voice.

He shook his head, slanting her a narrowed glance. "Don't put me in that category."

"You are rich. It's a simple fact." She tugged her fingers from his grip, her expression closing.

Frustration crawled through his belly. He wanted her to open up, to tell him why she reacted the way she did to money-eyed people when she made her living off their possessions. Was it revenge? Hate? She had secrets, he knew. So many things he didn't know. Seeing her with her sister had underscored how little he knew about her past, her life. He wanted to know, but so far she had divulged nothing and grew skittish whenever he asked. She didn't trust him, not really, and he'd handed her a very large reason not to yesterday by asking her to be his mistress. It made his chest ache to consider it, so he settled for the question he thought she might actually answer. "Why do you want to go to this party?"

He watched her mouth twist and saw the moment when she decided to be bluntly honest. "Work. I need to meet with someone. I can manage it next week, but this is the perfect opportunity."

Shit. It was one thing to end up in a back-alley brawl by accident, another to willingly participate in something illegal. "You're not going to do any—"

"I just need to talk. Nothing more, nothing less." She lifted her hand and placed it over his heart, widening her smile. "I need information. No crimes will be committed while in your company."

He grunted, keeping his gaze on her face to catch even the minutest nuance of expression. "This is cutting into my week. I had plans for what we could do this evening. And I hate these kinds of parties."

"I'll make it worth your while." Her smile turned coy with promise.

He tilted his head, narrowing his gaze. "I'm not certain that's possible."

"It is." Her lashes fluttered, her fingers stroking against his chest. "I have this dress you'll love. I can have Lorelei send it over. And I won't be wearing anything underneath it."

"Mmm." His body had a very predictable reaction to her words, his cock hardening to the point of pain. He hadn't had her in hours. Too long. But he knew if he let her distract him, he'd never get the information he wanted. "All right. We can go."

She blinked, wondering what that game was. Tilting her head, she tried to catch his eye. "Just like that?"

"Just like that." He waited a beat. "You realize that Carnac probably will be there."

She sucked air between her front teeth, curling her lip in disgust. "He seemed the type to like that kind of knobfest."

"I'm sorry you had to deal with him." His gaze met hers, the gold sparking in the brown irises.

Her shoulder jerked in a shrug, tightening her grip on the pillow that was her only cover. This wasn't how she expected this conversation to go. He'd resist, she'd seduce, he'd give in. She shook her head at her only foolishness. Since when did Hunter do what she expected him to? "He's a rich man just like every other."

The tone of her voice was as frigid as she could make it. This was not a topic she wanted to discuss. She was here to be his fuck toy for the week, which meant his business associate hadn't been so very wrong about her. She didn't want to hear Hunter's apologies or excuses for the man's behavior. It wasn't anything other than what she'd come to expect from people with more money and entitlement than they knew what to do with.

"You don't like rich people very much, do you?" As usual, Hunter ignored her warning tone—which was exactly what she would have done to him before the last twenty-four hours had mangled things in her mind. Now, she wasn't certain how to act with him—having him in her world should have scared him away, but instead he'd fought beside her. All of it made him more appealing and left her in a tailspin.

"Why would you ask that?" Widening her eyes at him, she flashed an innocent smile.

He snorted. "The sneer on your face and the snide tone to your voice every time you mention my wealth were my first clues."

"Maybe I just don't like you." She hugged the pillow like a lifeline as she sought a light, mocking tone of voice.

A hot, knowing smile curved his lips and made the light cast shadows on his saturnine face. "You wouldn't come so often if you didn't like me."

Her eyes narrowed to dangerous slits. She didn't like the smug confidence in his voice. It was too much like all the other rich men she'd known. She hated that he was in that category. "Good sex is good sex, it has nothing to do with how I feel about you."

"How do you feel about me, then?" He shifted his weight on the bed, making the mattress dip.

Caught in her own verbal snare. Shit. She hissed at him. "That's not your business."

His eyebrow arched, and he tilted his head in that hawk-like fashion he used when she said or did something he didn't quite understand. "Well, being rich is my business, so tell me why you don't like wealthy people."

"No." Her jaw jutted stubbornly and she continued to glare at him. He couldn't *make* her talk about this.

The other eyebrow rose to join its twin. "What do you mean, *no*?"

Now it was her turn to snort. "No one has ever told you no before? Why am I not surprised, rich boy?"

"I've been told no before." Some of that smugness dissipated and he shifted on the mattress again, something close to discomfiture on his face.

"Did you take it for an answer or did you force them to give you your own way?" She scooted away from him on the wide bed until she was just outside his arm's reach and let the pillow drop.

Swallowing, his gaze zeroed in on her exposed breasts. He blinked several times before he shook himself and returned his gaze to her face. "I . . . convinced them that giving me my way was in their best interest."

She shook her head at him. "In other words, no one has ever told you no and made it stick."

"Perhaps not. Not since my uncle died, anyway." He sighed, but she had to respect that he didn't deny the truth just to win an argument. And she was annoyed at herself for searching for redeeming qualities in him, even though he'd discard her like trash after a few days of fucking and he was everything she'd always hated in a man.

If her long-buried conscience whispered at what a lie that was, she squelched it quickly enough.

She rolled her eyes at him. "That's the way it always is with rich people."

"Well, even though you're still here, you told me no yesterday. So, stop playing, kitten." His gaze met hers, and the expression in his dark eyes made her unable to lie. He sat forward so he could stroke his fingertips down her cheek. "You don't like us much, do you?"

"No," she said baldly.

That earned her a small smile. "We're not all bad."

"Mmm." The noncommittal noise she intended to make emerged as almost a low moan as his other hand slid up her hip and pulled her into his lap.

Arranging them so he sat cross-legged in the middle of the bed and she straddled his thighs, he kept his gaze on hers. His fingers trailed up and down her spine. "I mean it."

The gentle way he touched her almost broke her. It also made the deep-seated anger come bubbling out. Too many ugly memories had resurfaced in the last day and her voice shook when she finally forced the words out. "Tell me that when you have to watch your sister be a rich man's plaything in order to feed herself and you." Her fingers balled in his microsilk shirt. "Tell me that when they think they own you. Tell me that when you watch them make your mother love them, and then play her for a fool, break her heart, and leave her with nothing." She shook him a little, her voice rasping. "Tell me that when they take whatever they want from you and use you up and leave you to pick up the pieces."

Her rage guttered out as quickly as it had come, and she cursed under her breath for revealing so much. This was none of his business. Her chest heaved and her skin dampened with sweat. She should have kept her mouth shut.

Deus help her, the pity she'd expected to see in his eyes never surfaced, just calm, quiet understanding. "Now you take whatever you want from them."

"Maybe." Her shoulders twitched in a quick shrug, refusing to admit even to herself that it mattered what he thought of her and her past. Her life was what she'd made of it, and she'd accepted a long time ago that there were many people who would find her distasteful because she broke the law for a living. "They have what's worth taking. They played the game with my family. It's not my fault we learned to play the game better."

He was quiet for a moment, his brow furrowed in thought. "What did they take from you?"

"What?" She frowned at him, anger beginning to simmer again. Hadn't he heard a word she said? Wasn't what her family lived with every day enough?

"You talked about what they did to your sister and mother." His thumb smoothed over her cheekbone. "What did they do to you?"

She shook her head, terror squeezing her chest. No. She couldn't talk about that. She wouldn't. No one knew except Lorelei. No one could ever know except Lorelei. "Doesn't matter. It was a long time ago."

"Things that happened a long time ago can still affect us." An ironic, too-knowing smile twisted his face and made the scar on his cheek stand out in the light. "It matters to me."

"No, it doesn't. Not really."

"Tell me anyway." He held her gaze so long she had to look away, fearing he'd see the secrets in her eyes. His palm slid up and down her back in soothing circles, and she shuddered.

"I can't," she whispered, closing her eyes.

He cuddled her closer. "Please."

A watery chuckle slipped from her throat. There was a word she'd thought no rich man knew how to use. The problem wasn't that she shouldn't tell him, the problem was that she *wanted* to tell him. Everything. She wanted him to know her, wanted him to like her as much as she liked him. Too much.

If he knew, he could hurt her far more than he could with her attempted theft of his ruby. If he betrayed her, it would wound her far more deeply than she'd like to admit. And still, she wanted him to understand. That loneliness in his eyes called to something deep within her, and the ruthlessness she'd seen in him made her believe he *could* understand.

If she let herself trust him.

Her hands shook so badly she balled them into fists on her naked thighs. She stared at them so she wouldn't have to look at him when she spoke, so that a small part of her could deny that she was doing something stupid. Her throat tightened until she had to swallow several times to get the words out. "There were always men who thought they owned me because they paid for my mother or my sister for a while. After my mother died, my sister made it clear that I wasn't for sale. They could have her, but I was untouchable. She didn't want me in that life. She wanted me to make my own choices." She shook her head, smiling at the thought of Lorelei. Her touchstone. She flicked her gaze up to Hunter, saw that he watched her with that calm, controlled expression. "Once you're in the system as a jade, it never goes away, you know. It never gets expunged from your ident file, whether or not you only did it for a month thirty years ago, it's still there and it'll always be there to haunt you." She shrugged and looked away again. "It's legal, yeah, but it's not exactly respectable unless you're at the very top of the profession. Even then, people know you've been bought and paid for. My sister learned that one the hard way. Hell, there's not much the Chase women don't learn the hard way."

"You're avoiding the question." His hands still stroked her skin in soothing circles. Sweet pleasure wound through her, but it didn't make the memories easier.

"I'm getting to that." She sighed, pinching her eyes closed. "So, one of the rich men who'd bought Lorelei decided he'd paid enough and he could have us both. Who would believe a jade if she accused him of lying? No one. Who would care enough to do anything even if they did believe? No one."

He tensed underneath her and his chest expanded in a deep breath. "What happened?"

"No one takes what I'm not willing to give, Mr. Avery. I don't give a damn how rich you are. *That* rich man learned it the hard way." Her eyes flared open, and her voice held more bite than she intended, but she was past caring. "I might have been young, but I had sharp enough claws to make sure he never took what wasn't his ever again."

But she still remembered the feel of his hands on her skin, the pain when he'd struck her to keep her pliant, the ripping of her clothes as he tore at them, the scent of his breath as he'd held her down and tried to kiss her. The way his skin had parted like water under her claws, his screams, the iron stench of blood.

Nausea bubbled up in her throat, and she tamped it down and forced herself to breathe through it. She'd survived, and so had her sister. No one ever knew the truth about what happened to him and that was the way it stayed after they dumped his body in an alley and fleeced his pockets to make it look like a mugging gone wrong. He was just another statistic of being in the wrong place at the wrong time in the wrong part of town.

The memory didn't plague her much anymore. She'd done what she had to do. It was hard. It was unfair. It was just life in the Vermilion. She pulled in a deep breath and let it ease out. When she looked down at her hands, they'd stopped shaking.

"Good." Hunter's growl pulled her back to the present, his body vibrating with rage.

Her gaze met his, and she could see that his pupils had contracted to pinpoints. The ebony flecks in his eyes seemed to darken them to icy black pools. Her hands fisted again and she leaned away from him warily. This was the second time in under twenty-four hours she'd seen that look of cold anger on his face. First with Carnac and now with her. Still, he didn't scare her. Some deep part of herself trusted him not to hurt her. She never would have told him her ugliest secret if she didn't. She sensed his rage wasn't directed *at* her, but the intensity of it made the hairs rise on the back of her neck. "Good?"

"I'm glad you could protect yourself, and I'm sorry you had to go through that." His voice dropped to almost a soundless whisper and the muscles in his arms shook as he pulled her tight to his broad chest. "There's scum in every social class. Rich, poor, doesn't matter."

She shivered and rested her forehead against his shoulder. She sensed he was talking as much about his uncle as he was about the man who'd hurt her. "Yeah."

It felt good to have his arms around her. Relief slid through her that her faith in him wasn't misplaced, that she hadn't misjudged him. For so long, it had only been Lorelei and her. For so long, Delilah had only relied on herself to protect her sister from what she did for a living.

It was terrifying and exhilarating to let someone else in, even a little.

7

"Incredible." They were alone in the lift that took them to the ballroom, but Hunter hadn't been able to stop staring at her since the moment she'd stepped out of his bedroom tonight.

Delilah smoothed a hand down the curve of her hip. "I clean up all right."

The woman was insane. She was stunning. He'd gone hard as soon as he saw her. The pale strands of her hair were slicked close to her scalp, baring the thick, sparkling earrings in both ears. One of them also bore delicate whorls of mercurite chains that looped from the lobe to attach to the top of her ear. The flame-red dress she wore molded to every micrometer of her form and was short enough to make her legs look obscenely long. The characteristic feline grace in her movements made her a wanton goddess. And only he would touch her.

Impossibly, inevitably, his cock grew even harder, tenting the fly of his slacks. He stepped out of the lift with a painful wince. Running his hand over the line of buttons that marched down the front of his knee-length black jacket, he tucked a finger in the mandarin collar and tugged at the uncomfortably tight fit. He didn't like the constraint and he wanted nothing more than to drag Delilah back to his bed, strip them both bare, and spend the rest of the night burying his straining erection in her wet heat until she screamed his name.

He let the erotic images linger in his mind a moment longer, while she tucked her slim fingers in the crook of his elbow. Her touch did little to ease his current discomfort. He looked down at her and her breath caught at the desire he let show on his face. "Are you sure you don't want to—"

Her palm lifted to press against his chest. "Think of it as foreplay."

"So, you intend to tease and torment me with that dress, is that right?" He let himself savor the feel of his mate's hand on him. He'd rather it was on his naked skin, but he'd settle for this in public.

She grinned, her exotic eyes tilting even more, the cosmetics she was wearing making them an even more prominent feature on her lovely face. She patted his chest again before letting her hand drop. "You need to play a little more, Hunter."

"I haven't heard you complaining." He knew he was more serious than she was, less adept at letting his tension go and enjoying the moment. But even in the handful of days he'd had with her, he could feel that changing. The prospect of change, of bending to meld his life with hers, wasn't all that horrifying anymore. Not if it meant she was there to fill in some of the holes in his life. She'd stepped into a place that had always been reserved for her and only her. Losing her wasn't something he wanted to face. She'd become important in the time he'd known her, and he loved the moments when he could laugh with her, talk to her, touch her. Every moment he spent with his mate was one where he felt as though he was walking on a razor's edge and one false move would eviscerate him. But the other option was to walk away, and he was honest enough with himself to admit that was no longer a real option for him.

"I'm not complaining." She glanced aside, and her gaze caught, her nails digging in to his sleeve.

"What?" He followed her gaze to a gorgeous woman in a floor-length, sheer, white microsilk concoction that revealed far more than it hid. Her dark hair was piled up in an intricate pattern on top of her head, making her look inviting and untouchable all at once. He somehow doubted the effect was accidental. "That's her?"

"Yeah." She glanced up at him.

He looked at the woman again before meeting Delilah's eyes. "A jade?"

"No, she's not being paid to be here any more than I am." She straightened her slim, bare shoulders. "Though people will assume it about us both."

He lifted his fist and coughed. "They won't assume that about you. Not after the discussion I had with Carnac."

"Ah." But the look she gave him was filled with questions he couldn't answer. He wasn't about to tell her that he'd explained in excruciating detail what Delilah was to him, and what would happen to anyone who treated her as anything less than the mate of Hunter Avery. He was certain the word had spread—people in his world weren't as discreet as they liked to pretend.

He arched his eyebrow. "Who is she?"

She sighed and refused to meet his gaze. "Felicia Tamryn. Tam."

"And she is?" He recognized the name Tank had given her the night before, but that told him little about who or what she was.

"A cheetah, actually." Delilah grinned. "Her speed is really handy in certain circumstances."

That told him precisely nothing, so he repeated, "And she is?"

She sighed, her mouth twisting. "A grifter."

"Interesting." He waited a beat, very certain that he did not like how dangerous her line of work was but equally certain she'd have found a more illegal way to contact the cheetah if he hadn't agreed. Delilah's work was a problem—one he didn't yet know how to solve, but something would come to him. It had to. "She's who you need to meet for information on the . . . collector's item."

"Yeah." Her fingers drummed against his arm. "Looks like she's on the grift. Her mark is younger than her usual. Handsome, too."

He squinted, recognizing the tall blond man with Tam as a very savvy and unforgiving man he'd done business with occasionally. "Well, he doesn't do a thing for me, but Breckenridge isn't going to take it well when he finds out."

"Then let's not be the ones to break it to him." The look she gave him was so hopeful he didn't have it in him to tell her no. It was both amazing and horrifying what a man would do for a woman.

He'd be kicking himself for this later, but he sighed and gave in anyway. "Wouldn't be sporting of us."

"No." Her radiant smile made his chest ache and his cock throb. Deus, the woman did it for him. He choked on a groan when she licked her lips. "Tam'll assume I'm on the job as much as she is."

"Ah." He tugged at his collar again, wanting to be anywhere but here. But here was where Delilah was, so he sighed and led her into the heart of the room. He hoped this meeting of hers was as simple and fast as she anticipated.

But then it was his turn to freeze in place. Luckily, it was a good moment to pause as several other couples passed in front of them. Delilah glanced up at him, a question in her eyes, but he shook his head and gave her a wink.

He didn't want to explain that he'd just seen Tarek from across the crowded ballroom. The man's black hair was greased to his scalp, his tuxedo the most expensive creds could buy. He was tall and wiry, looking exactly like the snake that he was. But he was wealthy enough to be invited to the gala and to pay to cover up any of his nastier indiscretions. Hunter had seen vidpics of what happened to Tarek's first wife, and the memory was enough to make him grateful he hadn't had dinner. The woman had mysteriously disappeared a week after the pics had been taken. Tarek had a talent for making evidence disappear, didn't he? Hunter and Pierce would know that better than most—they'd both been digging long enough. His jaw locked and he bared his teeth in a smile when the other man met his eyes. A smirk crossed the viper-shifter's face and he lifted his champagne glass in a toast. When his gaze dropped to Delilah and his eyes narrowed, Hunter moved to block the other man's view of her. He had no right to even *look* at Hunter's mate, and every protective instinct roared to life. The hawk wanted to attack the threat, and the man wanted to even more.

He sucked in a deep breath and firmly led his mate away from Tarek's assessing eyes.

This was just the reason he hated these kinds of parties. He saw people that he'd rather not, that he'd rather throttle the life out of. The mingling, the noise, the close contact with others. He hated anyone touching him except Delilah, and he'd have to shake hands with every grasping little up-and-coming business flunkey. Hell, this was why he didn't like leaving his penthouse. All he needed was some reporter following him around trying to get a story for a newsvid to make this night worse.

He slanted a sour glance at Delilah as they moved across the polished marble floor. "You owe me for this. More than you know."

"I promise I'll make it worth your while. Before we leave here, if you like." Delilah felt the muscles in his arm go rigid under her fingertips, and she could smell his excitement. It was never far from the surface with either of them, and she was as eager as he was to get this night over with.

Her gaze swept the room, trying to keep Tam in sight. A holo chandelier rotated high above the ballroom; the vaulted ceiling was polished mercurite, diffusing the light around the wide room. It made the jewels every guest wore twinkle like stars. It was a pickpocket's dream.

Fleecing these people would be far too easy. Kitten's play. A wry smile curved her lips. She'd thought the same about the ruby job. That had gotten complicated rather fast. It was still complicated.

More complicated than she knew how to deal with. What was she doing here? She shook her head. Focus on the job. Hunter was just here as a cover. A willing cover. Well, willing with some incentive from her. A wicked little grin quirked her lips, and she let her gaze slide over his big, delicious body.

He looked gorgeous normally, but in a tuxedo he looked magnificent. The black fabric made his shoulders look even wider, his hips impossibly narrow, and his legs longer and more muscular. Perfection.

"Look at me that way much longer, and I'll take you right here in the ballroom." The timbre of his voice dropped to a sexual rumble that sent a shiver down her spine.

"Mmm." She pursed her lips and gave him a coy look from under her lashes that would have made her mother proud. "You'd like all of your friends to watch? Not usually my preference, but I'm flexible."

He growled low in his throat. "I'll keep you to myself, thank you. How much longer do we have to stay here? I don't enjoy these peacock parties."

"Peacocks are tasty." She licked her lips. Teasing him was too much fun, and he seemed to enjoy it. She'd watched him carefully since she told him about her past, but there'd been no withdrawal as there had been when he'd confessed about his uncle. In fact, he'd been more open, which she liked far more than she should. "Peacock tastes like rooster, actually."

"Delilah . . ." He burst into laughter, the rich sound rippling over the crowd. More than one person turned to stare, a mixture of surprise and interest on their faces.

She felt herself tensing at the unwanted attention. Standing out was not part of the plan. "Why is everyone looking at you?"

He shrugged and gave her an easy grin. "Because you look beautiful."

"Or more likely because none of us have ever heard you laugh. And rarely seen you smile."

She turned to see the approach of a tall, older man. He smiled widely, obviously accustomed to charming others. She recognized the type. He transferred the smile to her, his gaze sliding over her. Not in the slimy way Hunter's last business associate had, so she returned the grin and offered her hand. He bent over it with practiced elegance, kissing her fingertips. "I am Luc Bessinger. It's so wonderful to meet the woman who taught my old friend to laugh."

"Delilah Chase." She'd decided to use her real name so Hunter didn't have to play into any kind of con for her. It was enough that he'd brought her here.

"I'm so pleased you both could make it this evening." He offered his hand to Hunter, and the way his muscles continued to vibrate with disquiet told her it was unlikely he was as friendly with Luc as the man wanted. Luc glanced at Delilah again. "You gift my home with your presence."

Her presence was a gift? She struggled to hide her disbelieving grin. The man was trying too hard.

Hunter didn't bother to hide his grimace. "You can thank Delilah for our presence. She was very . . . interested in the benefit."

"Oh. Yes. It's a wonderful cause." She had no idea what the "cause" of this particular rich-people soiree was, but she brightened her smile and hoped no one asked her opinion on it.

"I agree. There's nothing more noble than saving the endangered lake slugs."

She bit the inside of her cheek so hard to choke off her laughter she was surprised she didn't draw blood. Hunter's shoulders shook, his eyes shining with tears of mirth.

"Excuse us, please." Tucking her hand back into the crook of Hunter's elbow, she steered him away from Luc and toward an alcove that lead to a wash closet.

She shoved him through the door and slammed it closed behind them. The autolight flickered to life, painting the sharp planes of his face in shadows. He bent over, braced his hands on his knees, and howled with laughter. "If—If you could have seen your face when he said *lake slugs.*"

She swatted his shoulder. "You could have warned me that's what the party was for."

Chortles continued to break from his throat, and he wiped the tears from his eyes. "You wanted to come—you should have asked."

She snorted. "Fine."

He straightened and let his gaze slide over her body. "You truly do look lovely."

"Thank you."

"I had to talk to Lake Slug Luc." He tugged at his collar again. "I think I deserve a bit of a reward right now."

"Oh?"

He grinned, hot and feral.

She knew that look, knew it meant she was a few nanoseconds away from an orgasm—and in that moment she forgot about Tam and a job and needing information. Wetness slicked her sex. It was amazing how quickly she'd become accustomed to Hunter providing sexual release. She shook the thought away and stepped forward to press her hands to his chest. Her fingertips drifted down the microsilk covering his muscular chest, his body heating the smooth fabric. Her hand slipped lower, into the split of his long jacket, bumped over the waistband of his pants, and curved as far around the long shaft as she could reach. She stroked up and down his cock, teasing him.

"Delilah."

"Yes, Hunter?" She tugged at the seal on his pants, dipping her hand inside to stroke the hard length of him. The pad of her thumb rolled over the tip, and she savored the contrast of soft skin over hard flesh. "Anyone who comes down this hall is going to know what we're doing."

A shudder rippled through him, and she glanced up to meet his gaze. His pupils expanded so that only a thin ring of brown showed, and his eyes glittered with hard lust. "I don't give a damn what people know."

"Neither do I." The fact that they might get caught only made it a bit more thrilling. She'd never been much of an exhibitionist, but at that moment, she'd have been willing to fuck Hunter in the middle of the ballroom. She couldn't stop a shiver at the thought, heat winding tight inside her. Her nipples beaded into hard points. She wanted his hands on them, his mouth. "I want you."

A breath hissed passed his clenched teeth. "I appreciate that about you."

She laughed softly, and he caught the sound with his mouth, turning it into a moan as she arched her body against his. Her tongue flicked out to meet his, their lips moving together desperately. Her arm was trapped between them, and she stroked her fingertips over his dick. He gathered her dress in his hand, working the hem over her hips and up to her waist. Cupping her ass, he slipped between her cheeks to delve into her sex from behind.

"So wet," he whispered against her mouth. His chest heaved as he panted, his warm breath brushing her cheek.

"Yes." She pushed her hips back, opening herself to more of his sensual exploration. He ran a finger up and down her slit, parting her damp lips to sink into her pussy. She moaned, squirming until he was touching her in just the right way, in just the right spot. Tingles raced over her skin, made her rub her palm over the head of his cock. "I've been like this since you first saw me in this dress. The look in your eyes made me hot."

A harsh sound jerked from him, tension tightening his muscles as he worked his fingers deep inside her pussy. Backing her up until her buttocks hit the polished vanity, he lifted her onto the cool surface. She shivered as his fiery body molded to her front while she settled on the icy marble counter. "Hunter, hurry."

"Yes." He shoved her thighs apart so he could step between them.

Grasping his cock with shaking fingers, he guided himself to her opening. The tip slid over her slick lips, and need sliced into her with vicious claws. She wanted him, needed him, craved him. Leaning back on her palms, she levered her hips up in offering. "Hunter."

"I love it when—"

"Hunter!" she cried when he thrust hard and fast into her, stretching her wide.

"Yes. That." A grin curved his lips, and it warmed something deep inside her. Something beyond the sexual cravings. Something far more terrifying.

But he rolled his hips, and thought dissolved into meaningless nothing. All that mattered now was Hunter's hands and Hunter's mouth and Hunter's cock driving her faster and faster toward orgasm. Molten lava raced through her veins with each pounding heartbeat. Sweat beaded on her forehead, sliding down her temples and the back of her neck. She shivered at the sensation.

A knock sounded on the door, and both she and Hunter froze where they were. She struggled to pull in a steady breath, to find her voice enough to answer. "There's someone in here."

"Oh. Will you be much longer?" A female voice that was reedy with age responded.

Delilah had started to slide off the vanity when Hunter stopped her. He grinned wickedly and began moving again, hard and fast. Her head fell back and her mouth opened in a silent scream, her fingers biting into his shoulders. Hunter's lips opened on her exposed throat, placing damp kisses down the side until he reached that sensitive spot where her neck met her shoulder. His teeth bit down lightly on the tendon there, and her body jolted, her pussy fisting around his thrusting cock.

"Deus, that's amazing," she breathed.

He chuckled against her flesh, flicking his tongue over the area he'd just bitten. The gentleness coupled with the rough was enough to send her spinning into orgasm. Her pussy pulsed around his hard length, and she clung to him as she rode out the white-hot intensity of it.

"*Delilah*." A shudder racked him, and his fingers bit into her hips as he came deep inside her. "My Delilah."

The sentiment should have sent a warning screaming through her, but a harsh aftershock of orgasm went through her. Her pussy clenched around his cock, and they both groaned. She threaded her fingers through his hair, resting her forehead against his as they gulped in air.

Time stretched in the long, quiet moments it took for her heart rate to slow to normal. All the while she stared into his eyes, watching the gold and ebony flecks brighten in the chocolate irises. His gaze softened, promising things she knew he wouldn't—perhaps *couldn't*—follow through on. It was emotional suicide to think otherwise, and she knew better than to let herself even dream of such things. This man was not for her, and he never would be. All he wanted was sex, and that was all she *should* want, too.

His hand rose to cup her jaw, his thumb brushing her cheekbone. "Something is wrong."

"Why would you say that?" She pulled away with a breathy laugh, shaken despite herself.

"You always do that, avoid personal questions." He shook his head, his eyes darkening with disappointment.

Her heart tripped, hating that she'd put that look there. It wasn't that she didn't want to tell him the truth, just that she couldn't and shouldn't. "I told you things I haven't told anyone ever before."

"I know. I want more than one moment of honesty, though." He stepped back, his cock sliding from her body. She shivered at the glide of flesh on flesh. He tucked his dick back in his pants and resealed them, straightening his jacket. "In this case, you were with me one moment, and then you were gone. So, something is wrong."

"I haven't gone anywhere." She spread her arms and motioned down at herself. "See? I'm here."

He gave her the kind of look reserved for very dense children but didn't press any further. She sighed, relief winding through her. It was something she couldn't explain to him. He wouldn't understand, and it wasn't his fault that she suddenly wanted more than their bargain would ever allow. More than he would ever allow.

Slipping down from the vanity, she smoothed her dress down until it danced around her thighs once more. A glance in the mirror made her groan. She did what she could to repair her hair and makeup, but there was little that would save it aside from washing her face and starting over—unlikely in this tiny wash closet.

She shrugged. It wasn't as if she were here to impress Hunter's friends. Though she'd yet to see him look at or treat anyone like a friend. Then again, besides Lorelei, she didn't have many she could truly put in that category, either. She turned away from the mirror to find Hunter watching her intently, his arms crossed over his broad chest.

"What?"

"Nothing." He shook his head, forked his fingers through his disheveled hair, and flipped the door open so she could exit in front of him.

The sight of a small old lady standing outside the door brought her up short. She'd completely forgotten their interrupter. The woman harrumphed when she glanced over Delilah's shoulder to see Hunter. "It's about time. Hunter Avery, is that you? Shame on you!"

"Mrs. Willets." Hunter didn't spare the woman so much as a glance as he walked past. When they were out of earshot, he groused to Delilah. "That woman is a nasty old hyena."

"Literally or figuratively?" She shot a grin over her shoulder, gave her skirt a last twitch, and led the way back into the ballroom.

A low chuckle rumbled out. "Both."

She laughed with him, but heaved a sigh of relief when she saw Tam and the man Hunter called Breckenridge were near where they entered the ballroom from the short hall to the wash closet.

The look of utter panic that flashed across Tam's face was gone so fast Delilah could almost convince herself she imagined it, but even in her wildest dreams she'd have never put such an expression on the other woman's face.

She let a quiet smile form on her lips, and decided to play the situation as though she'd never met Tam. Whatever the woman was into, she obviously didn't want Delilah interfering.

A few fawning socialites and business types tried to waylay Hunter, but a deadly glare from him and they scurried back wherever they came from. He steered Delilah around until they stopped about a foot from Tam, and Delilah had a polite greeting hovering on the tip of her tongue when the other woman spoke.

"Excuse me for just a moment." Tam's normally smooth

English accent was clipped. She flashed an overly bright smile and scurried away.

"I'll have to introduce you when she comes back." The blond man frowned at Tam's retreating form, but offered them a smile when he turned back.

Frustration raked over Delilah's temper. She wanted to get this over with and have Hunter take her back to his quiet flat where the two of them could pick up where they'd just left off. Chasing after Tam wasn't exactly subtle, so she'd have to hope the other woman really did come back soon so she didn't have to track her down.

Hunter nodded a greeting. "Breck."

"Avery." The blond man held out his hand and the men shook. Hunter's body didn't subtly tense the way it had when Luc reached for his hand, so she offered Breck a welcoming grin as he looked at her. "And who is this?"

Hunter's palm moved to slip down her back. "Delilah Chase, this is Constantine Breckenridge. Breck, this is Delilah."

"Hello." She wiggled her fingers in a little wave. "I can see why you go by Breck."

"My father has a sadistic streak."

"Those can be fun at times." She shrugged delicately and pursed her lips.

His eyebrows arched and a deep laugh rumbled out. His blue eyes twinkled with obvious delight. "Oh, I like this one, Avery. Keep her."

"I am."

"For now." She nudged him with her shoulder, damning herself for the way her heart tripped. The only thing he'd keep her as was his mistress, and she wasn't that kind of girl. She would never put up with the kind of shit Lorelei did in her line of work—she wasn't that tolerant.

"Good." Breck's smile widened. "How's business?"

"Always up." Hunter's fingers drew circles on her back and made her shiver.

Breck shook his head. "You play it far too safe, old man. You may have stayed at the very cutting edge of the fields you're involved in, and your profits are doing well, but you haven't expanded beyond them in the last decade. You should diversify even more."

"Hunter? Refusing to expand his horizons and *change* anything? No!" Delilah widened her eyes comically and Breck laughed again while Hunter pinched her ass. She giggled, jumping forward.

Hunter's arm wrapped around her waist and reeled her back in. "Breck's investment strategy is too reckless for my taste, kitten."

"Stay too long in one market, and the world passes you by." Breck rolled his eyes.

Hunter snagged two champagne flutes from a passing waiter and handed one to Delilah. "Invest in commodities people will always need, develop them so you're always on top of the market, and you don't have to worry about being left behind."

"That just makes my brain hurt." Breck sighed, shaking his head. He turned as Tam approached, his eyes softening. "Now, then. I'd like you to meet the most beautiful woman in the solar system. Tamryn."

"Only this solar system?" Her smile managed to be coy and adoring at the same time—something Delilah wouldn't have pulled off in a million years. She'd never been very good at conning people. She preferred quick, clean jobs over those that required feigned emotion.

"All of them, beloved. All of them." Breck lifted Tam's fingers to his lips and kissed the tips.

"A pleasure." Tam shook hands with Hunter and Delilah, but didn't meet either of their gazes.

Delilah squeezed Hunter's arm, and he reacted without further prompting. "Breck, if you have a moment, I would like to discuss a business matter with you. Privately."

"Of course. Ladies, if you'll excuse us." He pressed a kiss to the back of Tam's hand, lingering for just a nanosecond too long. The heat and intimacy in his expression made Delilah feel both envious of Tam and a deep pity for Breckenridge. When he found out the truth about Tam, the affection in those eyes would turn to ugly bitterness. Rich men scorned were not a pretty thing to deal with.

She tilted her head at Tam, indicating they take a walk on the balcony. "Tank says you have some information that might be useful to me."

Her mouth worked for a moment. "Yes."

Delilah waited a beat for the cheetah to speak, but nothing else was forthcoming. "Hunter's only going to be able to stall your mark so long, Tam."

"Breck," Tam hissed. "His name is Breck. Don't call him—"

She stopped herself from finishing the sentence, her mouth snapping shut.

Delilah blinked, uncertain how to deal with this side of her normally cold, methodical associate. She'd always respected that about the other woman. Better to get this over with and get out. "Do you have information for me or don't you? If you don't, then we can just talk about the weather or something until the men get back."

The torment of hell's fire was in Tam's luminous eyes when she finally let the words jerk from her throat. "I have the information you need. Breck . . . Breck has a shipment coming in with the Gutenberg you've been looking for. For an auction he's hosting." She swallowed. "I can encrypt the data for you to downlink. The usual network location."

Reaching out to take Tam's hand, Delilah gave her an out she never would have considered before she met Hunter. "You don't have to do this."

"Yes, I do." Desperation contorted Tam's face, and Delilah could relate to that feeling. Wasn't that what drove her to seek out another job immediately? To drag Hunter to a party he'd hate and put him in a situation he'd loathe even more?

"Tam. I don't know what's going on, and we aren't the kind of people who would care, but . . . you don't *have* to do this. I'm not going to need a payout for quite a while after this."

"That man. Avery. He's your mark?" Tam's fingers shook in Delilah's grasp before she withdrew them and patted down a wisp of inky hair.

Delilah tilted her head, considering her answer. "Not like you have marks, but yes, he has merchandise my client requires."

"Right. Of course." The other woman's chin dipped in a jerky nod. "Your business isn't to make them love you."

She sighed and rested her elbows against the balcony railing. "Most of the time, my business is to make sure they never see me."

"We're doing well this time, aren't we?"

She tapped her short fingernails against the marble surface, glancing back at the cheetah. "Your Breck looks like he loves you, so you're doing better than I am."

Tears welled in Tam's eyes and her slim, elegant hand rose to cover her mouth. "I-I'll send you the information. I . . . need to go."

Spinning, the cheetah moved so fast even Delilah's cat eyes had trouble following, but she stopped dead when Delilah called after her. "You're in love with him, aren't you? It's not an act this time."

A shudder rippled down the woman's spine, and she turned her head enough for Delilah to see her profile. "Yes. Deus help me. I love him."

And then she was gone.

It left Delilah more confused and upset than she would have liked to admit. Was everyone going crazy lately? Tam was the most meticulous, ruthless professional Delilah had ever met. She stole men's heart and their money without a single qualm that Delilah had ever been able to detect in the many years they'd known each other.

If a consummate con artist like Tam could fall for her mark, what hope did that leave for Delilah?

Emotion she didn't want to feel squeezed around her heart. It hurt so much, fighting it, but she didn't have a choice. The moments she had left with Hunter slid away like the relentless hum of her chrono.

"Delilah." Hunter's strong hand settled on the curve of her hip, drawing her into the warmth of his embrace.

She shook herself, flashing him a smile she hoped looked genuine. "Sorry to keep you waiting. I know you don't want to stay here any longer than necessary. We can go now."

Crooking a finger under her chin, he forced her to meet his gaze. "Your friend looked upset when she blew past me. You don't look very happy, either. I take it she didn't have the information you needed?"

"She did. It's not that."

"Then what is it?"

She pulled her chin from his grasp. "It's nothing."

"Liar." The word was more weary than angry, and it made her heart twist. He shook his head and sighed. "Let's go home."

"It's your home. Not mine." She hissed the reminder more fiercely than she should have, but couldn't seem to maintain any kind of control around him. It scared her. He scared her. "I live in a jadehouse."

"I know that." A wicked little smile creased his lips, and he rubbed his palm in soothing circles against her back. "I remember every detail of your room, in fact."

She swallowed, recalling the time she'd spent there with him. Every erotic sensation was burned into her memory. She didn't know if she'd ever be able to walk into her own room and not smell his intoxicating scent or lie in her own bed and not feel the weight of him crushing her into the mattress. Not remember how she'd strained against the kleather bonds to get closer to his mouth and hands.

He'd only been there once, and she wasn't sure the memory would ever fade. She wasn't even sure she wanted it to, and that terrified her more than anything else. She already knew she was too close to the hawk, she just didn't know when she'd stopped wanting to pull away.

It was stupid. She was going to end up as twisted up as Tam was—as spun as her sister had worried she was—if she didn't leave soon. Now.

She could do it. A hundred ways to escape this fancy party formed in her mind. She'd been in this business so long, she automatically looked for exit routes.

Hunter dropped his forehead against hers, his arms tightening around her. "We only have a few nights left together and this is not where I want to spend them. Come home with me."

"You seemed to like the water closet well enough." She pressed her mouth to his in a slow, soft kiss.

He chuckled against her lips. "We can stop off there on the way out if you like."

"No. No, I want to leave." She should have jerked away and run as far and as fast as she could. She should race back to his penthouse, snatch his ruby, dump it with her client, and then disappear, leave New Chicago and lie low until Hunter forgot all about her.

Instead, she let him lead her away from the balcony, make their excuses to their host, and take her home with him.

Unlike Tam, Delilah doubted even Deus could help her now.

8

At dawn the next morning Hunter found himself sitting on his couch looking out at the city beginning to come to life. He let his head fall back against the cushion and rolled it so he could look at the sculpture his mother had commissioned to display the ruby.

He should move the furniture to where it once was, but he had no desire to get up and do it. Instead, his gaze went back to the pink and amber streaks that lightened the sky beyond his windows.

The room was an excellent metaphor for his life lately.

Nothing was as it should be, nothing was as he expected it. Everything had changed. The thought would have made his gut clench a few days before. Now, he had his hands so full with his mate, the arrangement of furniture was the least of his concerns.

It felt good.

The ache in his chest, the wound that never seemed to heal, wasn't as painful now. It hadn't been since Delilah landed in his life. The crushing weight didn't seem as heavy anymore. He missed his family, and he always would, but the loss wasn't burned into his flesh like acid. Knowing how Delilah's past mirrored his own, how she'd had to kill to protect herself the way he had from his uncle, somehow made it easier to bear.

He felt less alone in all of this, because of her. And she was right. He'd blamed himself for what he hadn't been able to do to protect his family as a young man, but he had a choice—he could either let it eat at him until he was as dead as his parents or he could learn to live with his regrets and find a way to be happy anyway. His parents would never have wanted him to suffer. It was because of them that he knew what love was at all. Forgiveness, hope, self-sacrifice. They hadn't been perfect, but they'd done the best they could. They'd tried. Hunter had given up on everything but wealth and ambition long ago. He collected things—art, technology, cred accounts—but he didn't love, appreciate, or need any of them.

Would his parents be proud of who he had become?

Perhaps. His father would have been glad to see the business thriving, but he'd have taken more risks than Hunter ever had. His mother would have been upset to see how isolated he'd become, to see that he'd chosen to cut himself off from the world and even the possibility of finding his mate.

Fate had a twisted sense of humor that way. If Hunter was unwilling to seek out his mate, Fate would be certain she could literally steal her way into his life. He snorted and shook his head.

Delilah wasn't a comfortable woman. She was never going to stay in her place or accept that she had boundaries in his life. If she didn't like a rule, she broke it. She arranged the world around her to suit herself—they had that much in common— but if he wanted her to stay forever, he had to convince her she wanted it as much as he did. He had to give her everything. Not the money—he understood her well enough now to know she'd rather steal her own than be kept by his. No, she'd want everything. His heart, his soul, his love. Trust, commitment, fidelity. She deserved those things from any man she chose to love.

If he wasn't prepared to give them to her, then he needed to let her go at the end of their week.

As much as he recognized that, it made his hands shake to consider needing someone that much. Yet his gut twisted at the very thought of losing her.

To never see her face again, never wake up wrapped around her, never talk to her, touch her, fuck her, kiss her. Nothing. Never again.

He forced himself to imagine going back to life as it had been only a few days before and realized again how bleak his existence had become. No warmth or laughter or joy. He hadn't wanted those things, and he always got what he wanted.

It had taken her breaking through the wall he kept between himself and the rest of the world to even notice. He'd lived so long this way that it felt normal.

He winced at how pathetic that sounded, but made himself own up to the fact that he had been avoiding *life* for almost half the years he'd been on Earth. Since he'd killed his uncle. He'd taken the easy way out, in matters of the heart and in matters of business. Always choosing the clear path, always considering every consequence before he acted. He avoided risks. He'd stagnated.

Perhaps it no longer mattered what his parents would think of him, but what he thought of himself.

Did he like the man he'd become? Would he do it all over again if he had the chance to go back?

No and yes. He wanted to change who he was now, but he couldn't regret the decisions he'd made up to now if it meant he had Delilah.

She was his one true thing. No lie or excuse or amount of

money would change who and what she was to him. She was his mate.

He couldn't stop the smile that formed on his face.

This was the joy he should have felt at the beginning, he knew, but better late than never.

And now was as good a time as any to start with bringing his past, present, and future into alignment. He rose from his seat and padded on silent feet into his bedroom. Delilah lay sprawled facedown across the mattress, her back lifting and lowering with each slow breath that indicated she was still deeply asleep.

Turning away from his mate, he stepped up to the painting that covered his safe and swung it away from the wall. He keyed in all of the authentication codes, swiped his ident card, and pressed his palm to the vidpad for a scan. The safe popped open quietly, the internal gears whirring as the door swung wide.

He walked out to the main space, the weight of the ruby heavy in his hand.

Reaching out, he set the stone in its place, balanced precisely on the mercurite sculpture. It gleamed, its beauty showcased by the brilliant silver metal.

He stepped back, let out a quiet breath, and waited to see how it felt to have it there. Good, not as painful as he would have imagined. He had Delilah's gentle, but completely unsubtle, prodding to thank for that.

His chest tightened, emotion cinching around his heart until he could barely breathe. He'd already admitted to himself how much he craved her and wanted her to be with him forever. By choice, not by the dictates of his instincts. But now the full truth hit him square in the chest.

He loved her. The little thief had stolen his heart. He snorted a soft laugh and shook his head. He'd never imagined giving his heart away. Not even to a mate. Lust, amazing sex, possession, yes. But the tenderness caught him unawares . . . and something deeper, hotter, purer. *Love.* It was madness. He'd assumed it ended with the physical need. Emotions were dangerous. They tangled a man up, made him make irrational and illogical decisions, made him vulnerable.

He'd never wanted that.

He'd learned long ago that the only decisions to be made were those schooled by patience, tempered by reason, and honed by ruthlessness. In business, irrational decisions cost money and cost jobs. Occasionally, they cost lives. He wasn't interested in any of those consequences.

In this case, it didn't seem he had a choice. Delilah wasn't one for half-measures. He'd wanted everything from the moment he met her, and he loved everything about her. Her fierce personality, her uncompromising loyalty to those few whom she loved, her disregard for any rules she didn't like.

She was so damn perfect for him it made his chest band tight with emotion. Everything about her fit him. Not just physically—though that was even more phenomenal than he'd ever imagined—but everything else as well.

"You left me alone in bed." Delilah's grouchy comment preceded her out of the bedroom door.

He caught the lynx close when she stumbled against his chest, rubbing her eyes sleepily. "I'm sorry, kitten."

"It was cold without you." She yawned, relaxing bonelessly in his embrace. He felt her lashes flutter against his skin, then he felt her tense, and blink hard. "You put the ruby back."

"That's where it goes, isn't it?" He grinned, enjoying a moment where he'd dumbfounded his little cat burglar.

She leaned back and stared up at him. "You're not afraid that makes it that much easier for me to steal it?"

"If you wanted to get it out of the safe, we both know you could have." He shrugged, grinning at the shock reflected in her gaze. It felt damn good to have the upper hand for a moment.

"You could have sent it somewhere else." Her mouth set in what could almost be called a pout. Not that he'd ever tell her that. She might decide to skewer him with her claws.

He let his hands drop to her ass and pulled her tight to his body. "If you really wanted to, you could track it wherever I sent it, but I trust you not to take it, and it belongs here."

Just like she did. Belonged in his home, in his arms, in his life. The ache in his chest expanded outward, and he had to have her. Again. Always.

He slanted his mouth over hers and dragged her to the floor. Rolling her underneath him, he caught her laugh with his lips. She arched against him, her long legs snapping tight around his hips. "Now, Hunter."

"No."

"No?" Her eyebrows lifted and she rubbed her slick lips against the head of his cock. Deus, she was already wet for him.

His breath shuddered out, his muscles locking tight as he fought the need to slam home within her. He moved his hips away from the temptation she presented. "No. Not yet."

Pressing his lips to hers, he kissed her gently, reverently. A hum of surprise vibrated up from her throat, but her body softened beneath him, her hands coming up to cup his jaw. He grunted, showing her with his mouth and body everything that he didn't know how to say to her. Even if he could, he wasn't sure she'd listen . . . or believe him. Especially after his suggestion that she become his mistress *and* with what he now knew about her past with men in his position.

He spread kisses down the soft underside of her jaw and throat. When he reached her breasts, he kneaded the small mounds, lifting them so he could suck the pink crests into his mouth one after the other. He batted them with his tongue, and they hardened to tight points. His fingers slipped down her silky flesh to delve into her hot slit. Pumping inside her, he added a second and third finger.

She writhed beneath him, her hands fisting in his hair, tugging until sharp, hot tingles radiated up his scalp. "Hunter!"

He winced, but the pain twisted with the pleasure inside him. He glanced up at her, watching her pupils dilate with passion. He struggled to keep his voice even. "Yes, Delilah?"

"I don't . . . I can't . . ."

"I do. I can. Just lie back and enjoy it." Working his way down her torso, he took her navel ring in his teeth and tugged until she choked on a breath. He flicked his tongue over the butterfly nanotat on her hip. The wings beat faster with her excitement, fluttering wildly. When he reached her pussy, he stroked his tongue over her clit and her hips bucked.

"Oh. Oh. Oh! Hunter, yes . . . I love it when you—*oh*!"

She closed her knees over his ears, so her cries were muffled, but he could still hear them. He smiled against her sex, loving the way her heat and slickness increased. He hadn't even begun yet.

Every flick of his tongue over her clit made her thighs jerk, and he continued to push his fingers into her sex. The way her pussy clenched around his thrusting digits told him she quivered on the very edge of orgasm. He wasn't going to let her go over without him. He wanted every moment of this to be theirs. Together.

He sat back on his heels, cupping her thighs in his hands as she whimpered a protest. She arched toward him, her eyes glazed with desire. Emotion fisted in his chest, and he welcomed it. He loved her so much, and it felt so good. He drew her legs up to drape them over his shoulders. Her sex gleamed with juices, and he groaned at the sight. He pressed his cock to her entrance, easing into her hot channel. The slick feel of her made his jaw lock and his muscles shake with need.

Her legs flexed against his shoulder as she tried to take him deeper. "That feels so fucking prime."

"You have no idea." He pinned her thighs against his shoulders and shoved his dick into her in short, hard jabs. Rotating his pelvis, he changed the angle of his penetration

"I have a very good idea, actually." She laughed, pressing her palms flat to the floor and she lifted herself into each thrust. "Hurry up and make me come."

Deus, he loved her. He had to tell her, the words crowded onto his tongue, demanding to be spoken. "Delilah, I—"

She screamed, and her sex convulsed around his cock. He had no choice but to follow her into orgasm, the rush of it better than anything else in the universe. He emptied himself into her, letting go of the old pain and loneliness to embrace here and now with Delilah. Every muscle in his body clenched tight as he came, the sensations going on for eternity. When it was done, there was nothing left but her. For the first time in as long as he could remember, he was content and exactly where he wanted to be with exactly who he wanted to be with.

Sometimes, life was good.

Delilah stared at her wavy reflection in the windows over-looking the city. Same short blond hair, same green eyes, same robe that she'd liberated from Hunter's 'fresher closet. But it wasn't the same Delilah, was it? The mercurite and ruby sculpture was reflected in the windows as well, mocking her.

When was the last time anyone except Lorelei had ever trusted her to do the right thing? Her clients trusted her to be dishonest. They expected her to lie, cheat, steal, break the law, and generally be a horrible excuse for a human being. But Hunter? He expected her to do the right thing, to not steal from him, to not hurt him.

He had no right to expect those things from her, and the guilt of what she'd had every intention of doing ate at her soul a little. She'd been so angry for so long, so certain that every rich person alive had it coming, that she hadn't been prepared for someone to prove that they were as human as she was.

Hunter had changed everything, just by being himself.

He wasn't what she expected. He should have hurt her. He hadn't. He should have turned her in. He didn't. He should have been a rich asshole like every one of her sister's clients. He wasn't. He shouldn't have given a damn about her, should have discarded her as worthless. He hadn't. He'd been kinder to her than she had any right to expect.

He was everything she'd never known she wanted.

She loved him.

Deus help her. She loved him with every scrap of her twisted, broken, mercurial, feline soul.

Tears pressed against her lids; she was angry at herself for the weakness. *Never let your heart get involved.* It was her sister's first rule. She knew the rules, knew the score, knew the consequences of every one of her actions, and she'd fallen so fast she'd never had the chance to run. How could she have known? She never would have suspected for even a nanosecond that she'd lose her heart to a man she'd been paid to rob. A rich man.

If that wasn't the least likely situation to fall in love, she didn't know what was.

And it was just her luck.

She sighed, resting her forehead against the cool window. She couldn't do it. The ruby was right there, unsecured, just waiting for her to walk the two meters between it and her and take it. But . . . she couldn't do it.

Pulling her palmtop out of the pack she'd dumped on the couch, she cued the vidscreen and keyed in a message she would have cut her own fingers off before she'd have typed last week.

Tarek: your retainer fee has been refunded in full. Could not acquire the merchandise you require. Contract terminated.

She swallowed and pressed the button that would uplink the message to a secured location her client could access.

Hunter would never want her the way she wanted him, never love her, but she wouldn't give him a reason to hate her. He'd had almost everything important stolen from him in his life, and she wouldn't be one more in the line waiting to take what was his. She just . . . couldn't do it.

She loved him too much.

And this was the last day she had left to savor him.

When she heard the shower water cut off, she flipped the palmtop closed and tucked the device into her bag. Grabbing her pack, she entered the bedroom and tossed it onto the chair Hunter had occupied the first time he went down on her. Her pussy lips dampened at the carnal reminder, swelling and sealing together with her own juices.

The wash closet's door opened and Hunter stepped out tugging at the sleeves of a full business suit. His hair was pushed back off his face, which emphasized his sharp features and the scar running down his cheek, and he looked every centimeter the dangerous, wealthy hawk that he was. She arched an eyebrow. "You're dressed."

"I'm delighted you noticed." He drew close to her, a serious expression on his face, but still winced and hooked a finger in the tight collar and tugged a bit. That was the Hunter she knew. She wished that meant that everything was as it should be, but it wasn't. Everything had changed in a few short days, and she wasn't sure she'd ever get the old Delilah back. She wasn't even sure she wanted to. She only knew she'd miss Hunter.

She stuck her tongue out at him as he drew near, reaching for some of the playfulness she was usually so good at. He swatted her backside, so she hooked her leg behind his to tumble him back onto the bed. She came down on top of him, her legs straddling his hips as she gave him a sassy smile. He rolled them until he was on top and made to rise. Her legs snapped around his waist to hold him to her as she ran her hands down the expensive fabric covering his chest.

"I have to go to a—" Whatever he would have said was cut short when her lips met his. She licked her way into his mouth, and he gave a ragged groan. One hand cupped the back of her head, the fingers massaging her scalp and raising goose bumps on her flesh. She lifted her hips into his, tightening her grip. He thrust against her, his clothing stimulating her skin. But she didn't want the barrier between them. She tugged at his pants, but with his weight against her, she couldn't open them. She bit his lip.

"Shit." He jerked back, frantically reaching for his fly. Then he was on top of her again, thrusting deep inside her. She hissed at the hot press of his flesh within hers—exactly where she wanted it. The rhythm he set was almost punishing in its swiftness, just the way she needed it.

"Hunter," she breathed in his ear. *I love you, I love you, I love you so much.* But his mouth caught hers again, and she didn't say the words out loud. Probably for the best, but it made her heart bleed to deny the sweetest damn thing she'd ever experienced.

Their time was coming to an end, and she felt each second slipping through her fingers like grains of sand. Never to touch him again, never to kiss him again. A sob exploded from her throat, desperate agony slicing through her. So she stroked her hands over him, determined to wring every last sensation out of the moments she had left in his arms. Her body arched harder against his, taking him as deep as she possibly could. Her walls closed around him, gripping him tight.

His mouth broke from hers on a low groan. "Fuck, Delilah."

"Yes. More. Please, more." Her gaze met his, and she begged shamelessly. "I need you, Hunter . . . please."

A rough shudder racked his body. "Anything for you, kitten. Anything."

Deus, she wished it were true. Anything? More likely nothing. But she couldn't think of that now. And then she didn't have to think at all. He ground his hips against her until he hit her clit just right. She screamed as ecstasy hit her in a rush so hard and fast she was swept under. Her pussy flexed in pulses so intense, it was almost painful. She held on to Hunter as if he were her only anchor in the storm, and he pistoned in and out of her, riding her through her orgasm.

"Delilah!" Lust pulled the skin tight across his sharp cheekbones, making his eyes burn bright. His body bowed in a hard line between her thighs as he came deep inside her. His arms gave out and he crashed down on top of her, crushing her into the soft mattress. She hugged him tight, grateful he couldn't see the tears that pricked her eyes.

For a long time, she just breathed him in, loving every moment with him and pushing away the inevitable moment where she had to walk away from the only man who had ever burrowed his way into her very soul. A shaky sigh slid past her lips, and she smiled. It hurt, yes, but it was more than she'd ever expected to have. It would have to be enough.

Hunter groaned like a man who'd taken a shot to the face from her poison canister. She laughed. It had been only days ago since she tried to hit him with that stuff. He chuckled and slowly heaved himself to his feet.

"I have a meeting to go to. I'm going to be late." He fastened his pants, smoothing a hand down his shirt.

"Okay. You should go, then." She bit her lip and stared at his groin, running her fingertip from her collarbone down to her breast to circle the areola.

"Okay." He reached into his 'fresher for his jacket and slid it on. "I'm leaving now."

Her gaze ran up his body until she met his eyes. "Kiss me good-bye first."

"I'll be back in a couple of hours." It didn't matter. What they had was coming to a swift and painful close, but she still wanted her kiss. One last time. She watched the muscles in his shoulders tense as he resisted temptation. "I shouldn't."

Arching an eyebrow, she grinned and plucked at her hardened nipple. "So? Do it anyway."

Closing his eyes, he swore under his breath. When he opened them, they sparkled with chagrin and suppressed laughter. He braced one palm and one knee on the bed, careful not to touch her. Then he bent forward for a quick kiss. She cupped his jaw, angling her head to deepen the contact. One short kiss became two until he was feasting on her mouth with long, slow drugging kisses.

He jerked back, breathing hard. "Woman, you are dangerous."

"Don't you forget it, either." She licked the flavor of him off her lips.

He laughed, stroked his fingers down the top of her thigh, and beat a hasty retreat before she could reach for him again.

She lay there for a long time after he left, pressure tightening in her chest until she wanted to scream. She wished she could cry, wished there was a way to release all the pain and love and grief whirling around inside her, but the wound had cut too deep and the tears wouldn't come. There was no relief for her.

Forcing herself to rise, she pulled in a deep breath and turned away from the bed that still smelled of sex and Hunter. She wasn't going to make either of them suffer through a long good-bye. Opening the 'fresher, she pulled out her bodysuit and boots and wriggled into them, then she grabbed her dress and shoes from the gala to stuff into her knapsack. She bent over the pack, tucking in a strap from her shoe and sealing the bag. Pulling it over her shoulder, she groped for something else to do before she left, but there was nothing to keep her here.

It was time to go.

A sense of foreboding crept down her spine and she froze in

place for a long moment. She cast a surreptitious glance around the room, shielding her eyes with her lashes. Nothing. Her senses told her nothing. No odd smells, no movement. But still that instinct that told her danger was near wouldn't fade. Her muscles tensed, ready for an attack from an unseen assailant.

The softest whisper of noise sounded behind her and she whipped around.

Too late.

Hunter was not in a good mood when he stepped off the lift into his penthouse. He wanted to rip something apart with his bare hands. What a bitch of a meeting. Tarek was at it again, looking to undercut his business interests. The viper really knew how to live up to his nature.

Hunter couldn't wait to burn off his frustration in Delilah's arms. He needed her more with every passing moment. Touching her only increased the craving, and he didn't care. She was meant to be his until the day he died. His mate.

Tilting his head, he tried to sense where she was, but the flat was deadly still.

She wasn't here.

"Delilah?" He called her name anyway, dropping his jacket on a side table as he searched every room. Nothing. No note, no vid message. She was just gone. He sat on the bed heavily, running his hand over the indentation in the covers where they had loved earlier.

Would she have gone back to Tail? If not, surely her sister would know where she'd gone. He'd have to convince Lorelei to tell him. He didn't think he could wait for an investigator to track her down. His belly cramped with the pain of it. She'd left him. He was alone. Again.

The vidscreen in the wall flickered to life, chiming to indicate an incoming message. Delilah? His heart thumped hard in his chest, and he struggled for calm. "Display cache."

A vidpic flashed on the screen. Delilah, nude, her green eyes narrowed, frozen in place with a slim silver blade to her throat. A single bead of crimson blood trailed down her neck from where the knife touched her flesh. Lines of text appeared under the pic.

She didn't get me the ruby, so I'll take it out of her pretty hide. I always get what's yours, in the end.

Shards of ice stabbed at his soul. He knew that hand, that blade. Tarek. The viper-shifter had Hunter's mate.

Fear unlike anything he'd ever known before fisted in his gut. Delilah in the hands of a madman.

Hunter had seen the things Tarek would do to people when he was displeased. He didn't even want to imagine what he would do to Delilah. A thief who'd failed him. Mate to his biggest rival.

The hawk within him scrabbled for control, wanting to hunt, to kill. He and the hawk were in complete agreement. He gripped his rage tight, chilling it to cold, methodical calculation. If there was a chance to save her, it had to be done now before the viper was done toying with his prey. There was no time to lose.

Bile burned the back of his throat as he cued the vidscreen to make a call. "Pierce, I need a favor. Fast."

The government operative didn't show so much as a flicker of emotion on his face at the abrupt greeting. "What do you need?"

"Tarek. I need to know where he is now, and I know you keep constant surveillance on him. He has someone who belongs to me." Before he'd even finished speaking, Pierce had reached over and begun tapping his fingers against a vidpad out of Hunter's line of sight.

Pierce paused in his movements, hands suspended above the pad. "Some*one*?"

"My mate." He met the man's gaze, let all the agony he felt show in his eyes. He wasn't going to hide what Delilah meant to him. Not from himself or anyone else. Especially not from her, if he could save her. *When.* He forced himself to hold tight to the tiniest scrap of hope. For her. He'd tell her he loved her *when* he saved her.

"I see." Pierce resumed what he was doing, his fingers flying faster than before. Then he stopped again. "I have him. I'm coming with you."

10

"Your retainer fee was returned to you, Mr. Tarek. The matter is closed." She tried to keep her voice level, but everything about this man sent chills down her spine. He'd knocked her unconscious and while she was out had brought her to a building somewhere near the lake, to judge by the scent and sound of water. When she'd awoken, she'd found herself stripped down to her bare ass and strapped her to a hardened mercurite chair bolted to the old cement floor. Then he'd taken vidpics while wielding that nasty little knife of his. The tiny slice he'd made in her throat burned like acid, but the excitement he didn't bother to hide at the sight of her blood made her stomach heave. Two of the windows in the room were broken out, and the frigid wind tore at her flesh. Cold sweat broke out across her forehead, made her hands clammy. She clenched them tight. She knew better than to let an enemy see her fear.

He paced in a tight circle around her, running the cold edge of his knife along her skin. She bit back a hiss of pain as her flesh parted and blood welled. He chuckled, the sound not quite sane. "I normally don't like to soil my hands with this sort of thing, but for you, I made an exception."

"This sort of thing?" *Keep talking, Delilah. Keep thinking.* There had to be a way out of this. Her heart pounded, her muscles beginning to ache at the unnatural angle they'd been forced to assume when he bound her.

"Yes, I like to keep myself at arm's length." He slid the flat of the blade down her biceps, then twisted his wrist and slashed a shallow, agonizing cut down to her elbow. "Makes it less messy for me, less incriminating."

She blinked, struggling to focus above the pain, to think, to have all the pieces fall into place. "You're the man who's sabotaging Hunter's business."

"Very good. You are as sharp as they claimed." The sharp point of his knife drew a line from her arm to the base of her neck, and her throat closed so tight she couldn't breathe, couldn't scream, couldn't vomit. "Too bad you proved completely useless in your original capacity, but I've found a better one for you."

"I'm sure you could hire another thief to steal the ruby." She twisted her wrists in the tight kleather bindings, struggling for the hundredth time to free herself. Again, they didn't give so much as a micrometer. She could feel the blood trickling down her arm and around the kleather to drip from her fingertips.

He chuckled low in his throat, and it came out edged in a reptilian hiss. "My dear, it was never about the ruby."

"Oh?" She didn't really care what it was about, she just wanted to get the hell out of here. She wanted no part in whatever new capacity he'd found for her. She needed to escape the pain. And she knew it could only get worse from here. Her mind raced, her thoughts bouncing around like a bliss addict's.

He squatted in front of her, slapping the knife lightly against her inner thigh. His gaze focused for a moment on her naked sex, and he smiled to himself before he met her eyes. "It was about taking the thing Avery valued most. The buzz is that you're that thing now."

The hysterical laugh that bubbled up in her throat emerged as a choked sob. A whore's daughter, a professional thief, the most valuable thing to one of the richest men alive? He'd wanted her as his mistress, a fuck toy, nothing more. The buzz was off this time. Way off. It might even be funny if it didn't put her in an even worse situation. But the endgame didn't change. She was on her own. No one was coming to save her, no matter how valuable Tarek might think she was to Hunter. A little relief trickled through her that Hunter would be safe from this asshole. This time. She pulled in a deep breath, locking her thoughts down.

Meeting Tarek's eyes, she knew without a single shred of doubt that he was going to kill her. Slowly.

She was bound, she was locked in, she was bleeding, and the way he looked at her told her exactly what he was going to do with her before he killed her.

No way in hell.

She swallowed and cold hard realization slid through her, washing away whatever grain of hope that remained. There was no escaping. She wasn't getting out of this. There was only one option left, because there was no way she was going to let this piece of shit steal the one pure thing she had in her life. Hunter. The way his hands felt on her body. The way he looked at her when he slid his cock inside her.

Her tongue rolled around in her mouth until it pressed against the right tooth. The escape plan. Everyone in her profession had one; they all just hoped they never had to use it.

Figures she'd be the one who did. That was just her luck lately. A sad smile curled her lips, and she pushed away the self-pity, pushed away the worry that Lorelei would never know what happened to her, pushed away the regret that she hadn't told Hunter she loved him, until there was only the under-standing of what she had to do now to save herself. Not from death, but from a death not of her choosing.

Something else she wouldn't let this man take from her.

Her choice.

Her body relaxed into the chair and she tilted her jaw until she could bite down hard on the false tooth. A sharp pain and blood filled her mouth as she bit a little too hard. And then poison she'd concocted herself coated her tongue. It mixed with the blood, coppery sweet, and she forced herself to swallow it.

Blackness edged into her vision as the poison did its work. She would feel no pain, no suffering, she would just be numb, and then it would all be over.

She'd mixed the poison herself, after all.

She knew it would work.

For a moment, Hunter's face wavered before her eyes, and she smiled. Deus, she loved him so much.

And then there was nothingness.

Hunter didn't wait for Pierce once the building came into view. Third floor, southern corner room. He shifted to hawk form and launched himself skyward with a deep beat of his wings. The wind sliced more fiercely this close to the lake, but it took him only a few moments to sweep past the correct window. The sight that greeted him stopped his heart and made him wish his vision weren't so accurate. Tarek. Standing over a bound and blood-soaked Delilah, her head hanging limply on her neck.

Swirling up in a draft of wind, he gained the altitude he needed, killing rage pumping through his system. Then he stooped into a swift strike, diving in through a broken window.

He hit his mark. His talons plunged into Tarek's eye, shred-ding his soft flesh. The viper screamed, blood splattering the ground to mix with Delilah's. He dropped that vicious little knife of his as he clamped his hand over the empty socket that used to hold his eye. Hunter swooped up and away, circling to watch for another opening to attack.

Tarek shifted into his viper form, hissing a reptilian warning. Hunter didn't heed it—he was beyond warnings. The viper had hurt Delilah, and he was going to die. Tarek coiled tight, waiting to strike, fangs bared.

A shriek ripped from Hunter's beak and he dove forward. He didn't give a damn if the snake bit him. He'd wanted to take what mattered to Hunter, and he'd succeeded. This went beyond levelheaded business decisions. Delilah was everything, and there was no patient waiting for a mistake this time. This time, Tarek would pay.

This time Tarek would die.

It was over too quickly to satisfy him. Tarek lunged. And missed. Hunter's beak snapped around the viper's neck, letting his weight carry them to the ground. He ripped and stabbed at the scaled body with his beak and talons until nothing remained but a bloody mass of flesh.

"Avery. Avery! Get ahold of yourself and get over here!" Pierce's roar sliced through the fog of rage that held Hunter in its grip.

His head snapped around to see the wolf-shifter running his hands over Delilah's limp, bloodied body. He checked her vital signs, a graver look than Hunter had ever seen settling over the dour man's face. His gray eyes met Hunter's as he shifted back to human form. He stepped over Tarek's mangled body, the viper forgotten in his need to get to Delilah.

Pierce moved back, his palmtop already in his hand as he quietly requested medical support. Hunter's breath tangled in his throat, acrid fear coating his tongue. His hand shook as he stroked her soft hair. "Delilah? Open your eyes, honey. Look at me. Please."

"There's not that much blood." The wolf-shifter watched as

Hunter ran his hands over Delilah's nude body. "So, where did he bite her?"

A bitter laugh strangled out of Hunter's throat as full realization struck. "No, she did it to herself. Poison. She . . . uses poisons in her work sometimes."

"I see." And Pierce said no more.

Her breathing was so shallow he had to put his palm between her breasts to feel her chest move with each inhalation. Her pulse was thready and weak under his fingers.

She was dying.

His gut clenched at the mere thought of losing her. No. He couldn't. Life without Delilah was no life at all. It was empty, colorless. Meaningless.

He needed her.

"Delilah," he whispered. "Kitten, can you hear me? Open your eyes."

Her lashes fluttered, her green eyes locking on his face for a moment. Her fingers twitched, and he lifted them to his mouth, kissing the tips. A wan smile curved her bloodless lips. "I didn't think you'd come."

"Foolish woman." Because she thought he didn't care. Because he'd been too much of a coward to tell her the truth.

"Fuck you."

He laughed, but tears stung his eyes. He blinked, focusing on her lovely face. "You will not die. Do you hear me? I refuse to let you."

"Sorry, birdie." Her fingers flexed, brushing over his cheek. Her gaze softened, warmed in the look he liked best from her. She swallowed, those wide eyes blinking slowly, and then she was gone.

"Delilah." He grabbed her shoulders, shook her, waited a moment, shook her again, but her eyes didn't open again. "Delilah!"

Nothing.

He cut a glance at Pierce. The man had turned away to grant them some semblance of privacy. He stared out the window. "The medics are here."

"Tell them to hurry." Hunter's voice was no more than a harsh croak.

Pierce spun away, left the room, presumably to do what Hunter had told him to.

Please, Deus, don't let them be too late. Please, Deus, let Delilah be saved.

He lifted her into his arms, cradled her close, and breathed in the essence that was Delilah, feeling the fading warmth of her soft, soft skin.

II
———————————

Delilah burned. Every centimeter of her was on fire, pain eating her from the inside out. She felt as though she might explode from her skin at any moment.

It was the only way she knew she wasn't dead. Dead people couldn't hurt.

She wished for death, sobbing and pleading with whatever deity who would listen.

And Hunter was there in her dreams, squeezing her fingers tight, smoothing her hair away from her sweaty face. He begged her to stay with him, demanded it, cursed her and told her he loved her in the same breath.

Sweat slid down her face, the salty fluid burning her cracked lips.

Hunter.

She wanted to see him again. One last time. Feel his skin under her fingertips, whisper his name in his ear, kiss him. It was the one thing stronger than the pain, the one thing she could latch on to and hold tight until the darkness swirled in to take her again.

A cough rattled her chest, made shrieking agony rip through her body. The darkness peeled away layer by layer as the pain became more real, and she felt it in every micrometer of her skin, her legs, her arms; even her hair hurt. Her eyes felt as though they'd been sealed shut. When she managed to pry them open, it was to see Lorelei slumped in a chair beside her bed.

No, beside *Hunter's* bed.

She frowned, but the movement hurt. Opening her mouth, she tried to speak, but couldn't even manage a whisper. Her throat and mouth were a desert and rolling her tongue around did little to help.

A masculine hand appeared on her other side, offering her a drink with a straw in it. She sucked greedily, the precious liquid ambrosia flowing over her tongue. When she was done, her head fell back against the pillow and she was weak and shaking. "Thank you."

"Of course." The quiet voice had a roughened edge, but she sensed no threat from the man. Everything about him was gray. His hair, his eyes, his clothes. Silent, ghostly, and watchful. Wary of everyone and weary with the world.

But there was something about the way he looked at her sister, some flicker of emotion he quickly hid. He reached out and gently touched Lorelei's shoulder. She jolted, her hand snapping up to catch his wrist before her eyes even opened.

"Pierce." She sighed, a small smile curving her lips. Then her gaze dropped to Delilah and her mouth dropped open and tears sheened her eyes. "Hey, baby girl."

"Hey, yourself." The voice was rusty and too soft, but it was there. A triumphant smile curled her lips. She flicked a glance at the watchful male. "Interesting man, that Pierce. Yours?"

"No." Lorelei gave him the kind of smile that would drop most men to their knees with lust. "But he helped save you."

Pierce froze, staring at Lorelei. The look was so intense,

Delilah felt as though she'd interrupted a private moment. Then he shook himself, snapped around, and walked away.

She lifted an eyebrow, and Lorelei just shrugged. "Well, I didn't say he was talkative."

"No, I guess not."

"I don't care." She just stared at Delilah for a long moment, her green eyes bloodshot. "I told him he had free drinks waiting for him at Tail whenever he wanted. You're here and you're safe. That's all that matters."

"I love you, too, big sister."

Lorelei squeezed her hand tight, swallowed hard, and pressed her free hand to her shaking lips. "I want to tell you to *never* do something like that again, baby girl, but in your line of work, I don't think it's fair to ask for that kind of promise."

"I wouldn't agree to it. I couldn't." Delilah sighed and used what little strength she had to tighten her hand around her sister's fingers. "I'd do what I did again in the same circumstances."

"I know." A sob was quickly suppressed, and Lorelei pulled in a deep breath that made her breasts strain against the confines of her outfit. "And I would want you to save yourself from rape and murder, but . . . I don't want to lose you, either."

Delilah nodded even though it hurt, but there was nothing to say. They both knew the score, they both knew what the other did. They didn't lie to each other.

"I'm glad you're alive and safe. I love you."

"You, too." A movement in the doorway caught Delilah's eye. Hunter stood there watching them, his arms crossed, his shoulder braced against the doorjamb. Her eyes catalogued every centimeter of him. He looked exhausted, lines bracketing his eyes and mouth.

She met her sister's gaze. "Can you give us a moment?"

"Actually, I have to get back to Tail. Someone's got to keep the customers in line." She gave Delilah's hand a last pat, rose, and smoothed down the purple sheen of her skintight dress. "I'll be back to check in on you." She glanced at Hunter. "Tomorrow."

He nodded, straightening. "I have someone ready to take you home. They're at your disposal—they'll bring you back whenever you want."

"Thank you." She stepped toward the door, brushing a kiss to Hunter's cheek.

He patted her shoulder gently and moved aside so she could leave. His gaze never left Delilah. He entered the room, sliding into the chair Lorelei had abandoned. "Pierce told me you were awake."

"Oh." She rubbed the microsilk sheet between her fingers, her mouth working as she tried to find the right words. "What am I doing here? I mean . . . our week is over."

"What the hell is that supposed to mean?" Hunter straightened in his chair, the hawk's feathers clearly ruffled. "You thought I was just going to let you be murdered by a man who hated me? What kind of person do you think I am, Delilah?"

"A good one." She turned her head on the pillow so she could see all of him. "One who didn't turn me in when he could have. One who takes his responsibilities seriously, but I'm not your responsibility."

"We can argue about that later." The anger drained away from his face, and he looked even more tired than he had moments before.

"What if I want to argue about it now?" She tried for a weak smile, but ended up blinking back tears instead.

She was alive, and Hunter was here.

His mouth worked, but nothing came out. He didn't have the words. If the woman wanted to argue, he'd sit here and debate until she was satisfied. Just then, if she'd wanted the moon, he would have gone to get it for her.

"I'm just . . . glad you're awake." His voice emerged harsher than he'd intended, but it was such a wonder to see those green eyes open and focused on him.

"I am." She blinked and ran her fingertips over the sheets. "I shouldn't have woken up, Hunter. I mixed that poison myself."

He nodded, reaching out to fold her hand in his. "The medics . . . the medics said we may have gotten to you just in time. The cold and the fact that you were naked slowed the spread of the poison. They did what they could, but after three days, they didn't think you'd make it. That's when I brought you ho—here."

He'd almost said *home.* He'd brought her home. It was so right to have her here. Those first few days, he'd come in, paced the echoing silence, but couldn't sleep in a bed that smelled of her. The whole penthouse was covered in her scent, but it was empty, barren. There was no laughter here, no life. There was nothing without Delilah.

His mate, the woman he loved, the woman who'd been so certain he'd leave her to die, she'd poisoned herself.

His gut fisted at the thought, an echo of sheer agony ripping through him. She thought she meant nothing because he'd been too afraid to tell her the truth—that she meant everything. That he now measured his life by the moments he spent in her presence, that he couldn't see beyond the pain of losing her to even imagine an existence without her in it.

"Don't ever try to leave me again, Delilah." The words emerged little more than a tortured whisper. Moisture flooded his eyes as the reality of *her* finally sank in. She wasn't going to die, the warmth of her hand in his wasn't a fleeting sensation while the life slowly drained from her slim body. She was here, she was alive, she was talking to him. He closed his eyes briefly. Deus help him if she was ever in danger again, let alone injured.

She narrowed her gaze at him. "I was kidnapped—you can't blame me for that."

"That wasn't what I was talking about and you know it."
He stroked his fingers down the back of her hand.

"I know."

He swallowed, unable to stop the painful words from tumbling from his lips. "You thought I'd leave you to be raped and butchered by him."

"It wasn't—I didn't—" Her eyes closed for a moment, and she swallowed. "I couldn't let him do that to me. It was just like before, only I was tied down, and there was no Lorelei, no Hunter, no one to help. So, I took the only way out I had." Her voice tripped over a sob. "I didn't want the last thing I remembered to be *that* with him, instead of making love with *you*."

"Delilah . . ." He needed so badly to hold her, his arms shook. He sat beside her gingerly, sliding his hand over her silken hair. She dove against him and clung with surprising strength.

Then she cried. Every sob sliced into him like a white-hot blade, making him wince as her tears soaked through his shirt. He pulled her on to his lap, wrapped her in his embrace, and rocked her gently. He held her until her sobs slowed to hiccups and she collapsed against him, spent. Still, he didn't let her go. He breathed in her scent and felt the warmth of her body seep into his. Burying his nose in her soft hair, he closed his eyes for the first time in days and relaxed. The tension left his body by degrees as he listened to the steady rhythm of her breathing.

"This is nice," she said, her voice softening with sleep.

He ran a hand up and down her back, if only for the pleasure of touching her. "Yes."

Three weeks later, she was crawling the walls in her need to get away. But she was never alone, not for one moment. Lorelei, Pierce, and Hunter sat with her in shifts to make sure she followed the medics' orders of bed rest. Hell, even Nolan took a turn babysitting her.

She'd finally been given a clean report of health, and Hunter stood over the bed, arguing with the medic about how he was certain she needed more rest. She threw aside the covers and the shirt she'd stolen from Hunter fluttered around her thighs as she stepped between Hunter and the frazzled medic.

"You can go now," she said to the medic, who took the reprieve and scurried away.

Hunter snarled, his fists clenching at his sides. "I wasn't done talking to him."

The anger didn't quite mask the torment in his eyes, so she cupped his face in her palms. "You saved me, Hunter. I'm all right. It's not like your parents."

"They were good people, good parents." He closed his eyes, letting his forehead drop against her. "Rich or not, they didn't deserve what happened to them. Though my uncle did. And Tarek."

"I would never say your parents deserved anything, Hunter, no matter how wealthy they were." She sighed, wrapped her arms around his neck, and tried to find words to explain that the anger she'd locked up inside for so long was now all but gone. "I was . . . it's not about money, you're right. It's about people who think they deserve whatever they want. It annoys me that wealthy people cover it with a veneer of civility while calling people from the Vermilion filthy animals. Then they come down to Tail, put on a mask, and pay their creds to fuck Nolan up the ass in front of the whole jadehouse."

"Hypocrisy." He bent forward, scooped her in to his arms, and settled on the bed with her in his lap and his back against the headboard.

"Yes." Her finger gripped his shoulders tight, grateful that he understood, that he knew she wasn't some whack job on a crazed vengeance spree. "That's what I hate. If you're going to do bad things, at least be honest about it. Or as honest as you can be without getting arrested."

He chuckled and kissed her. "I promise not to pay to fuck Nolan up the ass."

"You, he'd probably fuck for free." She flicked her tongue over his bottom lip. "And then I would have to kill him for touching you. Lorelei would be upset. She has a soft spot for him."

"I understand."

She pulled back to meet his gaze and decided to lay everything on the line. She should be dead by now, never to see his face again. If he rejected her, then he did, but it wouldn't be because she was too scared to ask for what she wanted. "It would just be a bad thing for you to touch anyone except me. I wouldn't like it."

"I'm willing to be exclusive if you are." His mouth slanted over hers, the kiss hard and possessive. Exactly what she'd been craving during all the days that he hadn't done anything more than hold her hand.

She shifted in his lap until she straddled his thighs, letting her head fall back so he could nip and suck on her throat. "So, you decided to keep me, is that it?"

"I'm not looking to start another collection or to make you a kept woman, so that's not exactly what I had in mind. I'm sorry I ever insulted you with that offer, kitten." He swallowed audibly, his hands stroking her back.

She tried to smile and failed, pinning her gaze on his chest. Hope surged inside her. So far, he was saying exactly what she wanted to hear. So far. "What did you have in mind, exactly?"

Nudging her chin up with his hand, his eyes met hers. The amber in his dark gaze glimmered. "Will you marry me, Delilah?"

Her breath seized in her chest, every muscle going absolutely rigid. She stared at him for so long his brows contracted and uncertainty flickered to life in his eyes. It wasn't a look she was used to seeing on his features. But of all the things she'd expected him to say, those words weren't among them.

That he wanted her to stay with him, that he cared. Admitting that he wanted her for more than just a sexual convenience was the most she'd ever dreamed of, but this . . .

"I love you, Hunter." Then she covered her face with her hands and cried.

"Kitten." His hand cupped the back of her head, his palms moving frantically over her shoulders and back. "Delilah? Honey, what's wrong? We don't have to get married if you don't want to. We'll do whatever you want. Just promise to never leave."

"I won't." She wrapped her arms around his neck and twined her legs around his waist. "I can't. Hunter."

"I love you." He held her close, his body shaking. "You're my mate. There's no living without you."

"Wh-what?" Another shock hit her and she swayed against him. Tears made spikes of her eyelashes so she blinked to see him clearly.

He squeezed her tighter against him. "I'm a red-tailed hawk, kitten."

"I know that." But it had never occurred to her that *she* might be his mate. Not until he said it. Pulling back, she stared at him, her mind spinning. It all made sense, finally. Things he'd said and done that she hadn't understood at the time, that seemed so out of character for him. Including making her stay in the first place. "They mate for life."

Meeting her gaze directly, he nodded. "Yes. *We* do."

"And you sensed I'm your mate?" Her heart hammered in her chest, her hands trembling with the shock.

His gaze never wavered. "Yes."

Her mouth dropped open and outrage rippled through her. She leaned back and smacked the side of his head. Hard.

He jerked away and gave her a glare. "What the hell was that for?"

"Why didn't you tell me before? Deus, Hunter, you offered me a position as your whore!" Her lips pressed together and tears welled up again. "I thought I was nothing to you."

"Everything. Never doubt it, even when I'm an idiot and say the wrong thing. Even when I screw up. Even when I hurt you. You are everything to me." His eyes closed, but not before she saw a sheen of moisture form. "When I thought . . . when they said you wouldn't make it . . . Kitten, I am so sorry. It's all my fault. If I had lost you, it would have been my fault. You're right about my parents, you're right that I couldn't save them, but you? You would have died because I lied to you, because I didn't tell you that I love you so fucking much it hurts. Your death would have been my fault, and I never would have forgiven myself."

"I love you, too." A tear trailed down her cheek. "I even love you when you're stubborn and when you say the wrong thing. You make up for it."

He huffed a short yawn. "Yeah? How?"

A derisive snort almost erupted, but she stopped it. It occurred to her that he might actually need a list of his good traits. When was that last time someone said anything nice to him or about him that wasn't looking to get paid? "You don't judge people, no matter what their profession. You managed to make room for me in your life, you welcomed Lorelei into your home, you saved me, you took care of me, you fought beside me. You listen when I tell you you screwed up and you care enough to try to fix it. There are a lot of people who don't bother."

"I didn't start out wanting to do most of those things." A self-deprecating smile curved his lips.

"But you did them anyway. You didn't have to." Her palms lifted to cup his strong jaw. "In the end, you *chose* to be the man I love."

He laughed softly, leaning into her touch. "Well, I'm not going to argue with a woman who wants to give me everything I want."

"Smart, too. Let's add that to your good qualities." She favored him with a cheeky grin.

Swooping down on her, he slanted his mouth over hers and kissed her. Their tongues twined together, savoring the taste of each other. She slid her palms down his chest, feeling the warmth of his hard muscles beneath his shirt. Tugging the hem out of his pants, she broke the kiss to pull it over his head. Then there was nothing between her fingers and the rough silk of his flesh.

His hands closed over her thighs, and he jerked her legs tighter around him until she could feel the heat and length of his erection through his pants. She squirmed to get closer, to rub herself against his hard cock. Flames licked at her flesh, and after so many weeks without him, her need sliced through her with fierce claws.

Grabbing one of his hands, she shoved it between her legs, pushing his fingers and hers inside her to stroke her wet folds. Her moisture slipped down the insides of her thighs, and she moaned when he ground the heel of his palm against her clit. "Please."

"You want more?" He used his teeth and his free hand to jerk open the shirt she was wearing.

A naughty laugh spilled from her, but she managed a nonchalant shrug. "I'm a thief. I always want more."

"Good." He unsealed his fly, his knuckles still rubbing against her sex. She rolled her hips forward to keep the constant contact on her clit.

Sweat beaded on her forehead as her anticipation reached a boiling point. His cock sprang free of his pants, and neither of them was willing to wait for him to slide inside her. He thrust deep, gripping her hips to push her down as he thrust upward.

Her breath hissed out. After weeks, the stretch was painful, but it was so good. Exactly what she needed. Her knees clamped on his flanks and she began to ride him hard. She was so wet, and she wanted him as deep as she could take him.

Tightening his arms around her, he pulled her close and every movement of their bodies stimulated her nipples with his wide chest. She whimpered, closing her hands over his shoulders as she pushed them both faster. This was perfect, and she was going to have him for the rest of her life. The thought was enough to make her heart stumble and her sex clench tight.

She struggled to catch her breath and hold back the climax that threatened to swamp her. "I forgot to say . . ."

"What?" His hands dug into her hips, urging her even faster. His harsh breathing hitched with each deep penetration.

Goose bumps rippled down her limbs, and she knew she was going to break at any moment. "I'll marry you, Hunter."

His body froze for a moment, and then he groaned long and loud, coming deep inside her. It was enough to send her spinning over the edge into orgasm, her body arching against his as her pussy flexed on his cock. They moved together until both of them were spent, their bodies dripping sweat and their breaths no more than ragged wisps of air. They collapsed together on the bed, Delilah rolling onto her back to try to slow her galloping heart and suck in enough oxygen.

She closed her eyes for what she thought was only a few seconds, but when she opened them she found Hunter smiling down at her. He propped himself on an elbow, leaning over her as he followed the movement of her dragon nanotat with the tip of his finger. She hummed at the pleasure of having him touch her, but stopped when something occurred to her. She pulled back. "What about my work?"

Arching an eyebrow, he tugged on the glowing ring in her belly button. "What about it?"

"Hunter." She crossed her arms over her chest and frowned up at him.

"You know, kitten." He stroked his fingers over the plumped curve of her breast idly, a pensive frown on his handsome face. "There are people I know who would pay a great deal to have you test their security systems and then tell them how to keep you out the next time."

She blinked up at him, a slow, evil smile curving her lips. "People would pay me to rob them? Oh, I like that."

"You didn't think I was going to try to tame my lynx into a housecat, did you?" Bending forward, he pressed a kiss to the top of her cleavage.

Relaxing her arms, she gave him freer access to her breasts. The heat his touch generated within her began to fuzz her thoughts. "I wasn't sure."

"I like you wild, Delilah." His lips closed over one nipple before he trailed kisses to its twin. "I love you just the way you are, for exactly who you are."

She pressed trembling lips together, tears blurring her vision. "I can't think of a single thing I've ever done to deserve you."

White teeth flashed in a wicked grin. "I can think of a few things you can do right now."

She laid her hand along his jaw, turned herself into his embrace, and smiled back. Lifting her leg, she curled her thigh over his until she could press the bottom of her foot to the back of his leg, until she was wide open and ready for his penetration.

"I love you, Hunter."

He hummed in the back of his throat, his smile widening into something both hot and joyful. He looked younger than she'd ever seen him, less burdened. He kissed her quickly. "That is the sexiest thing you've ever said to me."

"I thought you just liked it when I said your name." She slid her foot up and down his leg.

Arching his hips, he slipped the flared crown of his cock inside her, but didn't press farther. "I do. That was better. Much better."

"I'll say it again if you stop teasing me and fuck me properly."

He chortled, holding her down so she couldn't gain the leverage she needed. "There's a proper way to fuck?"

"I can kill you with my claws, birdie." To demonstrate her point—all ten of them—she extended her claws and dug them in to his chest.

Flicking a glance down at her hands, his gaze only showed building excitement. She could smell it, and it made her wetter. A lazy smile twisted his lips. "Then you'd never get me to fuck you, properly or improperly."

"I'm going straight for you, Hunter." She circled his nipple with one claw and watched it tighten. "Make it up to me."

"Anything for you, kitten." He slid inside her, working his length into her soaking pussy. His eyes never left hers, and she watched the emotion play across his face. She gave as good as he did, letting him see how much she loved him, craved him. He was the only man she'd ever known who she didn't have to hide anything from, who wanted her just as she was.

It was the hottest thing she'd ever experienced.

His cock pumped inside her at just the right angle, at just the right speed. He knew her body so well, knew just what she needed. Heat roared within her, made her pussy contract, but she fought the orgasm that beckoned. She wanted this to last as long as it could, this perfect connection. The gold flecks blazed in his eyes, his pupils dilating. Their skin slapped together with each hard thrust, his fingers biting into her hips. She felt his talons score her flesh, and her tongue flicked out to press against the point of her fangs. The hawk claiming its mate, the cat writhing with a heat only he could give her.

The way his smile twisted his lips told her he knew she was putting off coming as long as possible, and the way his jaw clenched told her he was struggling with his own orgasm. For her pleasure and for his. Neither of them wanted to let this go. His skin pulled taut across his sharp features, and he groaned when she rolled her hips against him. She lifted her hand to cup his jaw, sliding her thumb up and down the slim scar that marred his face. His palms cupped her ass, pulling her as tight to him as he could and thrusting deeper than he had before. "Come now, Delilah. For me."

Bursts of light exploded behind her eyes, and she came so hard every muscle in her body locked tight. He groaned every time her walls fisted around him, but neither of them looked away. He was there with her when his orgasm took him, and she was there with him through every wave of climax that rolled through her.

"I love you, Hunter. I love you, I love you. Deus, I love you!"

"I love you, too, my mate." He moved one hand up to press against her back, to arch her forward so he could suck her nipple into his mouth. He rolled his tongue around it, batting it and shoving it against the roof of his mouth.

Orgasm crashed into her again and it was the sweetest thing she'd ever felt in her life. She was safe, she was whole, she was loved. She couldn't think of anything else she wanted right then. She had it all.

She had Hunter.

DEADLY
TEMPTATION

I

"*Mmmm... ooooh... yessss...*"

The long, perfect pink cock slammed inside Lorelei's soaking pussy. It was the exact length and girth she liked, big. She was so turned on she felt the blood pounding in her face. Beads of sweat slid down her temples to pool at the base of her throat. She flicked her nail over her nipple, cupping her breast and shuddering at the sweet, harsh feeling that reverberated through her body to pool between her thighs.

Orgasm gathered in her belly, drew her body in a taut line. So close. She was so close. A few more strokes and she would go over the edge. Sensations raced over her flesh, rushing through her in waves that matched the tempo of the thick cock moving within her. It was almost perfect... the only way it could be better was if—*no*! She forced her thoughts away from the tantalizing fantasy, ignored the pair of gray eyes that flashed in her mind, and the sudden desire to run her fingers through long, ebony hair. She moaned, squeezing her eyes closed to focus instead on the building pleasure, *not* on who she'd never have. Droplets of her creamy moisture slid down the insides of her thighs. She sobbed on a painful breath and her skin felt too hot to bear. Her hips rotated and squirmed on the smooth microsilk sheets, arching as she came so hard pinpoints of light exploded behind her lids.

Lorelei released a satisfied sigh and let her thighs relax, collapsing spread-eagle onto the mattress. Her body was still overheated, but her damp flesh cooled in the circulating air and she shuddered at the contrast in sensations. The walls of her sex clenched in a tiny aftershock of orgasm as she pulled the Phospho-Pink dildo out of her pussy and shut down the vibrations. She could probably just use a vibrator to get the job done, but she loved the feel of a big dick moving deep inside her. And Pinky was her favorite toy.

A melodious chime sounded through her suite, a reminder to get up and get on with her evening. Whorehouses did their best business at night, and she'd been working these hours so long, she wasn't sure she'd ever feel comfortable being active during the day. At least her nights were less strenuous now that she didn't make her living on her back. Five years of being a madam after sixteen of being a jade.

Deus, but the math made her feel old.

"I'm awake," she muttered when the chime sounded once more. She sighed again for a much less pleasurable reason and leaned up on an elbow, Pinky still clutched in her hand.

Throwing her legs over the side, she stepped nude from the bed and dropped Pinky into a compartment of her refresher closet. Then she flipped through her outfits, trying to decide which to wear.

The shoes were all-important. Strappy sandals with no heels for when she was on her feet all night, wickedly pointed heels for when she knew she'd be sitting. Typically, she worked behind the bar or as a dealer at the gaming tables. Tonight was the bar, so she tugged out a pair of flat silver sandals that laced to her knees. The dress needed to match. Her fingers drifted along the line of expensive fabrics in rich colors. She stopped on a pale green microsilk dress. The wisp of a garment was almost transparent, just what people expected a madam to wear.

And Pierce liked her in green. He'd once told her it complemented her eyes.

She swallowed and clenched her fingers into a fist. It shouldn't matter what Pierce Vaughn liked or disliked. The government agent was a customer like any other. And she had rules about her customers. She wasn't in the business of selling her body anymore, and sleeping with a customer of her technobrothel would be a bad idea.

Giving an impatient snort, she jerked the green dress out of the 'fresher. It was just a dress. She could wear it if she wanted to, and it didn't matter whether Pierce or anyone else especially liked it. She liked it, she'd bought it, and she could wear it. It pleased *her*, and that was the end of it.

A few minutes in the wash closet and she was bathed, dressed, and ready to start work. She'd pulled her hair back in a sleek chignon and smoothed a stray lock into place.

She entered her office through a hidden passageway in the wall and sat down to get some work done before the brothel opened for business. Bills to pay, orders to place, accounts to settle. Her fingers flew over a vidpad as she lost herself in the minutiae. It wasn't until a knock sounded on her door that she paused. "Yes?"

The metal door slid aside to reveal a man holding a large tray of food. Dishes steamed from its surface, and her stomach rumbled as the smell reached her nose. She stood and moved to sit on her red kleather chaise lounge, indicating he set the tray on the low table in front of her.

"You look delicious in that dress, Lorelei." The big man wore his hair in beaded braids down to his waist, the light glinting off the beads and the ebony skin that covered his heavily muscled chest. The adventurous bear-shifter was one of her most popular male jades. Not her *most* popular, though—that distinction went to Nolan Angelo—a man who was three parts dangerous to two parts sexy. Along with the sheer animal magnetism of his jaguar nature, he was a devastating combination. She'd known Nolan for most of her life, had worked with him at the same jadehouse when they were much younger, and had spent one incredible night with him and a customer who had paid for them both. A shiver ran over her skin, her nipples peaking at the sizzling memories.

She shook herself back to the present, rolled her eyes, and flapped her hand at the burly bear-shifter. "Don't waste your flattery on me; save it for the customers."

"Can't blame me for trying." He winked, set the food down, and backed out of the room. She picked up her utensil and began eating, her movements quick, efficient, and revealing a bit of the mink within. Her mind flickered from Pierce to Nolan to the bear who'd just left.

Another rule she had for herself. No sampling the wares. As gorgeous and talented at providing pleasure as her jades were, she knew exactly what their endgame was. Money. She'd been there, and she'd played the game better than most. She'd gone from working girl to madam, the ruler of her own little fiefdom in the middle of hell.

Because she worked a great deal and she had her rules, it meant she didn't get a lot of play anymore. She chuckled at that little piece of irony. She used to get paid for sex and she'd clawed her way up to never having sex.

Unfortunate, since the reason she'd been so good at her work was because she loved hot, feral sex. And slow, soft sex. And any kind of sex there was to be had. Rich men loved her intelligence, her ability to entertain at parties . . . and her willing eagerness to set aside all pretense of civility to fuck the night away once the party had ended.

But it had been a long, long time since she'd done that. It

had been far too many months since she'd had sex at all. It was just her and Pinky.

Which might explain her current fascination with Pierce. Nothing had rid her of her passion for Nolan since that one night, but there wasn't anything to be done about that. Nolan knew she'd never touch him as long as he worked for her, and he knew there wasn't a better place for a jade to be employed than Tail. Stalemate.

But Pierce. She had no excuse for him. She could only be grateful he'd done almost nothing to return or encourage her fascination. He was just so *different* from the men who patronized her place—gruff, remote, almost disinterested. And yet he came to Tail nearly every night. With as many men as she'd known in her life, anyone that stood out as different was . . . surprising. Interesting. Intriguing.

Dangerous.

Pushing away the tray, she stood to leave her office and do a final check of the main room. Music pumped through her prime-grade sound system as she passed the gaming tables, which were set and ready for her dealers; various vidgames; and caged-off areas where people would be bound, clamped, whipped, probed, and otherwise sexually stimulated with toys that put her Pinky to shame. The bar took up one whole side of the main room, a curving sculpture of polyglass that an old client of hers had created just for Tail. Behind the bar were several large iris doors covering round windows that looked in on bedrooms. The doors would open and close at intervals throughout the evening, giving people tantalizing peeks at the sexual escapades inside.

Everything in her hedonistic playground was in its proper place and ready for the raucous night to begin.

Lorelei was tending bar this evening. The bar was positioned on a platform that gave her a good view of the rest of the room. It also had security vidscreens built in under the polyglass surface; they showed her various angles of the main room and any room in the technobrothel. Similar vidscreens were embedded in one wall of her office. She liked to know what was going on in her domain at all times. Her business depended on customers returning, and she had to keep them happy. She also had a responsibility to her jades—keeping them safe was paramount.

New Chicago had decided that one way to "relieve the wildness" inside the predator shape-shifters that humans had morphed into over the last century was to allow prostitution as a means of letting off some pressure. A rueful smile curved her lips and she shook her head. The excuses politicians came up with to legitimize and justify their warped little fantasies. Still, she made her living on those fantasies. And she'd done well for herself. Very well.

Her gaze touched on the opulent surroundings. Much of it was an illusion. Outside these walls was the seething cesspool of the Vermilion District. But her business was fulfilling the fantasy, wasn't it? People came here to get away from reality, to pretend they were a sultan or a goddess in one of the private rooms, or to throw themselves into the raucous exhibitionism of the main room. It was all a carefully constructed mirage to enhance their pleasure and her cred accounts.

One of the vidscreens under the bar chirped to let her know there was an incoming message. "Display vid."

"Lorelei, I'm sorry to bother you, but roaches got into one of the older food lockers again." The heavily scarred face of Sienna, an old jade Lorelei had rescued from the gutters, appeared on the screen. Sienna ran the kitchens for Tail now, usually just feeding the jades but occasionally fulfilling a client's request for a certain dish. There were a few regulars with food fetishes and similar kinks. Lorelei groaned and poured herself a drink—the only one she'd allow herself for the night.

Bugs, rats, pests. It was a constant issue. She sighed. This was the other part of the illusion. Her customers would never know the reality that went in to the upkeep of the brothel. They didn't know that even as clean as her place was, simply existing in the Vermilion meant dealing with the vermin that made their home there—human and nonhuman. "Looks like we'll have to get new ones. It's costing me more in food than it would to just replace the older models."

"I'll handle putting in the order, since the doors are about to open." Sienna smiled and the vidscreen winked to black as she disconnected.

If they were opening for the evening, that meant Pierce would arrive in four hours, give or take a few minutes. Smoothing a hand down her skirt, Lorelei suppressed the girlish flutter in the pit of her belly. When was the last time any man had made her nerves dance? It happened very rarely. Not *this* much since the first time she'd turned a trick, and that was more out of fear than anticipation.

It was ridiculous. She was a professional, and here she was acting like a twitterpated child. Then she didn't have time to worry about anything other than entertaining her customers and serving them drinks. She kept one eye on the vidscreens under the bar at all times, but so far everything looked normal. As normal as a jadehouse could be on a busy night. Everywhere she looked there was sex, alcohol, and money being spent on gambling. It was going to be a lucrative evening.

She didn't know if it was instinct or something else that made her look up just then, but she knew when she did he would be there. He was tall and muscular, moving with the lupine grace of his predator side. His hair had once been dark, but had gone to salt-and-pepper gray. She wanted to feel it and see if it was soft to the touch or if it would prickle her palms.

She moved to the far side of the bar, where he usually sat. It had the best vantage point of the room, and let him put his back to the wall so no one could approach him from behind.

"Agent Vaughn." She nodded when he sat down directly in front of her.

The corners of his gray eyes crinkled in what could almost be called a smile. "Try not to say that too loudly. The Vermilion isn't fond of law enforcement."

"Can you blame us, Pierce?" She set a phosphorescent drink in front of Pierce. He'd become enough a fixture here that she knew exactly what he liked. "Are you sure I can't tempt you with one of my girls?"

He picked up his drink and sipped, those ever-watchful eyes sweeping the crowd. "No, thank you, Ms. Chase."

"They're nice, clean girls. And they like their work." Maybe if she saw him with one of her jades, she'd lose some of this sanity-eating craving she had for him. The fact that he came to drink but never touched her jades was something she didn't understand about him, something that made him even more intriguing. Which, to her mind, was not a good thing on several levels. She turned her most charming smile on him.

He blinked, but no real emotion shone on his face. "Clean wasn't always the rep of this place."

"The bastard who owned Tail before me had the jades tweaked out on bliss, but that was the first thing I changed. If I find drugs on any of them, they're out of here." She shrugged. It was one of the most unfortunate parts of her job, but it was still her responsibility no matter how hard or how much she disliked it. "No drugs, no exceptions."

"It's safer for everyone if there aren't dealers moving in on your business or trying to collect money from your employees." His tone was matter-of-fact, and she appreciated that he understood she didn't enjoy throwing people out onto the street.

"Exactly. I'm not a betting woman, and I don't gamble with our safety. This is the Vermilion, after all." She keyed a few buttons on a vidpad under the bar and waited for the machine to produce the seltzer water she wanted. Her throat was parched and she hadn't taken a break since she started. "Unlike the employees at a lot of technobrothels, my jades can leave at any time they want. If they feel the craving for bliss, they don't have to wait for me to fire them."

She shivered at the ugly memories of the brothel she'd rescued Nolan from when she took over Tail. Sex slave was a better description of what he'd been. Jades got paid, and he'd had to turn over everything he earned after he survived degradations that had made Lorelei's skin crawl when she heard about them. No, not all prostitutes were allowed to stay or leave as they chose.

Pierce nodded, frowning down at his drink. "How did you afford this place?"

"How do you think?" She gave him a gentle smile when he met her gaze. "The same way any jade affords anything."

He looked away, a flash of discomfort crossing his face. "Right. I shouldn't have asked. I apologize."

"I'm not ashamed of my work, Pierce." She took a sip of her drink, scanning the vidscreens out of sheer habit. All was as it should be. "This is the world I was born in, and I've done what I had to do to succeed here."

He pinned her with that silver gaze. "You could have gone anywhere else, done anything else."

She snorted, sliding a hand down her hip. "My mother raised me to be this. I started turning tricks at twelve."

"Deus." He closed his eyes, his Adam's apple bobbing as he swallowed hard.

"This is who I am. This is what I do." She made her tone matter-of-fact. She had no regrets about her life—she'd made the best of what she was given. Someone had had to take care of her mother and sister. Her mother's health had failed so quickly, and Delilah had been so young. It had fallen to Lorelei to make sure there was food to eat and a place to sleep. As Pierce said, she could have gone somewhere else, but leaving the world she'd known was a risk she'd couldn't have afforded to take. Not with people she loved depending on her. "I did what I had to to keep my sister out of the business."

It has been incredibly lonely to be the responsible one, but she knew she could rely on herself. Play by the rules, play it safe, and win. Relying on herself was a sure bet—everyone else needed to be looked after, so she did. The sacrifices were worth it. She was so proud of her sister, how strong she was, how independent. Lorelei wasn't above taking a hell of lot of credit for that—raising Delilah was the best thing she'd ever done. And while she didn't lament any of her choices, she wouldn't have wished her life on anyone, especially not her beautiful baby sister.

"How is Delilah?" Pierce seized on the opportunity to change the topic, and she could sense a bit of his relief. As a mink-shifter, she was good at reading emotions, but less able to react to danger as a better predator would be. And in the Vermilion, life was always dangerous. It just meant she always had to be on her toes, have her wits about her, and know every escape route out of any area of the district.

She flashed a grin at Pierce and refilled his drink, remembering her promise to him the first day they'd met. The agent had helped save her sister from a twisted madman bent on using her against her mate, Hunter. Delilah was Lorelei's only family, and they had always been close. She'd told Pierce he had free drinks any time he wanted at Tail, and while he'd taken her up on it the first night, he'd insisted on paying ever since. She was more grateful than she could ever say that he had helped Hunter get to Delilah in time. Lorelei's heart twisted at the thought of losing her precious and precocious sister. "She's good. She and Hunter eloped a few weeks ago."

Swirling the glowing liquid around in his glass, he took a long pull on the alcohol. "Good for them."

She tilted her head and narrowed her eyes at him. "You already knew that, didn't you?"

The ghost of a smile curved his lips. "Yes."

Movement behind Pierce drew her gaze. Nolan, in all his beatific masculine glory. She offered a welcoming smile, but noted that Pierce's body had tightened. Interesting.

"You know, I have male jades, if that's your preference." Wouldn't that be just her luck? The man she'd been lusting after for months liked men. If a dart of disappointment went through her, she quashed it. This was good news. If he liked men only, then he really was out of her reach. Even if she gave in to her desires, he wouldn't be interested. She should be relieved.

She wasn't.

He shot her a guarded look that told her nothing. "I don't have to pay for sex, Ms. Chase. I'm not interested, so stop offering."

Well, that was clear enough, though it told her nothing about his sexual preferences. She gave him and the approaching Nolan a nod before she turned away. "Fine. Enjoy your drink."

After winding his way through a crowd of men and women who reached out to stroke, grope, and pet him, Nolan slung his arm around Pierce's shoulder and leaned against him. "Hello, gorgeous."

Pierce's gaze went to the nanotattoos on Nolan's forearms, which were almost pressed to his cheek. Flames moved under Nolan's skin—the red, gold, and amber colors dancing from his wrists to his elbows. Then the wolf blinked up at Nolan, arched a brow, and sipped his drink, his silver eyes flashing awareness for just a moment before his face went carefully blank.

Ah, that was what Nolan liked to see. It was obvious Pierce wanted him, but he was fighting it. Hell, it was obvious the wolf wanted Lorelei as well or he wouldn't have spent the last couple of months sniffing around the place.

A twist of excitement went through Nolan at the thought of the three of them together, but he quelled it. As much as he enjoyed fucking either sex—or both at once—he knew it would never be with the three of them. No need to get himself in a lather.

He shoved his fingers through his freshly washed hair and sighed. This last job had been messy, and he'd needed to clean up before he walked in to Tail's main room. If it had just been messy sex, it would be one thing, but he didn't make most of his creds as a jade. No, he had much more dangerous and illegal work that he handled discreetly on the side. Assassin was a nice word for him, paid killer was probably more accurate. He was good at it, though, no matter how distasteful people might find it. He had enough in his cred accounts that he didn't need to serve as a jade anymore, but it was an excellent cover for his more nefarious work.

And he normally did a better job of keeping it quick and neat, but the man tonight had been a wilier quarry than Nolan had first surmised, and had the fighting skills to make him difficult. Nolan wouldn't make that mistake again.

Fortunately, blood washed away easier than memories. The look in a man's eye when he knew death was upon him wasn't one Nolan would ever get used to.

He cleared his throat, shoved the thought down to the deepest, darkest part of himself, and groped for something, *anything* to distract himself. Adrenaline still raced along his nerves, and he'd have to burn it off as soon as possible. Sex usually worked well for him. Being a jade did have a few perks.

"What brings you to our seedy side of town, *querido*?" A flirtatious smile curled his lips as he ran the tip of his finger down Pierce's arm.

"Just having a drink, Angelo." He shot Nolan a look and took a deliberate swig of his alcohol but didn't move away from Nolan's touch.

If there was anyone an assassin should avoid, it was a law-man like Pierce Vaughn. But Nolan couldn't seem to avoid the need to tempt the man. He was attracted and attractive, and standing this close to the wolf, touching him, made Nolan's cock go hard and his blood sizzle in his veins. Maybe it was the danger, maybe it was the challenge, or maybe he was just a twisted fuck, but he wanted Pierce with a craving he hadn't felt for anyone except Lorelei.

Lorelei. He glanced up to see her being her usual charming self and flirting with the customers.

Deus, she was luscious. Her auburn hair was up in some kind of twist tonight, but when it was down it fell in thick rip-ples to her waist. He loved watching it brush against her heart-shaped ass when she moved.

The filmy, low-cut dress she wore made it seem as though at any moment he could pray that her firm breasts might spill out. They never did, but he could dream. He had no doubt she'd de-signed the outfit to cause just such thoughts in her customers' minds. As the madam, she was now untouchable. It made her even more desirable. Every man—and some of the women—could fantasize about what it would be like to lick and suck and kiss that creamy, perfect skin, but they never could.

He'd known her before she was his boss, and he could tor-ment himself with more than just a fantasy. No, he had real mem-ories of touching her, tasting her. He wasn't certain if that made him the lucky one, or that much more unfortunate because he *knew* what it was like and he was still denied the privilege ever again.

She bent forward to refill an empty glass, and her skirt pulled tight against her ass. It was almost see-through. Almost. Just a tantalizing glimpse of the treasures beneath, nothing more.

Glancing over her shoulder at him, the exotic tilt at the cor-ners of her green eyes become even more exaggerated when she smiled. He couldn't help but grin back, feeling like an idiot the whole time. He should be more practiced than this. Normally, he was, but Lorelei was always an exception. He wanted to touch her when he shouldn't, and knew she'd never let him anyway. She was his boss now, and he was just another piece of flesh to be sold. If they had a history together, it just meant she knew his secrets and knew how to exploit them. Not that she ever had—she was a hell of a lot better than the piece of shit Xander she'd bought him from when she took over Tail.

What he'd never figured out was whether she knew the truth about him. The whole truth. What he did when he wasn't fucking people's brains out.

She might.

He admitted it to himself. She was smart enough to have put the pieces together, and smart enough to keep her mouth shut. But if she knew, why didn't she get rid of him? She could make up any number of reasons why she was cutting him loose, but she hadn't. He'd always assumed that must mean she didn't know. Sometimes, there was an emotion in her eyes when she looked at him that cut too deep, said too much. Scared him to death.

It would put her in danger if she knew the truth, if anyone knew the truth.

He shouldn't want her to know, but deep down, he wanted her to see, to understand, to soothe the parts of him that always ached. And the smarter, wiser parts of him wished he didn't feel anything at all. It was safer. No one cared what a jade felt, what an assassin thought. It didn't matter. He was a tool to be used, no matter what his profession.

She moved toward him, her walk as smooth as a corkscrew. He wanted to bracket those hips in his hands and lose himself inside her. He knew how good it would be, how good she was.

"How's your night going, Nolan?" Her voice was soft, throaty, and sexy without her even trying.

Everything about her made him think of sex, but that was one of the reasons she was the best at what she did. "My night? It's been productive. I had a house call earlier. The creds should be in your account."

Though he'd actually spent much less time with the customer than he'd ever admit and had handled certain other business between there and here. The timing had been difficult, but that's why he was the best at what *he* did.

"I got a notification of payment." She scanned the room, the gaming tables, the iris windows that opened and closed behind the bar to reveal her jades doing any imaginable carnal act with Tail's customers. The Peep Show, she called it. He liked working back there—the combination of exhibitionism and privacy made things interesting. After twenty years in the sex industry, he lived for the interesting.

Resting his wrist over Pierce's shoulder, he let his hand dangle over the wolf's chest just far enough so that he could "accidentally" brush the other man's nipple. Pierce's sharply indrawn breath drew both Lorelei and Nolan's gazes. It was the most overt reaction the wolf had ever given. A slow grin tugged at Nolan's lips. "Are you sure you're only here for the drink, *querido*?"

"Let it go, Angelo." The words were no more than a low growl, and Nolan sensed the warning from another predator. He was still debating whether or not he should heed it when someone spoke up behind him.

"Nolan, are you available for the night?" A couple that looked so bland it was painful approached the bar. The woman laid a tentative hand on his arm, her fingertip tracing one of the nanotat flames.

He slid away from Pierce's side to face the two. Upper-middle-class married couple who liked a little extra spice every now and then. They'd come to Tail for the first time a few years before, chosen Nolan for their foray into threesomes, and had come back many times since—not always to play with Nolan, but he was their favorite. He glanced at Pierce, an eyebrow raised. "I'm not sure. Am I?"

"Yes, Angelo, you are." The look he gave Nolan could have incinerated him, but there was a flicker of torment in the wolf's eyes.

"Voyeurism. I like it." Nolan swirled a finger from Pierce's biceps around his shoulder and up to the nape of his neck, wanting to touch him one more time. "Enjoy the show."

Pierce grunted, pinned his gaze on the bar in front of him, and took a deep drink.

"It's been a few months since we've seen you." Lorelei stepped into the tense silence with a warm, inviting smile. "Your usual room?"

The couple nodded and the husband handed over his ident card for Lorelei to swipe over a scanner and complete the transaction for Nolan's time. He rolled his shoulders, letting a little smile form on his lips as he gestured for the two to follow him down the short corridor that led to the Peep Show rooms. It might not be as exciting as playing with Lorelei and Pierce, but knowing they would both be watching added something to the occasion. His smile widened as he pressed his palm to a vidpad beside the proper door and let the couple precede him inside.

"After you." He didn't know their names, but he didn't need to. Only Lorelei would have access to that information from their ident cards, but Nolan didn't want it. Their names didn't matter, not really. *They* didn't matter—Nolan was just a means to a very pleasurable end for his clients, and they were just a means to getting paid for Nolan. One of his means. The legal one.

That didn't stop Nolan from enjoying his part in his customers' little games. Now that he had a choice in who he played with. Lorelei's rules. The jades decided, and someone was always watching to make sure no one got out of line. It didn't matter which room a client was in, they knew there were vidmonitors. If they had a problem with the rules, they were welcome to take their business to another technobrothel. They rarely did.

He let an easy smile form on his lips as he closed the door behind him. Bending forward, he unsealed his boots, stripped them off, and left them lying beside the door. When he straightened, he saw the couple swiftly shedding clothing. It was usually that way with these two. The first time was a rough, urgent spending of lust, and the rest of the night they savored slowly. He watched them kiss, devouring each other with their mouths, already consumed by the game. Watching them made his cock— still semi-hard from touching Pierce—go rigid. Just the thought of Pierce made him ache, and he hissed softly. The couple before him broke apart, their eyes gleaming with wicked intent as they looked him over.

"Let's take care of those clothes for you." The wife moved forward, reaching for his fly. She unsealed his pants and worked them down his hips so he could step out of them as the husband grabbed the bottom of Nolan's shirt from behind and wrenched it over his head. He brushed his long hair out of his eyes with one hand while lifting his other palm to cup one of the wife's pert breasts. He stimulated her nipple with his thumb and grinned when it tightened for him.

Advancing on her, Nolan let his grin widen into one that showed his predatory nature. She shivered and backed away until she bumped into the round polyglass window that faced out over Tail's main room. The iris doors over the window slid closed in a center point and would reopen in a few seconds. "It's exciting for you, isn't it? Knowing everyone will be able to see that prime little ass of yours and watch me fuck you up against the glass."

Her breath hitched, her pupils dilating with desire. "Yes."

"It's a thrill you don't get anywhere else but here, isn't it?"

He slid his tongue around his teeth, pressing it against the jaguar fangs that had slid down from his gums. He could smell her wetness, taste her sexual excitement in the air.

The husband's hands curved around Nolan's ribs, moving until he could twist the thick rings that pierced Nolan's nipples. "They'll all be watching you fuck her *and* me fuck you, Nolan."

"Deus, coming here is worth every cred," the wife whispered as she stroked a hand up and down Nolan's cock. Her cheeks were flushed and her eyes shone with heat. Her husband stepped aside for a moment and there was a small *pop* as he opened a container of the scented oils Lorelei stocked in these rooms. His palms dropped to cup Nolan's ass, spreading the cheeks to delve between them. Nolan groaned as two thick fingers eased into his anus, widening him for penetration.

He rocked between them, her palms working his cock hard as those fingers pistoned in and out of his ass. He lifted her so her back was pressed to the round window, which was now open for people to see in. She arched and gasped, her breasts crushing to his chest. Her legs snapped around his waist, tilting her pelvis so he could slide his dick inside her wet pussy. Her eyes flashed as she dug her nails into his bare shoulders. "Go fast, Nolan."

"Make it good for her, Nolan," the other man ordered as he nudged the head of his cock against Nolan's ass. This was about them, not him, and he never forgot it. He gritted his teeth on another groan when the husband sank into his ass. He shoved Nolan's hips forward with each thrust, pushing him deeper into the wife's sweet pussy.

He planted his hands against the cool glass on either side of the wife's shoulders and tightened his ass around the other man's thrusting cock, smiling when the husband gave a long, helpless groan. Nolan loved that he could make them react. It was his favorite part of these games. Some resisted, but in the end, they all gave in and screamed for more.

The husband's hands rose to Nolan's shoulders, holding him down while linking his fingers with his wife's. Her gaze went past Nolan, meeting her husband's. It left Nolan free to look down at the bar to see Pierce and Lorelei both watching. He knew they would be.

Fire fisted in his belly, and real craving twisted through him. They each tried to stop, glanced away, but their gazes came back to him every few moments. He ground his hips against the wife's clit, and Lorelei bit her full lower lip. She'd frozen where she stood, giving up all pretense of not staring. Her breasts lifted against the front of her dress and he could see the outline of her nipples. She licked her lips and he groaned, wanting that little pink tongue of hers on his lips, his skin, his cock. He ran his tongue up the side of the wife's neck, biting down gently right under her ear. Lorelei's hand flattened against her belly, her head tilting ever so slightly, as if to offer him access to *her* throat. He worked his dick into the wife's welcoming body, the need to come gripping him tight.

She squealed when he thrust deeper. "Yes. Just like that. Harder!"

But it was Lorelei's voice in his mind, calling out in mindless passion as she had the one night he'd had her in his arms. The window closed for a moment, blocking his view of the bar. When it opened again, his gaze went to Pierce. He sat looking down, hunched on his stool, but Nolan could see the fine tension running through the wolf's muscles.

Pierce glanced up out of the corner of his eye, and Nolan caught the flash of molten silver in his gaze. Nolan rocked his hips back into the hard cock, hissing each time his ass was penetrated. Still feigning disinterest, Pierce sat back and sipped his liqueur casually.

But the eyes gave him away, the way his hand tightened to a white-knuckled grip on his glass. His nostrils flared as though trying to catch Nolan's scent, and Nolan could imagine what it would be like to see the wolf rip loose of the civilized fetters. He would pound inside Nolan's ass, stretch him wide, and make him scream. Handing control of the game over to Pierce would be the hottest fucking thing Nolan had ever done, and he groaned as the husband's cock hit an angle that made Nolan's claws scrape against the glass. He held on to his control tightly, making it good for the wife as he'd been ordered. He shoved his hips back and forth, pleasing both his customers, fucking and being fucked.

"I'm coming, I'm coming!" The wife's pussy clenched around his cock, and he groaned in relief, finally able to give in to orgasm. He jetted deep inside her, closing his eyes because there was nothing like the feel of a woman's pussy milking his cock hard.

The husband snarled, whatever beast he kept locked inside him ripping loose as he released his come inside Nolan's ass. He slid out after a moment, making Nolan groan as he set the wife on her feet. The iris door closed again, cutting him off from Lorelei and Pierce, and the husband pulled Nolan away from the window to push him toward the bed. "Lay down. You're going to eat my wife's pussy while I fuck her ass."

"Oh, yes," she purred. She kissed her husband, moving her mouth slowly under his. Nolan turned, climbed onto the bed, and stretched out. He stroked his cock as he watched them fondle each other, rousing it for another round of sex.

Hours later, Nolan slung his shirt over his forearm and carried his boots out of the room. He didn't bother putting anything but his pants on. His customers had gone home fully satisfied, and the night was winding down at Tail. It was time for him to find his own bed and make use of it for some well-deserved sleep.

Yawning as he entered the main room and approached Lorelei at the bar, he set his clothes on the polyglass surface. He stretched his arms over his head, working out the kinks from a very active night. "Pierce left?"

"Hours ago." She arched an eyebrow, dropping a few empty glasses into a sanitizing unit. "You seemed to be having fun tormenting the man."

"I was. He wants to touch so bad he can taste it. I was just encouraging him to scratch that itch." Lorelei's gaze slid down his body, awakening it when he thought he'd expire from exhaustion. He leaned his hands on the bar and lowered his voice to a purr. "When was the last time you had sex, Lorelei?"

Her green eyes flashed at him as she shot back, "When's the last time you enjoyed it?"

"I always enjoy my work." He smoothed one hand down his chest and let a satisfied grin spread across his face.

She snorted, tucking a stray curl behind her ear. He wanted to see that gorgeous dark red hair fanned out over a pillow while he fucked her. She stepped closer, her gaze serious as she met his. "No, it's a game for you. You play it, you win it, but it's not about enjoying it."

"No one cares what a jade enjoys." He would know better than most. He hadn't even made it to an orphanage after his parents died in an accident at the fish-processing plant where they worked. The building and most of the docks nearby had burned after the initial explosion. The police officer who came to Nolan's school to tell him about the fire had taken one look at him and brought him to a jadehouse in the Vermilion to sell. He'd only been thirteen years old, and his childhood was over. There was nothing and no one but himself to depend on for protection after that. He had the wonderful justice system

Pierce loved so much to thank for what he'd become, and old angers he'd never be able to rid himself of flared in his chest.

Lorelei's fingers covered his on the bar, snapping him out of his reverie. "I do."

"Stop." He shook his head, jerking his hand away from her gentle touch.

Hurt filtered through her beautiful eyes. "Stop what?"

"Don't put something like that out there." It was one thing for him to want her physically. That he understood, but to *care*? No. Fantasies about her understanding him were just that. Fantasies. They weren't real. She didn't care and neither did he. He locked down everything inside himself, refusing to let his mind even go there. He picked up his boots and shirt off the bar, his fist clenching on the material so hard it ached. Because he never wanted to hurt the one person who'd done anything nice for him in decades, he managed to spit out the ugly truth. "It's easier to know that no one really gives a shit. It doesn't make you hope for something you can't have."

Her palm cupped his jaw, her emerald eyes soft with a sympathy he shouldn't crave. "I care, Nolan."

But he knew she wouldn't if she knew the whole truth about him. He stumbled back a few steps, turned, and fled as if the fires of hell chased him.

2

A week later, Pierce let his gaze sweep the street in front of Tail, his nostrils flaring as he took a deep breath. He forced himself not to gag on the rank stench of rotting garbage and human filth and instead focused on scenting anyone who might be watching. No one.

The latest case he was working on had connections in the Vermilion, so Pierce was even more paranoid than normal. Lev Barrone. He ran the details of his case through his mind—obsessing as he normally did about his job. White-collar crime boss who'd begun branching out from industrial espionage and had gotten into bed with some very dangerous organizations in this district of the city. Pierce was getting close to a break in the case, he could sense it. Lev Barrone *and* his Vermilion contacts would be going away for the rest of their lives when Pierce was done with them.

Which meant he shouldn't be in this district when he wasn't working. Knowing that didn't seem to stop him from ghosting down the street until he got to the entrance of Tail. He swiped his ident card and the huge iris door spun open to allow him in.

Then her scent called to him, luring him into her domain. Lorelei. It was the perfect name for her.

He settled in his usual spot, silently berating himself as he did every night for his weakness in coming at all. First, he'd come to learn more about her and Nolan. He'd met them both while helping Delilah recover from a nearly lethal dose of poison. He'd known the moment he met Lorelei that she was his mate. Gray wolves mated for life, and the predator within him had recognized her, wanted her, demanded her. The rational man had been surprised to find he had a mate at all, for many reasons—the first of which was his desire for both sexes. He'd always been that way, and had assumed there would be no single mate for him.

Then he'd met Nolan, and the same instinct had resounded within his soul. It made sense, even if it made him break into a cold sweat. Learning about them, about their pasts, their lives, had only made the dread worse. A madam and a jade turned assassin. Could there have been any worse mates for a man who dedicated his entire life to upholding the law?

Yet here he was. Again. He sighed. Once he'd known them, the wolf had refused to rest. The nightly visits were all that appeased it, but even that was beginning to fade.

A drink settled in front of him on the bar, and he didn't have to look up to know it was Lorelei. He could smell her, and his instincts flared to life. *Mate. Mine. Mate.*

She propped an elbow on the bar and leaned forward. Her breasts pressed against the confines of the black kleather corset she wore. The silver snaps that held it closed were going to give up the struggle any moment, and his cock went as rigid as hardened mercurite at the mere prospect. The flaming waves of her hair fanned over her shoulders, one lucky curl caressing the upper slope of her breast. Her eyes met his, the black ring that surrounded the green iris standing out in contrast. He kept his expression blank to keep her from seeing the direction his thoughts had been going. It was safer for everyone that she and Nolan never know the truth since Pierce didn't intend to act on his mating instinct. Her husky voice slid over his skin like microsilk. "All right, I have to ask. Why do you come in? I see you more often than not."

He arched an eyebrow. "Do you always hassle your paying customers that way?"

Those soft green eyes hardened to emerald, though a charismatic smile creased the corners of her mouth. "All my customers pay, one way or another, or they aren't my customers for long."

"I'm not going to ask what you do to those who don't want to pay with creds." The ruthless streak was as attractive to him as the feminine curves. The woman was a deadly combination.

The smile turned into an urchin's grin, the corners of her eyes crinkling. "Probably best you don't, Agent Vaughn."

"Just Pierce."

"Pierce." She tilted her head, revving up the charm. "I like your name. Have I ever told you that?"

"No." Deus, that smile of hers made his insides twist.

She reached under the bar and pulled out a glass of the seltzer water she liked to drink when she was working. "My mother named my sister and me after famous temptresses."

"Interesting."

"Is it? I always thought it wasn't very clever for a prostitute who expected the same of her daughters."

He merely nodded and said nothing more. The truth was he found her far more than interesting. He found her fascinating. He wanted to know everything, all of her. As deep as his background checks went, and as many people that had been willing to give him every scrap of buzz he wanted in order to stay on his good side, it couldn't replace knowing the woman herself. He knew her past, her favorite foods, favorite clothiers, favorite sexual positions, every detail of her financial and business background . . .

he didn't know *why*—why she'd made the choices she made, why she loved who and what she loved.

So, here he was in her jadehouse, talking to her, watching her, wanting nothing more than to be near her.

Fool.

No doubt when his other mate appeared, he'd be equally unable to pry himself away from the place.

Disgust at himself rippled through him, but there was little he could do. He'd tried to stay away, tried to appease himself with every little detail of their lives, tried watching from a distance, but none of it had satisfied the wolf.

It wanted to claim, to never allow either of them to touch another. Just the three of them. Forever.

But the man knew better than to trust "forever." There was no such thing in his world. It held only pain, bitterness, and an ugly end. No one got out alive—and very few got out naturally. He would know. With his job, he'd seen every imaginable ugliness visited upon people. That's just the way the world worked.

Nothing shocked him anymore. He somehow doubted that, in their lines of work, much shocked his mates, either. He liked that, liked that he didn't have to pretty up the world or his work for them to be able to accept him. They understood. Neither of them seemed to have a problem with his work, though they each had moments of wariness where they stopped midsentence and didn't tell him of things they did that were less than legal. As if he didn't know about all the infractions they'd ever been involved in. They could keep their illusions if they wanted, but he knew.

He wanted them anyway.

And that was the real problem. Not that he couldn't have them, but that he *shouldn't*. Neither of them wanted the problems that were involved in having a lawman for a lover. And he could kiss his career good-bye if he ever touched either of them.

He had no illusions about himself. In his line of work, that sort of thing would get him killed. He was a merciless, heartless bastard, he was good at his job, and he was both because he'd dedicated his life to being the best.

He was married to his work.

No mate he knew of would be willing to come second to a career. They shouldn't have to. So, he would never have one, let alone two.

The irony didn't escape him that he was mates with quite possibly the two most beautiful and sensually skilled people on the planet and he never intended to touch them. He should be the luckiest bastard on the planet and, instead, he was the most sexually frustrated.

Lorelei's nails drummed against the bar. "You never answered my question about why you come here. I do have customers who partake in more lucrative services, Pierce. I haven't been able to tempt you into those, and as wonderful as my bartending skills are, you could get better elsewhere."

"You have an interesting clientele." He took a swig of the phosphorescent liqueur he favored. If it wasn't mixed perfectly, it didn't glow, thus making it difficult to tamper with. Not that he thought Lorelei would, but there were plenty who would be happy to see him dead, especially in the Vermilion.

Her auburn eyebrows rose. "You like to watch?"

"Something like that." His gaze tracked Felicia Tamryn, a.k.a. Tam, a grifter who liked to use the gaming tables at various technobrothels to choose her marks. A large blond man swooped down on the woman as she walked across the room, spinning her around by the arm. Pierce didn't recognize the man, so he wasn't a regular, but he carried himself like a powerful man. His clothes screamed wealth and a great deal of it.

The two engaged in a heated discussion, but their voices were too low to carry above the crowd. Pierce's eyebrows arched, wondering what the grifter had done to scam the man.

Tam jerked at her arm, but the man held fast, pulling her closer. Then his mouth was on hers, and the kiss had the kind of passion behind it that could melt mercurite.

When they pulled apart, Tam had a dazed look of lust, confusion, and fear. Interesting. So, the man was more than a mark. The lust and confusion could be an act, but the terror wasn't faked. He could smell it, the ripe stench of it unmistakable.

Lorelei dragged his attention back to her by setting her hand on his arm and digging her nails in. Her green gaze was more fierce than he'd ever seen it. "If you're here to stake out the place and use my jadehouse as a way to arrest criminals, I will have you banned from the premises."

"Let's just say I like the drinks, I like the bartender, and I'm willing to provide extra incentive for good behavior if anyone knows who I am." He twisted his arm out from under her hand, not because he didn't want her touching him, but because he did.

"They all do."

He smiled, but it held no humor. "I know."

Motioning to the spectacle nearby, she frowned. "Tam's in trouble."

"He doesn't look like he's going to hurt her." Which wasn't strictly true. The man looked like he wanted to murder Tam, but he also had the anguished look of the lover scorned. Pierce sensed no physical threat from the man.

Lorelei snorted and gave him a glance that said he was being a stupid male. "It's not her body I'm talking about. She's in over her head with that one. Then again, I wouldn't bet against Tam. She lands on her feet."

"I thought you weren't a gambling woman." He struggled with a smile at the expression on her face. There weren't many who would dare to give him that kind of look.

She rolled her eyes. "There are a *very* few things that are a sure bet."

"Who is he?" He jerked his chin in the direction of Tam and her companion.

When Lorelei shrugged, it lifted her breasts until they were a micrometer away from spilling out of her corset, and he tensed in anticipation of seeing all that creamy flesh bared. His hopes were disappointed, of course, but he didn't know a single man who wouldn't have dreamed of it. She licked her lips. "I only know him as Breckenridge. He was a mark of hers, she convinced him she loved him and let him shower her with jewels, clothes, you name it."

He grunted and forced himself not to stare at her mouth. "Classic romance scam."

"Yeah." A dimple tucked into her cheek as her lips twisted. "But then she realized she really was in love with him, and she ran."

Now that made no sense to him whatsoever. A frown drew his eyebrows together. "Why not stay if it went from scam to legitimate?"

"You don't understand." She sighed.

"I just said I didn't."

"No, I mean . . . you work in that line of business and your whole existence is about playing the game. Making others fall for you, making them believe you feel the same, but you have to protect your heart. You can't really fall for any of them." Something close to horror flashed in her eyes, and she shuddered. "I can't imagine how terrifying it would be to give your soul to a man you were trying to scam."

He shook his head. "I still don't understand why she left if she really loved him and he loved her."

"How long would it have been before what she was came out?" Now her gaze reflected impatience at his density. She tucked a curl behind her ear. "Once it did, do you think he'd believe she loved him?"

"No, I don't suppose he would." Pierce didn't know much

about love—he'd grown up with parents as married to their jobs as he was now, he'd left to join the military at eighteen, and he'd returned home only twice after that. Once for his mother's funeral and then for his father's. Still, he couldn't help feeling a pang of sympathy for Breckenridge. Poor bastard.

Lorelei glanced over at the arguing couple before she met his gaze, hard sympathy settling over her features. "This way, she ends it and walks away before the lie blows up in her face. Poor thing."

He narrowed his eyes at her, considering. "Is that what you did when you were a jade? Made men believe you loved them to get things from them?"

"Yes and no." She blinked at the abrupt change in topic, but recovered quickly. "I was honest about what I was. They knew they'd have to pay for my favors. They didn't expect my love any more than I expected theirs. I had *feelings* for some of them, but I never loved them. Not romantically. It's one of my rules. Never let your heart get involved."

They both jolted and turned when Tam stormed up to the bar. "Lorelei, this man is bothering me."

Breck's hand closed over her shoulder, spinning her until her back hit the edge of the bar near Pierce. He shoved his face into hers, snarling. "What bothers you more, Tam? That I knew you were playing me from the beginning, that I played you back, or that I beat you at your own scam and now you love me so much you want to rip your own heart out just to make it stop?"

"Shut up. Shut up, Breck." The woman's English accent deepened as she shoved at his broad shoulders. "You have no idea what I think or what I feel."

He swallowed, his voice vibrating with emotion. "I know *exactly* how it feels, Tam. How do you think it's been for me since you ran away?"

"No. That's a lie. You were playing me from the start, you even said so." She twisted her head around, desperation in her eyes and voice. "Lorelei, I want this man removed. Call your security."

"Do it and I will shut this place down, Ms. Chase." Breck shot Lorelei a fierce look, cold intent on his face.

Pierce pushed to his feet, shrugging his shoulder to expose the weapon and badge under his jacket as he faced the couple. The sympathy of a moment before vanished. He didn't give a damn that the other man outsized him, the wolf protected what belonged to it. "Are you threatening a local businesswoman, Mr. Breckenridge?"

The man's gaze snapped to him, taking in the gun and badge. "I know you. The agent who saved Avery's mate."

"Ms. Chase is his mate's sister." Pierce bared his fangs in a smile that made some of the blood leach out of Breck's face. "I doubt Mr. Avery would appreciate you threatening her or her business for a lovers' quarrel. I suggest you make your private affairs a bit more private. Do I make myself clear?"

"Fine." Breck pulled in a deep breath and glanced at Lorelei again. "Ms. Chase, do you have a more *private* room I can rent?"

Tam struggled in his arms, trying to kick him but failing. "You can enjoy the room by yourself, Breck. I'm not going anywhere with you. You can't make me."

"Oh?" Breck's voice dropped to a silken whisper, his grip tightening around her waist. "I can make you do many things, Tam. I can make you scream, I can make you come, I can make you beg."

Her breathing hitched, and Pierce could clearly scent her arousal. "Let go of me, Breck."

"No. I won't, and I never will."

"I hate you."

"I hate you, too, Tam." If possible, the cold rage on his face intensified, making him look even more dangerous. "And I'm still not letting you go, not now, not ever. But I'll tell what I *am* going to do."

"Let. Me. Go."

"I. Said. *No.*" He pushed her against the bar until her body arched back, and he shoved his knee between her thighs. "The rooms with the windows."

"What about them?" Her chest lifted in little pants, her lips almost touching his. The muscles in her neck strained, but she neither moved closer or farther away; the internal struggle was visible on her face.

"I'm going to take you inside one of them, and I'm going to fuck you up against the glass until no one in this jadehouse could doubt you are mine." With every word, the muscles in his thigh flexed as he rubbed against her sex.

A whimper slid from her lips, and she twisted her hips to get closer. "Breck, please . . ."

"I will please you. Don't I always make you purr?" He worked his leg faster against her.

"You can't do this." Her pelvis ground down, her body no longer fighting what her mouth still protested.

He continued as if she hadn't said a word. "After I'm done with that, I'm going to tie you to the bed and fuck you until neither of us can stand up. You love it when I tie you up, don't you, Tam?"

A sob ripped from her throat, a single tear slipping from the corner of her eye. "Breck."

He stopped moving his leg, holding her still so she couldn't rub herself against him. "Don't you, Tam?"

"Yes. I love it." A shudder ran through her when he started working her again. "Deus, I hate you."

"I know. As I said, the feeling is mutual." His mouth slammed down over hers, kissing her thoroughly enough that no one could doubt the possession in the act. Tam kissed him back, her movements as rough as his. She shoved her fingers into his hair, wrapping her arms around his neck and her legs around his waist.

Lorelei cleared her throat, her fingers dancing over a vidpad built into the bar. "Room Three is open for you, Mr. Breckenridge. Have a good evening, Tam."

The couple didn't even look up as Breck walked blindly toward the corridor that led to the windowed rooms. Just the thought of those rooms reminded Pierce of the week before, of watching Nolan get fucked from behind, of the look on his face that dared Pierce to look away. The mere memory was so powerful it made molten lava flow through his veins, made his dick harden to the point of pain. He shook himself back to the present, shoving away the lust he'd never expend.

"Huh." He leaned against the bar and sighed. "Those two are going to have an enjoyable night."

Lorelei's shoulder lifted in a delicate shrug. "I've never liked being bound. Or spanked, for that matter. Though there have been plenty of times I was . . . not in a position to protest."

"Someone hurt you?" The wolf within tensed with the need to hunt, to rip apart the men who would have forced her.

An easy smile curved her lips, acceptance filling her eyes. "It was a long time ago. I have no ill feelings. And, you're right, I'm certain Tam will enjoy her evening."

He arched a brow at her calm reaction. "You're unflappable, Ms. Chase."

Her eyes crinkled at the corners and her grin widened. "I was a jade for years, and I'm a madam now. I've been in every conceivable sexual situation, so not much surprises me anymore." She tilted her head. "If Tam hadn't been willing, Breck would have been shown the door, threats, money, and all."

He was more interested in all those sexual situations she'd mentioned than Breck and Tam. Pierce wanted to try all of them with her—and Nolan—and find out which ones they liked best. It was one thing to hear about it through a secondhand source, another entirely to experience it himself. And he wanted to so much it made his body ache.

He jerked when Lorelei's fingers brushed the back of his hand. He hadn't even noticed her move, and a sharp growl warned her away. It was rare that anyone touched him, and his reflex was to attack anyone who got too close. He got a stranglehold on the reflex as his instincts fed him conflicting information. Attack the threat, claim the mate. The soft contact with her made his body and instincts scream for more. *Mate.* It hit him again, and sweat broke out on his forehead. His hardened cock chafed against his fly. "Yes?"

Uncertainty flickered to life in her eyes and she dropped her hand, her smile fading as she took two quick steps back. "I asked if I could get you another drink. I didn't mean to startle you. I apologize."

"No, it's fine." More than fine. It was too good for his peace of mind and reminded him just how fine a wire he was walking here. "And, yes, I'd like another drink."

"I'll be back in a moment." Nodding quickly, she moved away to check on the other patrons lining her bar. Her face wore the mask he was learning to see through, but he regretted that he'd scared her enough to feel she had to throw the barrier up between them. She was a woman, petite and soft, and even in animal form, she was a lesser predator. Her vulnerability sliced through him, along with the ever-present worry for her safety. The Vermilion was no place for someone like her. There was no good reason why she had survived—no, *thrived*—in this environment. She was smarter than people gave her credit for. Wily. So was he.

He watched her glance at the chrono on the wall. It was the third time she'd done it in the last five minutes. He checked his wrist chrono against the one on the wall as she set a fresh drink in front of him without meeting his gaze. He caught her arm, stroking his thumb against the inside of her wrist in apology. She nodded, tugged her arm from his grip, and looked at the chrono again. It was then that he realized what was wrong, what was missing. "Isn't Nolan supposed to be here by now?"

"Maybe he got tied up with a customer." Her grin was knowing, her gaze devilishly teasing, but her hands told the real truth. They clenched to hide the sudden trembling. "But he should have been back a long time ago."

He could smell a hint of fear, concern, and that was enough to have him shoving to his feet. "When did he leave and from what door?"

She blinked at the bark of command, but pointed to the rear of the building. "The employee entrance. Four hours ago."

"Deus." They couldn't make it easy on him, could they? He swore under his breath the entire way, employing every one of his honed senses to track his mate.

For the first time in his entire career, he dismissed his work and the fact that Lev Barrone might have people watching for him in the Vermilion and chose to find his mate over doing his more prudent duty.

He *had* to know that Nolan was safe. At that moment, nothing else mattered.

Nolan knew he was going to die.

Resignation slid through him. It was bound to happen sooner or later. If you tripped up in this business, death was the only possible result. He understood that, accepted it, and now he got to deal with the consequences of his choices.

The job had gone down the shit chute pretty quickly after he'd set up on the roof with his high-powered, state-of-the-art rifle. A deal was going down between two rival gangs, and he'd been paid to take out the leader of one of them. He hit his mark, they all started firing, and no one knew who was responsible for the first shot.

Easy.

But then the feds showed up with helicopters and spotlights and his safe position got not so safe in a hurry. Just his luck that while he was hiding his rifle one of the gang members decided to take the stairs to the roof of *this* building. Nolan's arm was grazed by a stray bullet in the cross fire and he'd been slammed back into an old antenna. The metal bent in half, dumping him over the side of the railing. Only his cat reflexes saved him, and he'd managed to catch the metal rod. So, there he dangled, ten stories up, held up by a half-broken piece of metal and some wires, surrounded by feds and gang members, and thoroughly fucked.

Rain fell in torrents, the acidity of it burning slightly as it hit his skin. His gloves helped him keep a firmer grip on the wet pole, but his sweating fingers were beginning to slide in the kleather. Even a cat couldn't fall from this height and survive. A bird-shifter, yeah, but a cat? He might land on his feet, but he wouldn't survive the impact. This side of the building was a smooth, windowless expanse of cement. Nothing to hold on to. Nothing to help him. Swallowing, he pushed every emotion away. Looked at rationally, there was only one choice to make. It was inevitable in his profession. You got out or you died. It looked like he was going the messier of those two routes.

"Nolan Angelo."

Oh, Deus. He knew that voice. Nolan squinted into the glare of a helicopter spotlight, making out the outline of a short man with one foot braced on the building's railing. "Marconi."

The spotlight moved away as the aircraft did, circling to find more fleeing gang members. Nolan could see just as well in the dark and he watched Marconi drape his forearm across his bent knee. "It's crazy seeing you here. I heard there was a shot fired before we made our move. You know anything about that?"

"Not a thing." He tried to keep his voice casual, shifted his grip on the antenna, and fought the pain in order to hang on.

"I'm just hanging out. Wrong place, wrong time. You know how it goes."

Marconi gave a booming laugh. "Right. Sure. I'm actually glad I caught you here. I've been meaning to have one of our little talks again."

"Fuck you." There were no "little talks." Marconi had been trying to recruit Nolan into working for the government for years. They wanted the best working on their team, doing their dirty work for them. It was always the same. Marconi threatened, Nolan walked. The agent had no evidence, so he couldn't arrest Nolan, but he knew about the jaguar's extracurricular activities. He couldn't prove anything . . . though tonight might change that.

It had been especially bitter when Nolan found out Pierce worked for the same agency as this pissant. Another good reason for him to stay away from the wolf, but staring death in the face made him wish he'd pushed a little harder to get a taste before he died.

Nolan's muscles began to shake with the strain, sweat sliding down his forehead along with the rain. It slicked his skin and made it that much more difficult to hang on. The wound in his arm shot agony straight to the base of his skull in pounding, nauseating waves.

"Join us, or I'll leave you here to die." Marconi's eyes were colder than his voice. "I don't have any reason to protect a man who doesn't work for me. You're just another criminal, one that someone else is going to be kind enough to take care of for me. If you don't fall first."

"You son of a bitch."

A humorless smile quirked his lips. "I'm a coyote-shifter, so it's truer than you know."

Be a slave to the system that put him into prostitution in the first place? They'd tell him who to kill and when. They'd own him. He'd be ground under by the corrupt machine of justice. Bitter hatred made his stomach heave, his throat burning on the bile. No. He couldn't do it. "My answer hasn't changed, and you still don't have anything you can pin on me."

"Suit yourself." The coyote straightened and kicked the base of the antenna hard before he turned and walked away.

Nolan dropped another meter, the metal bending even more, but it didn't break. How long did he have before it did? He didn't know. He could hear the sound of Marconi's footsteps fading, and then the metal door that led to the roof crashed as he closed it behind him. Nolan was alone.

Sliding his hands along the slick pole, he tried to work his way closer to the building. The metal groaned with each shift in his weight, so he moved slowly and carefully. He was a good meter and a half from the side of the building when his good hand slipped off the pole, and he bit back the agonized scream that threatened to rip free. The antenna's metal squeaked as he swung wildly, the muscles in his wounded arm giving way, and he barely caught the pole with his other hand before he took the plunge.

But the antenna finally snapped, and Nolan knew it was over.

He hit the side of the building hard, a few wires still hanging on, but he could hear each one pop in rapid succession.

Here it came. The ten-story drop to a quick splatter on the wet pavement below.

The pole jerked, moving upward. Nolan blinked through the pouring rain, but he couldn't make out more than a shadow. If it was a gang member . . . torture if he was caught. He looked down again. It was a faster and better choice.

"Don't you fucking let go, Angelo." The rough voice made Nolan's breath seize in his lungs, and the first tiny spark of hope burned through him.

"Pierce?" It couldn't be. There was no way in hell the wolf would help him even if he were working this case. Nolan was delusional. But he had to grit his teeth as the moving pole jarred his arm.

"Give me your hand." Pierce's face was hard with determination and strain when he finally came into view. Rain dripped off his chin, plastering his short hair to his skull. "Come on, Angelo, give me your hand."

Nolan swallowed. It could be a trick, something Marconi cooked up. His fingers started to slide again, and he knew he wouldn't be able to hang on much longer.

Those silver eyes snared his, one hand reaching while the other secured the broken antenna. "Please."

He took the hand, snapping his fingers around the wolf's forearm. Pierce let go of the pole, latching on to Nolan's arm with both hands. Together, they got Nolan back over the railing and onto the roof.

Closing his eyes in relief, he slumped against the rough cement surface for a moment to catch his breath.

"We have to move. It's not safe for you here."

Nolan opened his eyes to see the wolf bending over him. He nodded and let Pierce haul him to his feet. Bracing himself under Nolan's good arm to steady him, Pierce directed them to the door that would lead to the staircase. Nolan didn't mention his stashed rifle. He could come back for it later or call it a loss. There was no way to trace it back to him even if Marconi found it.

The trip down the stairs was a quick but painful one. They exited the building, and Pierce skirted them around the agents while Nolan kept his gaze moving to look for anyone that might ambush them. There were a lot of dangers in the Vermilion, especially with Nolan leaving the scent of blood in the air behind them. Thankfully, the rain would disguise and help

214 / Crystal Jordan

wash away their trail. The few predators not driven away by the presence of lawmen and the acidic deluge skulked in the shadows, staring after them with hollow eyes.

Nolan knew he should say something, maybe thank Pierce for coming for him. They were several blocks away from the crime scene and neither had spoken. Nolan's mouth worked, but he didn't have the words for a moment. At this point, the wolf had to know what he was, what he did. And yet Pierce was here, saving him. It all came down to one simple question. "Why?"

Pierce said nothing, just kept walking while a muscle twitched in his jaw. The closed expression didn't waver for a moment. Nolan pulled to a stop, and Pierce stopped with him. The wolf swallowed audibly, but still didn't meet Nolan's gaze. "Why does it matter? You're alive, aren't you?"

"You could be throwing away your career by helping me. I'm a criminal." He spoke the words baldly, not letting the older man deny or pretend to mishear what he'd said.

Those gray eyes met his then. There was a torment there Nolan didn't understand, a deep agony. He knew pain and suffering, but why Pierce might feel that about Nolan was beyond him. "What do you care what I do or why? Let's just get you out of here."

He resisted Pierce's attempts to start moving again. "Because I have to know. How do I know you're not just going to turn me in when you come to your senses in the morning? Or your conscience reboots?"

"*I would never do that.*" But the words had a contained violence that made Nolan's eyebrows arch. Pierce sucked in a deep breath. "If I wanted you dead or imprisoned, all I had to do was stay at Tail and do nothing."

"Pierce." Nolan waited for the wolf to meet his gaze again. "Tell me why."

"No." Pierce boosted his shoulder under Nolan's arm, tightening his grip to the point that Nolan knew he'd be dragged if he didn't move this time. "You'll just have to trust that I'm a man of my word, and I said I wouldn't turn you in for this."

"I do trust you. You're an honest man." Or he trusted Pierce as much as he trusted anyone, which probably wasn't much by most people's standards. They walked a few more steps. "I don't know that many honest men. In fact, you might be the only one."

Pierce grunted. "Not that honest, apparently."

"Is it because you want to sleep with me?" Nolan felt Pierce tense against his side, rage vibrating through his muscles. But it was an honest question. What other reason would the other man have for saving him? He didn't understand any of this, and that made him suspicious. No one helped him out the of the kindness of their hearts—everyone had an agenda, an angle they were working. What was Pierce's?

"I didn't do this for a free fuck." A low growl vibrated from his chest, and he jerked them to a stop this time. "I could have had you the same way everyone else could have."

"Only if I said yes," Nolan retorted. "Lorelei doesn't force her jades to fuck anyone. I would have had to be willing to fuck you, for free or for creds."

"You would have been willing." Pierce shot him a glance, one that raised the hairs on the back of Nolan's neck. It had awareness to it, revealed the sensual man behind the cynical mask. That was the man Nolan had always wanted to touch. "If I had wanted to pay."

What was he going to pay with now? If not creds, then his career. Nolan might not know everything about Pierce, but he knew the man was more in love with his job than he was with any person—man, woman, or child. Not that Nolan expected love from anyone, but he also didn't expect anyone to sacrifice what they loved for him. With Pierce, that meant his career.

A lopsided smile formed on Nolan's face, and he let his gaze slide leisurely down Pierce's lean form. "I guess everyone has their price."

"Shut your mouth and walk, Angelo." They started again, ghosting down alleys and avoiding main thoroughfares that might have nosy law enforcement officers. Other than Pierce, of course.

Nolan tightened his grip around the wolf's shoulder, leaning on him even though he didn't actually need to. Only his arm was hurt, and the shock had worn off almost a kilometer ago. But if Pierce wanted to touch him, he wasn't about to protest. "I love it when you order me around, Vaughn."

That earned another growl. "Fucking cat."

A laugh tripped out, relief that he was alive finally breaking loose. He'd been so sure he was a dead man. "Not yet, but—"

Pierce's glance was more acidic than the rain which had thankfully slowed to a sporadic drizzle. "You're trying to make me regret saving your feline hide, aren't you?"

"Is it working?" Nolan ran his free hand down his face, wiped away the droplets of water, and winked at the wolf.

"Walk, Angelo."

3

"My name is Nolan."

"I know what your name is." Pierce shot another glance at the jaguar, checking to make sure he was steady on his feet and that he was, indeed, safe and sound. The relief that sluiced through him made him angry at himself for feeling it, and angry at Nolan for putting him through the hour of hell it took to track him across the Vermilion District. His voice emerged gruffer than he intended, "I know more about you than you'd like."

"Clearly." Nolan snorted, but his midnight gaze met Pierce's as they walked. "But let's not talk about me. . . . let's talk about you. You risked a hell of a lot to come save me, but keep Lorelei and me at arm's length by calling us by our last names. Yet you insist we call you Pierce. Something doesn't add up here."

Pierce swallowed, knowing it was true, and knowing there wasn't a single response he could give that wouldn't damn him more than his actions tonight already had. "Fine. Nolan."

A smile quirked the taller man's full lips, and Pierce had several very sexual thoughts about things he'd like that mouth doing. None of which required talking. Still, his mate looked . . .

different tonight, and it disturbed some deep part of him to see it.

The jaguar-shifter's hair was pulled back in a short, tight ponytail at the base of his neck. It made him look dangerous, deadly. Exactly what he was. It took away the veneer of charm and civility he wore in his other line of work.

This Nolan wasn't playing games, teasing, and flirting his way into bed with high-priced clientele. *This* Nolan was undeniably the assassin. His clothing was black, his shirtsleeves long enough to conceal his nanotats, and he wore military-grade body armor, pants, and boots. Black gloves stretched like a second skin over his hands. Hiding evidence, but not impeding his movements at all. Smart. The kind of criminal Pierce usually tried to corner in the act because they were damn good at covering their tracks.

This was the first time he'd ever seen that side of Nolan, and he realized what a dangerous game of denial he'd been playing about who the jaguar really was. Oh, he'd known he was an assassin, but seeing it, experiencing it, was different from understanding it intellectually.

Deus help him, it did nothing to suppress the craving within him.

"So." The midnight gaze cut Pierce an incisive glance. "How much *do* you know?"

He could lie. Good man or not, having this job didn't mean he couldn't lie with the best of the pathological criminals. He just conned the cons for the government. But he didn't want to lie to his mates any more than he had to. "Everything. Except why."

Nolan blinked and looked away. His voice went soft. "The first time . . . the first time was an accident." He slid his fingers down his hair, obviously at a loss for words. "I was with a client, things got rough, and . . . before I knew it, he was dead."

"Did he hurt you?" Pierce did *not* want the answer to his question, but he had to ask.

A bitter laugh rippled out. "Did he rape me, do you mean?"

"Yeah." The word was a gruff exhalation of air.

"No, not him. But there were others. It happens in the Vermilion."

"I know. I'm sorry." Acid burned through Pierce, knowing there was nothing he could do to rid his mate of the suffering he'd gone through.

Nolan nodded, took a breath. "Apparently, the client had a bounty on his head. They thought I'd killed him on purpose, posed as a jade to get the job done. I never knew how they knew it was me, just got a vid in my cache and a lot of creds in my account the next day. A thank-you for smoothing out an inconvenience for someone."

"How did that turn into more?" That was the hard part for Pierce to understand. Accidents happened, self-defense was one thing, but a hired killer . . . was something else.

"The second time, I was approached by a man whose daughter was kidnapped, raped, gutted, and dumped in Lake Michigan. Her body washed up, the father knew who did it, had evidence, but the lawyers didn't think they could make the charges stick." Nolan's shoulder rubbed against Pierce's when he shrugged. Even that simple a contact sent awareness snapping through Pierce's body like an electric shock. He willed his cock not to harden. And failed.

Swallowing, he forced himself to keep with the topic at hand. This was important. This was information he'd wanted for months, since the moment he found out what Nolan did. "They were paid not to."

"Yeah." Nolan sighed. "I knew the guy and even if he hadn't done the daughter, he'd done plenty else that more than earned him a trip to the morgue."

"That's not your place to say."

"The law did so well?" Nolan's expression went stony.

Pierce closed his eyes for a moment. "It's not a perfect system, but the alternative is worse."

"The alternative is me." The jaguar's gaze reflected a comprehension and self-deprecation that was hard to watch. "From there, it was too easy to keep going."

"Slippery slope."

He just nodded. "I don't take every job that comes my way. I never did. I don't kill women or children."

"That's something." Pierce let a sigh ease out, so many conflicting emotions ricocheting through him that he wasn't sure which to deal with first. The worst part was he had no right to feel most of them at all. He should be hauling Nolan's ass in for questioning. But he didn't and he wouldn't and he knew it.

"Everyone has their price, Pierce. I do what I have to do to look myself in the mirror every morning. I'm not like you. I'm not an honest man, I'm not even a good man."

"You're better than most would be under the same circumstances." Which was the hard truth. There wasn't a lot of good in the world, and unlike Nolan, Pierce did his best to protect what was left of it. Cynic that he was, he was still bound by the oaths he'd taken to uphold the law.

Nolan snorted. "Pierce, that system you love so much is what put me here. I don't believe in your laws, even though I pretend to follow them. The laws have never protected me— the system chewed me up as a kid and spit me out in a jade-house."

Deus. Pierce had read that in the ident files, but hearing the other man say it made his gut twist tight. He didn't have a fucking thing to say to something like that. Yet, what the jaguar did was still wrong. What a mess. For all of them. "Nolan—"

"I don't want your pity." The jaguar's expression flattened to nothingness.

DEADLY TEMPTATION / 221

A laugh straggled out of Pierce's throat, squeezing past the tangled mass of conflicting emotions in his chest. "I don't pity anyone. Not anymore."

"Good." Clearing his throat, Nolan made an obvious effort at his usual playfulness. "I'd hate to have to kill you."

"That isn't funny."

He smirked. "Maybe not to you."

"You're not an evil man, Nolan." Pierce had been around the younger man long enough to know. There were some things people just couldn't hide, and most didn't bother when they lived in this district. It would be better for Nolan if he was outwardly evil, but he chose not to fake it.

"Maybe. I don't like to think about it much." Nolan rocked his hand back and forth. "It's not a black-and-white world, is it? It's all gray area. I guess that's what I am. A gray area. Not good, not evil. Not anything."

That was how Pierce felt most days. He was long past the point where he had much idealism left. He'd done things in his work that, if he didn't work for who he worked for, would be illegal. Was he really any better than Nolan? He wasn't sure. Hell, the agency he worked for had people like Nolan to do their wet work. Off the record, of course, to preserve public deniability, but that didn't change who paid the bills. "I know what you mean."

"I somehow had a feeling you would, or I wouldn't have said anything." Nolan smiled his charming smile and winked, but Pierce recognized the kind of trust it had to take for the jaguar to have told him as much as he had. It shook him to realize how much he wanted his mates to have faith in him, especially knowing how much *faith* could cost a person.

"You're going to have to ditch the body armor." They were close to Tail, and it was one less question to answer when they got there.

Nolan sighed, some of the tension easing out of his body. It was obvious both of them had needed a change in topic. Too many undercurrents ran through their words, things they couldn't—or wouldn't—tell each other. "I'm not the only one who wears it in the Vermilion. It's not that uncommon."

"It is for you to wear it." At least when he was at Tail. A part of Pierce was grateful his mate protected himself when he was doing his less legitimate work. The rest of him wondered how this night had gone to hell so quickly.

"True." Nolan dropped his arm from around Pierce's shoulder, stepping behind a corroded Dumpster to unseal the vest and strip it and his gloves off. He tossed all of it into the overflowing piles of garbage.

Pierce coughed and forced his gaze away from the shirt that encased Nolan's hard muscles. His instincts lit up again, and his cock went hard in nanoseconds. Deus, what he wouldn't give to have the right to order the jaguar to finish stripping, get his hands all over that tight body, and lose himself in the hot channel of Nolan's ass.

And Pierce knew he wouldn't let himself reach out and take what he wanted so badly. After he left Nolan with Lorelei, the smartest thing Pierce could do was take himself home to his downtown flat. He'd already crossed too many lines tonight.

"Patrol," Nolan hissed. He fisted his fingers in Pierce's shirt and shoved him up against the alley wall and away from the passing police officers. He was close enough that he could see the flecks of black in those gray eyes; he could count every eyelash. Their breaths mingled and he could smell the lust Pierce always tried to hide. Nolan swallowed and held tight to the reality of the danger they were in if discovered. "If they stop us, tell them you're my client."

"I know what to tell *mmph*—"

He smothered the sound with his mouth, shoving his tongue between Pierce's lips. If he had one chance to taste the man, he was going to take it. The wolf's body went absolutely still, and for a moment, Nolan was certain Pierce was going to finish the job Marconi had started. Nolan might be bigger, and he knew how to fight dirty, but he had no illusions about the wolf's ability to take him out if he wanted to.

A low warning growl slipped from the wolf's throat, but he didn't try to pull away. Nolan smiled against his lips and took that for the invitation it was.

He could feel the rough bristles on Pierce's unshaven chin, and the scent of the wolf's arousal increased by the moment. It made Nolan's cock ache to make this man react to him. He'd been practiced at making men and women want him enough to beg since he was barely old enough to maintain an erection, but there was something different about Pierce. Something more intense. Nolan didn't know why and he didn't care. He just wanted more.

The hard length of Pierce's erection burned against Nolan's thigh. He shifted his hips until he could rub their cocks together through their pants. They both groaned, and fire exploded in Nolan's veins. He rolled his pelvis in a rhythm he couldn't stop, and he shuddered when Pierce moved with him. The friction as their dicks slid alongside each other was so fucking good.

One of Pierce's hands grabbed a fistful of Nolan's hair, ripped it free of the tie that secured it, forced his head into a new angle, and took control of the animalistic kiss. They weren't gentle. They bit and sucked and grunted at the painful ecstasy. Nolan ground his hips into Pierce, the movement shoving him toward orgasm. Pierce's other hand ran over Nolan's chest until he found a nipple. He flicked the tip, making Nolan's body jolt. When he was on a job, Nolan wore only studs in his pierced nipples, but still, they were incredibly sensitive. The wolf pinched hard and twisted.

"Pierce," he groaned against the other man's mouth. His

224 / Crystal Jordan

muscles locked as he came in his pants, his cock jerking against his fly. Pierce arched his hips and dragged another tormented groan from Nolan. He clenched his jaw as the sensations went on for an eternity and ended far sooner than he would have liked. Deus, he'd never been so aroused in his life.

A hiss of pain he couldn't quiet ripped out when Pierce's hand clamped over his wounded arm. He stumbled back a few steps and bent to brace his good palm on his knee. Pierce's fingers closed over the back of his neck, and he dropped to his haunches beside Nolan. "I'm sorry. I didn't mean . . . Are you all right?"

Nolan nodded, pushing himself upright. Pierce was there, slipping back under his arm to help him stand. They started moving again, and within a few minutes were walking up the alley that ran alongside Tail. He glanced down at the hard lines of Pierce's features, at the flush of lust running under his skin, at the muscle that twitched in his jaw. "You didn't come."

He hadn't asked it as a question, but Pierce answered anyway. "No."

"I'll do better next time."

The wolf stumbled before quickly righting himself. "That will never happen again, Angelo."

The rear door of Tail flew open as they approached, cutting off any response Nolan might have given. Lorelei stood in the doorway, the light behind her turning her hair to flame and making her sheer skirt irrelevant. Her gaze slid over both of them, assessing any damage before she motioned for them to follow her.

The halls were deserted as they skirted around corners until they reached Lorelei's office. She jerked her head to indicate they should precede her into the room, but her face wore the carefully emotionless expression he knew disguised deep feeling. What those feelings were, he couldn't guess. Was she angry? Scared? Hurt? He wished he knew. Dropping his arm

from Pierce's shoulder, he entered the office first and felt the
wolf fall into step behind him. Nolan turned to watch Lorelei
close and engage the security locks on the door.

Easing himself down on the red kleather chaise, he sighed as
his sore muscles relaxed into the comfortable seat. This night
had already been insanity and he was more than ready to sleep
it off and pretend it never happened.

Pierce paced the confines of the office like a caged animal, all
but vibrating with whatever thoughts were roiling around in
that lupine head of his.

"You're bleeding." Lorelei's small hands settled on Nolan's
forearm, moving his arm so she could see the wound. Even that
gentle contact burned and he fought a wince. "I have a med kit
in the cabinet. I'll get it."

She walked toward a wall of vidscreens that showed various
images of rooms in Tail and bent to open a long cabinet underneath them.

"It's just a scratch." It would hurt like hell for a while, but
he could tell it wasn't that deep and if he slapped a nanopatch
over it, he'd be fine. There wasn't much else to do for it. He'd
had a lot worse.

Pierce paused in his ceaseless pacing to glare at him. "Sit
there and let her take care of you, damn it."

"Yes, sir," Nolan drawled.

"Don't be a smartass."

He arched an eyebrow. "*Querido,* my ass does a lot of
things, but I don't think smart is one of them. You can check
for yourself if you want, though."

A growl was the only response he got. Lorelei knelt on the
chaise beside him, the kleather creaking beneath her knees. It
brought her breasts tantalizingly close to his mouth when he
turned his head to look at her. Every time she took a breath,
those soft, full mounds pressed against the top of her corset.

His cock hardened again, and he fought a groan. He'd just

come and still he wanted more. Of all the people in the world he could fuck, why did he crave these two? Was it the challenge they presented, the fact that they both fought their desire for him and each other, or that he just didn't like that they wouldn't give him what he wanted? He didn't know anymore.

Lorelei tsked as she peeled up the bottom of Nolan's shirt so he could take it off. Dried blood caked around the shallow furrow where the bullet had grazed him. "Deus, you're a mess."

She had no idea.

"Well, at least it didn't mess up my tat." He flexed his forearm, making the flames dance even more that usual.

The look she gave him was cutting, and she snorted. "The fire's a good metaphor for you, Nolan. Vibrant and beautiful, but dangerous and likely to consume everything around you until there's just darkness left."

Opening his mouth to shoot back a response, he bit off a curse as she cleaned the wound before affixing a nanopatch. His erection died a swift death as the pain rocketed through his body. He gritted his teeth so hard he was certain they'd crack, clenched his fingers into fists, and was sweating when it was over. The cleaning almost hurt more than getting shot in the first place.

Jerking to his feet when she was done, he spun for the door. He was more than ready for this night to be over and wasn't interested in the questions he saw in Lorelei's eyes . . . or any more comments about how he was consumed by darkness. He didn't have answers or assurances that would satisfy her. He wiped his forehead on the back of his good arm. "Thanks, Lorelei. I'll see you—"

"You're not going anywhere yet." Pierce stepped in front of him, and Nolan just kept moving until he was a hairbreadth from the other man. Even with his arm on fire, it didn't stop his body from reacting. Again.

He leaned forward a bit, until his face was right in Pierce's.

He was too fucking tired and in no mood to deal with some alpha wolf's suppressed lust. "What are you going to do to stop me, Pierce? Hit me, restrain me, kiss me again?"

"Again?" Lorelei interjected with a breathy catch to her voice that just made Nolan's cock harder.

Pierce's gray eyes flashed to molten silver, and Nolan watched the internal struggle make a muscle in his jaw start to tic. It didn't mask the scent of his arousal—a scent that hadn't faded from the moment he'd made Nolan come in his pants.

"I can smell how turned on you are and we both know you're harder than mercurite right now." He slid his hand down the front of Pierce's fly and grasped his straining erection. Both men groaned and Nolan heard a soft whimper from Lorelei. Stroking Pierce's cock through his pants, Nolan lowered his voice to a coaxing, seductive purr. "What I don't understand is why you don't just take what you want. To hell with whether or not it's a bad idea. You've already had a few bad ideas tonight. Why not one more?"

4

"Damn it. Damn you." And then Pierce broke, planting his palms against Nolan's chest to slam him against the wall next to the door. Their lips met in a wild rush of anger, pain, and longing. They bit at each other, the kiss as violent as it was urgent. Nolan shoved his tongue into Pierce's mouth, and he couldn't fight a helpless groan. He wanted this so badly, and now he'd have it. Just this once, he'd have it.

Nolan's hands were already busy unfastening Pierce's belt and pants, sliding in to grasp his hard cock. He thrust into those talented fingers, fire boiling hot and wild in his veins. Nolan pushed Pierce's pants down around his hips, the weight of his gun and badge pulling them down further, and freed his dick for Nolan to stroke it more fully. The wolf inside him howled, demanding he take his mate. Now.

For the first time in his life, he couldn't find a good reason not to give in to his baser instincts.

He pressed his palm to the jaguar's flat belly and slid it up his torso. The heat of smooth flesh stretched taut over thick muscles made him groan. He reached the small disc of a nipple and stopped to explore the thick stud that pierced it. He tugged gently, twisting it. Nolan jerked under his touch, hissing softly. Bending forward, Pierce flicked his tongue over the flat, brown nipple, grazing it with his teeth when it tightened for him. He sucked it hard, and Nolan arched.

"Oh, shit." Nolan groaned, panting for breath. He fisted his hands in Pierce's jacket, pulling him closer. His fingers turned into claws, the points shredding the cloth and biting into Pierce's flesh.

The pain was nothing compared to the pleasure twisting inside him. Nolan's passionate reaction and the fact that he could *feel* Lorelei's gaze on them, watching them give in to their lust, just made Pierce burn hotter.

He ripped open the seal on the jaguar's pants, shoving them down to his thighs. "Turn around and face the wall."

"Deus, Pierce." Nolan obeyed and braced his hands against the wall, looking back over his shoulder. The flames on his forearms had turned into a raging inferno, a contrast to the stark white walls of Lorelei's office. "Fuck me, please."

Pierce kicked Nolan's legs open as far as his pants would allow, cupping his ass in both hands. His cock slid into the cleft of those muscled globes, and he shoved the length deep into the tight anus. Nolan groaned at the roughness of his entry, but his hips moved to take all of him. The muscled ring scraped maddeningly against Pierce's dick as he thrust over and over into the jaguar-shifter's body. They grunted each time their skin slapped together, sweat sealing their bodies. Nolan hissed when Pierce bit his shoulder hard.

In his wildest wet dreams, he'd never once imagined fucking his mate would be this good, this intense. The feel of Nolan's ass closing around his cock was so amazing he thought he'd die, and he knew he'd go out a happy man.

Nolan's claws scrabbled against the smooth wall and his head dropped forward as he shoved his hips back into Pierce's groin. "Fuck, that's good."

"Yeah." Reaching around the jaguar's chest, Pierce ground those pierced nipples between his fingers. A jungle cat's scream rent the air. "Like to have these played with, don't you, Angelo?"

Nolan just groaned and shuddered. Pierce laughed, feeling better than he had in years. Deus, he wanted it like this forever, it was so good. Hot, hard, sweaty, and feral. His thrusts became shorter, harder, and he was right on the verge of orgasm.

He groped for Nolan's cock, releasing his nipples. He wrapped his fingers around the thick shaft to stroke it in time with his thrusts into the jaguar's ass.

"Oh, Deus." Lorelei's soft exclamation was almost a moan, and he damn near came then and there. Having them both here, knowing they were as hot for this as he was, got him higher than a hit of bliss. "Harder, Pierce. Faster."

"Lorelei," Nolan groaned. His hips rocked faster; he impaled himself on Pierce's cock and pushed his dick through the circle of Pierce's fingers. "Pierce! Yes! I need it harder, just like Lorelei said. I need it so much."

Need. His mate *needed* him, even if only for the sexual release he could grant him. The words set Pierce off like a biobomb and he exploded into Nolan's ass, pumping his come as deep as he could. He felt Nolan give in to his own release, snarling catlike while his come bubbled through Pierce's tight grip on his cock.

He dropped his forehead against the muscled planes of Nolan's back, flicking his tongue out to taste the sweat-slicked flesh. The flavor of Nolan was embedded in Pierce's psyche now, something that his instincts would never forget and that the wolf would always crave.

Nothing in his life had ever been so right and so wrong at

the same time, but he'd thrown his protests out the window, and he was going to take this night and squeeze every last sensation out of it that he could.

It was the most arousing thing Lorelei had ever seen in her life.

She sat on the chaise, crossed her legs to savor the lustful ache, and watched them touch, kiss, fuck. It was all she could do not to slip her fingers under her skirt and stroke herself. Her clit burned, the lips of her pussy swollen and slick with juices. She closed her eyes and dragged in a deep breath, but the musk of sex and pheromones in the air did nothing to calm her.

"You should see the look on your face, Lorelei." Nolan's voice was a deep purr of satisfaction.

She opened her eyes to see the men had pulled apart, and Pierce was using some of the supplies from her med kit to clean himself up. He stood in profile to her and seeing his hands move over his still semi-hard cock made a whimper bubble up in her throat. Instead of straightening their clothes, both men finished shedding them.

Her mouth dried as she watched the smooth, hard muscles gleam under the lights. She'd seen Nolan naked before, and he had never failed to make her hot. Tonight was no exception. He was huge, his legs flexing with heavy muscles as his pants and boots dropped to the floor. Every micrometer of him was bare, sculpted pecs, sloping abs, long cock. Even as her gaze touched him, his shaft hardened, darkened. Deus, he was beautiful. His skin a deep golden hue, his nanotat a rippling contrast in color, and his midnight eyes and hair accented a nearly perfect face. The nipple piercings were new since the last time she'd been allowed to touch him. Her hands flexed with the need to twirl a fingertip around a small areola and tug on the jewelry. Her own nipples were so tight they throbbed, and her skin felt too tight to hold in the heat that boiled within her body.

232 / Crystal Jordan

Pierce was a revelation, though. He looked on as Nolan stripped, his eyes giving away how much the jaguar aroused him. His cock grew rigid and a shudder shook him. He looked at her, and her breath strangled in her throat. The heat she saw snared her, made her body flame everywhere the silver gaze touched. His jacket hit the floor and the metal of his gun and badge clanked against the polyglass of her low table. His fingers flicked open the closures on his shirt, reaching behind him to pull it out of his pants and over his head. He was leaner than Nolan, but his ropy muscles left no doubt about the deadly force his body could wield. She wanted to slide her hands over him, feel the vital heat of him under her palms. A light smattering of hair stretched between his flat nipples and bisected his torso to trail down to his impressive dick. She wondered if she could get her mouth around it—she knew she wanted to try. It wasn't as long as Nolan's, but it was nearly twice as thick.

As he bent to ease his pants down his legs, she could see the ripple of muscle in his broad back, the tight globes of his ass, the long, masculine legs. He tossed his clothes aside and straightened, rubbing a hand over the back of his neck as they stared at him.

Nolan groaned and moved to stand near Pierce, giving her the kind of look that would have scorched her if she weren't already burning. "Come here."

She swallowed, shaking her head. Her gaze never left their hard, naked bodies, though. "That's a bad idea. I have rules. No touching the jades or the customers. You're one of each. That's a bad bet if I've ever heard of one."

Nolan strolled around the long table that stood between her and them, feline grace in every movement. He offered her a wicked, delicious smile, his dark gaze slipping over her curves. She stood when he got around to her side of the table, stumbling backward. Deus, if he touched her, she might come before he ever got inside her, she was so turned on. Her hormones clamored in agreement with that idea, while her mind knew what a mistake it would be. He kept coming, stalking her like so much prey. It made her heart pound, excitement revving inside her.

He backed her up against her desk. She scooted up onto the smooth surface, the cold of the polyglass biting into her thighs, and he laughed. "Just where I want you."

"No," she gasped.

He put a hand behind her, not touching her, but not letting her go any further without touching him. "What's wrong, Lorelei?"

"Stop it, Nolan." Her back straightened to a rigid line, her eyes narrowing and her chin lifting to look down her nose at him. The command was unmistakable, an order from a displeased employer.

His eyebrow arched, and he leaned closer. Her eyes flared wide with trapped panic, need raging through her system. "Oh, I think we're beyond madam and jade at this point, Lorelei." He moved so his mouth was a hairbreadth from her ear. "Don't you?"

"Nolan." She tried to think, but her thoughts were drifting like smoke on a breeze. She could smell the heavy wetness of her desire and the deepening musk of his. It was intoxicating. She wanted him so badly her sex ached.

"You remember what it was like, don't you?" The tiny hairs at the nape of her neck moved when he whispered against her skin. She shivered, biting back a moan. "How good it felt that night? How you screamed and clawed my back?"

Deus, yes, she remembered. Every. Erotic. Detail. It was seared into her memory. She fisted her fingers, trying to hold on to some control. She had her rules for a reason. They protected everyone, including her. "We were performers in someone else's show. We were just entertainment."

"You can't fake that kind of enthusiasm, Lorelei. Don't even

234 / *Crystal Jordan*

try to lie to me." The heat of his big body enveloped her, made her want to slide her legs open and let him ease the ache between them. Surely having Pierce and Nolan now would slake her craving, and she would know—finally—and be able to put the fantasy of all three of them together behind her. Yes. No. She didn't know what was right and what was wrong anymore. Nolan's dark eyes flashed with the same heat that she felt. "I know what's real and what's not. You liked it when I touched you. You wanted it. You begged me for more."

She whimpered. "I . . . I . . ."

"You? Tell me what you want, Lorelei. Tell me how you want me to eat your creamy pussy again. Tell me you want my cock in your mouth, in your cunt, in your ass." The liquid heat inside her exploded like a volcano as he painted images in her mind. She needed to come so badly she thought she might die, and he kept tempting her with that low, sinful purr. "Tell me you want Pierce and me to fuck you until you can't even remember your own name, let alone all the reasons why you think this is a bad idea. Tell me how you want it, how you like it, and I'll give it to you."

One last weak protest fell from her lips, but the words came out a throaty moan. "I have rule—"

"Damn the rules. We're beyond those, too." And then he kissed her, slipping his fingers into her hair to cup her head gently. He moved his mouth over hers worshipfully, and any resistance she had left melted into nothingness.

She had wanted this, fantasized about this, *craved* this for so long. Her hands rose to wind through the silkiness of his long hair, holding him closer, meeting his tongue with hers. His hot breath rushed against her skin, and she arched her torso into him. The tightness of her corset restricted her movements, frustrating her need for contact.

Her hand tightened in his hair when he pulled back. "Nolan, please."

"Shh." He dropped a soft kiss on the top of each breast, and her lungs seized when he bit her. His nimble fingers deftly popped open each tab on her corset, spreading it wide to look at her. She let her head fall back, arching herself in offering. "You have the most beautiful breasts I've ever had the pleasure of sucking."

She chuckled and the movement increased her awareness of how painfully tight her nipples were. "You haven't sucked them yet. You should."

"I will." He suited actions to words, dipping forward to suck one nipple into his mouth. He batted the taut crest with his tongue, shoving it against the roof of his mouth. Then he bit her, oh so gently.

A cry tore from her throat, and she leaned back on her hands to push herself closer, deeper. The softness of his lips contrasted with the sting of his teeth, driving her wild. A low growl sounded to her left and her chin jerked to the side, her breath catching. She felt Nolan turn his head to follow her gaze, and they both saw Pierce stroking his cock as he watched them, pale fire burning in his gray eyes. "Don't stop, Nolan. Keep playing with her pretty nipples."

"Pierce." She shuddered as Nolan did as he was told. The dynamic changed, the air almost electrifying around them as Pierce caressed them with his gaze. Her hips rocked in sensual abandon, and she was almost incoherent with lust.

Her slim claws scraped against her desk as her fingers flexed with every swirl and flick of Nolan's talented tongue on her nipple. He teased her beaded flesh with exquisite skill, the wetness he left behind cooling as his hot mouth closed over the peak of her other breast.

"Fuck me, Nolan. I want you inside me. Right now." And she wanted Pierce to watch Nolan take her, fuck her until she screamed. Shivers raced down her limbs, leaving her breathless and tingling.

"Deus, you made me wait long enough." He groaned, his fingers jerking her corset away to fling it to the floor. He made short work of her skirt, ripping it from her body with a sharp tug. A purr rumbled his chest as he slid his palms over her naked flesh. "I've waited forever to get my hands on you again."

Scooting as close to the edge of the desk as she could without sliding off, she parted her legs in blatant invitation. She licked her fingertips and slid them between her thighs to stroke herself, the first touch on her clit making her moan.

"Oh, no, you don't." Nolan caught her wrist and pulled her hand away.

"Then hurry up." She twisted her arm until she could grasp his fingers and press them between the folds of her sex. They both groaned, and he quickly thrust his long digits into her slick channel. It felt too good. It had been so long since anyone touched her like this. Her inner muscles clamped around his stroking fingers. "Deus, *please!*"

He kissed her again, and this one was pure fire. Shoving his free hand into her hair, he held her still while he thrust his tongue and his fingers in the same enticing rhythm that drove her to the edge of madness. She bit his lip hard and he hissed, dragging his claws down the inside of her thigh as he withdrew his hand. The head of his cock nudged against her wet folds and she spread her legs wider. He entered her a micrometer at a time, and she whimpered into his mouth. She gripped his shoulders, her claws digging their points in.

Wrapping her legs around his waist, she drew him deeper into her pussy. Then he gave her what she desired. He rode her hard against the desk, shoving his cock deep with every swift thrust. Her body jolted as he slammed against her, and her inner walls flexed on his dick. The drag of his flesh moving within hers excited her beyond measure, and she struggled to hold on to the moment, to savor the heat, the rawness, the sweat, the pure animalistic drive toward orgasm.

She shuddered when she felt Pierce's hand slide down her back. His skin was so hot she felt branded by it. She turned to look at him, and his fingers tangled in her hair, making the tips tickle her flesh. A shiver rippled through her. His gaze was hotter than his skin as it burned over her and Nolan. A little smile kicked up the corner of his mouth while he watched them fuck.

If there was anything that could have excited her more, it was *this*. Deus, she had wanted them both for so long. The thought of both of them stroking her and working their cocks into her at the same time almost pushed her over the edge. She held tight to what little remained of her control while she let go of Nolan's arms. Lying back on the desk, she crooked her finger at Pierce. "Come here."

Moving around the desk, he stepped within Lorelei's reach. She tilted her head back, bowing her body over the edges of the polyglass surface. It gouged into her hips and shoulders, but she didn't care. The discomfort was worth having what she craved. Her fingers curled around Pierce's jutting cock, stroking the length of it as she pulled the head into her mouth. He was almost too big for her, but she relaxed her jaw and throat, taking all of him. The musky tang of him slid over her taste buds, and her sex spasmed in response. She closed her eyes, working him with her tongue. He cradled the back of her neck, supporting her while she suckled his dick. A groan ripped loose while his hips began to move, pushing into her throat.

His hands closed over her breasts, teasing the nipples with his thumbs and forefingers. Or were they Nolan's hands? From her arched position, she didn't know, couldn't tell. And she didn't care. Her world hand come down to pure carnal sensation. Fingers stroked her, a thick cock slid over her tongue, and another dug deep into her pussy. The scent of Pierce and Nolan and herself, their passion mingling, overwhelmed her and she knew she wouldn't be able to hold on to her control much longer. She didn't even want to. She wanted to go where they would take her, wanted to let them burn the fire out of her.

Nolan's hands pinned her thighs to the desk as he hammered into her. He rotated his hips, grinding against her clit. Her low moan was muffled by Pierce's cock. A few more thrusts and she would go over. Contractions gathered in her belly, the desire spiraling tighter and tighter.

Pierce pulled from her mouth, and she didn't even have time to protest before he bent forward to suck her nipple into his mouth, biting, grazing the tight crest with his teeth. Her hands lifted to clench his muscular thighs, her body twisting as the sensations mounted. Nolan rolled her clitoris with his fingertip, and she screamed, writhing against the desktop. They knew just how to touch her to bring her to the very brink and hold her there. It was everything she'd ever imagined it could be with them and more. Some wall deep within her crumbled, but she didn't have time to assess the damage. Stretched between them as she was, all she could do was experience their sensual worship of her body. Nothing had ever felt so incredible. A tear slid from the corner of her eye.

"Please," she breathed.

Nolan pinched her clit, extending a single claw to flick over the hardened nub. She arched and screamed, sobbing as her pussy fisted around his cock. He groaned and continued to move his claw over her sensitive tissue, pumping into her as he came. She cried out, holding tight to Pierce as her orgasm went on and on. He sucked her nipples, blowing on the hot, damp flesh until she shuddered. Tears continued to slide down her cheeks when they finally let her loose, utterly spent.

Pierce scooped her into his arms, sinking into her desk chair. She wrapped her arms around him, shivering. "Pierce," she whispered.

She reached back, her hand groping for Nolan. He folded his fingers around hers, kissing the center of her palm. "Lorelei, are you all right?"

"Yes. No." She buried her face against Pierce's neck, a shudder running through her. "I don't . . . I don't know."

It was all too much, everything she'd needed and shouldn't have. The desire was sharper than ever, not fading as she'd hoped. Touching them once hadn't been enough. How could she have been so stupid? Another tear slipped from her eye.

The more important question was: what would she do now? Pierce's rigid cock pressed against her leg, and Nolan's fangs lightly scored her palm. Tingles swept up her arm and she swallowed a moan as her body reacted to their nearness, to the scent of their desire.

It was too late to go back now, too late for any of them. There was no way she could pretend this hadn't happened. And she wanted more—as much as they could give her. Her heart twisted, a warning of the pain she'd feel when it was over and they walked away. She knew these men as well as she'd known any in her life, and she knew how consumed they were in their work, their pasts. There was no future with these men, there was only now.

She would take it and deal with the consequences later. There were always consequences when rules were broken.

5

"Why don't we take this somewhere more comfortable? I actually have a bed in my suite." Lorelei had been silent for so long, Pierce had thought she'd drifted to sleep. She stirred, gingerly hauled herself up off his lap, and brushed her hair out of her face.

"Will you have to get dressed for that?" Pierce's gaze swept over her naked form. His erection hadn't eased the entire time she'd been in his arms, and it pulsed painfully at the visual orgy she presented. She was even lovelier than he'd imagined, all soft curves and silky skin. Her full breasts were topped with shell-pink nipples that he wanted to suck again. They'd darkened to raspberry, beading under the lash of his tongue. Those long legs had wrapped tight around Nolan's hips . . . Pierce had never seen anything more erotic than Lorelei with her mouth stuffed with his cock while Nolan pumped his dick inside her.

A husky laugh erupted from her throat. "No, I have a direct passage behind that mirror."

She pointed to a wide piece of mercurite surrounded by a decorative frame. Stepping over to it, she pressed her palm to the surface. It wavered, the reflective surface clearing in an outward ripple from her touch to reveal a room beyond. Then it slid aside, and she stepped over the mirror's frame and into the well-appointed room.

The men followed her through the opening, stepping into her private sanctuary. Her rooms were decorated in deep colors and smooth fabrics. A fountain gurgled from some hidden corner; Pierce could hear the water running, but couldn't pinpoint the location. Bronze microsilk wallpaper covered the walls, and a wide alcove off the main space was dominated by a bed with diaphanous green covers. Everything that could be mounted to a wall was, including the bed. Gleaming mercurite beams attached the head and foot of the bed to the wall. This was a true indicator of Lorelei's taste. Not the cool, professional, almost sterile office, but the rich, passionate colors of her suite.

He liked it, his shoulders relaxing in the quiet space. What would it be like to come into this place every day and have his mates waiting for him? Dangerous thought, that. He shied away from it. He already knew he shouldn't be doing this, shouldn't touch them, should *never* have touched them. It was too late now, and he wasn't walking away. Not yet. He'd take tonight, and worry about tomorrow when it arrived.

It was a novel approach, one he hadn't tried before.

"I like your bed." A wide smile curved his lips. The movement felt unnatural, but that wasn't unusual with the way this night had been going.

Lorelei's eyebrows lifted, a grin answering his. A sinful little sparkle flashed in her green eyes. "Do you?"

"Yes." He caught her around the waist, tossing her onto the enormous mattress. Her surprised laugh was cut short when she bounced, her thick red curls fanning out across the bed coverings. Her thighs fell open, baring her slick pussy, and she bowed her body toward him. He could see the lips of her sex were still dewy with Nolan's come. Wrapping his fingers around her calves, he pulled her to the edge of the bed and pressed her knees flat. Then he leaned forward to taste.

The essence of her, of Nolan, exploded in his mouth and the wolf couldn't hold back a growl at the intoxicating flavor of it. His. Always his. Both of them. He could hear Nolan moving around the room, opening cabinet doors and rifling through drawers, but Lorelei's deep moan wiped anything else but her from Pierce's mind. He slid his tongue into her wet slit, stabbing into her tight channel. Her muscles clamped around his tongue, and when he growled against her sex, she arched off the bed. "Pierce! Oh, Deus! *Pierce!*"

Lorelei's fingers slid against his scalp, holding him close to her pussy. He bent to the task, licking her sweet juices from the swollen folds. His cock was so hard, it was dripping. He loved the little sounds she made as her pussy spasmed against his lips. The contractions came faster, and he knew she would come soon. He wanted to feel it against his mouth, wanted to taste every nanosecond of her pleasure. She pulled him closer still, one hand on his head, the other gripping his shoulder as she gasped at each movement of his tongue over her hot flesh.

He didn't normally let anyone touch him. If they were close enough to touch him, they were close enough to attack him. Too close.

Even when fucking his lovers, he usually held their hands above their heads or took them from behind so they couldn't reach for him. He'd even bound more than one to make sure they didn't get the chance to touch him.

But not with Nolan and not with Lorelei. With them, he wanted to be petted, stroked. The need went beyond the mere physical, touching something so deep inside him, even the predator within writhed in ecstasy.

He shuddered when Nolan's hands pressed to his naked back, stroking down until they could part his ass cheeks. He went rigid, every muscle in his body locking as he waited.

Lorelei moaned a protest as he stopped moving his mouth. A single fingertip swirled against his anus, some kind of oil heating as it met his skin. He could smell the spice of it, a fragrance Lorelei used sometimes. He groaned and he heard her breath catch as the vibrations stimulated her sex.

Nolan's low, seductive purr filled the room. "Have you ever let another man fuck you, Pierce?"

"No." He didn't like for anyone to touch him, let alone trust them enough to allow those kind of liberties. Fire slammed into his gut at the thought of Nolan taking *him*. Deus, the things these two did to him, *for* him.

"Let me." Nolan's lips pressed between Pierce's shoulder blades. "I want all of you tonight. Let me."

Pierce choked on a breath when the very tip of that slick finger eased into his ass. His muscles shook, his head dropping against Lorelei's inner thigh. "Yes."

A rush of hot, damp air kissed his skin as Nolan let out the breath he'd been holding. "You won't regret it, *querido*."

Pierce closed his eyes and willed it to be true. Even for a moment, he wished he could *believe* that he wouldn't wake up regretting every second of this in the morning. Still, if this was all he would ever have, this one night, then he would take it.

"Don't stop pleasuring Lorelei. She loves to have her pussy licked." The finger slid deeper within him, working up to the second knuckle. The oil eased his passage, and Pierce pushed his hips back to take more. Nolan dropped a violently pink dildo on Lorelei's belly right in front of Pierce's eyes. "And here's something else to make it a little more interesting."

"Nolan, you are such a—" Lorelei's sentence choked off as Pierce gave her pussy a long, slow lick. Her hips squirmed closer as he suckled her hard clit, the slick flesh blooming against his mouth. He scooped up the dildo with one hand and flicked a few of the controls at the base. It vibrated, it glowed a phosphorescent pink, it swiveled and twisted. Excellent. He slid it deep inside her, watching it part the wet lips of her pussy. When he flicked it on and sucked her clit at the same time, she arched off the mattress.

Nolan chuckled quietly, and Pierce didn't have to look to know a wicked smile crossed the younger man's face. He added a second finger to Pierce's ass, stretching the muscles for his long cock. The thought made anticipation burn through Pierce, and he growled against Lorelei's pussy and pressed a higher control on the dildo to light it up. She sobbed on a breath, her fingers tugging on his hair again as she writhed against the microsilk covers. "P-Pierce, please!"

He smiled, batting her hard little clit with the tip of his tongue. Thrusting the dildo in and out, he matched the rhythm Nolan set with his fingers. He swirled the thick digits around in Pierce's anus before delving even deeper. It wasn't enough. He needed more. He needed everything. Lifting his mouth to blow on her glistening red curls, Pierce barked, "Quit teasing, Angelo."

"Yes, *sir.*" Nolan's fingers withdrew and he fitted his hands around Pierce's hips. The head of Nolan's cock probed for entrance in Pierce's ass and he groaned at the painful stretch of his flesh while Nolan's dick sank deep. "You know, I love it when you order me around."

"Deus, *Deus.*" But Pierce's words were muffled against Lorelei's pussy. The wolf in him almost howled with rapture as Nolan slowly withdrew, the drag of their flesh making Pierce groan.

The first few strokes were to let Pierce adjust, but soon Nolan picked up speed and force, driving deep each time. Pierce grunted at the sharp impact of Nolan's thrust, the agonizing pleasure like nothing he'd ever experienced before. He dropped his hands from Lorelei's sex toy, let it vibrate deep within her pussy, and fisted his fingers in the bedcovers beside her hips while Nolan rode him, his movement growing wilder as he ground himself against Pierce's backside.

Pierce worried her clit between his teeth, and her fingers jerked at his hair hard enough to make his eyes water as she came hard against his mouth. He continued to lap and tease and suckle her through her orgasm until he felt her twisting again, until she was building toward another peak. He grinned against her pussy, loving that he could push her so hard so fast and she stayed with him every moment.

He'd never imagined it could be so good, and some terrified part of him realized that the trust he was giving them both now showed just how far over the line he'd gone tonight. Hell, he wasn't even sure *when* he'd crossed the line or even where the line was anymore. Good and bad, right and wrong, wise and foolish. Pleasure and pain. It had all begun to twist and blur.

The harder Nolan thrust into his ass, the harder he suckled Lorelei's wet flesh, nudging his chin against the vibrating dildo to stimulate her, flicking his tongue over her little clit. She screamed over and over again, begging him to stop, begging him to never stop. She'd come so many times, he'd lost count, but a hot rush strummed through his body every time she did, every time Nolan pumped into him. He fought to hold off his own orgasm. He wanted this to last as long as possible—his time with his mates.

His mates. Another rush of pleasure, of some unnamable emotion, went coursing through his veins. Nolan's claws raked down Pierce's hips as he sank deep and came hard. Pierce balled his fingers in the covers and turned his head to press his forehead to Lorelei's thigh, gritting his teeth to keep his control. The roar of his heartbeat in his ears and the ragged panting of his own breath were the only things he heard for long, long moments.

"You didn't come?" Nolan's voice broke the silence. He

eased his cock out of Pierce's ass and a deep-throated purr rolled forth. The jaguar's claws scraped lightly up Pierce's ribs. "That's a very bad habit of yours, *querido*. I think Lorelei and I can help you with that."

"I don't—"

But Nolan pulled him upright and pushed him back against one of the beams that held Lorelei's bed off the ground. She pulled out the dildo and shut it down, slithered off the mattress, and joined Nolan so that both of them dropped to their knees before Pierce. The jaguar's fingers wrapped tight around the base of Pierce's dick while Lorelei's little pink tongue trailed after a bead of come that seeped from the head.

It was the most incredible sensation in the world having both of his mates suck his cock at once. His fists clenched at his sides, his muscles shaking. Deus, his whole body was shaking. His hands were shaking. He'd faced every imaginable deadly situation and been certain he was going to die more than once and he'd never flinched.

His mates touched him and he wasn't sure his legs would stay under him long enough for him to come.

So, he buried his fingers in their hair and held on for the ride. His cock throbbed with a need so intense it burned. Lorelei sucked the head between her full lips, working her tongue along the shaft. Nolan's mouth was almost rough as he mouthed the balls. His claws sank into Pierce's thigh, and he shuddered at the pain with his pleasure.

They worked him in perfect tandem, setting just the right rhythm to have him on the verge of orgasm within moments . . . and to keep him there without letting him come. Sweat slipped down his face, and he panted for breath. Blood rushed hot and fast in his veins, and his hands tightened in their long hair to urge them faster.

They slowed down.

A low growl rumbled in his chest. Deus, they were good. "If the two of you don't let me come . . ."

"You've always seemed to enjoy prolonged agony, *querido.* We're just giving you what you like." Nolan's lips brushed the base of Pierce's dick when he spoke, and Lorelei's hum of agreement vibrated along the entire shaft.

A rough howl ripped from his throat, and he wasn't certain he'd survive this with his sanity intact. And he didn't care, if it meant the last thing he remembered was his mates sucking him off. He closed his eyes and groaned, rolling his head against the beam. "Deus, hurry the fuck up before I die."

Lorelei let his cock slip from between her lips to slide her hot tongue down the underside of the shaft. Nolan's mouth closed over Pierce's dick, sucking him hard until the head nudged against the back of his throat. The jaguar's deep purr was the last thing Pierce heard before his world exploded around him. He came hard, his hips arching again and again, and their mouths continued to wring him dry. His hands cradled the backs of their heads as he shuddered.

He knew, somewhere in the back of his mind, that nothing in his life had ever been as perfect as this moment. Contentment wound through him and he smiled, a real, wide, genuine smile. Then he laughed, a rusty bark of sound that was echoed by Lorelei's musical giggle and Nolan's soft chuckle.

Sometimes life was very, very good to a man. This was one of those rare times.

Nolan watched the wolf sag against the mercurite beam on Lorelei's bed. They knelt before Pierce and worked to steady their breathing, the scent of sex ripe in the air. She leaned her head on Nolan's shoulder, slipping her hand down to curl her fingers around his. He had no idea why, but the simple touch made his heart trip. Squeezing her slim hand in his much bigger one, he brought them to his lips to kiss her fingers. Her green eyes lifted to meet his, and a soft smile that was just for him curled her lush lips. He opened his mouth to say something, but nothing emerged.

When he looked up at Pierce, the quiet pleasure in the wolf's gaze as he looked back down at the two of them made Nolan's heart clench tighter. He didn't know what any of it meant, but he liked it. It would be far too easy to become accustomed to. He shook that thought from his head and made a lazy smile quirk his lips.

Pierce straightened and stretched, a grin flashing his white teeth. "I don't know about the two of you, but I could use a shower."

He proffered a hand to each of them, and Nolan caught his wrist to let himself be hauled to his feet. Lorelei slid her fingers into Pierce's hand and rose gracefully. They formed a circle, the three of them. United. It was a disturbing and tantalizing notion. Nolan dropped his hands as Lorelei's laugh bubbled out. "In addition to the bed you like so much, I happen to have a shower, too."

The wolf lifted a brow. "Do you?"

"I also have a whirlpool." She leaned closer to him and he dropped a quick kiss on her lips.

"Now, that's interesting." He kissed her again, slower and deeper. "I don't think I've ever seen one of those outside a penthouse like, say, Hunter's."

She hummed in her throat, smiling against his lips. "I had one installed in the Turkish Bath fantasy room my clients can use. At the same time, I had a private one embedded in the floor of my wash closet."

"Let's not let it go to waste, then." He laughed softly, lifting his free hand to stroke her jaw as he kissed her.

Something sweet tightened in Nolan's chest as he watched

them banter. He'd never seen either of them so . . . open, so relaxed. Never felt so at ease himself. It made him crave something he didn't even understand, didn't even believe was possible.

It was stupid. This wouldn't last past dawn, it never did. There was no permanence. There sure as hell wasn't such a thing as forever. Not for him, not for any of them. They were too dark, too damaged. Even Pierce, for all his upstanding goodness.

But Nolan felt as though there was something more there, if only he knew how to reach out and take it, the way he'd told Pierce to tonight. At the time, he'd meant sex. Now, he wasn't so certain.

Dragging in a deep breath, he turned for the wash closet. "Last one in takes it up the ass."

"Nolan!" Lorelei's laughter bounced around the room as they all jolted into a half-run and tussled with each other to get into the whirlpool first. Pierce leaped past both of them into the water, splashing around until he came up beside Nolan and jerked his legs out from under him. He shouted a laugh and tumbled into the whirlpool, coming up sputtering. Lorelei grinned and hopped into his arms.

He caught the light sound of her giggle with his mouth and dipped them both beneath the waterline. The wet heat flowed around them, sliding over their flesh like a liquid caress. That, added to Lorelei's tongue twining with his and licking the inside of his mouth, made him groan. Her legs snapped around his waist, bringing her pussy up against the rigid arc of his cock. Stroking the head of his dick over her slick lips and clit, he teased them both with heart-stopping efficiency. He slid his fingers up her back to tangle in her hair. His lungs began to burn from holding his breath so long, but he couldn't make himself stop kissing her. Her slender claws slid forth to bite into his shoulders, and she wrenched her mouth away from his. A hot twinge shot through his injured arm, the first time he'd noticed the wound since they'd begun their sexual games.

Shoving his feet against the bottom of the pool, he propelled them upward. Both of them sucked in oxygen, and he smoothed her sodden curls back from her face. Her arms linked behind his neck and she pressed her forehead to his, the quick rush of her breath cooling the water on his skin. "Well. That was exciting."

He chuckled and the vibration of it rubbed his cock against her. A little smile played over her full lips and she rotated her torso to slide her tight nipples against his chest. The stimulation made his cock ache, and he flexed his hips to enter her with the tip. She hummed in pleasure, moving with him in infinitesimal strokes. His jaw locked at the feel of her inner muscles closing around the head of his dick, fisting each time he withdrew as though trying to keep him within her and draw him deeper.

"That is possibly the sexiest thing I've ever seen." Pierce's voice was little more than a sub-vocal wolfish growl. Nolan turned to see him lounging against the side of the whirlpool, his arms lying along the rim. His eyes had turned to fiery silver while he watched them.

Lorelei pushed at Nolan's shoulders, and he let her swim away from him. "I thought you both said you wanted to wash up."

"Ah, yes." Pierce grabbed a bar of soap from the edge of the pool and tossed it to Nolan. Nature and years of honing his reflexes made it a simple thing to snap out his hand to catch it.

Gliding through the swirling water toward the wolf, he worked a soapy lather between his hands, dropped the bar into the water, and ran both palms down Pierce's body. The wolf kept his arms up on the ledge and let Nolan touch him, wash him, but his gray eyes betrayed how much he liked what Nolan was doing to him. He spent far too much time washing the wolf's thick cock before he slid his hands around to the taut globes of his ass. His finger slid into the muscled ring of

Pierce's anus much easier than it had an hour ago. Both men groaned. Nolan jolted when slim hands slid between his own ass cheeks and probed him the same way he had Pierce. "Lorelei."

Her other hand stroked slick soap up and down his cock, while Pierce's hand dropped down to help her. It felt so good, he purred. The wolf's thumb rolled over the tip while Lorelei's finger set a swift rhythm in his ass. When she pressed on his prostate, he choked, snapped his arm around her waist, and dragged her through the water until she was sandwiched between Pierce and him. "You know, I don't think our dirty girl here has bothered to wash herself. We should make sure nothing got missed."

"Of course." Pierce pulled her legs over his thighs one at a time. It spread her wide, opening her to both their exploring hands. "We'll be very thorough."

"Yes, we will." Nolan cupped her soft ass in his palms, massaging it and letting her know exactly what he had in mind for her. "Plus, she *was* the last one in the water."

"Oh, no. I'm in for it now." She chuckled and let her head fall back on his shoulder, arching her torso toward Pierce. He caught a taut nipple between his teeth and bit down hard enough to make her cry out. Her hand reached back to fist in Nolan's hair, using it for leverage to lift herself out of the water and into the wolf's mouth.

Grabbing her hips, Nolan sank into her pussy from behind. The wolf's teeth flashed in a white smile against her breast as her body jolted with Nolan's quick, rough thrusts. She moaned each time he penetrated her, rolling her hips to push herself toward orgasm, and he grinned. He wasn't even close to done with her, and he wasn't going to make it that easy for her to come.

Soon, but not just yet.

As swiftly as he'd pushed into her sweet heat, he pulled out.

Her fingers twisted in his hair. "Nolan, I am going to hurt you if you—"

Her squeal turned into a moan as Pierce obviously lived up to his name. Nolan slipped his hands down the smooth skin of her back and between her buttocks until he reached the tight recess of her anus. He worked one, then another, finger into her ass, pressing against the thin wall that separated him from Pierce's cock. He rubbed her and the wolf at the same time. They both shuddered, groaning. A fierce smile parted his lips. After wanting them so long, he *loved* that he could make them respond so strongly.

Pulling his fingers away, he pressed the tip of his dick to her anus. Pierce stopped moving, jerking her legs wider to give Nolan greater access. Their gazes met and they shared the moment of supreme masculine triumph that came with making a woman scream with pleasure. He pushed in slowly, not wanting to hurt her. Neither he nor Pierce was a small man, so he eased one micrometer in at a time, gritting his teeth the whole time as her ass bore down on his dick. He could feel Pierce's cock deep within her as well, and it just intensified the moment for him.

Somehow, with them, everything was better. This wasn't the game that Lorelei accused him of playing with his clients—this was more serious than he'd ever been in his life. It wasn't just fucking, it was a *connection* to these two people. And it was amazing.

He'd always known Lorelei had a soft spot for him, and after Pierce had saved him tonight, he was fairly certain the wolf cared. That dangerous word again, the thing he avoided. Caring. Emotion. But there it was, wrapping around his twisted, scarred soul until he couldn't breathe. He could only move his body and show them how he felt in the only way he knew how. Sex.

Lovemaking.

Deus, the thought alone was enough to make him freeze,

make cold sweat blend with the hot steam coming off the whirlpool's water. Lorelei glanced back at him, her eyebrows lifting, a question in her emerald gaze. He could still feel Pierce moving within her. He tried to smile, but the emotion expanding in his chest made it impossible. Pushing her hair away from her shoulder, he bent to kiss her damp, satiny flesh. The rough speed and urgency had been cast aside. Lorelei and Pierce. Pierce and Lorelei. They were different. He ran his hands down her arms. She'd been used for careless pleasure too many times in her life. She needed to be cherished, worshipped.

Both of them did, these people who had insinuated themselves into his soul.

He slowed his thrusts, grinding his pelvis against Lorelei until she mewed with pleasure. Her fingers tightened in his hair when he penetrated her, and she moaned when both he and Pierce entered her at once. The wolf had followed Nolan's lead without a word, without question, some instinct telling him what his lovers needed.

Lust pulled the skin taut across Pierce's sharp cheekbones, made his eyes gleam silver. He met Nolan's gaze and the secrets there, all the things the quiet man never said, seemed to crowd his expression. His mouth opened, and for a moment, Nolan thought he'd finally say what it was he'd been hiding since they met. He balanced on a razor's edge of anticipation, but Pierce's mouth closed again. Then he looked away, and the moment was lost.

Disappointment he knew he shouldn't feel shook through Nolan, and he closed his eyes to hide it. He sucked in a deep breath and began rocking his hips more solidly into Lorelei. Her inner muscles clamped around him and she worked her hips with his, with Pierce's, to find the ecstasy their bodies had promised her. He kissed her shoulder again, opening his mouth to taste her salty-sweet flavor. His fangs slid forward to score her flesh as her ass clenched tight around him on his next thrust. The water swirling around them only enhanced all the sensations ripping through him, and beads of sweat and steam slipped down his face.

Fire and ice raced through his bloodstream and his heart pounded hard. Hearing her gasps and the wolf's groans only drove him onward. He slammed deep, rotating his hips.

"Nolan!" she screamed and arched hard. Pierce took the opportunity to suck her nipple into his mouth. She sobbed, her body shaking. "Pierce!"

Her hips jerked, jolting back and forth as she demanded without words that they make her come. The two men worked together, pistoning at a hard tandem rhythm into her sleek body. The water splashed and sloshed around them as they moved faster and faster.

The hot press and drag of his flesh inside her tight ass was enough to shove him over the edge and he slammed deeper than he'd ever been as he came in long jets. Pierce's thrusts reverberated through all of them, nudging Nolan's cock through the thin layer of Lorelei's flesh that separated them. She screamed when Pierce buried himself as deep as Nolan had, her muscles clenching and unclenching as she reached orgasm. The wolf growled as he joined them, his body shuddering.

Starved lungs heaving for breath, Nolan dropped his forehead to Lorelei's shoulder until the shaking stopped. It was the best he'd ever had, and it still wasn't what he wanted. Needed.

He didn't even know if he could handle getting what he needed. Hell, he couldn't even admit what he needed to himself in the privacy of his own mind. He swallowed and closed his eyes, hoping against hope that this time he was right to trust, that this time he wouldn't be betrayed when he was least prepared to protect himself.

6

"Open up!" A fist slammed against the door and Pierce arched out of bed, using the adrenaline rush to shift into his wolf form. He hit the ground on all four paws, whipping around just as Lorelei's bedroom door exploded inward.

Baring his teeth in a low growl, he waited to see who came through. A young man wearing an armored vest with the name of Pierce's agency emblazoned on it stepped inside. He knew this kid—something Reagan. He'd just made agent and been transferred to Pierce's field office. Shit. He stifled a groan, shifting back into human form and rising to his full height. "Reagan."

All the blood leached from the young man's face and he looked like he just might crap himself. He recovered himself quickly enough and holstered his weapon. "Agent V-Vaughn, sir."

A flicker of movement caught Piece's attention and he watched Nolan stretch catlike and rise from the bed. The smile that curved his lips didn't reach his dark eyes, but the jade's charm oozed from his body language. "Really, Vaughn, if you needed a wake-up call, we could have arranged for a much more pleasant one."

Pierce grunted, not amused in the least, and stomped through the open passageway to Lorelei's office, snatching up his clothes, gun, and badge.

The young agent moved forward so he could keep Pierce within view. "Agent Vaughn, you know these people?"

"Obviously," he growled, stuffing himself into his pants and sealing the fly. His thoughts whipped in endless circles of turmoil, and he was glad of a few semiprivate moments to lock down his emotions and smooth his expression. A cold ball of dread sank to the pit of his stomach. He jerked his shirt and shoes on before he secured his weapon on his belt. Then he rejoined the others in the bedroom.

Reagan's brow creased as he motioned between Pierce and his mates. "I didn't think you were the type for jades."

"You don't know me." Wasn't that the truth? Hell, after the night he'd had, Pierce wasn't even certain he knew himself anymore. The ball of dread expanded until Pierce could feel nothing else. This was why he'd never touched his mates before, why he *should never* have touched his mates. The one thing that had ever truly mattered to him was his job, and being caught with his mates might not ruin his career, but staying with them would.

He was a fool to have indulged himself, and in the process, hurt them all. His gut twisted and he fisted his fingers to still their shaking.

"No, sir. Of course not, sir." Reagan backpedaled so fast it would have been funny if Pierce's mind weren't churning. "I apologize. Sir."

He grunted again and gave the kid a stony look. It wasn't his fault that he'd brought to life Pierce's worst nightmare, but it was difficult to remember that when he saw how quickly his perfect night had shattered around him.

Reagan swallowed and rushed to speak. "I-I need to ask Mr. Angelo where he was last night."

Lorelei rose from the bed unhurriedly and the young agent's face flushed, his eyes glazing as he stared at her nude form. Every movement of her body was calculated, and Pierce could see in her eyes that she'd discerned far more than either he or Nolan would like. The woman was far too cunning for her own good. She pulled on a robe, a small smile gracing her face. "Isn't it obvious where all of us were last night?"

"Right." The agent blushed, finally averting his eyes. He coughed into his fist. "You were all here between ten and twelve last night?"

"I was over on Crighton around ten." Nolan folded his arms and didn't bother to cover himself, but he tilted his injured shoulder away from Reagan's line of sight. "Working another job, you understand."

"Ah. Yes." The agent swallowed, but didn't flinch as Nolan gave him a very obvious once-over.

Pierce arched an eyebrow. His mates were both a bit too clever, but keeping Reagan off-balance might make this a lot quicker. "And that's where I picked him up and brought him back here for our appointment."

Lorelei jumped in with her most engaging smile. "I was waiting for them here at about ten thirty. We haven't left all night."

Reagan's gaze flicked back to Nolan. "Can you provide the name of your first . . . uh . . ."

"Client?" He supplied helpfully. "No. I never knew his name. I don't ask, they don't tell. It's best for all concerned that a jade be discreet." He slanted a very pointed glance at Pierce—

a reminder to Reagan that discretion would be appreciated about Pierce's whereabouts the night before.

He almost snorted. As if that would save him. Buzz got around fast in the intelligence community. There was no doubt people knew of Pierce's sudden liking for jadehouses, and when they heard about him being found with a suspected felon and the most notorious madam alive ... Well, it wouldn't look good. Sex was one thing, but mating? If he kept this up, he could kiss good-bye everything he'd ever worked for. Decades of service smeared by one night of lust.

"Yes, yes, of course. I understand." The kid nodded, glanced from Pierce to Nolan to Lorelei and back to Pierce. He looked more than a little dazed that his little break-in hadn't gone as planned. "I'll let you get back to your appointment."

"Thank you, Agent Reagan." He inclined his head toward the door in an obvious invitation to leave. "Close the door as best you can."

"Right. Uh ... sorry about that." Reagan slanted Lorelei an apologetic glance as he moved to leave.

When the door shut behind Reagan, Pierce turned toward his mates. He looked at them both, memorizing their faces. This was the last time he'd let himself see them. He'd gone too far, and he'd never be able to resist now that he knew what it was like to touch them, to taste them, to laugh with them, to hold them in his arms while they slept. Deus, he hadn't slept that well in years. Misery wrapped around his soul, a pain he didn't know how to handle. He needed his work more than anything. He always had, and he understood that about himself. If some part of him wished he didn't have to choose between that and his mates, it was better left unexamined and unmentioned. "I have to go."

Lorelei's fingers linked and unlinked in front of her, but her face was a cool mask of indifference. "I understand."

"No, you don't." A bark of bitter laughter ripped from his throat. "You don't understand anything."

Nolan sank down on the mattress with a heavy sigh. "I know this could be a problem for your job, but you're hardly the first federal agent to fuck a jade or two. Lorelei and I both have before."

"You're my mates." The words exploded forth before he could contain them, but he couldn't regret them. Maybe they deserved the truth before it was over.

Two voices breathed one incredulous word. *"What?"*

He closed his eyes, the dread and pain twisting together until he couldn't see straight. He wanted to run, but he doubted he could escape what was inside him. "You heard me."

Lorelei hugged her arms around herself. "B-both of us?"

"Yes." Pierce rubbed a hand over the back of his neck, a dull throb echoing through his skull. "Would I have ever come here if you weren't? You know by now *I'm* not the kind of federal agent who pays for sex no matter what the rest of them do."

And none of them wanted to mate with a jade. No, that was Pierce's own personal hell.

Nolan rose to his feet, some quiet light flickering to life in his dark gaze as he took a step forward. "Pierce—"

"I have to go. Now." Pierce met their gazes. "I'm never coming back, and I'm never going to see either of you again. I'm sorry it has to be this way. It's not either of your faults. I wish it was different—wish *I* was different—but I'm not." He dragged in a deep breath that threatened to strangle him, swallowing the bile that rose in his throat as the reality sank in of what he had to do to keep the life he'd worked so hard for. "I need to go to the agency and try to straighten out the mess I've made."

He couldn't look at them when he turned for the broken door, didn't want to see their reactions to his words. Perhaps they wouldn't care. Perhaps this was just another fuck for them. They had been jades for years. But he knew it was a lie. Lorelei had her rules, and Nolan had his side job, which meant neither of them would have touched Pierce unless they felt at least some of what he did.

He could only hope that the sharpness of the agony and regret would fade in time. Then he wouldn't have to feel anything at all.

7

Lorelei's thoughts spun in maddening circles. They were Pierce's *mates*? She'd known he was a gray wolf-shifter—one of the few who mated for life—but as a mink, the concept was totally foreign to her animal nature. It hadn't occurred to her that *Pierce* might sense . . . But it explained so much about why he'd made such a fixture of himself, didn't it? But he didn't want them to be his mates, didn't even want to *see* them again. It stung, even though *she* wasn't the one fighting her instincts and she knew she shouldn't let it bother her. In his position, would she be any different? He was a federal agent and she and Nolan were not included in even the broadest definition of upstanding citizens.

She'd known it couldn't last past the night, known that reality would rip apart the fragile and beautiful little fantasy they'd had together. Even knowing all that didn't change the fact that there was a man whose instincts said he was *made for her* and he just . . . didn't want her.

It hurt.

No amount of reasoning or justification made it not burn like acid etched into her skin.

He didn't want her. He didn't want Nolan. They weren't good enough for him. Her stomach clenched, and she pressed a hand against it, trying to maintain the cool professionalism she was known for. No one who grew up in the Vermilion survived without getting up close and personal with disappointment and loss, but somehow this felt worse. She shouldn't care, but she did. She should have known better, but it hadn't stopped her.

Pulling in a deep breath, she forced her mind back into order. There was no future with these men. Nothing could or would change that.

She followed Nolan into her office as he bent to snatch his clothes off the floor and stuff himself into them. Every jerky movement from the normally graceful man conveyed his inner turmoil, his anger. She just didn't know who he was angry with. Himself, Pierce, the whole situation, life in general? It could be any or all of the above with Nolan. His easy charm always hid a deep-seated rage, but he wasn't trying to hide anything right now. The bitterness was carved into the set lines of his face, the twitching muscle in his jaw. She watched his shirt cover the nanopatch she'd set over his wound.

"Why do you do it?" The question came out even though she'd promised herself she'd never ask.

He froze, a dozen emotions she couldn't name flashing through his eyes. "What?"

She lifted an eyebrow. "Don't make me repeat myself. You know what I'm talking about."

Yes, he knew. They both did. The little inconsistencies had all added up after a while. Lorelei wasn't stupid and she wasn't naïve—hell, she'd helped her sister cover up a homicide once, so she knew the kind of lies a person had to tell. It had taken her a while to figure Nolan out, but that was years ago. She just had too much of a soft spot for him. She always had. She'd told herself if it ever affected Tail, she'd fire him. She couldn't put herself and her other employees at risk for him. It was a gamble she couldn't take. Until today, he'd managed to keep the two halves of his life separate, and that had made her foolish little game of denial too easy. But the time for easy, for denial, for soft spots and weaknesses was over.

His dark gaze went blank before it focused on the kleather chaise. "For the money. You know what it's like to grow up with nothing, to *be* nothing. Now I have something. I decide what I do, when, and for how much. It's not much different than being a jade."

"Why?" Her derisive laugh came out a pained rasp. "Because you're still selling your soul along with your services?"

His jaw worked for a moment before he spoke. "You're one to talk, Madam Chase."

She flinched, folding her arms around herself. "You think my jades would be better off with someone else? I know what it costs them. They don't have to stay. I don't own them or lock them in like a prison warden."

"I know." Still, he didn't look at her. They both knew what was coming. "Any jade would give their arm to work at Tail. You're good to them. Us."

She shook her head, swiping at a tear she was ashamed to have let fall. "When does it end? When will you have enough?"

"Lorelei." He took a step toward her, concern on his face, his troubled gaze finally meeting hers.

Her spine snapped straight and she shook her head, denying whatever comfort he offered. "Killing people is illegal, Nolan. You'll get caught eventually. That's what happens to criminals."

A choked laugh strangled from him. "Is this what you used to tell Delilah?"

"Yes." Her sister had been a thief, and she'd worried every day she knew Delilah was on a job, terrified she'd lose her only family. Deus, she wished her sister was here now, wished there was someone who wouldn't make this so horrible, who wouldn't rip her heart out just by being themselves. "But Delilah isn't a criminal anymore. Hunter has her working for him now as a security expert."

The corners of Nolan's lips quirked in a humorless smile. "Rich people pay her to break into their own houses now and steal things, rather than other people."

"Yes."

He shook his head, cold, hard self-acceptance in his gaze. "I can't. This is what I do."

"I understand." She took a breath, forced the businesswoman, the ruthless madam to make the decision, and said the hardest words she'd ever had to say in her life. "Please go."

"What?" A flicker of panic entered his eyes, and anger followed on its heels.

"This just made me see how dangerous having you here is. I'm gambling with my life, my business, my customers' lives, my jades' lives. For what? So you can feel like you're worth something? A job won't give you that—killing people for money won't give you that." She made her voice steely, clenching her fingers into tight knots as she willed him to listen to her. "It's no different than fucking people for money. You have to find what's worth living for somewhere else. Somewhere *inside* you. Right now, you're just begging to throw your life away. I can't let you throw everyone else's away, too."

"You don't understand."

A sad smile curved her mouth and she shook her head, knowing she hadn't gotten through to him, knowing she never would. "Yes. I do. Better than most, and you know it."

Utter pain filtered through the hostility in his eyes, and it nearly broke her. "Please . . ."

"Please, what? This isn't negotiable, Nolan." She hugged herself tighter, wanting nothing more than to have some privacy to curl up, cry, and lick her wounds. She arched a cool brow instead. "You're welcome to come into Tail as a customer, but you don't work for me anymore."

"I—" His hand clenched and unclenched at his sides, and she could see that he was willing the rage to win out over the pain and loss. It was so much easier to be self-righteously angry and bitter, wasn't it?

This was how it always ended. This was why she could only rely on herself to make good choices. Nolan was a bad bet, and knowing she'd let her guard down with him and Pierce even a little scared her to death. Breaking the rules, taking a risk, trusting anyone else to do the smart thing—it was futile and she knew better. "Are you going to give up your work as an assassin?"

The muscle began twitching in his jaw again. "No."

She nodded. She'd known what his answer would be, and no matter how much she cared about him, she couldn't afford to keep him. It gave her a whole new perspective on Pierce's decision to leave, but didn't help her feel any better. It just made her feel worse. Poor Pierce. Poor Nolan. Poor all of them. "Then . . . please leave."

"Don't do this." He took another step toward her, and she retreated. She wasn't strong enough to take any more today. It was over. All of it. And she just felt empty, sad, and more alone than she'd ever been in her life.

"It's done." She closed her eyes, swallowing. Turning for her bedroom, she walked away from him and didn't let herself look back. "Go. Now."

Nolan stormed after Lorelei into her room, so many emotions he didn't *want* to feel roiling inside him. It couldn't end like this. It couldn't.

She spun around with a soft gasp as he approached, the same agony he felt reflected in those green eyes. It just made him even angrier. What happened to how much she *cared* about him? What happened to Pierce setting aside his duty to help Nolan? What happened to all the sweet hope that he'd felt only hours ago? He didn't even know what he should feel anymore, everything had been flipped over and over and he'd been dumped out like the trash he'd been since he was thirteen.

A snarl built in his throat as he invaded her personal space, moving close enough to feel her warm breath brush his lips. "Fine. I'll leave, but there's one more thing."

"What's that?" She didn't back down, but her breathing sped, her gaze darting from his mouth to his eyes and back again. He could sense her excitement and how she tried to master it. She might want him to leave, but she also just *wanted* him.

A smile kicked up one side of his lips. "Kiss me good-bye."

"Nol—"

He cut her off, slamming his mouth down over hers. Her hands lifted, her nails digging into his shoulders as he jerked her close. Her soft curves rubbed against him and a sound somewhere between a hiss and a purr rumbled up from his chest. She struggled against him, bit his lip, tried to kick him, but she was no match for his strength.

The idea of it being over, gone, tormented him. He'd always known this moment was coming, but he had to hold on for a while longer, had to have one last taste. He kissed her until she moaned into his mouth, until her tongue twined with his, and the deepening scent of her desire was almost enough to make him come.

He stumbled back until the back of his knees hit a chair, pulling Lorelei with him when he collapsed into it. The kleather creaked under their combined weight as he jerked her on to his lap. Her breathing hitched in little gasps, passion flushing her cheeks. He shoved her robe off her shoulders and ripped open the seal on his pants, letting his cock spring free. She stared at him, her lips swollen and damp from his kiss, and his fingers bit into her hips as he positioned her over his cock. "Ride me, Lorelei."

"This is a bad idea." But her slim fingers wrapped around his shaft, rubbing the head of his dick against her soaking pussy. Then she sank down on him, taking all of him in one swift plunge.

His head fell back on the chair, his fangs erupting as he hissed. Deus, it felt so good. It always felt good with Lorelei.

And this would be the last time.

No. He refused to think about that. There was only her, only this. Right now, nothing else mattered.

The muscles in her thighs bunched and flexed against his as she rode him hard. He lifted his hips into each movement, meeting her halfway. The feel of her slick walls closing around his cock made him think his head was going to explode. His blood rushed too hot and fast through his veins, his flesh felt too tight. He groaned as he entered her pussy again and again, loving every vivid, overwhelming sensation. It was too fucking good to be real. Their skin slapped together with each thrust, and no other sound broke the silence in the room. They didn't speak, just clung tightly to each other as they moved, his claws digging into her skin and the points of hers scored his shoulders.

Their coupling was harsh and desperate. For two professionals, there was no finesse, no coy seduction. This was animalistic fucking, a need for closeness that neither of them could have.

She rolled her hips, grinding her clit against his pelvis. Her breath caught and he felt the deep contractions of her orgasm around his dick. Her gaze lost focus, a sob breaking from her. His body locked tight as he came with her, groaning as it, like everything good in life, ended far too soon.

They clung to each other, too many years of friendship tangling with too many lies. He felt the moment she came back down to earth, her muscles tightening as she withdrew in every possible way. Some desperate part of himself wanted to haul her back into his arms. How could it all be over so soon? How had he managed to keep her this long before she dropped him?

Pierce, he knew he'd never see again, but if he could hold on to *one* thing. His voice dropped to a low, cajoling rumble. "Lorelei—"

She shoved her hair out of her eyes, anger vibrating through every movement. "No! I said you have to leave, and that's final. You know as well as I do that good sex isn't what it takes to have a future together. Please, Nolan. Don't make this harder than it has to be. Pack your things and *go.*"

The tears shimmering in her green eyes were enough to stop his heart. In all the years he'd known her and all the extreme situations he'd seen her in, he'd never once seen her lose her cool.

She didn't wait for him to reply; she spun on her heel, shifting as she went. In the blink of an eye, she'd become a mink. Her claws scrabbled against the smooth floor as she ran. A flash of sleek auburn fur was the last thing he saw before she darted into a hidden hole far too small for him to follow through, even if he'd tried to pursue her.

He didn't.

For a long time, he sat there and stared at the bed he'd spent the night in with Lorelei and Pierce. Their mingled scents still permeated the air, and he imagined if he ran his hand down the sheets, he could feel the warmth of their skin.

The best night of his life, and it resulted in the same thing he always received from something he wanted badly. Rejection. It burned the pit of his belly, and his fingers clenched into tight fists on his thighs. Rage, bitterness, grief, and utter emptiness expanded inside him until he couldn't draw breath.

He loved them. And they didn't want him.

Typical.

8

Nolan rented a room in a crumbling building at the edge of the Vermilion. It had about fourteen quick escape routes if he needed them and a lot of convenient places to hide his gear. Perfect for his needs, and just right for a down-on-his-luck jade.

It also reeked of urine, had things growing on the wash closet walls that he didn't want to get near enough to identify, and he'd yet to find a comfortable enough position on the narrow bed to actually get much sleep. Then again, it could be that every time he closed his eyes he was haunted by the memories of Lorelei and Pierce, of a few fragile moments of hope and trust, of the looks on their faces when they shattered his soul.

His palmtop computer vibrated gently, the screen lighting with an incoming message. The number belonged to one of his regular johns, but all that mattered was that it wasn't Lorelei or Pierce, so he swallowed, closed his eyes, and tamped down on the hope that cut like a ragged blade. It had been a week. He'd assumed this *feeling* would have begun to fade. It hadn't.

He needed to get back to work, needed to get past what had only been a fantasy and get on with his real life. Sucking in a deep breath made him gag a bit on the stench, and he scooped up his palmtop to access the vidcache. His client wanted to know if he was free for the night. His stomach twisted a bit at the thought of being with someone besides Pierce or Lorelei, but he ruthlessly reminded himself that neither of them would care what he did with his time.

This client was the perfect way to get over whatever hang-ups Nolan might have now about fucking for creds. Longtime john who only liked to watch, no touching. It gave the man some deniability in his own mind about wanting other men. Nolan huffed out a laugh. Whatever they needed to tell themselves to sleep at night. Gritting his teeth, he keyed in an acceptance and a meeting place on the palmtop's vidpad and sent the message before he could talk himself out of it.

He threw on some kleather pants and boots and slid the thickest rings he had into his nipples and lit them up. A confirmation from his client was all he needed before he escaped out into the night for his rendezvous. If there was one thing he could count on, it was his work. He'd always done it and had always been good at it. The lies were easy after so many years. A little flattery here, a smile there, and he could have any customer eating out of the palm of his hand.

His belly cramped when the man took him to Tail, intent on playing the wild vidgame, Space Race. Nolan couldn't blame him, it had always been fun for them. But the last place he wanted to be was back in Lorelei's realm. The familiar scent and sound of the place wrapped around him the moment the large iris front door parted to allow them in. It was a comfort and a torment.

Deus help him.

A huge vidscreen was embedded in the wall in front of the game players. He watched two other couples playing the game and refused to look at the bar to see if Lorelei was working there. Each client used controllers to try to kill each other's spaceships on the screen. Every time they took out the opponent's ship, a narrow platform the jade straddled thrust a large phallus into them. Repeatedly. While the platform vibrated. It was usually the jades' favorite game to play, but Nolan couldn't muster an ounce of enthusiasm. *Why* did he have to be *here*? His luck just wasn't improving. What if Lorelei was watching? He could smell her, but refused to allow himself to look for her. What if she'd seen him and turned away so she wouldn't have to watch? Did he sicken her now that she'd had to accept what he did when he wasn't playing the jade? He didn't know. He didn't know anything anymore.

After one team managed to kill all of the other's ships, it was Nolan's turn to play. They waited a few moments while the game self-sanitized its gear. Another couple—this time two customers rather than a customer and a jade—approached the other player station. Nolan smiled and nodded to both of them as he shoved aside the sick feeling in the pitch of his stomach, stripped, and swung his leg over the narrow platform. Seating himself in just the right place, he settled into the familiar position. He knew how this worked, it was all rote. He only hoped that helped him survive this. He flicked the test switch, and the lubricated mercurite phallus built into the platform pressed into his anus.

The inhuman metallic cock stretched him wide, but the slide was smooth and sent a shudder through his body. A few slow pumps got him used to the feel before the rough ride began. He shifted, adjusting the fit of the game's phallus. Then it withdrew, the vidscreen lit up, and the game began.

His stomach clenched tighter and tighter until he thought he would vomit. Each time his client made a ship explode, he was impaled. The platform bucked and vibrated underneath him and his cock hardened at the stimulation of the mecurite cock riding against his prostate. But it was biological, not passionate. He put on the prerequisite show, yelling and cheering the way he'd be expected to, but it was empty. His soul ached, his body had betrayed him.

Everyone had.

He swallowed, his body shaking, but not with orgasm. His client looked at him, looked at his raging erection. He closed his eyes for a moment, then forced a flirtatious smile to his face. He was going to have to get off, whether his body wanted to or not. That was what his client wanted.

He was a sure thing. He always had been. He gave his customers what they wanted, and he always got off on how he played them.

Not tonight.

Frustration crawled through him. This wasn't like him. Why wasn't he aroused by the game the way he'd always been? Why did even the thought of coming for someone else make his chest ache? Anger and pain and too many other feelings he didn't want slammed through his system.

Orgasm. He had to do it, so he swallowed, curled his fingers around his cock to stroke the length of it, and forced his mind to the most erotic images he could think of.

All he could see was Pierce's face, the hard planes of his features tightening with lust. Lorelei's body arching between them. Her hands, her smile, her eyes sparkling with heat and desire. Her mouth suckling Pierce's cock while Nolan slid deep inside her. He choked, the memory so real he could almost touch it.

He wanted it to be real.

And Lorelei could be watching now, just as she had been the night she and Pierce had looked on while he fucked that couple in the Peep Show. Deus, having them near had made him burn, so he focused on that, thought about how good it would be if

Lorelei was watching him now, how her gaze would slide over his skin like a caress, how her lips would part as her breathing sped.

Pressure built behind his eyes, anguish and lust fisting in his gut until he wanted to howl. He pumped himself hard with one hand while the claws of the other hand dug into his thigh, slicing the flesh, and he welcomed the pain. It gave him something to feel besides the agony that had been twisting and twisting inside him for days.

He threw back his head, a jaguar's scream ripping from his throat as he came hard. The hot fluid bubbled between his fingers and splattered his stomach and thighs.

When it was over, the only thing he knew for certain was that he couldn't do this again.

It took him almost an hour of drinking his client under the table to shake himself loose for the evening. Walking through the Vermilion half-drunk wasn't the most intelligent thing he could do, but the alternative was staying at Tail with a man who wanted him to perform more sexual favors and risking a run-in with Lorelei. None of it sounded even remotely palatable to Nolan just then. So, he'd have to take his chances on his way back to his flat.

He was only staggering a bit, not enough for most people to notice, and he stayed to the well-lit areas. It didn't make him any safer, but it would be harder to sneak up on him.

It didn't save him.

The hairs rose on the backs of his arms, pinpricks of awareness pressing into his skin as he froze beneath a dingy streetlight. Whispers of movement came from the dark alleyway to his left. Men. Large and moving with the near-silence of true predators.

Shit.

He blinked hard and tried to clear his mind of the alcohol, but he knew he wouldn't be sober quickly enough. And this time, there'd be no Pierce to pull his ass out of the fire. Time slowed down to a single heartbeat, to a single nanosecond.

"Nolan," the voice that emerged from the shadow had a slick quality that froze Nolan's blood in his veins.

He turned on his boot heel to face the man he couldn't yet see. His old owner, the man Lorelei had paid a small fortune to save him from. Of all the jadehouses he'd worked in since that police officer had sold him into prostitution, none had been worse than this man's. "Xander."

"You remember me. I'm touched." A wiry man in an expensive suit edged into the light. The mandarin collar on his jacket made his neck look too long for his body, but nothing would make those pale blue eyes less menacing. This was a man who would kill without blinking.

The scrape of a boot against the cement was the only warning Nolan got before a hard fist slammed into the back of his skull and drove him to his knees. Black spots swam before his vision, but he caught himself with his palms before his face planted on the filthy ground.

His arm was wrenched behind his back as whoever hit him dragged him to his feet. Back arched, he could do little to keep from being propelled into the alley. Shaking his head to try to clear the pain and the booze, he watched Xander approach through the inky night. "What do you want?"

"You, naturally." He slid his palm up the front of Nolan's pants to cup his cock. "Since you no longer work for Tail, you can have your old position back at my brothel."

"No, thanks. I prefer being a free agent." He'd prefer death to being Xander's sex slave again, but he saw no need to confess that to a man who would take it as an invitation.

"Xander don't like free agents. Bad for business." The thug behind Nolan twisted his arm hard enough to nearly rip it out of its socket.

Xander let a finger drift up Nolan's stomach and chest to circle his piercings. "These are nice. I'll let you keep them."

"I'm never going to work for you again, Xander." He kept his voice cool and collected, but his ears still rang from the hit he'd taken, and his thoughts swam with too much alcohol. He wasn't sure he was going to be able to get out of this.

The smile Xander gave him made the hairs in Nolan's arm lift again. "I wasn't asking, but I think it's time you got acquainted with your new handler. Until you learn to behave again, he'll make sure you do as you're told. Right now, that means being in your old room at my place."

A cell was a better description of what he'd slept in at Xander's technobrothel. He'd spent his first month there tweaked on bliss and chained to a bed while men forced their cocks into his ass—as many men as Xander deemed appropriate for the night. It had taken Nolan a long time to get the bliss out of his system. His assassin work had ground to a standstill until he'd proven he was well-behaved enough to get around his handlers. The things he'd done to prove himself to Xander had the power to make even his stomach turn. Nolan's heart pounded, sweat dampening his flesh. All he could think was that he couldn't go back to that. Not ever.

He watched a sharp smile curve Xander's lips as he ripped open the seal on Nolan's pants. His fingers slid in to grasp his cock and Nolan's stomach curdled. "I think I'll go first. I want to see if you're as good as you used to be. When I'm done, it's his turn."

Nolan hissed at him, and the thug whipped him around to slam his face into the alley wall. Crumbling brick ground against his skin, scraping it away.

Xander laughed, and the sound was chilling. His hand came around Nolan's middle, dove into his pants against, and wrapped around his cock in a crushing grip. "Oh, good. He likes it when they fight back. It's good of you to make it more fun for him."

Something snapped inside Nolan's head, and a deep jaguar's scream exploded from his throat as Xander jerked Nolan's pants down. No one but Pierce would ever fuck him like that again. No one. He'd die first. His claws and fangs slid forward, and he slammed his foot back to pop the thug's knee backward. He squealed, but the sound gurgled to a stop as Nolan broke his grip and slashed his throat with his claws. The copper scent of blood filled his nostrils, fueling his rage.

Xander stumbled back, spinning to flee. The first hint of fear Nolan had ever seen from him flashed across his cruel face. A painful laugh tore from Nolan's chest, and he was on Xander before he cleared the alley. The jaguar's roar sounded again as he shoved his face into that of the man who had tormented him for so long. "You're lucky that, unlike you, I don't like to toy with my prey."

That didn't mean that Nolan didn't have to listen to the death screams, see the haunted, empty look fill those blue eyes as the life drained from Xander's body.

It didn't mean that Nolan didn't have to live with more blood on his hands and another scar on his already battered soul.

Lorelei had to get out. Her sanctuary was overridden with memories she couldn't make go away. It had been nearly two weeks since she'd seen them, but every corner of Tail held reminders of Nolan and Pierce. There wasn't a single piece of furniture in her office or her suite that didn't haunt her with memories of them.

And watching Nolan play Space Race with his client had been both arousing and agonizing. She wanted to see him so badly, but having to witness him playing with someone besides Pierce or her had hurt more than she could ever admit to anyone. Who would understand? Nolan was a jade; she'd seen him work for years. But things had *changed* in their night together.

DEADLY TEMPTATION / 277

She couldn't make that change disappear. She couldn't make either man change who he was, and she couldn't make herself stop remembering every detail of her time with them.

So, she did the only thing she could. She fled Tail and went to see her sister.

The Lakeshore District was on the other side of the city, but it might as well be another planet for all the similarity it had to her neighborhood. Here, the buildings weren't crumbling prewar relics eaten away by acid rain. The mercurite and polyglass could stand up to the corroding atmospheric punishment and remain pristine, gleaming gems on the skyline.

Hunter's skyrise tower was one of the tallest in the city, and he and Delilah lived in the penthouse. Lorelei strode through the lobby and nodded to the building manager. He smiled, flushed, and tugged at the collar of his uniform. The woman standing beside him winked and indicated that Lorelei could use Hunter's private lift.

She pressed her palm to the vidpad beside the lift doors and waited the few minutes it took for the car to come down the hundred-plus stories to the lobby.

The doors parted and she took a step forward to walk inside. But a man was in the lift, moving to leave as she entered.

Not just any man. Pierce. He drew up short when he saw her, and her breath strangled in her throat. Her mouth worked, but not a word came out. All of that charm she was so famous for evaporated into nothingness.

Pierce. He was here. Her mind gibbered uselessly, her thoughts bouncing from one memory to the next. Pierce's smile, Pierce's rare laughter, Pierce and Nolan fucking her senseless, Pierce telling them they were his mates, Pierce *leaving.*

"Lorelei." That gravel voice slid over her nerves like rough silk.

She swallowed, gathered together the few wits she had left, and managed to speak. "Wh-what are you doing here, Pierce?"

Making no move to exit the lift or get any closer to her, his silver gaze slid down her body. "Avery asked to be kept informed while we were tying up loose ends on a case he was involved in."

"Tarek," her voice dropped to a toneless whisper. Concern drove her into the lift with him, and her hand closed around his forearm. "The man who tried to murder my sister. Is—is everything all right? Hunter's not in trouble for killing him, is he?"

The corners of his mouth quirked, his gaze flicking to the doors of the lift as they slid closed. The lights dimmed when no command came for it to move. "Hunter is fine. Other than that, I'm not at liberty to specify."

"I understand." A blush heated her cheeks, and she dropped her hand, hoping his wolf eyes couldn't see her clearly in the dark. "I'm sorry. I shouldn't have asked about your work."

His all-important work. She wished she could dredge up some bitterness, but there was only an open wound that she hoped would heal someday.

Touching him had been a mistake. It reminded her too much of what it was like to let her palms slide over his naked flesh and hear his deep groan of pleasure at the sensual contact. Her body reacted to the erotic mental imagery, a vortex of heat expanding inside her. She bit her lip to stop a whimper of need. It had been too long since he'd touched her—one night had been enough to addict her to the feel of him. She missed him so much. Pierce. Nolan. Her soul craved both of them, and seeing Pierce now only increased the ache.

"You don't have to apologize." His breath whispered over her cheek as he leaned closer. "But I can smell your desire, Lorelei. Do you have any idea what it does to a man to know he doesn't even have to touch you to turn you on?"

She swallowed, folding her shaking hands together. "I can speculate."

"Then you know what I want to do with you now?" This time when he spoke, his lips brushed her jaw.

Excitement exploded inside her, weakening her knees. Deus, she wanted him. It was so wrong, so stupid, but she knew she'd regret it forever if she didn't touch him one last time. "I don't care to speculate. I want you to show me."

Only because he was so close did she hear the slight catch in his breath. His fingers slid against the nape of her neck, twining through her hair. His other hand cupped her hip, turning her so her back was to the wall of the lift. "This doesn't change anything."

"I know. I don't care. Touch me." She moved as he directed her, wanting nothing more than to *feel* again. It had been so long since anyone had made her tremble with want that she'd forgotten how good it could be. She shivered as his fingers drifted through her hair, bringing a lock to his nose to inhale the fragrance. Her eyes slid to half-mast and she hummed when his body pressed against hers. The heat of his flesh leached through their clothing, and the hard muscles of his chest molded to her softer curves.

"I've missed your face." His fingers bracketed her jaw, forcing her to look at him.

It was so sweet. It wasn't enough. She offered a wavering smile. "Kiss me, Pierce."

He did. His lips met hers and pain lashed her soul as ecstasy whipped through her body. Her breath hitched at the first contact, and she opened her mouth a bit to let him in. He took the invitation, sliding his tongue over her bottom lip before plunging it into her mouth. She moaned, loving the feel of him and the way he made her heart pound, her breath rush, her nipples tighten to aching points.

His kiss was soft and worshipful while his hands jerked at

her skirt, pulling it up to her waist. He groaned when his fingers slipped between her thighs and he found she wore nothing underneath her clothing. "Spread."

Moving her feet as he'd instructed, she rolled her hips forward to push his fingers deep into her pussy. He stroked over her wet slit, delving into her hot, swollen channel. It wasn't enough to satisfy her. She gripped his shoulders, using them for leverage as she tried to climb him. "I want you inside me."

"*Yes.*" He cupped his palms under her thighs, lifting her against the wall. She snapped her legs around his lean hips, already moving to a carnal rhythm she couldn't stop. He growled deep in his throat, reaching between them to open his fly. "Hold on, baby."

He deliberately rubbed his knuckles over her swollen clit as he tugged open the seal on his pants. A low keen of need ripped from her and she threw her head back, arching her body forward. He sank into her with one hot plunge and she convulsed around him, tingles racing over her skin as her inner muscles milked his cock. She came again every time he penetrated her, his rough strokes driving her past her endurance. She clung to him in the madness that threatened to overwhelm her, her body reacting to his on a purely instinctual level. She moaned, shaking with the impact of each thrust, each orgasm. Tears slid down her cheeks, and she sobbed at the searing ecstasy. His mouth opened over her exposed throat, scoring her flesh with his fangs. Her pussy flexed at the sweet pain that sliced through her. She felt her short claws slide forward, digging into his shoulders as he rode her hard.

Sinking into her one last time, he groaned and filled her with his hot fluids. His body pinned hers to the wall of the lift, and he rested his sweat-dampened forehead on her collarbone. They gasped for breath, shuddering in the aftermath of their wild coupling. He didn't say a word as he straightened, unhooked her legs from around his waist, and set her on her feet.

She could feel their combined wetness between her thighs as she pushed her skirt down. Still, he didn't look at her, and she could feel his regret fill the lift. It was a cold blade to her heart, knowing one of the two men in her life she wanted *more* than sex from didn't even want her for that. His body might, but the rest of him? No. She was nothing more than a mistake he'd made. Again.

"Pierce, please." A sob tangled in her throat when he moved away from her, his eyes remote, his hands sealing his fly. It was far too much like her clients. Men who paid for the privilege to use her body for their pleasure, but this time it was Lorelei who paid the price. Deus, she was his *mate*. "Don't walk away. Not like this."

"I'm sorry, Lorelei. Nothing has changed." He swallowed, tapping his hand against the vidpad as he stepped out of the lift. He glanced back at her just as the doors slid shut again, an echo of the agony she felt reflected in those silver depths. "I just . . . can't."

She wanted to sink down on the floor and howl until the hurt burned itself out, wanted to sob, wanted to hit something. But nothing was going to help. Nothing but time. She slid her fingers in her hair and gripped it tight, allowing a few tears to slide down her cheeks as the lift sped her toward Delilah and Hunter's flat. Sucking in a deep breath, she wiped her eyes and tried to pull the pieces of herself back together.

Delilah poked her head up from where she was sprawled across a huge kleather couch as Lorelei exited the lift. A wide smile creased her face and she dropped the palmtop she had in her hand onto a low table. "Lorelei!"

Catching her sister in a tight hug, Lorelei clung for a long moment. "Hi, baby girl."

Delilah sniffed her delicately, holding her at arm's length to look down at her. "Well, it smells like you and Pierce had an *uplifting* rendezvous."

"I'm not at liberty to specify." A smile that held no mirth flashed across her lips as she reiterated Pierce's words.

"Right." Delilah rolled her eyes and snorted. "So, if you just got fucked through the wall of a lift, why do you look so miserable, big sister?"

Blinking back tears she refused to let fall again, Lorelei shook her head. "Can we talk about something else, please?"

"Do you need me to kill him for you?" All amusement fled her sister's face, and her Chase-green eyes narrowed to deadly slits.

A watery chuckle slipped from Lorelei's throat. "No."

Delilah ran a hand over Lorelei's hair, tugging on one of the curls while sympathy shone in her gaze. "You are so spun over him."

"I know." The laugh Lorelei managed was a little fuller this time, and she remembered warning her sister not to get too spun over Hunter because she worried the rich hawk-shifter would hurt her sister. It looked like her baby sister had a better grasp on who to fall for and who not to than she did.

"Well. If we're not going to talk about Pierce, we should come up with new ways to get you sexed. Moving on is the best way to get over someone." A wicked little grin curled the corners of Delilah's mouth. "What happened to that itch you've been unwilling to scratch with Nolan for the last, I don't know, decade?"

Lorelei closed her eyes for a moment as pain fisted around her heart. Of course Delilah would know about Nolan. Too bad she didn't know he was as verboten a topic as Pierce. "It itched. We scratched. I fired him."

"Ouch." She lifted her pale eyebrows. "His performance wasn't as prime as you were hoping?"

"It was prime." Lorelei couldn't stop the sinful smile from forming. "Very."

Her sister winced, sliding a hand over her short platinum blond hair. "The assassin thing, then?"

"You knew?" *That* caught her attention, but even as she voiced the question, she wasn't surprised. Delilah had always been too inquisitive, too smart, and far too knowing.

"I knew he was into something other than prostitution, but Hunter was the one who dug up the rest." She shrugged ruefully. "He was worried about you getting hurt by whatever Nolan was doing."

"That's . . . sweet of him." Which wasn't a word Lorelei would ever have imagined applying to her brother-in-law. She followed her sister when she motioned her into the kitchen and keyed the food storage units to dispense two beverages.

Delilah handed one to Lorelei and winked. "Yes, but don't let him hear you say that."

"Men." She rolled her eyes and settled herself onto a tall mercurite stool.

Saluting her with her drink, Delilah took a sip as she leaned against the counter across from Lorelei. "It's too bad it's mostly illegal to kill them."

"In the Lakeshore District, yes." She let the icy fizz of the drink tickle down her throat. "Come over to my side of town and the rules become a bit more . . . flexible."

Delilah shook her head. "It sounds like you flexed a lot more than your rules lately."

Ah, her coveted rules. Almost as coveted as Pierce's job and Nolan's bitterness. The three of them were one big ball of messed up. "I did."

"Are you all right?" Delilah's hand reached over the countertop and squeezed Lorelei's.

"I don't know." Her lips trembled and she pressed them together. The truth she'd scarcely allowed herself to admit to herself slipped free, and a single tear slid down her cheek. "I love them both. And they love each other, but they're too wrapped up in their own issues to see it."

"All three of you, huh?" Other than an arched eyebrow, Delilah's face didn't show more than a flicker of surprise.

Lorelei nodded, wiped the stray tear away, and sighed. "It's insane."

"Love is, big sister." Her sister's fingers squeezed tighter and she waved her free hand around to indicate Hunter's palatial flat. "Look where it landed me."

The hawk's voice boomed from his office doorway. "You sound like that's a bad thing."

"As long as you're in the ivory tower with me, sweet prince, I'll be your damsel." Delilah pressed her hand to her chest and batted her eyelashes at him.

"I don't know why, but I somehow doubt your sincerity— and your ability to be anyone's damsel in distress." He grinned and walked toward his wife, pausing just long enough to pop a kiss on Lorelei's cheek as he passed.

Delilah stuck her tongue out at him.

He caught her close, bent her backward over his arm, and kissed her senseless. They were both laughing when he let her up for air.

Their obvious love and happiness made a huge lump form in Lorelei's throat. Deus, what she wouldn't give for just a little of that. As much as she missed seeing her sister now that she didn't live at Tail, it might have been a mistake to come here. It might not remind her of Pierce or Nolan, but it did remind her of what she was missing in her life. She slid off her stool and let a cha-grined smile crossed her lips. "I don't want to intrude, I—"

Hunter frowned and waved an imperious hand. "You're staying for dinner. Sit down."

"You'll have to forgive birdie, here." Delilah thrust an elbow into the hawk's flat belly, making him grunt. "He sometimes forgets he's not the boss of everyone who walks in the door."

"What?" He lifted an eyebrow and rubbed a palm over his abused midsection. "She came over. She's staying for dinner. Why make the trip across town otherwise?"

So, Lorelei sat and had dinner with them, and let them tease her and joke and make her feel better, which was exactly what she'd hoped for when she arrived. If they cast each other concerned glances when they thought she wasn't looking, she chose to ignore them. There was nothing she could do to assure them she was all right because the truth was she was *not* all right, and she didn't know if she ever would be again.

9

Nolan didn't like being at loose ends. It gave him too much time to think. He paced the close confines of his flat like the caged jaguar he was. Even in human form, the room felt too small. His heavy boot heels rang against the cracked concrete floor with every step.

How long would this go on? How long could he exist like this before he went insane? He couldn't work as a jade, and every time he thought about accepting one of the hits he'd been offered, the look on Lorelei's face when she asked him *why* flashed through his mind. He could retire, leave New Chicago, and never come back. He had more than enough creds in his encrypted account to disappear, but where would he go? This was the life he knew, and he couldn't quite bring himself to put that much distance between him and the only two people in the whole world he loved.

Which just made him angrier and angrier with each turn around the room, a snarling hiss spewing from his mouth. *They* had done this to him. Made him care, made him hope, made him *love*. No one in his entire adult life had ever managed to break through the protective wall he'd built in the first few years in the Vermilion, but now? Deus, he couldn't make it stop. Pierce had saved his life, turned his world upside down, told him he was his mate, and then *walked away.* What kind of man did something like that? Didn't he know how much that burned? Didn't he give a damn?

No, and that was the problem, wasn't it? Nolan had fallen in love, but he'd fallen alone. Pierce might have rescued him from the drop off the side of the building, but he'd left him to shatter when the night was over. And Lorelei. She'd just kicked him out of her life, kicked him when he was down after Pierce left.

He wanted to rip his own heart out and throw it away as easily as Lorelei and Pierce had. Anything to make the pain stop, to kill it forever. Where was the bullet for that? Why wasn't it as simple to wipe away emotion as it was to wipe away a man's life?

He snorted. It wasn't that they didn't care about him at all, it was that they didn't *want* to care about him. They didn't want *him.*

His palmtop vibrated and he hissed at it. No doubt another job he couldn't take. Someone who wanted to fuck him, someone who wanted him to make their problems go away. Tension coiled through his every muscle as he snatched the device off his bed. He downlinked his vidcache to erase the message.

He blinked, his eyebrows arching at the figure that scrolled down his screen. A job. A very lucrative job. More than he'd ever made on a single hit in his entire life.

He could take it, sever at least one tie he had with Lorelei and Pierce. Pain echoed hollowly in his chest. He'd spent his entire life being abandoned, left, discarded. It shouldn't matter anymore, it shouldn't hurt. But it did.

Closing his eyes, he swallowed. Deus, why did it hurt so damn much? Why couldn't he let it go, walk away as easily as he always had? He knew better than to let anything get under his skin. He knew better. He'd fought so long and so hard to not feel worthless, and still to the people he worked for he was worthless. In both his professions, his clients could dispose of him easily. He didn't matter to them and they didn't matter to him. They were a means to an end to each other.

Not to Lorelei. Not to Pierce.

He, *Nolan,* mattered to them. But hiring himself out as a killer was one thing they couldn't accept about him. He opened his eyes, letting a heavy gust of breath out of his lungs.

As if he'd conjured the man, Pierce's image appeared on the vidscreen in front of him. It took him a long moment to process what he was seeing.

Pierce.

On a vid from a man who wanted Nolan to kill someone.

And the someone was Pierce.

Shit.

Icy sweat broke out on his forehead, made his scalp itch. He pulled in a deep breath. Two. Rage began to boil slowly in his veins. His hands shook, and he clenched them tight. He couldn't remember ever being so angry in his life. Not at Pierce and Lorelei, not even at Xander. Nolan's gut fisted tight, and he sat there for long, long minutes staring at the screen.

Pierce stared back at him. The eyes were hollow; they had none of the intensity of the man. Just the way they would look forever if his life were snuffed out.

Nolan's stomach revolted.

He swallowed the gorge that rose in his throat and forced himself to read the attached documentation. Lev Barrone. The man had paid him well and often to eliminate problems for him. It appeared Pierce had become a problem. A humorless smile quirked his lips. The lawman was a problem for every-one. He didn't know when to quit. He was relentless, dedi-cated, and . . . it was going to get him killed.

Sweat slid down Nolan's face.

He should do it. Pierce was a problem, not just for his client, but for him. Anger burned in his chest. The man had made Nolan want, made him care, made him love, and then left him alone again. Always alone. Always apart. Always on the outside looking in.

And now he had the perfect excuse to pay him back for betraying him.

This was it. He had a choice. He could take it and truly become the man he should be. A man with no heart, no soul, no feelings. Nothing.

He'd truly be nothing.

Calm settled over him as the final decision swept over him. He knew, without a doubt, what he had to do.

Sliding his fingers over the palmtop's vidpad, he keyed in a number that had been burned into his memory.

"Marconi." The coyote-shifter's face filled Nolan's screen, and tension screamed through him at dealing with an old enemy who'd hunted his skills for so long.

Forcing himself to maintain a blank, cold expression, he met the agent's gaze. "This is Angelo. I'm taking you up on your offer."

"It's about time." A satisfied smirk crossed the coyote's face, the look of a man who'd gotten what he wanted at no real expense to himself. Bastard. It stuck in Nolan's craw to give over, but some things were more important than a coyote's gloating.

Nolan cleared his throat. "There's a condition."

Marconi settled back in his office chair, stroking his fingers down his chin. "Name it."

"I decide which assignments I take." Nolan didn't let his gaze waver. "I decide who, I decide when."

"Fine." The coyote's grin widened. "You'll be off the record anyway. Each contract is individual, you decide which to take.

You get burned and you're on your own. You're not on our payroll, we don't know you. But you don't work for anyone else."

"I understand." That was the government, wasn't it? They had their cake and ate it, too. They demanded exclusivity, but no protection for loyalty. Not for people like Nolan. He clenched his fists tight, reminding himself what was really at stake here. Something worth more to him than what little was left of his pride and dignity.

The coyote sat up. "Good, then I—"

"I want Lev Barrone. He'll be my first job." Double-crossing his client was a move Nolan couldn't take back. He knew exactly what he was doing, exactly what he was sacrificing to save Pierce, and even though it was a secret Nolan would never tell, it was what he had to do to save what was left of his humanity—the part of him that Lorelei always loved best.

Now Marconi hesitated for a long beat, pulling in a deep breath. "We have an ongoing investigation that could net us more people if we waited."

"Those are my terms. That's the deal I'm offering. Take it or leave it." It was that simple. Nolan didn't give a damn about the political implosion he might cause in Pierce and Marconi's agency. If Barrone stayed alive much longer, he was going to have Pierce killed. If Nolan didn't do it, Barrone would hire someone else who did. Maybe even someone who didn't specialize in quick, painless, and clean.

That couldn't be allowed to happen.

"I'll take it." Marconi gave a crisp nod, his fingers already flying over the vidpad beside his vidscreen.

"Fine." Nolan disconnected, and within seconds, his palmtop lit with new instructions. Barrone's face appeared to replace Pierce's.

So, Nolan would be doing what he did now, only he'd do it for the government, the system that had flushed him into a jadehouse as a child. He'd turn away from his old bitterness to save the man he loved. His life had spun around again because of Pierce. Nolan stored the instructions on his palmtop and returned an affirmative receipt to Marconi.

Then he stood up, walked over to the commode, and vomited his guts up.

He came at Pierce from the shadows of a burnt-out shipping yard. Karlson, one of Lev Barrone's men.

Pierce almost smiled. The wolf within him growled for a fight, and there was nothing Pierce wanted more right now than to kick someone's ass.

His case had gone to hell when Barrone turned up dead with a single gunshot wound to the head. Obviously a professional job, but no one had taken credit for the hit, and not a hint of buzz had reached Pierce's ears about who might have done it. Instead, Pierce had been scrambling for days to make what he could of the evidence he had at hand. Most of Barrone's people were in the wind, and Pierce had warrants out for their arrest, but the crime boss's death had ruined the case.

Once Karlson's ident file has been flagged by New Chicago's street surveillance, it had only been a matter of time before Pierce tracked him down. The man was stupid not to have left town like his comrades, but Pierce would catch up with all of them eventually. For now, he'd satisfy himself with this one.

Bracing himself for the attack, he blocked Karlson's first punch. Deadly talons tipped the falcon-shifter's fingers, and they ripped through Pierce's sleeve on the next swing, carving slashes into his flesh. He grunted and almost welcomed the pain. It sharpened his focus, dragging his mind away from the weeks of misery and onto the task at hand.

Then he did smile, shoving the falcon over an ancient wooden crate that splintered on impact. Pierce kicked the wood out of his way as he perused his prey. "Get up."

Adrenaline hummed through his system, demanded a fight, an outlet for his pent-up emotions. Baring his fangs, he growled appreciatively when the falcon obeyed, his eyes narrowed.

"I'm going to kill you." Those taloned fingers flexed and he balanced on the balls of his feet, waiting for Pierce to make the next move.

He shrugged, letting his smile widen. "You can try."

They feinted, swiping at each other with fists and claws as they danced in circles. They both sported nicks and cuts that oozed blood, but neither had the advantage. Loose gravel, metal debris, and broken glass crunched under their feet. Pierce sensed the exact moment Karlson lost patience with their fight. He lunged for Pierce, who let himself be caught around the middle and dragged to the ground so he could drive his elbow into the falcon's spine.

Glass dug into his flesh as they rolled, punching and kicking. The falcon butted his head against Pierce's, making stars swim in front of his eyes. He swung blindly and heard the sickening crunch of cartilage as he broke the other man's nose. Karlson slammed his foot into Pierce's thigh, and he returned the favor by jabbing his fingers into the falcon's ribs. His breath whooshed out and he choked when he sucked dirt and splinters back into his lungs. Grinding his face into the gravel with grim relish, Pierce pinned him down.

The falcon began shifting and Pierce set his knee on the back of the man's neck and twisted an arm behind his back hard enough to break it. "Try it and I guarantee you will not like the tiny cage I find to lock you in."

"Fucker." Karlson choked, but relaxed against the ground in defeat, snorting up blood from his broken nose.

Pierce grunted, more drained than he should have been by the fight, and unable to muster an ounce of enthusiasm that he'd won and was putting a mobster behind bars. "I've been called worse."

An hour later, he shoved the restrained man toward a junior agent. "Take care of this."

"Yes, sir."

Pierce didn't even wait to see if his order was obeyed. He just . . . didn't care. A short lift ride and he stepped out onto his floor of the agency's field office. Karlson might be in custody, but it just meant more paperwork for Pierce. Grit burned his eyes as he hunched over the vidscreen in his office, the noise of the agency ebbing and flowing outside his door. The words on his screen blurred, and he couldn't make sense of them. He pressed his fingers to his eyes and then scrubbed his hand down his face. Deus, he was tired. Exhaustion dragged at his bones, made them feel too heavy to move, and made every single micrometer of him ache. He hadn't slept in days, and not well since the night he'd been with Lorelei and Nolan.

"Nolan . . ." At first he thought the word was an echo in his mind, but his thoughts didn't usually come with the nasal flavor of Marconi's voice. Closing his eyes, he tilted his head and let his wolf's hearing come to the fore. ". . . joined to save Vaughn."

Shock rocked through him, and his body jolted. They were talking about *his* Nolan. What had he joined? What had he saved Pierce from?

"Agent Vaughn?" Reagan's fresh-scrubbed face peered in through Pierce's doorway, and he fought a groan. The kid was far too eager and had gone out of his way to try to befriend Pierce since the morning he'd broken into Lorelei's rooms. Though Pierce had to admit the little explosive the kid had built to pop the lock on her door had been . . . inspired. It had damaged only the door and nothing else. Very clean and neat. But Pierce wasn't in the mood to be *inspired* by a newbie. He wanted to know what the fuck was going on with Nolan.

Pierce grunted, not encouraging the kid to talk to him and hoping he would go away.

He didn't. Instead, his expression turned to the almost sly one people got when they were going to tell Pierce something they knew they shouldn't. "The man you were with . . . Angelo?"

That got his attention. Pierce jerked his chin toward a chair across from his desk. "Sit. Talk."

"I'm only telling you this—"

"Because I'm a senior agent and you want to impress me." He interrupted, not willing to play at being patient today. He glanced at his chrono. Tonight. Deus, when did it get that late? "So, impress me."

"Barrone was going to have you killed."

Pierce shrugged. That wasn't news to him. Half of his cases resulted in someone wanting him dead. It was just the job. "So?"

"He hired Angelo to do it."

And all the pieces fell into place. Barrone hired Nolan, Nolan joined the agency to save Pierce. But what exactly had the jaguar signed on for in order to save him? Nolan hated the system Pierce worked for, and his anger ran deep. Pierce met Reagan's gaze. "Thanks."

"So, you're impressed?" The kid gave a cocky grin.

"Yeah, now get back to work so you can impress me some more." Pierce shoved himself to his feet, walked straight into Marconi's office, and closed the door behind him. The man's eyes popped wide with what might have been panic . . . or fear. Pierce frankly didn't give a shit. He wanted information and Marconi was going to give it to him. He sat in the flimsy chair across from the coyote and offered a cool stare.

Flicking a hand over his vidscreen's controls, Marconi swallowed and tried for a weak smile. "Vaughn, what can I do for you?"

"You recruited Nolan Angelo." He hitched an ankle onto the opposite knee. "Tell me about that."

"Ah, your late-night lover." The knowing smirk that curved Marconi's face made Pierce want to slam his fist into the coyote's face.

"He's my mate." For the second time, the words just fell out, words he'd never imagined saying out loud to anyone except Lorelei and Nolan, but he couldn't take them back. Maybe it was the exhaustion, but he didn't even want to take them back.

"*Mate*?" the coyote squeaked. His eyes bulged as the information processed. "Ah . . . gray wolf."

"Yes." Leaning forward, Pierce gave the other man the kind of look that was more than a threat. Then he bared his fangs in what he knew no one in their right mind would call a smile. "Tell me about my mate. Now."

"He . . . ah . . ." The color leached out of the coyote's face, leaving him ashen and even uglier than usual. "I've been trying to recruit him for years. He was very good at his work. His other work, you know."

"I do. What else?"

Marconi fiddled with a framed vidpic on his desk, not meeting Pierce's gaze. "He agreed to join us."

"Did you threaten him?" He let his voice go deadly soft, but his stomach tightened at the thought of what the coyote might have done or said to Nolan to get him to become a cog in the machine he hated. His jaguar wouldn't have broken easily.

"No!" But the vehemence behind the word told Pierce that Marconi *had* threatened Nolan before. "He came to me."

"Because of Barrone." Guilt slammed into Pierce with the force of a hurricane, sucking him into a deeper darkness. Deus, Nolan had turned on a contract to save Pierce *after he left him* for his own job. Too many emotions to name ricocheted inside him. Shame at himself, pride in his mate, fear, anger, hurt. Love. He closed his eyes as it all swept through him.

"Yes. Because Barrone took a hit out on *you*." Marconi

cleared his throat. "Angelo will be working as a contract operative for us."

He didn't specify what kind of work Nolan would be handling for the agency, and Pierce didn't ask. They both knew and that was the end of the discussion. The government had its assassins, thieves, and con artists the same way everyone else did. Hell, Pierce had captured more than one criminal by running the same game on them that they ran on their victims. It was amazing how they didn't see it coming when it was their turn. "So, same job for him, just a new client."

"His only client." Marconi shrugged. "And he's legal. Any involvement he may have been *suspected* of in older cases is gone. Addendums to his ident file have been removed. As far as anyone knows, your mate is a good little citizen now."

Pierce nodded and stood, turning for the door. He let himself out while Marconi's disgruntled voice sounded behind him. "You're welcome."

Pierce shut the door in his face. Disquiet churned through his gut. He grabbed his coat out of his office, shut down his vidscreen, and left the agency. He didn't want to go home, didn't want to face another night alone. So, he let his mind wander, put one foot in front of the other, and just walked the streets of New Chicago. It was always alive and bustling, no matter what time of day or night it was. He needed to lose himself in that sea of humanity, to just think.

His mate had put himself in danger. Pierce's jaw locked tight. He'd known he was on Barrone's shit list. But the thought of what might have happened to Nolan if he'd failed, if Barrone had found out he'd been double-crossed, made bile burn Pierce's throat, and he almost choked when he swallowed. It killed him to think he'd had a hand, however inadvertently, in putting one of his mates in danger. *He* was supposed to protect *them*.

The gears of his mind spun, tormenting him. What would he do if he lost them? Forever? They could die any moment of any day. There were no guarantees, especially considering where they worked and what they did. Would he regret leaving them? Yes. The answer punched him in the solar plexus.

Somehow in the months he'd known them, they'd become the center of his world. Being without them was something he wasn't strong enough to handle. Anything but that. Anything but losing them. Not even his job was more important than that. He snorted, self-disgust ripping through him. It had taken him long enough to figure that out, hadn't it?

He was an idiot.

But he had to see them, had to apologize even if they never forgave him for throwing them away in the first place. They deserved that and so much more from him. He winced, but made himself face the truth. Memories that flayed him open like razor whips flashed through his mind. The spark of hope in Nolan's eyes when Pierce said he was their mate. The way Lorelei's lips shook when she begged him not to leave her in the lift. He'd hurt them both because he couldn't see what had become most precious to him.

Them.

He had to tell them. Peace settled inside him, snapping the band that had cut tighter and tighter into his soul every moment he'd been away from his mates. They were his and he was theirs. It wasn't even the mating instinct that made it so. He'd walked away from that weeks ago, denied it for months before that. No, it was *them*. Who they were and what they brought out in him. They were the best parts of himself, and he'd be damned in every possible way if he ignored that truth.

Pulling in a deep breath, he considered what this would mean to his career. It was all he'd known, all he'd worked for, for more than half of his life. And somehow it had become meaningless. What had once been his whole life, wasn't. He'd tried to bury himself in it, but it wasn't enough for him anymore. He needed his mates. It was as simple as that. If his agency kicked up a fuss, then he would deal with it when the time came. Lorelei and Nolan were irreplaceable; his job was not.

He wasn't willing to waste his life on regrets. He knew what he wanted, what he needed, and if they could forgive him, he'd spend every nanosecond he had left making it up to them.

When he looked up, he faced the entrance to Tail, the blue glow of lights bathing his face. Shaking himself, he glanced around. He couldn't believe he'd walked through the Vermilion and hadn't noticed. It was suicidal to not be on his guard in this district.

He snorted and shook his head at himself. It looked like his instincts had decided where he needed to be tonight. The human side of him couldn't agree more. He fished out his ident card, swiping it to open the door.

10

Lorelei ached. Every particle of her, every moment of every day. The misery was almost more than she could bear.

Oh, she laughed, she smiled, she did everything she was supposed to do to keep Tail running and successful. But, inside, where no one could see, where no one would know, she bled. And she'd begun to suspect the wound would never heal.

Not without them.

Pierce and Nolan. Nolan and Pierce.

The two filled in pieces of herself that she hadn't even known were missing. Now that she'd had them, it was a thousand times worse because she knew how wonderful she felt when she was with them. Nothing had ever been so good. And nothing had been so painful as losing them. She'd gambled on them and she'd lost. Vivid memories of the last time she'd seen them pushed to the front of her mind—Nolan in her jadehouse with someone else, not three meters from where she sat now; Pierce in the lift, fucking her and then leaving her all alone.

Knowing she was probably better off without their driven

bitterness in her life did nothing to ease the agony that sliced through her every time she thought about them.

She loved them. She hated them and the way their stubborn refusal to let go of the past meant she couldn't keep them. And she loved that their stubbornness was what had kept them alive and whole in a world gone mad. A tiny part of her knew she deserved the pain she was going through—this was what happened when she denied her own rules. She had no one to blame but herself.

Flipping her hair over her shoulder, she forced a coy smile to her face as a customer flirted with her. Her fingers flew as she dealt gaming pieces to the half dozen players sitting at her table. "The house wins."

A few players groaned. She grinned at them and nodded when one of her employees gave her the signal that her dealer shift was over. Standing to leave, her smile widened as another round of groans went up and the woman who'd been flirting with her sighed. "Oh, don't leave us hanging, sweetness."

"Sorry. I promise the next dealer's even prettier than me." Lorelei winked and let a light laugh tinkle out. It was *almost* natural. Anyone who didn't know her well wouldn't be able to tell the difference. Nolan and Pierce would have known.

She sighed, suddenly tired, but she had at least another hour before she could let herself go to bed. Not that her rooms gave her any measure of peace anymore, but going through the motions was her only option.

Rounding the end of the bar, she stopped to pour herself a glass of seltzer water. She snapped straight when she smelled *them* enter her domain. Pierce from the front door, Nolan from the employee entrance. She'd forgotten to remove his ident card access from that door. Panic flared inside her and she squeezed her eyes closed. She wanted to run, wanted to hide, wanted to see them again so much it terrified her.

But it was too late for her, and she knew it. Even if she fled now, she'd never escape the hold they had over her, the love that had been tearing her apart for weeks.

When she opened her eyes, Pierce stood before her, leaning against the bar as he had so many times before. He looked as tired as she felt, dark circles under his eyes and lines bracketing his mouth. She wanted to smooth them away with her hands, soothe whatever pained him. She balled her fingers into fists on the bar to keep from touching him. His gaze met hers and something softer and sweeter than she'd ever seen before shone in those gray depths. His hand covered one of her fists, coaxing it to open for him. Tears welled in her eyes when he twined his fingers with hers. He gave her a crooked smile, but said nothing as they both turned to wait for Nolan.

She could smell him drawing closer, but she couldn't yet see him through the crowd. Then she found out why when a huge jaguar leaped onto the bar. The jungle cat's golden gaze locked on the two of them, deadly power and feline grace in its every movement as it stalked them. The lights overhead gleamed on its silky tawny-and-black-spotted coat, and a shiver rippled up her spine as she heard its claws scrape against the polyglass bar with each stride. It ignored the gasps that followed it, the way people took a hasty step back as it passed; it was focused only on the prey it hunted. The jaguar stopped as it reached them, its intense gaze taking in the way Pierce cradled Lorelei's hand.

"Nolan." A laugh bubbled up in her throat, but came out sounding closer to a sob. "You always did like to make an entrance."

Pierce lifted his free hand to rub his knuckle along the underside of the cat's jaw. Nolan leaned into the caress, his eyes closing in ecstasy. A murmur ran through the crowd at Tail as they watched the exchange, and Pierce finally spoke. "Let's go to your office, Lorelei. We're going to need some privacy for this, I think."

Her fingers shook when she ran them through her hair.

Dragging in slow, deep breaths, she stepped out from behind the bar and led the way to her office. Butterflies winged through her stomach as memories of the last time she'd taken them to her private space assaulted her. Deus. *Deus.*

Nolan bumped his head against her fingers and she looked down at him. His steady gaze gave her strength. Tears filled her vision as she stroked her palm down his silky fur. He purred and bumped into her legs, urging her to continue. She walked, blinking away the moisture in her eyes and trusting him to guide her as they turned down Tail's various hallways.

She keyed her security codes into a vidpad beside the door, and she and Nolan stepped into her office when the door popped open.

They were here. They were *here.* What did it mean? What did they want? Hope and anxiety tangled within her, knotting so tight she feared she'd be sick. She spun to face them the moment the door closed behind Pierce. Nolan stretched his front legs out before him, his jaguar body twisting and morphing back into his human form. He rose to his feet, nude, staring at Pierce with a rapid succession of emotions flickering through his gaze. His mouth opened and closed again, and he shook his head helplessly.

The wolf's silver eyes gleamed as his hand shot out, wrapped around Nolan's forearm, hauled him into his arms, and held tight. "It's all right. I know you killed Barrone for me. It's all right."

She could see the shock flash across Nolan's face, the vulnerability, before he buried his face in Pierce's shoulder and snapped his arms around the older man, fisting his fingers in the back of his shirt. The flames on his forearms danced in fiery arrays of color the way they did when he felt deeply about something. The two men stood there for a long time, none of the macho backslapping that normally came with a male hug. They just held each other, both shaking.

Her thoughts whirled. Nolan had killed Barrone? She's heard

about it on the newsvids, but Nolan? And for Pierce? There was so much going on that she didn't understand, including why they were here in the first place.

"*Querido.*" The word came out a broken whisper and Nolan's fingers bunched tighter in Pierce's shirt. "Don't hate me."

"I couldn't." The wolf-shifter's hand stroked down the back of Nolan's hair. "You didn't have to do it. Not for me."

"Yes, I did." His chuckle was strangled, nothing like his usual smooth laughter. "Killing him was easy after all this time."

"No." Pierce knotted his fingers in Nolan's hair, using it to pull his face up. He leaned his forehead against the jaguar's. "I didn't mean the killing. I meant joining the agency. I never would have expected you to do that."

Lorelei could hear Nolan swallow and his Adam's apple bobbed. "It was the only way. To save you. To save myself."

"I know." Pierce's voice was a gentle rumble. "I love you, too."

That choked laugh erupted again, and a tear slid down Nolan's face. He pulled back, a smile quivering on his full lips as he pressed his fingers to his eyelids. "I didn't . . . I can't . . ."

Pierce shook his head, caught Nolan's hand, and pulled it away from his face. Those gray eyes were sadder and more serious than ever before. "It's all right. After what I did—" His glance included Lorelei, and she moved forward until he caught her hand as well. "—after what I said to you both, I don't expect you to trust me. I don't expect you to forgive me. I just . . . wanted the chance to tell you—"

"That wasn't what I meant." Nolan shook his head, his ebony hair brushing his shoulders.

"Will someone tell me what's going on?" Lorelei squeezed Pierce's hand and pinned Nolan with a look. "You killed someone for Pierce, that much I got, but why?"

Nolan's eyes darkened to black ice. "Barrone. The bastard tried to hire me to take out Pierce, so I killed him."

"It's more than that," the wolf broke in. "He went to my agency—went legit—and got them to order a hit on Barrone."

"Yeah, I'm a good guy now." Nolan twisted his lips in a self-deprecating smile.

The announcement stunned Lorelei and she stared at Nolan. He'd joined a *government agency*. She knew what that meant to him, how little he trusted the establishment. He'd actually chosen something—some*one*—over his anger. Now she understood Pierce's reaction when they came in the room. Lifting her fingers, she brushed them over Nolan's cheek. "You are wonderful."

He shook his head slowly. "I still kill people for money. Don't make me into something I'm not."

"We wouldn't dare." Pierce's mouth twitched at the corners.

Nolan snorted. "How did you know I would be here?"

"I didn't. I didn't even mean to come here tonight." The wolf blinked. "How did you know?"

His broad shoulders rolled in a shrug, the self-deprecating smile reforming on his beautiful face. "I couldn't stay away no matter how much I wanted to."

Lorelei's insides pinched at their words. It hurt to hear how badly they'd wanted to stay away from her. They didn't have to be here if they didn't want to be. They could leave. This was *her* place. And yet, they *were* here, but she still didn't understand why. They seemed to need to talk to each other, so why drag her into her office with them? Too many questions, not enough answers, and too much repressed aguish to try to sort it all out in her head.

She let her hands fall away from them, biting her bottom lip. Her arms wrapped protectively around herself and she moved back a step. Would the pain never stop? Would she ever be whole again? She didn't know. She only knew she was tired of wanting something she couldn't have.

The room had gone quiet, and when she looked up, both men were looking back. "What?"

Nolan's dark gaze flicked from her to Pierce and back again. "I was here a few weeks ago. After . . . after."

"I know. I saw you." With someone else. Someone who wasn't her and wasn't Pierce and had no right to touch what was *theirs*. Her arms squeezed tighter as the ugly envy threatened to strangle her.

"Were you watching the whole time he had me on Space Race?" He took a step toward her.

She took a quick step away, digging her nails into her biceps. "Were you hoping I was watching?"

"Yes."

She flinched, swaying so hard she stumbled back and collapsed on her kleather chaise. "You wanted me to see how easy it was for you to move on? You liked that I saw you with someone else?"

"Were you jealous?" He moved until he loomed over her, some unnamable emotion glimmering in his gaze.

"I wanted to scratch your client's eyes out," she snapped and looked away. She was tired of playing games with him. It looked like some things didn't change. She was glad he'd made strides in overcoming his distrust of anyone with a badge, but that didn't spare her heart. She dragged in a deep breath. "I saw everything on the vid monitors."

Nolan dropped to his knees before her, caught her hands in his larger ones, and waited for her to meet his gaze. "It was the only way I got through it, by imagining you watching me. By remembering you and Pierce watching me from the bar so many times. I could always see in your eyes how you were thinking about our first time together, and I could always see in his how he wanted to be the one fucking me but didn't let himself."

"I will now." Pierce moved to the other side of her, hemming her in on the chaise. Their masculine scents assaulted her senses, and she couldn't stop herself from growing wet. The wolf's rough growl only increased the need. "I'm going to put you on that machine and make it fuck you until you run out of come. I'm going to have Lorelei suck me during the whole game and then I'm going to let you watch while I have her hold on to the front of the platform and fuck her from behind."

A shudder went through Nolan. "Deus, I'm going to come just listening to you talk about it."

"Can we just get right to the part where I'm getting fucked? I'm not in the mood for games." Self-loathing ripped through Lorelei at her own weakness. Breaking her rules again. More pain, more loss. She just needed them more than she needed air. A sob caught in her throat and she tugged her hands out of Nolan's.

"That's for later." Pierce ran a fingertip down her shoulder, nudging the strap of her dress down. "After we've burned off the weeks of craving."

The jaguar's palms cupped the outside of her thighs. "Now is a good time to start the burning."

"No." Pierce dropped his hand, shooting a look at Nolan, who followed suit. "We can't."

She couldn't suppress the sob this time at the loss of their touch. Closing her eyes, she waited for them to leave her. She just wasn't strong enough to watch them walk away again. None of her rules covered what to do when her heart crumbled.

"You're right." Nolan sighed. "Not yet."

Not yet? How long were they going to drag this out? She was so tired of not understanding what was going on with them, tired of being caught in the middle of their angst and anger, just tired of it all and unable to stop loving them despite the anguish it caused her. Damn it. Lorelei gritted her teeth and opened her eyes to narrowed slits.

Each man linked his fingers with one of her hands. Pierce spoke first. "We have a few things to settle before we pick up where we left off. First, I want to tell you both how sorry I am—how *wrong* I was—to have left you. I never will again.

Not ever. Not for any reason. I'm yours and I always will be. I was the moment I met you, I was just too stubborn and too stupid to admit it." He swallowed, his silver eyes open and honest. "I hurt you, and you didn't deserve it. I don't deserve your forgiveness, but I want it anyway. I love—" His breath caught and he cleared his throat softly. "I love you both so much."

"What about your career, *querido*?" Nolan asked the question that hovered on the tip of Lorelei's tongue. "Things haven't changed *that* much, even with my new job."

"I'll resign if they want me to." Pierce set his free hand on Nolan's shoulder, his fingers tightening around Lorelei's. "I'm so sorry that you even have to ask that question—that I ever for one moment made either of you feel like you weren't more important than a paycheck."

Her chest was so tight, she could barely force words out. "It's more than a paycheck to you."

"Not anymore." He lifted her hand and kissed the middle of her palm. "It's important to me, yes, but not so important I'd choose it over you."

A watery chuckle ripped out of her. It was everything she'd always wanted him to say, to do, but never dreamed he would. Reality sank in and it struck her that they were *here* tonight because they wanted what she wanted, no matter how they'd tried to run from it and deny it. Emotion swamped her soul and the first tentative tendrils of joy unfurled inside her. "I love you, too. And I forgive you."

"I do, too. On both counts." Nolan leaned in until his bare body brushed against her equally bare legs. Her heart stopped at the hot contact.

Those gray eyes squeezed closed. "Thank you."

"We were both wrapped up in our own shit, Lorelei." The jaguar captured her with his gaze. "But when you look at us, you *see* us. Not Pierce's gun and badge—"

Pierce drawled, "Or Nolan's pretty face and steady trigger finger."

"Or that." Nolan tossed him a small grin before looking at Lorelei again. "You see *all* of us, the good parts and the bad, and you like us anyway."

"You want us anyway, which is a miracle all by itself." The wolf's gaze slid over her in a gentle caress. "You can count on us to make the right decisions, Lorelei. It's not just you taking care of everyone else anymore. We'll take care of each other. We can make this work."

Nolan nodded. "That's why I'm here, that's why I needed to come tonight. I had to see you and touch you again, had to tell you that I'd done what I could to be the kind of man you always hoped I would be. I . . . wanted to see if joining Pierce's agency could make you change your mind about keeping me."

Something close to desperation shone in those eyes, and it occurred to her that, for all his seductive charm and smooth confidence in her attraction to him over the years, he might not know how desperately she had wanted to keep him all along. Her heart twisted tight. "Nolan, all those years when I knew what you were doing, when I was breaking my rules by letting you stay, when I told you I *cared*? It was because I loved you. Probably from that first night we touched, and getting to know you for the last decade-plus has only made me love you more."

He dropped his head into her lap, wrapping his arms around her to pull her close. "Lorelei . . ."

She stroked her fingers through his hair. "I love you, Nolan. I never want you to leave again. I want you with me."

His broad shoulders shook and he rocked her gently. He didn't look up, didn't speak for a long, long time. "Don't ever change your mind."

"I won't." She tugged on his hair until he met her gaze. Moisture sheened his beautiful dark eyes. "I'll make loving you one of my rules."

He barked a short laugh. "Can we throw the rest of the rules out?"

"You've always been the exception to my rule. I just never told you until now." She squeaked when he hauled her off the couch and into his embrace. Her thighs straddled his as she made full, startling contact with his cock. "You're hard."

"And you're naked under this dress." His lids dropped to half-mast and he rubbed himself against her. The slide of his hot flesh between her legs made her squirm to get closer. Deus, she was wet and ready in nanoseconds. More than ready. Eager. Needy. His breath rushed over her lips. "Tell me again."

She spoke slowly and clearly, arching her hips so that the flared crest of his cock slipped inside her. "I. Love. You."

The muscles in his jaw bulged and he clenched his teeth, shuddering in sharp reaction to her words. "I love you, Lorelei."

His fangs lengthened and she watched the man wrestle with the jaguar for dominance. She knew the moment the man won—he sank his cock deep inside her, and she threw back her head to scream. Her claws scrabbled for purchase on his muscular shoulders, raking down his chest.

The wolf knelt beside them, shoving his fingers into Nolan's hair to pull him down for a kiss. They weren't gentle with each other, their kiss more of a taking, a claiming. Nolan rocked himself inside her, and her head rolled back on her neck as she savored the exquisite pleasure of his penetration. Every micrometer of her tingled. The fingers of Pierce's free hand brushed down her back until they slipped between the globes of her ass. Her breath froze as he teased her anus before sliding farther forward. Both Nolan and she moaned as Pierce stroked her damp lips and Nolan's thrusting cock. Then he dragged his fingers to her anus and used her own moisture to ease his passage. Her claws sank into Nolan's flesh as Pierce plunged into her.

"Deus, I can feel your fingers." Nolan ripped his mouth free from Pierce's, his pupils dilating to consume his irises.

A brilliant, wicked smile flashed over the wolf's face. He twisted his digits inside her ass, rubbing both her sensitive flesh and Nolan's cock through the thin membrane that separated her channels. "I know."

Nolan groaned, moving faster as he sought that deeper touch. "I love you, Pierce. I love you so fucking much."

Lorelei sobbed for breath, her inner muscles clenching. It was too much. Their sudden return, their apologies, their love. It was everything she wanted and more. She twisted in Nolan's arms. "Please . . . please . . ."

Jerking to his feet, Pierce stripped in nanoseconds before he slid onto the chaise behind her. He bracketed her waist with his hands. Nolan looked over her shoulder at the wolf and smiled. His palms cupped her thighs and together the two men lifted and spread her. She choked as they lowered her on to Pierce's cock, the broad shaft stretching her ass until she arched at the intense sensation. And she knew they'd only just begun with her. She whimpered when Pierce pulled her back against his chest, opening her for Nolan.

He leaned in and sealed his lips over her pulsing clit. She shuddered, heat exploding inside her. "Nolan!"

His ebony gaze sparkled with promise and he purred. She screamed, wetness slipping from her pussy. She was so close. If Nolan would suck her a little harder, if Pierce would *move*, she could come. Instead, the jaguar teased her with his tongue, flicking it over her lips, lapping at her slit, sliding down until he licked the rim of her anus and the base of Pierce's cock. She sucked in a breath, bowing her body to press herself against him. But he pulled back before she could get what she needed. He chuckled at the frustrated cry that broke from her throat.

A smile curved her lips at the rich sound of his laughter. She'd never really believed she would have this again. She'd dreamed, she'd wished, she'd fantasized, but she hadn't *be-*

lieved. The reality of it made her vision mist with tears. She loved them both so much and here they were. Hers.

Turning her head on Pierce's shoulder, she swallowed a low sob. "I was miserable without you."

"Every moment was a torment." His palms slid over her body through her dress, and with Nolan's claws slashing through the fabric and Pierce's hands ripping it, they'd stripped her bare and tossed her ruined garment aside in moments. Pierce cupped her breasts, tweaked the nipples, but still didn't move from his position planted deep inside her ass.

Nolan lunged upward, pressing the head of his cock against the soaking lips of her pussy. He sank all the way to the hilt in one slow push. "Let's not do that separation thing again. I don't like it."

They laughed and groaned as it vibrated all the way down to a very central location. The men's hands were all over her, pushing and pulling, lifting and lowering, pleasuring her, pleasuring themselves. She closed her eyes and held on for the ride. The two huge cocks stretched her past bearing and she didn't give a damn. It felt too good to care about agony or ecstasy. Experiencing their touch again after so long without them was already exquisite agony. Nolan sucked her nipples as he filled her pussy and ground his pelvis against her clit. Sweat sealed her back to Pierce's chest, adding to the friction as he moved and she moved and Nolan moved.

The scent of them was heady, masculine, overwhelming. She wanted to lose herself in it, in the sensations they sent spinning through her. One dick stretched her, then the other, and she cried out when they thrust into her at the same time. Every muscle in her body strained and throbbed. They pushed into her over and over again, and she lost all sense of time and place. She only *felt.*

"Deus," she moaned.

Nolan's tongue batted at a beaded nipple, biting down enough to let his fangs scrape her flesh. He purred low in his belly, and she felt it quiver all the way up the length of his cock. Pierce groaned and froze with his cock buried deep in her ass, and he filled her with hot jets of fluid. When Nolan slammed forward and they both penetrated her at once, her control snapped and she spasmed around their cocks. Her muscles flexed in rhythmic pulses and tears slid down her face. Nolan jerked against her as he came hard, shuddering repeatedly. He panted and dropped his forehead between her breasts. He held her, bent at an awkward angle, his arms lying on top of Pierce's as they circled her.

"I love you," they both spoke the sentence, voices deep with satisfaction.

Shivers ran through her, making her pussy clench in little aftershocks of orgasm. Nolan groaned, Pierce shuddered. Their arms tightened around her, holding her, cosseting her. Loving her.

This was it. This was peace, this was perfection.

They were everything she'd ever wanted and never thought she'd ever have. As a jade and as a madam, she'd always been the one alone, looking out for everyone and making sure they were all safe, all cared for, all following the rules. But she'd broken every rule for them, and she couldn't muster a single regret. Not if it got her *them.*

She wasn't naïve enough to think they wouldn't have their share of problems, that they'd faced all their demons, but their love made them three against the world now. Those sounded like good odds to her.

She'd bet on them every time.